A Dreamspun Christmas

FIVE NEW STORIES BY

Marilyn Campbell

Justine Davis

Carole Nelson Douglas

Edith Layton

Emma Merritt

D0210164

A TOPAZ BOOK

TOPAZ

Published by the Penguin Group
Penguin Books USA Inc., 375 Hudson Street,
New York, New York 10014, U.S.A.
Penguin Books Ltd, 27 Wrights Lane,
London W8 5TZ, England
Penguin Books Australia Ltd, Ringwood,
Victoria, Australia
Penguin Books Canada Ltd, 10 Alcorn Avenue,
Toronto, Ontario, Canada M4V 3B2
Penguin Books (N.Z.) Ltd, 182–190 Wairau Road,
Auckland 10, New Zealand

Penguin Books Ltd, Registered Offices:
Harmondsworth, Middlesex, England

First Published by Topaz,
an imprint of Dutton Signet,
a division of Penguin Books USA Inc.

First Printing, November, 1994
10 9 8 7 6 5 4 3 2 1

Topaz is a trademark of Dutton Signet,
a division of Penguin Books USA Inc.

Printed in the United States of America

PUBLISHER'S NOTE
These are works of fiction. Names, characters, places, and incidents either are the product of the authors' imaginations or are used fictitiously, and any resemblance to actual persons, living or dead, events, or locales is entirely coincidental.

Marilyn Campbell—the award-winning author of two Topaz Dreamspun romances, *Stardust Dreams* and *Stolen Dreams,* she also writes psychological suspense. Her March release, *Pretty Maids All In A Row,* published by Villard, is a Literary Guild Alternate.

Justine Davis—author of a Topaz Dreamspun futuristic romance, *Lord of the Storm,* she also writes contemporary romances for Silhouette. Her heavenly hero in *Angel for Hire* won her both a RITA and *Romantic Times* Award for Best Romantic Fantasy in 1992.

Carol Nelson Douglas—author of many romance, mystery, and fantasy novels. Her mystery *Good Night, Mr. Holmes,* won a number of awards and was chosen as a *New York Times* Notable Book for 1991.

Edith Layton—historical romance author, winner of numerous awards including the first *Romantic Times* Award granted for Best Short Story Author in 1992.

Emma Merritt—bestselling author of thirteen contemporary and thirteen historical romances. Her historical romance *Viking Captive* was nominated for the RITA Best Book of the Year award in 1991.

Contents

A Dreamspun
Christmas

Ghosts of
Christmas Past

❦

Marilyn Campbell

1

Janice Fowler lifted her foot off the gas pedal of her vintage Volkswagen Bug the moment she saw the sign:

WELCOME TO HAVERSHAM, VERMONT
Founded 1710, Pop. 956

Her first task was to absorb the atmosphere of the town from border to border, before examining anything specific at closer range. Obeying the posted speed limit of twenty miles per hour, she spoke into her tape recorder:

"Looks like a typical small town with the usual combo buildings lining Main Street. Correction, Haversham Street. State Road One Hundred became Haversham Street at the welcome sign. On one side, there's May's, a cutesy diner with ruffled curtains in the front window. Then there's a general store slash post office. The city hall slash police department slash fire station is on the other. Next to that is Haversham Public School. Pretty small building. Must not be many kids. Opposite the school is Chuck's Garage. No fast-food chain in sight."

It was close enough to lunchtime for her to wonder

what was on the menu at the diner, despite the ruffled curtains.

In less than five minutes, she reached the sign that read "Leaving Haversham." The last building at the edge of town was the Haversham Inn. She made a U–turn and took another look at that three-story, red-brick mansion. Four white columns supported a second-floor veranda, and two attic dormers jutted out of the gray-shingled roof. The old inn appeared to be meticulously cared for, unlike a number of the other so-called haunted houses she had visited so far on this trip. It was just as well that the story she was writing required her to stay there; it appeared to be the only thing in the area remotely resembling a hotel. *Gawd!* It was probably one of those bed-and-breakfast places, where she'd have to leave her room and actually speak coherently just to get a cup of coffee.

She proceeded to tour the side streets, which were primarily residential. The town was simply too quaint to be natural. There were actually white picket fences surrounding multihued clapboard houses with shutters, window boxes, and gingerbread trim.

This wasn't a town, Janice thought, grimacing. This was a set for a Disney movie . . . or a Stephen King novel. Personally, she was rooting for King. At least that would break up the tedium that had marked this whole project so far.

The fact that every inch of the damn town was decorated with gold garland and giant red bows made it even more nightmarish for her. Though it was daylight, she could see that every streetlight and every evergreen tree in every yard had twinkle lights strung around them. She didn't need the sun to go down for her to imagine how absolutely *charming* Haversham would be at night. The whole town simply oozed Christmas spirit.

There was nothing in the letter she had received from Wesley Haversham XII, the mayor of Haversham, Vermont, that prepared her for a fairy-tale village. His letter had been short and businesslike, with just the right enticement.

Mr. Haversham's letter mentioned that he had read her article in *Time* magazine regarding spiritualists who conned the elderly. He suggested that a visit to his inn the week before Christmas would alter her skeptical opinion of the existence of spirits. As an incentive to get her there, he offered free room and board.

That generous offer, along with her innate curiosity, set her to wondering whether Mr. Haversham had some ulterior motive for wanting her to come to his town at that particular time, which in turn made her more anxious to check it out.

She decided that a story on poltergeists and the living who shared space with them could be a natural follow-up to the article he'd referred to. Soon she had lined up overnight visits to a dozen places that supposedly had ghosts in them. To show how unsuperstitious she was, Haversham Inn was scheduled as number thirteen, the last on her list.

As she drove along, she played back the notes she'd recorded. Her voice sounded the way she felt—bored to tears. When she first hit the road a month ago, she had thought this article might bring back some of the old creative spark. But like everything else she'd tried working on in the last two years, it had so far failed to do the trick.

The story was a dud, and she didn't have the slightest hope that her stay at Haversham Inn would make a difference. However, anything was better than spending another Christmas Eve with family and friends. She preferred to spend that night in a town full of strangers, people who hadn't witnessed the most embarrassing hours of her life and didn't constantly spout phrases like "Poor thing." "Of all the nights in the year!" "I know how you must feel." Strangers wouldn't care whether or not she was "getting on with her life," or "throwing it all away."

If Haversham Inn turned out to be a disaster, she could always go elsewhere for the next four days, until Christmas was behind her. Maybe Boston, or Hartford. Anywhere but home.

She turned into Chuck's Garage and stopped next to the gas pumps to begin step two—personal interviews with the natives. Mechanics and gas station attendants were usually interested in her refurbished Bugmobile, and she often counted on the old car to act as an ice-breaker. Accustomed to self-service, she got out and removed the gas tank cap.

"I'll do that for you, ma'am," a portly, gray-haired man called as he came out of the garage. "Nice car," he said with a smile.

Janice smiled back and moved aside. "It's dependable. And economical. Fill it with regular, please."

While he got the fuel flowing, she closed the snaps on the front of her brown suede jacket and shoved her hands into the pockets. It felt colder than it had when she started out that morning. At this rate, there might even be snow for Christmas. Wouldn't that be just peachy!

"Are you Chuck?" she asked, to get a conversation going.

"Yep," he replied, keeping his gaze on the pump handle.

"You have a very nice station here, Chuck. I do a bit

of traveling, and I've got to tell you, that's one of the cleanest service bays I've even seen."

Chuck turned to her and grinned. "Thank you, ma'am. I'm proud of it."

"Have you been here long?"

"My father opened this station in 1932, the year I was born. Passed his name and the business on to me."

"I think that's great. You don't often hear things like that in bigger cities. Small towns seem to have more of a sense of tradition, I guess."

Chuck nodded. "Haversham's a town full of tradition, that's for sure."

"Really? Like what?"

He was obviously surprised by her question, but after a moment he replied. "Lord Wesley Haversham founded this town in 1710, and it's been managed by Wesley Havershams ever since. The current mayor is the twelfth in the line. Now *that's* tradition."

"Does anyone else ever run for mayor?"

"Nope." The pump clicked off and he returned the handle to its holder. "That'll be six dollars even. Cash or charge?"

"Cash," Janice said, pulling some bills out of her shoulder bag. "Where could I get something to eat?"

"May's Diner, down the street. The Haversham Inn serves breakfast and dinner, but no lunch." He glanced from side to side before adding, "May's the better cook, anyway."

She smiled as she opened her car door. "I'll keep that in mind."

"Have a safe trip, ma'am," Chuck said, and started walking away.

"Thanks, but I'm only going as far as the inn. I'm staying there for a few days."

Chuck stopped in his tracks and whirled around toward her. "You're staying?" His expression went from surprised to pleased when she nodded. "Then you must be that reporter-lady Wesley's expecting. Why didn't you say so? I thought you were just being nosy."

Janice laughed. "Reporters are notorious for being nosy. But actually, I'm a freelance journalist."

He came back and shook her hand. "Well, either way, welcome to Haversham, and if you have any other questions, you just stop by and visit any time."

"Thank you, Chuck. I'll probably take you up on that after I get settled in."

Chuck watched her drive away, then hurried inside. Within seconds, he had his wife, May, on the phone. "She's here," he told her excitedly. "Seems real nice, too."

"How old?" May asked.

"Hmmm, early thirties I'd say."

"What's she look like?"

"Now, May, you know I never look at other women," Chuck protested.

"Baloney. Describe her."

"Well, she was all bundled up, and her boots had heels on them, so it was hard to tell about height and weight, but I guess she was about average."

May clucked her tongue. "Was she *attractive*?"

Chuck thought out his answer before he spoke. This was the kind of thing that usually got him in hot water. "Her hair was reddish brown, kind of curly, down to her shoulders. I think her eyes were sort of green and she had some freckles on her nose and cheeks."

"She sounds perfect."

"I beg your pardon?" He could tell May was up to something, and as always, she was way ahead of him.

"What's the one thing Haversham needs?"

Chuck frowned to himself, then remembered what

had been decided by the town council. "Some tourist trade?"

"Besides that." She didn't wait for him to guess again. "We need another Haversham! And unless Wesley finds himself a new wife, there isn't going to be a Wesley Haversham the thirteenth."

"Now, May, honey, you know he's still grieving over Joanne."

"Only because there's no one around to take his mind off her. It's high time for him to be remembering his responsibility to this town."

Chuck didn't really want to know, but he asked anyway. "What scheme are you cooking up in that head of yours?"

She laughed lightly. "Don't worry. You'll hardly have to do a thing."

Janice turned into the paved driveway on the side of the inn and went around to the rear of the building. Only one car, an American sedan, was in a lot big enough for a dozen. The word REGISTRATION was printed on a small sign above a pair of intricately carved wooden doors. She parked in the space closest to those doors and pulled her suitcase out of the back of her Bug.

With a bit of effort, she lugged her case up the three steep steps to the covered porch and through the double doors. She found herself in a small foyer tastefully decorated with colonial pieces. On a narrow table was an open guest book and a ballpoint pen with a white feather coming out of its top.

She set her bag down and leafed through the pages. There weren't more than fifty names and addresses listed. She supposed it could be a new book, but the empty parking lot suggested that there was a dearth of guests at the inn. Chuck's instant assumption that she was the "reporter-lady" was also a pretty strong clue that visitors here were few and far between.

Using the fake quill pen, she inscribed her name in the book.

"Miss Fowler?"

Janice looked up to see a very striking man standing a few feet away from her. She wondered how he had approached on the wood-plank floors without her hearing him.

"Yes. I'm Janice Fowler. I have a reservation."

He held out his hand and smiled broadly, showing straight white teeth. "Welcome to Haversham Inn. I'm Wesley Haversham."

So, Janice thought, *this* was the man who wrote her the stiffly formal letter. He was not at all what she'd expected. "It's a pleasure to meet you, Mr. Haversham," she said, returning his smile. "Your letter was quite intriguing."

"I'm glad. And please call me Wes. If you'd like, I'll show you to your room and let you get settled. Then I'll be glad to give you a tour of the house. May I hang up your jacket for you?"

Before she had the snaps undone, he was standing behind her to assist. As he hung the jacket in the coat closet, she couldn't resist taking a longer look at him. She had assumed he'd be a stuffy old man with white hair and heavy jowls and a pipe sticking out of his mouth.

Wesley Haversham XII looked more like a model for a *GQ* layout—tall, with nearly black hair showing just a touch of silver at each temple. Because she was looking at his wire-rimmed glasses, she couldn't tell the color of his eyes, only that they were dark. She'd always thought that glasses made a man more interesting. His white knitted sweater and black dress slacks showed off a lean, fit body. And he seemed to be a real gentleman as well. Definitely *GQ* material.

As he picked up her bag and led her up the stairs from the foyer, she decided to take plenty of pictures of the inn—with him in most of them. If the ghost angle didn't work out, maybe she could sell an article on the owner. If not *GQ, Cosmo* would surely go for it . . . if he was a bachelor.

"Does your wife help run the inn?" she asked.

His step momentarily slowed, then resumed as he replied. "My wife passed away several years ago. But Louise Ludwig, my father's sister, lives here and keeps everything running smoothly. You'll meet her later."

"I'm sorry. About your wife," Janice said aloud, while thinking that a widower could be considered even more interesting than a bachelor or a divorcé.

He shook his head and smiled. "It's been a long time. Here we are." As he opened the first door on the second-floor landing, the hinges emitted a loud groan. "Darn. I forgot to oil those. I'll get it later."

He stepped aside and she walked past him into a room that could have been Dolly Madison's parlor. She hadn't expected a full suite, let alone such well-appointed rooms. There was no doubt in her mind that some of the pieces of furniture were valuable antiques.

"This is so lovely," she declared as she entered the bedroom and saw the fireplace and canopied fourposter. The heavy furniture was dark walnut and the colors were forest-green and ivory, with touches of red. Through the window she could see the Green Mountains, which bordered the town. Surely this place overflowed with skiers in the snow season. Valid story or not, this was where she was spending the next four days. "Quick, show me the rest of this museum!" she exclaimed.

"Don't you want to unpack?" he asked with surprise.

"I can do that later."

As he escorted her from room to room, words of genuine praise flowed from her tongue. The entire house was decorated à la eighteenth-century America. There were another three suites similar to hers on the second floor, one of which his aunt used. For guests on a budget, there were four small bedrooms in the attic, with one bathroom that had to be shared. Janice was certain that, for a lot of people, the price plus the view out the dormer windows was incredible enough to make up for the lack of a private bath.

The first floor had a spacious kitchen, a dining room that could seat thirty, a sitting room with game tables, and Wes's apartment, which faced the street.

On every wall of the dining and sitting rooms were portraits of Havershams, the eras of which could be estimated by clothing and hairstyles. The present Wesley bore an amazing resemblance to several of his male ancestors, right down to the glasses. When she remarked on it, he assured her that for each ancestor, he had a story he'd be pleased to tell whenever she wished.

She couldn't help but notice how his eyes avoided the most contemporary painting. He was obviously the man in the portrait, and the beautiful woman gazing up at him with adoration had to be his late wife. Janice thought he must miss her terribly.

He brought the tour to an end in the kitchen, where Early American furnishings were skillfully blended with modern conveniences.

"I absolutely *love* this whole place," she said sincerely. "What a marvelous writers' retreat it would make."

"You really think so? I never thought of—" Wes looked up at the ceiling. "Did you hear that?"

"What?" she asked, following his gaze.

"That tinkling sound. Like glass wind chimes. It's gone now."

Janice hadn't heard anything and admitted it.

"They were probably saying thank you for your compliments."

"They?" she asked, already guessing at his explanation.

"My ancestors," he said, with a perfectly serious expression. "They don't always make themselves known to strangers so quickly, but your appreciation of their home would make a difference. It's always been said that when you hear the sound of the wind chimes, it means the spirits are smiling."

"Well, I certainly hope I get a chance to meet some of them while I'm here. I think I should tell you, though, that this is the last of thirteen buildings I chose to investigate for my article, and I have yet to witness anything even vaguely supernatural."

Wes nodded his understanding. "Spirits are very independent. They choose who they want to communicate with, and no amount of pleading will convince them to perform on cue."

"I've been told that before. It's begun to sound like the standard excuse for why nothing strange ever happens when a reporter is nearby."

With a low laugh, Wes said, "I have a feeling your luck's about to change. I'm sure you have a lot of questions, but how about some lunch first? Aunt Louise won't be back until about four, but there's always something in the fridge."

"Actually, I thought I'd take a walk down to May's Diner."

"Good. I'll go along and introduce you."

Though Janice would have preferred to talk with some of Haversham's residents without him, she thought it might seem rude to refuse his company. Before heading out, he insisted on helping her don her jacket. It had been a long time since she'd enjoyed such gentlemanly treatment, and she decided she liked it. And when his fingers remained in her hair a moment longer than was necessary to free it from her collar, she decided she had no objection to that, either.

She had only met Wesley Haversham XII an hour ago, but he didn't seem like a stranger to her. She only hoped he wasn't a complete kook like most of the people she'd met in the past month.

2

"Are you sure you wouldn't rather ride?" he asked as he held the door open for her. "It's almost a mile."

"I spent the whole morning driving. I could use some exercise."

"All right. That will give me a chance to give you a bit of Haversham history as we go along."

His hand cupped her elbow as she descended the steps. Even through her suede jacket she felt the strength he could offer should she require it. When they reached the ground he released her; for a moment, she had the silliest wish that the parking lot was covered with ice so his steadying support would still be needed.

He began his narration as they strolled around to the front of the inn.

"The first Wesley Haversham was a wealthy British lord. He came over from Yorkshire in 1710 with his wife, Elizabeth, and their baby son, who as you probably can guess was named Wesley Haversham the second."

"If he was titled and wealthy, why did he leave England?"

Wes smiled down at her. "Because he was also insanely jealous. Elizabeth was so beautiful, every man that saw her fell in love. Her husband fought two duels over her before they left England. He thought if he took her to the New World to live among the savages, he'd have her all to himself."

During the brief seconds Janice had scanned the family portraits, she had been paying more attention to the men than the women, but it had flashed through her mind that all the women seemed uncommonly beautiful. "Did it work?"

He laughed. "Hardly. Lady Haversham liked people too much to be hidden away. She befriended the Indians, organized quilting bees with the women, and generally became the center of all social activity in the area. She encouraged her husband to put his energies into building a town and drew up the plans to get him started. Eventually he realized that she freely gave her friendship to anyone who desired it—male or female— but all her love was reserved for him."

"What a nice, romantic story. Is it true?"

Wes laughed again. "Who knows? It's been told for almost three hundred years. It's believed that they set the standard for marriages of all future Wesley Havershams. The Haversham men are traditionally jealous, the women have always been beautiful and goodhearted, and the stories about them are all of a romantic nature.

"Of course, you have to take into account the fact that the first couple had ten children, all of whom had large broods of their own. Practically every person living in Haversham today can trace their ancestry back to Lady Elizabeth and Lord Wesley, so only the positive aspects of the stories get passed on."

Janice thought he was about to say something else, something that made him sad, but whatever it was, he kept it to himself.

"Do Elizabeth and her husband haunt the inn?"

He waved a finger at her. "Uh–uh. They don't like the word 'haunt'. Or being called ghosts. They're spirits, and they reside in the home that was theirs to begin with. But to answer your question, *all* the late Havershams are still around."

"How can you tell?" Janice asked, making an effort to keep skepticism out of her voice.

"I've seen them."

She withheld the retort that came to her mind. He might be charming, handsome, and well mannered, but apparently he was loony as well. Too bad. She mentally switched gears from interested woman back to professional journalist. "What do they look like?"

"Exactly like they do in their portraits, clothes and all."

"How convenient." The sarcastic words slipped out before she thought better of it.

He stared down his aristocratic nose at her and cocked one dark eyebrow. "You really are a skeptic. No matter. They'll change your opinion soon enough. As I was saying, they're identifiable because of what they're wearing. Otherwise, it would be almost impossible to tell the men apart. As you might have noticed, we all look very similar."

"Are they trunslucent or solid?"

"Both. It varies."

Before she could ask another question from her mental checklist, they reached May's Diner. He held the door open for her, helped her remove her jacket and hung it up, then led her to a clean table, where he pulled out the chair for her and made sure she was comfortable before seating himself. Whether he was loony or not, she could still appreciate his old-fashioned manners.

Within seconds a waitress came up to them. She was no more than sixteen, but her body language and the expression in her eyes suggested she was considerably more mature. "Hi, Wes," she said, handing them each a menu. "You haven't visited us in ages. We've missed you." Her words were accompanied by a little eyelash fluttering and a hip shift that brought her thigh up against his arm.

He gave her a pleasant though nonencouraging smile as he unobtrusively increased the space between them. "Thanks, Stephie. I've been pretty busy lately."

A short, plump woman wearing a chef's apron came out of the kitchen. Her platinum hair was teased and piled several inches high on top of her head like an upside-down, woven basket. A pencil was sticking out of one side.

"Stephanie Ann! Stop flirting with Mr. Haversham. I'll take their orders," she said with a dismissing wave of her hand that sent the girl off with a pout. "Sorry about that, Wesley. If she wasn't my niece—"

"No problem," he said, cutting her off with a chuckle. "Let me introduce my guest. May, this is Janice Fowler. She's researching Haversham Inn for an article she's doing."

Might be doing, Janice corrected in her own mind. She held out her hand and May squeezed it. "It's a pleasure to meet you. Chuck recommended your cooking to me."

"He better recommend it or he'll be looking for a new place to sleep nights!" She extracted the pencil from her hair and pulled a pad out of a pocket of the apron. "What'll it be?"

They both ordered the vegetable soup and club sandwich special, then May headed back to the kitchen.

"In case you were wondering," Wes said in a low

voice, "May and Chuck have been married for about forty years."

She recalled Chuck's comment about tradition and Wes's statement that the people in town could all trace their ancestry back several hundred years. "I hope you don't mind my asking, but Chuck told me you're the mayor of Haversham and that the mayors have all been Wesley Havershams. Is that correct?"

He nodded. "It doesn't entail much. This is a small town with few problems. My job mainly consists of directing the monthly council meetings. It's more of an honorary position, really. Keeping up a tradition. Living with spirits for hundreds of years has kept most of the people rather superstitious. They tend to believe that everything will continue to go along fine as long as nothing ever changes."

Janice thought she understood. "So, a Wesley Haversham is always the mayor. And Chuck's a mechanic because his father was?"

"Exactly. Most everyone in town works at a trade or profession that was handed down to them through several generations. Chuck's grandfather had a bicycle shop where the garage is now."

Her first impression that she had driven into a Stephen King novel came back to her. "And no one ever changes *anything*? No one ever *leaves* Haversham?" She felt another story angle coming on, and this one was accompanied by chills.

It took him a moment to phrase his answer, and when he did, his voice was tinged with resignation. "That's the way it was for several centuries, but even the oldest traditions can face obsolescence. Some of our young adults have moved away in recent years. They wanted more than tradition for their children. I hope they find it."

That could explain the small school building. There really weren't many kids in town.

Stephie was still sulking a bit as she brought their soup and drinks to the table. When she walked away again, Wes said, "Stephie and her friends won't be staying much longer, either. There just isn't enough to offer here."

"Maybe they'll come back," Janice said in an attempt to lighten his mood. "After they've had a taste of the outside world, with its crime and dirt and unemployment, Haversham could look pretty good." She could see by his changed expression that she had chosen the right words. As they ate their soup, she took the conversation back to the subject that she had come here to research.

"You told me what the spirits look like, but *when* do they usually appear?"

Wes added a few shakes of salt to his soup, then said, "Actual appearances are few and far between. Usually they make themselves known in much less obvious ways."

"Such as?"

"The wind chimes, for one, and other noises. Or they move objects. A number of little things. If something is very important, they might leave a message of some kind."

May's appearance postponed Janice's next question. "Here you go. Two special clubs. Have you told her yet, Wesley?"

Janice raised her eyebrows at him. Intuitively she knew May was referring to something bigger than he had mentioned thus far.

"I'm getting there, May," he said with a wink. "But she's a real skeptic. Probably won't believe it till she sees it."

"Good," May stated firmly. "Then she'll just have to stay through Christmas." She turned to Janice with a smile. "Make sure he takes you to the Mountaintop Lodge over in Waitsfield while you're here. Chuck and I went there for our anniversary last month. They have a big dance floor, and the most wonderful band plays all the old music." For a moment, she closed her eyes and swayed to the music in her head. "And the food's not bad, either," she added when she opened her eyes. "You could take her there tonight, Wesley."

"Miss Fowler didn't come here to check out the restaurants in the area," Wes said with a slight frown.

"But she has to eat," May countered. "And your Aunt Louise, as much as we all love her, is a bit lacking in the cooking department."

Wes looked a bit embarrassed as he admitted to Janice, "It *is* a four-star restaurant with a great view of Camels Hump Mountain."

"I don't want to put you out," Janice replied without conviction.

"It wouldn't be a problem. I'd be pleased to take you."

May clapped her hands. "All settled then. You'll go tonight. I'll call and make reservations for you." To Janice, she said, "They dress up a bit there. If you need something, my friend Bernice owns the women's clothing shop down the street. I'm sure she has something pretty in your size. Then again, with that cute little figure, you probably look good in everything. Don't you think she has a cute figure, Wes?"

He sighed with obvious exasperation. "Did I hear you offer to make reservations for us? You probably should do that . . . *now.*"

Janice tried to hide her smile behind her hand as May waltzed back to the kitchen.

"Sorry about that," Wes said. "Are you sure you'd like to go tonight? I could stop her from—"

"I'm sure," she said. "It sounds nice. But I probably should visit Bernice's shop. I didn't pack anything but jeans."

"We'll stop by on the way back to the inn."

For a few minutes they ate in silence. Janice had the feeling he was still feeling some embarrassment over May pushing them into going out that evening. "If you'd rather not take me I could go—"

"No, no," he protested, quickly cutting her off. "I think it would be nice, too. I'm just a little surprised at May."

"Why? Is she usually more subtle?"

Wes laughed. "No. That was normal behavior for May. But I didn't expect her to try her matchmaking tricks on me." He paused a moment, then explained. "My late wife, Joanne, was her favorite niece. Our marriage was the apex of May's matchmaking career."

There was that sadness in his eyes again. "And you thought she'd never want you to look at another woman, even though Joanne is gone."

Wes shrugged. "*Gone* is a very relative term in this town. But yes, that's sort of what I thought."

Her natural curiosity had her wanting to hear more about his wife, but she didn't feel justified asking about her. Instead she returned to the spirit world. "May asked if you'd told me something yet. What was that about?"

"I was working up to it," he assured her with a slight grin. "Let's see ... as I said, the spirits don't often make personal appearances, and there has never been a way to predict when one might choose to become visible, except for one time." He paused and took another bite of his sandwich.

She gave him a few seconds, then prompted, "And that one time is . . .?"

"Christmas Eve. Or I should say, almost every Christmas Eve. They have been known to skip a year now and then, but they've never missed two in a row. Since they didn't visit last Christmas, we're fairly sure we can count on them this year."

Janet had no doubt that when no spirits materialized on Christmas Eve, he would refer back to this conversation, saying he hadn't guaranteed they would appear.

"At any rate, I won't spoil the surprise by telling you what they do, but it will definitely be worth your while to be here on Christmas Eve. As my guest, of course."

Though she had already decided to stay through that night, she let him believe his teaser convinced her. As they got up to leave, May popped out of the kitchen again.

"Your reservations are for seven o'clock, Wesley. And Janice, make sure he takes you to Montpelier while you're here. No visit is complete without seeing the state capital, and it's such a pretty drive."

Wes ushered Janice out of the diner before May could think of another excursion for them to take together.

"She means well," he said with a sheepish smile.

A few minutes later they were in front of Bernice's dress shop, and Janice assured Wes that there was no need for him to wait for her. He seemed oddly reluctant to abandon her, but eventually he headed back to the inn alone.

The little bell over the door announced her entrance. From behind a circular rack of dresses a tall, dark-haired woman greeted her cheerfully. "Hello. You must be Janice."

Janice's surprise must have shown on her face, because the woman laughed and explained herself.

"I'm Bernice. May called and said you'd be dropping by." She stepped around in front of the dress rack and scanned Janice from head to toe. "I must tell you, I thought May was exaggerating about how pretty you are. And such beautiful hair. It's the same color as my great-grandmother's mahogany tea caddy. I have just the thing for you to wear tonight."

As Bernice selected an emerald-green turtleneck sweaterdress with long sleeves and hung it in the dressing room, Janice wondered if the whole town was going to wait up for her and Wes to return from the restaurant so they could get a blow-by-blow account of the evening. It reminded her of how her family might act if *they* heard she was going out to dinner with an eligible man.

That thought replayed itself while she got out of her clothes and tried on the green dress. Was it possible that these people wanted to see Wes remarry as much as her family and friends wished that would happen for her? She could certainly empathize with him if they did. She had been harassed, nagged, and tricked into meeting dozens of bachelors in the last two years.

It wasn't that she didn't want to remarry. She just hadn't met a single man who wasn't totally and tiresomely predictable. Besides, they all had something about them that reminded her of her ex-husband, which was enough to disqualify them on the spot. That man was a *Pig,* with a capital *P.* Not only was he crude and self-centered, what he did to her two Christmas Eves ago was unforgivable.

As if it were yesterday, she saw herself sitting in their living room with all their family and friends. She had planned a big surprise dinner party for their fifth

wedding anniversary. By nine o'clock they ate the re-
heated dinner. By midnight, all the guests had departed.

He finally showed up at noon on Christmas Day, but
it was only to pack his clothes. Several more days
passed before she learned that he had gone home from
the office Christmas party with his secretary . . . to an
apartment he'd spent considerable time in already. This
time, however, he had decided to stay.

She shook off the anger that still accompanied
thoughts of his deceit and studied her reflection instead. Bernice was right; the dress was absolutely perfect. No need to try on another.

Suddenly she heard something that made her freeze.
She waited for it to be repeated, but all she heard was
Bernice humming a tune. She remembered the door to
the shop had a bell, but this sound was more like
. . .*glass wind chimes*. She pulled aside the dressing
room curtain.

"Bernice? Do you have wind chimes in here?"

"No, dear, just the bell on the door. Why?"

"Oh, nothing. I just thought I heard chimes."

Bernice's eyes widened as she noted the fit of the
dress. "My, my, but you do look lovely. They must
have been smiling at the sight of you."

"They?" Janice asked warily.

"My ancestors. Didn't Wesley explain everything to
you?"

Janice's gaze darted around the shop, looking for
something that could have made the sound she'd heard.
"Yes, he told me quite a bit already, but I was under
the impression that spirits don't move from building to
building."

"Maybe they don't in some places, but they do in
Haversham. You never know where they might show

up to do a little mischief. We're all quite used to it, though. Now, let's pick out some accessories, and you'll need hose, too. What about shoes and a bag?"

While Bernice bustled about her shop, Janice mulled over the idea of a ghost hovering in the dressing room while she was changing. How silly! She didn't believe in ghosts or spirits, or anything of the sort.

"I miss you, Jo-Jo," Wes said, staring at the woman in the painting on the dining room wall. He had hung the painting in there after his wife died, mainly because he seldom had cause to go into the room; thus he could avoid looking at it. Once in a while, though, he felt the need to talk things out with her.

That wasn't so strange, considering the fact that they had been friends from birth. They grew up together, attended school together, and on their wedding night, lost their virginity together. Theirs wasn't the kind of love that exploded with fireworks and passion. Rather, it was relaxed and comfortable, and if fate hadn't intervened, it could have been all Wes would have ever needed.

If only they could have had one child. Not that a son or daughter could have taken Joanne's place; it might have curbed the loneliness, however. But she couldn't conceive, and by the time they learned why, the deadly cancer had already spread beyond control.

He no longer asked why fate chose him as the Haversham descendant around whom three-hundred-year-old traditions would come to an end. Every previous Mr. and Ms. Wesley Haversham had produced at least three children early in their marriage, then lived happily ever after, until they passed on in their old age. His parents, however, had had only one child, and that was quite late in life. They died within months of each other when Wes was twenty-seven.

He had plenty of Haversham aunts, uncles, and cousins in town, but he had never felt as close to them as he had to Joanne. She was all the family he'd ever needed.

And now another long-standing tradition was being broken. In order to save the town from extinction, he had come up with a plan to turn their peaceful, reclusive town into a tourist attraction. And the residents—his family and friends—had wholeheartedly backed him. After all, he was Wesley Haversham XII. He *must* know what he's doing.

Everyone was counting on him to pull this off, and whatever it took—even a bit of trickery—he would do it, rather than let down his extended family.

"I sure wish you could give me your opinion of our houseguest, Jo-Jo. There's so damn much depending on her. She seems very nice, though. In fact—you'll love this—May arranged for us to go to Mountaintop Lodge tonight. Do you realize it will be the first time I've taken a woman out to dinner, other than you?"

It occurred to him that this was really why he had come in here—to let her know he would be with another woman. To be honest, it wasn't just that Janice was a woman, but that she was one who made his insides quiver when he first saw her. One that had him looking forward to the first slow song the band would play tonight, so that he could discover what it felt like to hold her close.

Guilt washed over him like a cold draft. Was that fear he was feeling? Or Joanne's way of showing disapproval? Perhaps it was still too soon. Perhaps it would be best to cancel tonight's—

"Wes? Are you here?"

Still wavering between backing out and diving in headfirst, it took him a moment to answer Janice's call. "I'm in the dining room."

She appeared in the doorway a moment later, her arms laden with bags. "Why the hell didn't you tell me the whole damn town was haunted?"

3

Wes placed his index finger to his lips to hush her. "You'll hurt their feelings."

Janice signed and scanned the portraits. "Haunted, shmaunted! What difference does it make what word I use?"

Wes shrugged. "They don't care for profanity, either."

"I beg your pardon?"

"You called it a *damn* town."

Janice was slightly taken aback. She used curse words all the time and—She aborted her thought when she realized her language had begun deteriorating only after her husband had walked out on her. "Okay. I'll be more careful. Now fill me in on whatever little details you failed to mention earlier."

Just then the sound of the outside door closing announced someone else's arrival. 'I wasn't keeping anything back; I just hadn't gotten to it yet. But first, let me introduce you to my aunt, Louise. I'm sure that was her coming in. Just set your packages down in here."

Janice did as he suggested, then went with him into the kitchen. A petite, white-haired woman was coming in from the other doorway carrying two shopping bags, each of which appeared to be heavier than she was.

'For heaven's sake, Aunt Louise," Wes scolded gently. "How many times do I have to tell you to get one of the boys to help you, or at least call me?"

She set down her bags and lifted her chin. "The day I can't carry groceries into the house is the day I stop buying them. And that day will only come when I'm laid to rest next to Mr. Ludwig."

Wes's exasperated expression told Janice they'd had this conversation before. "Janice Fowler, meet the stubborn Louise Ludwig."

"How do you do, Mrs. Ludwig?"

"None of that, now. I'm Aunt Louise to everyone in this town, and while you're here, you'll call me the same." She brushed her hands off on her coat, then grasped both of Janice's hands in her own. "How lovely you are, girl. And I've always admired people who can turn words into important sentences." Without releasing Janice's hands, she stared deeply into her eyes for several seconds. "Pretty and intelligent, but sad. Let go of the past, child. You have a beautiful future waiting for you, but you can't step into it until you get rid of the anger and hurt inside."

Janice was too stunned to respond, so she merely looked to Wes to rescue her.

"Aunt Louise is part gypsy," he said with a grin. "She reads tea leaves in her spare time.'

The elderly woman released Janice's hands and shook a finger at Wes. "You better watch your step, young man, or I'll put a spell on you. Now get out of my kitchen. I have things to do, and it's almost tea-time."

They started to go back toward the dining room when Wes stopped. "I almost forgot. You don't need to fix dinner for us—"

"Yes, yes, I know. Mountaintop Lodge. Seven o'clock. Dinner and dancing. Go on now."

Shaking his head, Wes and Janice left his aunt alone.

"How did she know about tonight?" Janice asked in a whisper.

With a grin, he said, "She'd tell you she's psychic, but more than likely she just came from May's."

"No secrets in a small town, huh?"

"Not one." He picked up her packages and nodded for her to take the lead to her room. At her door, he handed the bags to her rather than taking them inside himself. "Aunt Louise and I will be having tea in the sitting room in about fifteen minutes, if you'd care to join us. It's a pleasant tradition that she insists on maintaining."

Janice promised to be there, since he had yet to answer all her questions.

She closed the door but felt no need to lock it. As soon as she turned around to go into the bedroom, the warm beauty of the suite made her smile. This was the kind of environment she imagined would give her the inspiration to write the Great American Novel. Someday, she promised herself.

Her smile faded as she entered the bedroom and looked around. Her nightgown and robe were on the bed, her slippers on the floor. She remembered that Wes had left her suitcase sitting on top of the cedar chest at the foot of the bed, but now it was gone. She opened the closet door and found the case, but she also discovered that her jeans and blouses had been hung up. On top of the dresser were her camera, film, and writing supplies. On impulse she checked the drawers and saw that her underwear and sweaters had been neatly stowed away. In the bathroom, all of her toiletries had been put into the medicine cabinet or lined up on the counter.

She had heard of places where the maid unpacked for you, but there was no such maid here. Aunt Louise had been shopping, and Wes had been at the diner with her.

But Wes had come back while she was at Bernice's.

Could he have managed all this in the short time they were separated? It didn't look like the unpacking had been done in a hurry. Nonetheless, he had to have been responsible, and she didn't like the idea of him going through her things without her permission, even if he did it as a service of the inn.

Quickly, she dumped her purchases on the bed, hung up the new green dress, and headed down to the sitting room. He was lounging comfortably in one of the upholstered armchairs, looking very much like the man in the portrait behind him. In fact, Janice was fairly sure that the ancestor was sitting in the same chair Wes was. As soon as he saw her, Wes rose with a smile, but she was unable to return it.

"Look, I appreciate your unpacking for me, but I'd really rather you—"

"Excuse me?" he interrupted. "I didn't unpack for you."

She frowned at him. "You didn't?" He shook his head. "Well, *someone* did. I assumed it was you since your aunt was out."

"Aunt Louise?" he called. A moment later she came through the door, pushing a cart bearing an ornate silver tea service and a tray of cookies. "Did you unpack Janice's bag while we were out earlier?"

"Are you daft, boy? You were here when I left this morning, and you know I just got back. I didn't even know she'd arrived until I ran into Harriet in the grocery store."

Wes turned to Janice and filled in the blank for her. "Harriet was in May's Diner when we were there."

"Oh," she said, not questioning how he knew what she was thinking. "But then, who unpacked my suitcase?"

Aunt Louise handed her a delicate china cup of black tea and a linen napkin. "Help yourself to cream or lemon. It was probably your mother, Wesley. You know what a stickler she was for everything being nice and neat and in its proper place."

Janice's confusion was evident as she sat down in the chair to Wes's left and Aunt Louise took the one opposite him. Only then did he reseat himself. "You didn't tell me your mother lived here with you," Janice remarked.

He opened his mouth, but his aunt beat him to an explanation. "Wes's mother still lives here. You just can't see her. But she's forever rearranging the kitchen to please herself, knowing full well that I'll just put things back the way I like them."

Wes sighed. "My mother passed away eleven years ago. The two of them have been battling over the household ever since."

"Now wait just a minute," Janice said. "Are you telling me that a spirit—possibly your mother—hung up my clothes and put my toothbrush in the bathroom?"

Aunt Louise passed the tray of cookies to Janice. "Don't fret over it, dear. You'll get accustomed to their meddling after a while. If you live in a town full of spirits, you learn to expect the unexpected."

Janice was still certain there had to be a more tangible explanation. Short of calling them liars, however, she had no choice but to let the matter drop. "Speaking of a town full of spirits, I distinctly recall your letter, and the only place you mentioned anything about was the inn."

Wes set his cup and saucer down on the table in front of him. "I was afraid you'd think I was a crackpot if I told you the whole story in my letter."

"So Bernice wasn't putting me on? Everyone in town believes their dead ancestors are still hanging around?"

"Basically, that's about it," Wes replied.

"And this doesn't bother anyone?"

Aunt Louise chuckled. "The spirits only meddle with people they're fond of, and nothing they do is harmful. They just like to make sure we don't forget about them."

Janice had never heard of an entire town being haunted. If she could get enough examples of spiritual intervention from a wide variety of residents, this could make a great story after all. And it wouldn't even be necessary for her to believe any of it.

"How is it that no one's ever written an article about Haversham before?"

While Wes's aunt refilled everyone's teacups, he answered Janice. "It was always understood that what happened here was our secret and to reveal it to outsiders would be detrimental to both the spirits and the living."

"But you've obviously changed your mind now," Janice pointed out. "Why?" She could tell he was contemplating whether or not to respond truthfully, so she added, "The truth, please."

"All right," he said, and got up from his chair to pace a bit as he spoke. "I told you at lunch that some of our young people have moved away. The truth is that *most* of them have, for one reason or another. At this rate, Haversham could literally be a ghost town in thirty or forty years. Did you know that only two states, Alaska and Wyoming, have a smaller population than Vermont?"

She'd read that in the American Automobile Association's guide book, but hadn't given it much consideration.

"At any rate, we can't afford to lose any more people. The town council decided that drastic measures were needed to inject new life into the town, even if it meant revealing our secret."

"Maybe I'm a bit dense, but I don't get the connection."

Aunt Louise spoke up before Wes could reply. "Did you see the movie *Ghost*?"

"Didn't everyone?" Janice countered.

"Exactly. At one time people were spooked by the notion that a house could have ghosts in it. But suddenly it's all the rage."

Wes picked it up from there. "There are a number of towns throughout Vermont better equipped to attract tourists than Haversham. But none of them can offer what we can—a chance to commune with the spirit world. Like Haversham Inn, a lot of other old homes could easily be transformed into bed-and-breakfasts. The economy would improve and our young people might be more willing to stay put."

Janice could see the rationale, but something about it didn't sit well. "And what happens to tradition? Will it all simply be forsaken for commercial enterprise? Will Aunt Louise hang a shingle outside that offers psychic predictions? Or better yet, May's Diner could become a gypsy tearoom and Stephie could be taught to read tea leaves to the customers. Of course, Bernice will have to start carrying a whole line of new products—crystal jewelry and aromatic candles, that sort of thing."

"Obviously, you don't approve of my idea," Wes said, frowning as he returned to his chair.

Janice sighed and shook her head as she realized she had just done a complete reversal in her attitude toward the town . . . and she had been there only part of one day. That alone suggested there was something paranormal about this place. At least now her curiosity was satisfied as to his ulterior motive for getting her here. She decided that that evening, when they were alone, might be a better time to probe into his reasoning a bit further.

Seeing that he was still waiting to hear her judgment, she said, "It's not up to me to approve or disapprove. I'm sure it could be very successful. And my writing an article for you would certainly kick it off in a big way. Right?"

Wes and his aunt exchanged a guilty glance. "Right," Wes reluctantly admitted. "I thought if you wrote an article about Haversham's spirits, people would believe it."

"Because I'm a known skeptic?"

Though he looked somewhat uncomfortable, he nodded.

"But then you've got to realize, if I'm not convinced, I could write something negative instead of helpful."

"You won't," Aunt Louise said firmly. "They'll make sure you do what's right."

The grandfather clock in the corner bonged five times, much to Janice's surprise. She hadn't realized the lateness of the hour. She asked Wes, "When do we need to leave?"

"Six-thirty will give us plenty of time," he assured her with a forced smile.

"Then I need to excuse myself. Your mother may have unpacked for me, but I think I'd better take a shower myself." She was almost out the door when she remembered hearing the chimes in Bernice's dressing room.

"They do leave you alone in the bathroom, don't they?"

Wes laughed. "They have never been known to disrespect the privacy of the living."

Janice decided to take a very quick shower . . . just in case.

An hour later, she stood in front of the full-length mirror in the bedroom and critiqued her appearance. Bernice had talked her into buying a rhinestone-studded comb for her hair, and she had obeyed the woman's instructions about styling it with one side pulled off her face. The result was so inspiring that she had taken more care than usual with her makeup.

She decided she looked very nice, and that it had been too long since she'd thought that way about herself . . . as long as two Christmas Eves ago, when she had hoped that looking extra feminine would make her husband notice her again.

The black suede shoes Bernice had chosen had higher heels than she normally wore, but they did make her legs look good. And as tall as Wes was, the added height would make it more comfortable for them to dance together.

If he asked her.

She acknowledged that despite his belief in the supernatural, she found him very desirable and truly wanted to think of this evening as a real date.

The gloomy voice of reality whispered in her mind:

Wesley Haversham had invited her here to help promote a business venture, not for a romantic liaison. There was a strong possibility that he had lied about how her bag got unpacked. He was probably planning to spend the entire evening telling her fabricated ghost stories to sway her opinion. Besides that, he appeared to still be grieving over his wife. If May hadn't forced this "date,' it may not have happened at all.

Her confident mood effectively crushed, she picked up the little purse that matched the shoes and left the suite.

Some of her confidence returned when she noted that as early as she was, Wes was already waiting for her. It rose a bit more when his gaze crept from her toes to her hair, and his smile grew wider with each inch he progressed.

"Thank you," she said, smiling back. "That was one of the nicest compliments I've received in a while." As he walked toward her, she let her own gaze take in the cut of his charcoal-gray suit and light-blue shirt. "You look extremely debonair yourself, sir."

He took her hand in his and placed a featherlight kiss on her knuckles. "Would you care for a glass of sherry before we go?"

She liked the feel of his hand wrapped around hers and was pleased when he didn't release it after his gracious greeting. "No, thank you. I'm not much of a drinker."

"Then why don't we take advantage of the extra time to drive *very* slowly."

His eyes held such sensual promise that she swallowed hard and lowered her lashes. She had been hoping they might dance together that evening, but if she was reading the signals correctly, he was contemplating a considerably more intimate encounter. A flush of warmth flooded her body as she realized that her thoughts had turned down the same seductive path.

As he opened the closet door in the foyer, she grimaced at the idea of spoiling her outfit with her old jacket, but he made that worry disappear as well.

"My mother gave this coat to Aunt Louise, and she insists you wear it tonight."

Janice gasped at the sight of the full-length sable coat. The rich reddish-brown color nearly matched her hair. It might have been polite to protest a little, but she simply turned around so that he could put it on her. Wrapped in the magnificent fur, with a gorgeous man doting on her, she felt like a princess.

When they drove onto Haversham Street and she saw the myriad of twinkle lights, she forgot about the sarcastic thoughts she had had that morning. Tonight she was a princess, Haversham was her fairy-tale kingdom, and if she was very lucky, Wes would continue to play the part of her prince . . . at least for the next few hours.

Ghosts and haunted houses, commercial ventures and magazine articles, ex-husbands and deceased wives, they could all wait until tomorrow.

During the drive to Waitsfield, Wes commented on various points of interest, and when they arrived, he gave her a tour through the town. It was immediately evident that Waitsfield was more commercial than Haversham. There were two fast-food restaurants and a number of tourist-oriented shops. She liked Haversham better.

Janice didn't know how it had happened, but she had undergone a drastic change of attitude since her arrival that morning. Perhaps there really were supernatural forces at work in Haversham. . .something that had the power to make her want to believe in fairy tales again.

"Are you cold?" Wes asked.

She realized she was sitting there hugging herself and purposely relaxed her body. "Not at all. I was just thinking that there must be a way to save Haversham without turning it into a tourist mecca."

Wes was quiet for a moment, then requested a favor. "Would you mind if we didn't discuss it tonight? The subject of Haversham's future tends to spoil my appetite."

Janice smiled. *Not* talking business was just fine with her.

The Mountaintop Lodge, with its breathtaking view, turned out to be as elegant and romantic as May had promised. Heads turned as she and Wes were guided to their table, but rather than making her nervous, it boosted her good feeling a bit higher.

Wes ordered himself to calm down and look at the menu the waiter handed him. His stomach was jittery, his chest was tight, and he had the most ridiculous urge to throw every man in the restaurant off the cliff outside. How dare they all stare at Janice that way? Couldn't they see she was spoken for?

Suddenly he realized what was happening to him. He was jealous! Totally, irrationally jealous over a woman he'd only met that morning. It made no sense. He'd never reacted that way with Joanne, and she was as beautiful as a woman could be.

He peered over his menu at Janice. She was very attractive, but that wasn't what was causing these unfamiliar feelings. There was something drawing him to her that couldn't be seen. Something more elemental than physical beauty.

When he took Joanne out, he'd always felt proud to show her off. At the moment, all he could think of was how quickly they could finish dinner so that he could

have Janice to himself. The words repeated in his head
until he recalled that he had used the same phrase
earlier when telling Janice the story of the jealousy that
marked the marriage of the original Lord Wesley and
Lady Elizabeth.

Could history be repeating itself? Was he being
given a second chance to live up to the Haversham tradition? The possibility made itself at home in his mind.

"Do you believe in fate?" he asked.

Janice angled her head thoughtfully. "I don't know.
Maybe. Why?"

"No reason. I was just wondering."

The band struck up an old love song and Wes closed
his menu. "Would you care to dance?"

Her practical side hadn't been completely silenced
yet. "Shouldn't we wait to order first?"

He stood and held out his hand. "I've waited too
long already."

It was hardly an original line, and yet her intuition
told her he truly meant it. As strange as it seemed, she
felt the same way.

He led her onto the polished-wood dance floor, and
she glided gracefully into his embrace. From the first
step they moved as if they'd danced together a thousand
times before. When his cheek rested against her head, it
seemed perfectly natural for her fingers to stroke the
nape of his neck. As if they had done these things before as well. His warm hand caressed the small of her
back, bringing her close to him with only the slightest
pressure. It felt so right, so *familiar,* that Janice didn't
hesitate to align their bodies so that they each knew the
effect they were having on one another.

For several seconds after the band finished the song,
they remained entwined. And when they moved apart,

Janice saw her own sense of wonderment reflected in Wes's eyes.

Somehow the waiter got their order, they shared a bottle of wine, and ate some food, but Janice had no idea what any of it tasted like. She had been transported to a dreamy place where all that mattered was the way Wes was looking at her and how he repeatedly stroked the back of her hand with his thumb.

They spoke of inconsequential matters that had nothing to do with what was really on their minds. Eventually they gave up the pretense of enjoying the meal and returned to the dance floor, where there was no need for empty words.

Neither was anxious to give up the pleasure they'd discovered in each other's arms, yet their dancing soon took on an intimacy that was no longer appropriate in public.

"Shall we go home?" he whispered in her ear.

"Please." There was no need to say more.

During the drive back to Haversham, he held her hand, occasionally bringing it to his lips or giving it a squeeze. She didn't allow herself to think about what she was feeling, for fear it was only make-believe.

The inn was completely dark when they pulled into the lot and parked next to Aunt Louise's car.

"That's strange," Wes said. "I was sure Aunt Louise would be waiting up for us. I wonder why she didn't leave a light on."

"You don't think there could be a crowd of neighbors planning to surprise us, do you?"

Wes laughed. "Not even May would do that. She'll just drop by at dawn for her interrogation."

As soon as they entered the dark foyer, Wes flicked the wall switch several times without the lights responding.

"Probably blew a fuse. Wait right here while I go down to the basement and take care of it."

While he was gone she hung up the borrowed coat in the closet, but she didn't try navigating any further without light. It seemed as though she'd been standing there quite a while when an eerie, flickering light shone from the sitting room. Her heart skipped a beat as her imagination conjured up a ghostly presence.

Taking a nervous step toward the glowing archway, she hoped it was a friendly soul and not Wes's late wife coming to put a damper on their evening.

4

Janice gasped aloud as she and Wes nearly collided in the archway of the sitting room. The light was coming from a kerosene lamp in his hand.

"Sorry that took so long." He raised the lamp to illuminate her face. "Are you all right? You look like you've just seen a ghost." His expression and voice were both teasing.

"Very funny," she said with a frown, then realized it *was* pretty funny. "I gather it wasn't just a fuse."

"No. It must be a problem outside. It will have to wait until morning. In the meantime, I'll light a fire in your room for you." He set the lamp down on the table so that he could hang up his overcoat.

With the lamp in one hand, he put his other arm around her waist to guide her up the stairs. The sense of anticipation that had built up while they were dancing had faded when they reached the darkened inn, but the moment he touched her, it flared anew. She was uncertain as to how much she wanted to happen between them that night, except that she absolutely had to find out what his kiss tasted like.

She obeyed his hand signals to be very quiet lest they wake up Aunt Louise, but the squeaky door hinges weren't as cooperative. They both held their breath for several long seconds after reclosing the door, waiting to see if the noise had roused Aunt Louise.

"Fortunately, she's a bit hard of hearing," Wes murmured after he was certain they hadn't disturbed her.

Janice stood by the fireplace while he set fire to the logs and put the kerosene lamp in the bathroom for her.

"Are you cold?" he asked for the second time that evening.

Between the fire blazing at her back and thoughts of how good he looked, she was as far from being cold as she could be. "If I say yes, will you wrap your arms around me to warm me up?"

He took a few steps toward her.

"That would be a good excuse to hold you again," he said, removing his glasses and placing them on the fireplace mantel. "Or I could turn on the radio and we could go back to pretending we were dancing." He closed the distance between them. "Or we could just quit looking for excuses and do what we've both been thinking about for hours."

His fingers stroked her cheek so gently, she sighed and closed her eyes. As his hands tipped her head back, her tongue moistened her lips. By the time his lips touched hers, her pulse was racing with expectation. The tender peck she received did nothing to satisfy her curiosity, let alone her need. She looked up at him and saw restrained desire clouded by confusion. "What is it?"

"If I kiss you the way I want, I'm not going to want to stop there. Part of me knows we just met and it's much too soon to feel this strongly. But another part of me feels like I've known you forever, and there's nothing we could do together that would be wrong."

His words melted what little common sense she had

left. "I understand. I feel the same way. I hardly ever kiss a man good night on a first date, let alone . . ." She shyly bowed her head. "Let alone what I want to do with you."

Kissing her forehead while enveloping her in his arms, his words contradicted his actions. "Tell me to go, and I will. I can't promise it won't happen tomorrow or the next day, but it doesn't have to be tonight."

She raised her eyes back to his. "I can't order you to leave when I want you to stay so badly. Like you said at dinner, I've already waited long enough."

She slid her hands up the lapels of his jacket and around his neck, then pulled his head down to her. When their lips came together again, she was momentarily overwhelmed by the power she had unleashed. His mouth moved hurriedly over hers, pressing, withdrawing, and pressing again, tempting her with the promise of a deeper kiss only to pull back once more, as if he were afraid to take what he wanted.

Frustrated, she held his head still and took the initiative. With her mouth slanted beneath his, she slipped her tongue between his lips. That was all the encouragement he needed, for a second later he recaptured the lead, diving into an eating kiss that brought them both to their knees. His hands joined the assault, easing her the rest of the way down onto the plush carpet.

As demanding as his kisses had become, his caresses were even more so. One moment his hand skimmed up her stockinged thigh to knead her hip, the next it captured her breast. He was trying to discover every inch of her at once, and dear Lord, she wanted to help him. Her sweaterdress was already twisted up around her waist, and it only took a little maneuvering to get rid of it completely. As she tugged off his jacket and undid his shirt, he bared her breasts and learned their taste. In a tangle of arms and legs, the rest of the barriers between them were tossed aside.

"I want you too much," Wes murmured between hot kisses, his body straining against hers. "I should go slow—"

"No," she protested, and slipped her hand between their bodies to encourage him to act rather than think. "I never needed anything in my life as much as I need to feel you inside of me right now." She lightly grazed his sensitive flesh with her fingernails, and he gave in to the primal urge that was driving them both.

What had been desperate need was abruptly catapulted beyond anything definable.

They clung to one another as the raging winds of passion swept them away to a place where nothing mattered but satisfaction. Yet their hunger was too great to be appeased with one explosive release. Without pause, Wes took them to another, gentler plateau where all their senses were magnified and focused on each other.

When the ultimate pleasure was shared a second time and they lay breathlessly in the sweet afterglow, it occurred to Janice that what she had just done wasn't very smart. However, she didn't have the energy to scold herself over something so incredibly wonderful. And if she had accidentally gotten pregnant . . . well, would that really be so bad? Her ex-husband hadn't wanted children, and she had wanted them badly enough to have them without a husband who cared. No, it wouldn't be so bad if she had just conceived a child by Wesley Haversham XII.

Wes couldn't fathom what had come over him. In all his years with Joanne, as much as he had loved her, he had never experienced anything close to what he had just enjoyed with Janice. Nor had he ever had any interest in experimenting with any other women. What had just happened was proof that fate had surely had a hand in bringing Janice Fowler to Haversham. Perhaps his being so caught up in the fireworks that he forgot about protection was another trick of fate. Wesley Haversham XIII could already be on his way.

He gave her a long, sensual kiss, then murmured against her lips, "Marry me."

She smiled and nuzzled his neck. "Okay. Just so I don't have to get up and put clothes on."

He eased her away and waited for her to look at him. "I'm serious."

She blinked at him. "About what?"

"Getting married."

She stared at him long enough to be certain he wasn't kidding. Sitting up, she combed the hair back from his forehead with her fingers. "I didn't think they made men like you anymore. But believe me, I am a thoroughly modern woman. What we just did—and by the way, it was beyond a doubt the best sex I ever had—it was by mutual consent. You didn't compromise me or do anything that requires an apology or an offer to make an honest woman of me."

He sat up and grasped her hands. "What if I got you pregnant?"

She shrugged. "It would pose some difficulties, but I could manage. I wouldn't hold you responsible."

"That's a hell of an attitude."

"Careful. We don't want to anger your spirits by getting profane now, do we?"

He gave her hands a squeeze. "Stop it. I'm asking you to be my wife and you're making jokes."

"Wes, please. Be reasonable. Once your hormones settle back into place you'll realize that we were both simply stricken with a severe case of lust. It will go away, believe me."

His jaw tensed. "It wasn't lust."

"Was it love? Can you honestly say that, in less than one day, you fell madly in love with me? To have and to hold, till death do us part?"

"Yes."

She let out a sigh and mumbled, "I don't believe this conversation." Her mind fought to stay rational despite her emotions telling her to risk everything for a chance at happily ever after. "Look, I can understand how you might be anxious to remarry; it was obviously a good experience for you. But my first marriage was the pits. We mistook lust for love and put each other through torture for five years. I can't risk doing that again. I'm not sure I ever want to get married a second time ... to *anyone*. I like my independence."

"I can give you anything you've ever wanted in your life. I'm very wealthy."

"How nice," she said with a laugh. "What's next, do you show me a copy of the results of your last physical? I'm sorry. I know you're not trying to be funny, but you've really thrown me for a loop tonight. Can we just let it drop for now?"

He took a deep breath. "Fine. We can drop it for tonight, but it won't change anything. I love you, and I want to marry you. What happened with your first husband has nothing to do with us."

He got up, walked over to the bed, and turned down the covers.

Janice rose and went to him. Running a finger down his spine, she asked, "Another service from the friendly staff of the Haversham Inn?" She meant for the double entendre to lighten his mood, but when he turned around, she could see he had taken her remark as an insult.

"Is that what you think of me—a hotel amenity, like a swimming pool or lounge act? Maybe you're used to calling the concierge to send up a bellboy to service you, but—"

Crack. Her hand slapped his cheek before she could think about it. For several seconds, they stared at each other, breathing heavily.

"I deserved that," Wes finally said. "I apologize."

She shook her head and touched his cheek. "I shouldn't have slapped you. I've never done that in my life."

"And I've never behaved so ungentlemanly. You're the first woman I've been with since my wife died. And there was no one before her. I don't give my love lightly, Janice. It's important to me that you believe that."

She rose on tiptoes to give him a brief kiss. "I believe you, but that's all the more reason for you to slow down." She kissed him again, and this time he participated. "Will you stay with me?"

"I'd like to, but under the circumstances it would probably be best if I didn't. Besides, I'd just as soon not have Aunt Louise catch me coming out of your room in the morning. It would be all over town in an hour."

His grin let her know he was going to be okay, and she smiled back. Threading her fingers into the dark curls on his chest, she said, "Maybe you could just lie down with me for a little while."

"I really shouldn't."

She licked his one nipple, then the other.

"I'd probably fall asleep." His protest was not the least bit convincing.

Her hands trailed down his sides and around his waist to cup his firm bottom, and she felt his response against her stomach.

"Then again, I don't feel all that tired."

As his mouth came down on hers they tumbled onto the bed. The third time they came together was much slower, as they discovered the secrets of one another's bodies; but somehow the finish was even more powerful because of it.

Janice still thought it was lust, though it far surpassed anything she'd felt with her ex-husband.

Wes finally managed to part from her to spare their reputations, and despite a profound sense of loneliness, Janice eventually fell sleep.

She awoke in the morning with the pleasant kind of discomfort that can only be caused by great sex. She had the feeling Aunt Louise didn't need to catch Wes coming out of her room. As a woman, she'd know the minute she saw the smile on Janice's face.

She stretched and forced her eyes open. To her surprise, a red rose was lying on the pillow next to her. How in the world had he managed to find a rose in the middle of the night in December?

Two more surprises awaited her in the bathroom. First, the power had been restored. Second, the words *Janice Haversham* were printed on the mirror. The letters appeared to be fingerpainted on with some sort of gel.

Wes had a knack for walking around without making any noise, but she wondered how he had opened and closed the door to the suite without her hearing the hinges squeak. She must have been in an extremely deep sleep.

As she descended the stairs, she smelled bacon and coffee and heard a number of voices coming from the dining room. Before she reached the bottom step, however, Wes appeared and detoured her into the sitting room.

She opened her mouth to question why he had done that, but he pulled her into his arms and kissed her for such a long time, she forgot what she was going to ask.

"Good morning to you, too," she said quietly. His grin was contagious.

"Now maybe I can handle the crowd in the dining room."

From the way he said that she knew it wasn't good.

He kept his voice low as he explained, "The whole town council just happened to pick this morning to have breakfast here."

"Because of me?"

"Because of us."

"Oh. Are they angry because I'm an outsider? Surely they know I'll be leaving in three days."

He frowned at her. "We'll discuss the matter of your leaving at another time. But no, they're not angry. They're hoping our date last night was successful."

Now it was her turn to frown. "I don't get it. Why would it matter to them?"

Shrugging, he said, "I guess they want to see me happy. Do you accept my proposal of marriage?"

"*Wes* . . ."

"Not convinced yet? All right, but you'd make this a lot easier if you'd just say yes before we go in there." He held out an arm to escort her. "Shall we go face the inquisition?"

She went with him, but she had the uncomfortable feeling there was something going on that he wasn't telling her. "Wait," she said, tugging him back into the sitting room. "Thank you for the rose, but I think the message on the mirror could have been a bit more subtle."

He was completely bewildered by her comment. "What rose? What message?"

"Are you implying that you did not return to my room while I was sleeping, put a rose on the pillow, and write *Janice Haversham* on the mirror in the bathroom?"

His look of confusion was altered to one of awareness. "Was the writing done in a cloudy, jellylike substance?"

She nodded.

"That's great," he said happily. "They like you. They want you to be my wife."

She rolled her eyes. "Really, now! You think your ancestors were showing their approval by writing a message on the mirror? Look, I'm trying to be open-minded about this spirit business—"

"It was them. There are no roses growing here in the winter. The nearest florist shop is in Waitsfield. And that substance on the mirror is ectoplasm."

She shook her head. She didn't have a better explanation, unless he was lying, and her intuition kept telling her he was a completely honest man. Could Aunt Louise have been her stealthy visitor? That seemed highly unlikely. "I'm sorry. I just can't believe it. Maybe if I actually saw one of them, I'd feel differently. I don't know."

He arched one eyebrow and said, "Maybe one of them will decide to be obliging, if that's what you require before you believe you are meant to be my wife."

She felt ridiculously conspicuous as Wes took her into the dining room and introduced her to the group gathering there. She knew May and Chuck—Stephie and her mother were handling the diner—and Bernice and Aunt Louise. Everyone was friendly, but openly curious about her background, her career, her plans for the article on Haversham, and of course her opinion of the town, the inn, and especially their mayor.

Wes attempted to tactfully request that they respect Janice's privacy, but his efforts were ignored. If they had been the least bit rude, she would have refused to answer their questions, but they seemed genuinely interested in her, and their pride in the town was a pleasure to behold.

"I like Haversham very much," she assured all of them. "And I would truly like to help you, but I can't promise to write what you want me to. What I thought I'd do is visit with a number of you who believe you have had experiences with spirits, I'll take some photographs, and we'll see how it turns out."

"And what about you and Wesley?" May asked bluntly. "Do you two have plans for this evening?"

Janice couldn't stop the blush as she glanced at Wes. His plans for their evening were explicitly detailed in the steamy look he gave her. "We'll just have to see how that turns out, too."

During the next hour, Janice prepared a schedule of who she would see at what time and where. Wordlessly, Wes penciled himself in from two o'clock on each day.

She hadn't expected him to accompany her to each home or place of business, but she was pleased when he did. It gave her a chance to observe him interacting with his constituents, all of whom were either family or friends. Though it wasn't her primary objective, she also took the opportunity to listen to what the residents had to say about the future of their town. Not a single person voiced an objection to commercializing Haversham, but she picked up the unspoken concerns and fears that they would be losing something very precious in the process. Almost everyone she spoke to used the word "tradition" at some point during their conversation.

By two o'clock she had heard tales of ghostly appearances during times of great joy or sorrow. Wes had to stop several people from revealing what was expected to happen on Christmas Eve in order to keep the event a surprise. She also learned that the spirits could be mischievous or humorous, affectionate or reprimanding. The personality of the living didn't alter when they passed on. Ectoplasmic messages, like the one she supposedly received that morning, were rare, but two people she spoke to had received them when some vital decision had to be made. However, everyone had heard the glass wind chimes at some time in their life.

She also learned how well respected Wes was and how much he cared about each person's welfare. His gentlemanly demeanor went all the way to his core.

"What do you think now?" he asked her when they left the last appointment.

"Boy, you Haversham guys sure make it tough to remain a skeptic!"

He winked at her. "As someone once said, 'you ain't seen nuttin' yet!' Did you notice that the power had been turned back on this morning?"

"Of course. You must have been up awfully early to take care of it."

Wes shook his head. "I didn't take care of anything. *They* did. I guess they figured a fire would be more romantic than electric light." He pulled her close for a lingering kiss. "I think it worked very well."

After all the stories she'd just heard, turning the power off and on was a relatively minor feat for

Haversham's spirits. Maybe, just maybe, they really were hovering around.

Following May's suggestion, Wes took Janice to Montpelier for the rest of the day. The historic capital was as lovely as every other part of Vermont she'd seen so far. As he showed her around, he took advantage of every opportunity to hold her close and kiss her senseless. By the time they returned to the inn, she was weak with desire.

Their lovemaking was no less explosive than the night before, and Janice's resistance began to falter.

"Remember when I asked you if you believe in fate?" he murmured.

"Was that last night, or a hundred years ago?" She tickled his ear with her tongue and he laughingly repaid her in kind before replying.

"I didn't know how you'd react if I told you last night, but after everything you heard today, I think you're ready."

She eased back a bit. "Ooh. This sounds spooky."

He tweaked her nose. "Some months ago, I read your article in *Time,* then I threw out the magazine. Or I thought I did. The next day, I saw it on my nightstand, so I tossed it out with that day's newspaper. The next morning it was beside my bed again, only this time it was open to your article."

"Ancestor intervention again?" Janice asked. She was feeling less skeptical by the hour.

"What else? At any rate, you know what happened next. The point is, you were *meant* to come here, and the spirits gave fate a nudge. I had thought you were needed to help Haversham, but now I know you had to come for me as well." He kissed her tenderly, and she snuggled back into his embrace. "I love you, Janice, and I want you to stay with me forever. Please be my wife."

It would have been so easy to simply agree. Believe that fate and the spirit world had brought her to Haversham to be with him. But her natural skepticism and a disastrous marriage prevented her from giving in, even while his hands and mouth tempted her with the promise of a lifetime of pleasure. She could not say yes, and yet tonight, she couldn't say no, either.

Reluctantly, he accepted the small progress he'd made about their future and went back to enjoying the present. He stayed a bit longer that night, but again he returned to his own room.

Janice drifted off into a peaceful sleep moments after he left her alone.

"Janice."

She heard her name whispered in her dream, yet it didn't seem to belong there.

"Janice."

The repetition pulled her out of her dream, but she was too immersed in sleep to heed the call.

"Janice!"

The demand got through to her and she raised one eyelid. She didn't remember leaving a light on, but her room was no longer dark. Straining to focus on the source of the light, she was bewildered by what she saw. "Wes?" He was standing near the foot of the bed, and a soft glow surrounded him. When he made no move or sound, she blinked and squinted until she could see him a bit clearer. It was Wesley, and then again, it wasn't. His hair was brushed back from his forehead, he was dressed like a nobleman from eighteenth-century England, and he wasn't wearing his glasses.

She propped herself up on her elbow as she came fully awake. "What are you doing dressed like that?"

"Marry Wesley," he whispered, and smoothly glided through the bedroom door to the parlor.

"Wes!" she called, somewhat annoyed at his prank. "Come back here." When he didn't obey, she rose and went into the parlor, only to find herself alone there. She turned on a light and proceeded to search the entire suite, looking behind furniture and drapes, inside closets, even places he couldn't possibly be hiding.

Had she only dreamed that he was there, dressed up in a historical costume? Considering all that had happened in the last two days, it was possible that her dreams had become more vivid than usual.

No. He had definitely been there—and vanished—leaving only an odd, musty smell behind.

5

Janice quickly put on her robe to go pay Wes a return visit. As soon as she opened the door to her suite and heard the squeaky hinges, she was back to being confused. He couldn't possibly have been there and left without her hearing his exit.

A few seconds later, she was downstairs, knocking on his door. When he didn't answer immediately, she knocked a bit louder and called his name. "Wes, it's Janice. I need to talk to you."

The door opened and for a moment she forgot why she was there. He looked positively delicious. From his tousled hair and sleepy eyes to his sexy body, covered only with a pair of briefs, he had clearly been sound asleep. He gave her a welcoming grin, nonetheless.

"Couldn't sleep?" he asked, stroking her cheek.

"No. Yes. I—" She forced herself to think past the desire he had so easily reignited. "Were you in my room a few minutes ago?" she asked, despite the evidence to the contrary.

His fingers slipped behind her neck and urged her closer for a slow, sensual kiss. "A few minutes ago?" He moved his lower body against hers. "I feel like I haven't been with you in days."

She closed her eyes as his mouth returned to hers

and his hands sought out the sensitive places he had found earlier.

"Let's go back to your room," he said, lifting her into his arms.

That slight interruption was enough to remind her of why she had awakened him. "Wait. I have to tell you what happened. I woke up because I thought I heard my name being called. Then I saw you, or it looked like you, dressed up . . . in a Halloween costume, like some old English lord. And there was a strange light around you."

He set her on her feet and peered at her very intently. "Did the man you saw say anything?"

She made a face at him. "Yes. He . . . *you* said, 'Marry Wesley,' then you disappeared."

"Come with me." He led her by the hand into the sitting room and turned on a light. Waving his arm at the portraits on the walls, he asked, "See anyone familiar?"

What he was implying abruptly dawned on her. Her mysterious visitor was one of his ancestors! As crazy as it sounded, she was no longer able to deny the possibility. Her gaze scanned the painted images until she saw who she was looking for. "That's him," she declared, walking up to a portrait of a man wearing the same clothing as the one who had awakened her.

Wes smiled. "That's Lord Wesley. The only time he ever makes an appearance is on Christmas Eve, which proves how important it is for you to accept my proposal."

She sighed and shook her head. Spiritual endorsement or not, it was all too much, too fast. "I don't know what to think anymore."

"Then don't think. Just give in to the inevitable." He pulled her into his arms. "Say yes."

She looked up at him, and the adoring expression on his face almost convinced her to say the word. Her heart was ready. But her mind was clinging to practicality.

Now it was his turn to sigh. "All right. Tomorrow is Christmas Eve. I can wait until then."

"What is it that's supposed to happen on Christmas Eve?"

"Something that will change the mind of the worst skeptic," he said with a teasing smile. "Tomorrow night, at the stroke of midnight, you are going to witness a miracle."

"A *miracle*?" she repeated with a chuckle. "What do you call Lord Wesley's appearance in my bedroom? An everyday occurrence?"

"You'll see." He swept her into his arms again and headed for the stairs. "For now, let's just see what we can do about putting you back to sleep."

Nestled in his arms, she wanted him to understand why it was so hard for her to jump into another marriage. She told him about the very rocky relationship she and her husband had had, and how and when it had ended.

He kissed her then and promised that soon she would have a new Christmas Eve memory to help her forget the bitter one.

As it turned out, it was nearly dawn when Wes left her again.

By the time she came downstairs the next morning, Aunt Louise was the only one in the dining room.

"Good morning, sleepyhead," the older woman said with a broad smile. "Would you like breakfast or lunch?"

"Just coffee, please. I have an appointment in fifteen minutes with the Barringers."

"Not anymore you don't. Wesley let everyone know that all appointments were pushed back to this afternoon. He's out right now taking care of that."

"Oh. That was very kind of him."

"Hmmph! I'd say it was the least he could do after keeping you up half the night. All the spirits living in this house together never made as much ruckus as the two of you did."

Janice, the thoroughly modern woman of the nineties, blushed to the roots of her hair.

Aunt Louise walked over and gave her a motherly hug. "Now, now, there's nothing to be embarrassed about. It was meant to be. And now everyone can stop fretting." Without asking Janice's preference again, she broke two eggs in a frying pan. "Of course, it will be another month or so before you'll have any official results, but most people will take my word for the fact that it's already a done thing."

Janice wrinkled her forehead as she tried to interpret what Louise was telling her.

"Oh, my. You didn't realize it, did you? I suppose your being a skeptic keeps you from believing it without a doctor's report."

Frustration caused Janice to raise her voice. "What *are* you talking about?"

Aunt Louise patted Janice's stomach. "Why the baby, dear. Wesley Haversham the thirteenth. And don't worry yourself about what people will think about your having your honeymoon before the marriage. They'll all be too happy to hear that the Haversham tradition won't be ending with Wesley." She popped two slices of bread in the toaster, then got out a plate and flatware.

Janice's head was spinning. *The baby? Wesley Haversham XIII? The Haversham tradition?* Whether or not Aunt Louise was truly psychic was irrelevant. She could be pregnant, and it sounded as though the whole town was waiting to hear the good news. Yesterday morning's 'spontaneous' breakfast get-together came to mind. Everyone was so very happy to have her there, and so very interested in her and Wes's date.

Could it possibly be that saving Haversham involved more than building up the economic base? Did their superstitions go so far as to imagine that the town would die if Wes didn't have a son to carry on the tradition? A chill trickled down her spine and settled like a cold lump in her stomach.

"—to have children underfoot again, seeing them play hide-and-seek in the secret passageways, making noise . . . aah, I can hardly wait." Aunt Louise placed a cup of coffee and a plate of breakfast on a tray. As she carried it out to the dining room, she turned around and smiled at Janice. "Come along, little mother. You're feeding two now, you know."

Like a sleepwalker, Janice obediently went into the dining room and sat down. For some reason, she had been royally set up. But why her? Surely there were other women that would have been pleased to act as breeder for a handsome, wealthy man. Instantly she knew the answer. Other women might not have been able to help promote the town!

If the nefarious scheme didn't directly involve her, she might have admired Wes's ingenuity. With her, he could handle two problems at once. No wonder he never took any precautions with her and was so very anxious to tie the knot. *Love!* Bah humbug.

Her brain busily sorted out the previous two days' events. As she swallowed her breakfast without tasting it, Aunt Louise continued chattering away happily across the table from her.

If he lied about loving her, he could have lied about everything else—her bags being unpacked, the ectoplasmic message, the ridiculous explanation about the magazine article. And of course if the whole town was in on the plan, they would have all lied about their experiences.

Suddenly an image of the ghostly Lord Wesley flashed in her mind. Examining it critically, she saw what she had missed when she was half asleep. The eerie glow was the same as she had seen created by the kerosene lamp the first night, and the "lord" had kept one arm behind his back, as if he were hiding something. A ghost wouldn't have need of a lamp, but a real man playing a ghost might use one to create a spooky appearance.

Yet if her visitor had been Wes after all, where had he gone from her bedroom, if he didn't walk out the door? "Aunt Louise, did you just say something about secret passageways?" She tried to sound innocently curious, so as not to alarm the woman.

"Yes, yes. This old house is full of hidden passages. There's a whole maze behind the walls. Children always love to play hide-and-seek in them. Don't worry, though, they can't really get lost, since all the passageways lead back to one place eventually."

Still maintaining a calm front, she asked, "And that one place?"

"The front room—Wes's bedroom. You'll have to ask him to give you the behind-the-scenes tour when he comes back."

"Yes. I'll have to do that." Janice couldn't remain seated another second. "Please excuse me. I think I'll go back up and lie down, since I don't have an appointment to rush off to."

She didn't wait to hear Aunt Louise's parting comments. The moment she reached her room, she began a thorough examination of the parlor walls. Knocking every few inches, it didn't take long to find a panel that sounded hollow. A few seconds later she discovered that pushing on the right side caused the wall section to pivot like a revolving door. And it was completely silent!

Immediately inside the tunnel, she found a light switch, then two narrow, winding flights of stairs, one going up and one going down. Through trial and error, she eventually found herself in Wes's bedroom. Following her intuition, she inspected the contents of his closet, armoire, and chest of drawers. She discovered the secret to his silent walking—rubber-soled shoes. To spare the wooden floors, perhaps? Or to frighten visitors with unexpected appearances?

It wasn't until she lifted the heavy lid on an old cedar chest, however, that she found the final piece of damning evidence. Right on top of a pile of old clothing was the outfit Wes had worn in her room last night. Now she realized that the odd smell she had detected was a mixture of burning kerosene and cedar.

She considered going back upstairs and clearing out before Wes returned, but that would strip her of the opportunity to curse his black soul to hell with the rest of his ancestors. So she sat down in the chair beside the open trunk, a spot from which she could see Haversham Street out the window.

Less than a half hour later, she saw his car pull into the drive. The minutes ticked by as she imagined him greeting Aunt Louise and learning his patsy had gone back to bed. She was beginning to wonder if she had guessed wrong about his going to her room to awaken her when he stepped through the passageway. His worried gaze darted from her to the open trunk and back. "I can explain everything."

"I don't doubt that," Janice said in a voice laced with as much hurt as anger. "You're very good at explaining things ... as long as you don't have to be honest."

He strode across the room and knelt before her. He tried to take her hands, but she bolted out of the chair and away from him.

"Cut the theatrics, *Lord* Wesley. I'm not buying them any more. I only stayed here to let you know that if you did manage to get me pregnant, you will *never* see this child. I'll swear I was with three other men this week, if that's what it takes to deny your rights of paternity."

Wes rose and walked toward her, looking utterly baffled. "What on earth are you talking about? I thought you might be upset if you guessed what I had done last night, but I was desperate to convince you to marry me. I would have confessed ... eventually. But what's all this about paternity rights?"

In crisp, concise language, she informed him of her conversation with Aunt Louise and the conclusions she had drawn.

By the time she was finished, he was pacing the floor and scraping his fingers through his hair. "I can't believe this. Yes, I can. I've lived my entire life in a town full of busybodies, who mean well. These are good, honest people, who wouldn't know how to pull the kind of scam you're talking about. They're just superstitious and believe in spirits and the mysterious workings of fate. Aunt Louise probably thought that you'd be happy to know that everyone wanted you to stay and be the mother of the next mayor. *They* consider it an honor."

He marched over to her and grasped her shoulders before she could evade him again. "Think about what you just said, Janice. Every single person in this town lied to you? *Every one*? All those friendly, uncomplicated people you met yesterday are all expert liars, whose greed could provoke them to encourage me to seduce a woman for the sake of the town? Do you honestly believe that?"

He was breathless as he stood there waiting for her response.

She felt herself weakening and willed herself to walk away. Before she reached the door of his apartment, however, he blocked her exit.

"Where are you going?" he demanded.

"I'm leaving."

"You can't leave until tomorrow. You have to be here at midnight tonight."

She stared at him, steeling herself against the desperate need she saw in his eyes. "Please let me by." When he didn't move out of her path, she tried to step around him, but he moved as well. Making an about-face, she headed for the passageway. He rushed in front of her and closed the panel.

"At least hear me out first. The only supernatural occurrence that I or any other living person has been responsible for was Lord Wesley's visit last night. Everything else was absolutely legitimate. I realize what a mistake I made, but I can't undo it now. I did it for a wholly selfish reason. It was strictly meant to benefit me, not the town. I love you, and I was willing to do anything to keep you here with me. I was just so afraid that if you went away after Christmas the way you planned, I'd never get you back. And if you'll recall, I didn't lie to you about being in your suite. I only changed the subject. Everything I've ever said to you has been the truth."

"Is that it?"

He rubbed the tension out of his forehead. "No. I'm sorry Aunt Louise was indelicate. And I'm sorry if you truly believe I seduced you with nothing in mind but perpetuating the Haversham tradition. I'll admit it occurred to me, but only after it was too late to go back and take preventive measures.

"I don't know what else to say. There is nothing I would enjoy more than to see a child of our making growing inside your body, but not because of any tradition. I loved Joanne and respected her memory enough to let the Haversham line come to an end rather than replace her in my life with someone I had lukewarm feelings about.

"But then you came along, and it was as if I'd been struck by a bolt of lightning. What I felt for Joanne was good, but entirely different from how you make me feel. You aren't just a convenient means to an end. You're a dream come true for me."

She was doing her best not to listen to the words coming out of his mouth, but he was making it more difficult by the minute.

Taking a deep breath, she said, "I was married to a man who played me for a fool for five years. I can't let that happen to me again."

"Tell me what to do," he pleaded. "What can I say to convince you that I love you?"

"I don't know, Wes. How do you earn back someone's trust after you've ripped their heart to shreds?" His look of dejection almost swayed her, but she turned and walked out of the apartment.

She packed as quickly as possible, holding back the tears for a time when she was far away from Haversham, Vermont. With some effort, she managed to haul her suitcase down the stairs, but Aunt Louise caught her before she made it out the door.

"Janice, dear, whatever do you think you're doing with that heavy thing? Consider the poor babe."

"Spare me, Louise. I've had enough nonsense for one week." She ignored the stunned look on the woman's face, but she couldn't ignore the man leaning against the archway of the sitting room.

"Janice has obviously decided to leave us, Aunt Louise. She is of the opinion that we have all been part of an enormous hoax to take advantage of her talents and her virtue."

Louise's mouth dropped open with an expression of quite believable shock. "A hoax? I don't understand."

"Your nephew can fill you in," Janice said as she got her old suede jacket out of the closet. Her hand brushed against the sable coat, and the memory of Wes wrapping her in the magnificent fur made her heart clench, but she pushed it out of her mind.

"Please don't go," Wes said quietly.

"You were meant to be one of us," Aunt Louise added.

Janice simply shook her head and opened the door. She didn't make it out, however, for half the town seemed to be standing on the porch and in the parking lot between her and her car.

"We heard you were planning to leave," May stated incredulously. "You mustn't do that. If you and Wes had a little tiff over something, I'm sure it can be worked out."

Janice turned around and frowned at Wes.

"Don't be upset with him, dear," Bernice said, pushing her way forward. She was holding a dress box with a pretty red bow on it. "Wes called to ask me to bring this over immediately, so naturally I wanted to know why the rush. I mean, it was his gift to you for tonight's party. So he *had* to tell me why, you see. Then I told May, and—"

"All right," Janice said, holding up a hand to stop the explanation. "Please. I have to leave. I'm sorry."

They made a path for her despite the fact that they all looked as though she were taking away their last hope. And maybe she was, but that wasn't her problem.

Without looking back, she forced the big suitcase into the back of her Bugmobile. She then got behind the wheel and turned the key in the ignition. If she didn't get out of there soon, she was going to burst into tears.

Click. Click.

This can't be happening, she thought. Not a dead battery. Please don't let it be a dead battery.

"Sounds like a dead battery," Chuck shouted beside her door.

She rolled down the window to talk to him. There was no way she was getting out of the car again. "Can you fix it?"

"Of course. Soon as I get a battery to fit this model. I'll be able to make a run up to the parts store in Waitsfield first thing Monday morning."

"Monday morning?" she cried. "But this is only Friday. Why can't you get it today?"

"Sorry," Chuck said, shaking his head. "No can do. They close at noon today for the holiday." He pushed the sleeve of his coat back to check his watch. "That was a half hour ago."

She groaned and closed her eyes. The thought occurred to her that Chuck probably sabotaged the battery himself, but since she couldn't prove that, or physically force him to repair her car, it was hardly worth the effort to accuse him.

"Best come back inside," he said gently. "It's starting to snow."

That did it! A white Christmas in a fairy-tale village was exactly what was needed to round out her week. With no enthusiasm whatsoever, she climbed out of the car and wended her way back through the crowd. "You win, Wes," she told him as she passed. "I'll be staying a few more days." Climbing the stairs, she spoke in an imperious tone, "Please notify the cook that I'll be taking my meals in my room. I would appreciate not being disturbed otherwise." She heard the anxious murmurs of the crowd begin as she reached her room, and did her best not to listen.

Her last order was almost immediately disobeyed by a knock on her door, which she had no intention of answering.

"Miss Fowler? It's Chuck. I have your suitcase."

"Just leave it outside the door," she called back. After she was certain he was gone, she brought it in herself, then relocked the door. Next, she tried to think of a way to block the passageway, but any furniture heavy enough to prevent the door from opening was too heavy for her to move. She supposed it would have been futile anyway. If Wes really wanted in, he probably had a key to her door.

Slumping down on the sofa, she was suddenly overwhelmed by fatigue. Was it depression or an early sign of pregnancy? *Damn!* She didn't want to think about that yet. Unable to fight the urge to escape into sleep, she stretched out and closed her eyes. She didn't even realize she had dozed off until another knock at the door awakened her. Glancing at her watch, she was surprised to note that it was four o'clock.

"Janice? It's teatime. I brought you a tray." Aunt Louise paused for a response that didn't come. "You hardly ate a thing this morning. I have tea, some cheese and crackers, and some pretty little cakes that May baked."

Janice's stomach demanded she accept the offering. "Please leave it outside. I'll get it shortly." Again she waited a short time before opening the door, but this time, her visitor hadn't departed.

"It appears that I'm the cause of the problem here," Aunt Louise said, nudging Janice aside so she could carry the tray into the parlor. She set it down on the table in front of the sofa, then perched on the edge of a chair. "I'm not leaving you alone until I have my say, so you may as well join me."

Janice took a deep, exasperated breath, but she sat down on the sofa and poured herself some tea. Just because she was upset didn't mean she had to go hungry.

"Good girl," Aunt Louise declared with a nod of her head. "Now, it seems to me that you're in a snit for reasons that make no sense whatsoever."

"Hah! You have no idea—"

"Wes told me everything. It was very foolish of him to try such a silly trick to convince you to marry him, but it was done for love. *You're* the one who has no idea of what's happened here. Wes was a lost soul when Joanne passed on. We thought we would never see him smile again. And if you haven't figured anything else out, you must realize that we're one big family in Haversham. If our most important member is sad, we're all sad.

"Your arrival changed everything. People had hope. Wes came back to life. The town felt happy again. No one lied or made up stories to deceive you, least of all Wes." She paused a moment to be sure she had

Janice's attention. "When I first met you, I sensed the anger inside of you. You've let it rule you for so long, you've forgotten how to be happy. If you'll just quit being angry and let yourself feel the goodness around you, you'll know the truth. Wes loves you. The townspeople respect you and want you to stay. Look deep inside your heart, Janice, and you'll find a woman who could be extremely happy here."

Janice felt the tears about to flow and bit her lip to hold them back.

'I'll go now," Aunt Louise. "You just give what I said some thought."

For some time, Janice sat there as the tears trickled down her cheeks. She knew Aunt Louse was right about the anger. When Wes offered her a fresh start, she couldn't accept it for fear of being hurt all over again. And when she discovered his deceit, all the anger resurfaced.

Perhaps more than was justified.

Wes and Aunt Louise had said the same things in different ways. Did she *really* believe every person in Haversham had lied? That May and Chuck and Bernice were actually wicked, greedy con artists hiding behind masks of friendliness? She pictured them as she had seen them earlier that day. If they were faking sincerity, they should all win Academy Awards for superior acting ability.

And what about Wes? Did she honestly believe he had tricked her into having unprotected sex? She knew she could have stopped him at any time. She recalled the look on his face and the sound of his words when he told her she was the only woman he had been with since Joanne. Had that been a lie? Had his lovemaking been only pretense? The mere thought of his kiss made her shiver.

And yet the fact remained that he had brought her here to promote the town, and he did resort to a low trick to convince her to marry him and bear his child. Besides that, she had no proof that any of the other stories were true.

Dear Lord, what was she to believe?

6

Snow continued to fall for several hours, turning Haversham into a winter paradise. Janice sat by the window most of the time, thinking and rethinking. She was watching the street when all the twinkle lights came on and the snowflakes stopped falling. Aunt Louise brought her dinner, but there was nothing more the woman could say to help settle her mind.

The nap she had taken prevented her from going to sleep, so she was still gazing out the window when Wes came through the passageway at eleven-thirty.

"You've pouted long enough," he said firmly. "It's time to come downstairs. The party begins in thirty minutes."

He didn't come close, and that disturbed her. If he had, she might have given in, just to feel his arms around her one more time. "I don't feel like partying," she replied.

"Neither does anyone else at the moment. They're all too upset about you. This is the most wonderful night of the year in Haversham, and I will not permit you to ruin it for everyone. If you don't have it in your heart to be cooperative for their sakes, consider it research. I'm sure you've never seen anything like what's about to happen."

The guilt had her rising from her chair. Curiosity took her the rest of the way. When Wes offered her the sable coat, she didn't have the willpower to turn it down.

Before they went outside, though, she had to tell him the results of all her introspection. "I apologize. I've thought about it all day, and I've decided that I over-reacted. You were right. These aren't bad people. I'm not saying I believe everything I've been told, but I know there was nothing mean behind anything that happened."

The stern expression on his face softened a bit more with each of her admissions.

"You hurt me. But I suppose I understand. If I thought dressing up as Lady Elizabeth would make everything turn out the way I wanted, maybe I'd have done the same."

He smiled then, and put his arms around her. "I have Elizabeth's dress packed away in the attic if you want to try it on later, but I'd rather have Janice Fowler to-night."

"Am I forgiven?" she asked unnecessarily.

He gave her a light kiss. "Forgiven. On one condition."

She raised her eyebrows. "Oh?"

"First, do you believe I love you with all my heart and never meant to hurt you?"

She looked into his eyes and saw the truth that her anger had concealed. "I believe you. And you wouldn't have been able to hurt me at all if I didn't love you just as much."

His answering kiss was quick and hard. "Thank you. Now the condition. Accept my proposal. Say you'll share the rest of your life with me. Hurry. It's almost midnight." Her slight hesitation caused him to add,

"We can leave Haversham and live elsewhere if you wish." Her shocked expression prompted him to make a final concession. "And we don't need to name a single one of our children Wesley."

Shedding the last of her doubts, Janice hugged him with all her strength. "You'd give up three hundred years of tradition for me? You must be crazy!"

He held her away so he could see her face. "No. I'm in love . . . and waiting for an answer."

"Yes," she whispered. "I would very much like to be Mrs. Wesley Haversham the twelfth. And if Aunt Louise's psychic powers are accurate, number thirteen will be arriving in nine months. Damned if I'm going to rile any of your dearly departed by breaking even one tradition. We'll name him Wesley, and he'll grow up right here in Haversham, just like all the rest of the little Wesleys."

His head bent to hers, and as their lips touched, she distinctly heard the sound of glass wind chimes. His smile against her mouth told her he'd heard it, too.

He reluctantly ended the kiss. "Time to go."

Before they even reached the street, she felt the anticipation in the air. Lined up on both sides of Haversham Street were hundreds of people. Every single resident from the elderly to the babies were there, waiting for the miracle.

She was a bit embarrassed when Wes tugged her out into the middle of the street and faced the crowd.

"Ladies and gentlemen of Haversham," he shouted. "I have an announcement to make. Janice Fowler has graciously agreed to be my bride."

A cheer rose up at their end of the street and traveled as people spread the word along. She thought she would never again see or hear anything so incredible as that, but she was wrong.

A chorus of angelic voices suddenly burst into song behind her. *"Joy to the world ..."* the lyrics began, and she turned to see the carolers.

It couldn't be! Her eyes had to be playing tricks on her. Standing before her was another throng of people, but these were somewhat translucent and dressed in old-fashioned clothes. Most of the men in the front of the line looked very much like Wes, and she had seen the faces of the women next to them in the portraits on the inn's walls. The man and woman in the center could be none other than the spirits of Lord and Lady Haversham. As she gasped at the lord, he looked directly at her and winked!

When the ethereal gathering finished the first carol, they went on to another and began promenading down the street. Wes held Janice close while the spirits of his ancestors walked by, smiling their approval.

One woman, dressed in a contemporary fashion, stopped and turned around in front of them as the procession continued. Janice felt Wes's body tense, and she realized the woman was Joanne. His late wife smiled at the two of them, blew Wes a kiss, then mouthed the word "Good-bye." Janice felt Wes relax and understood they had been given a blessing he had needed very badly.

By the time the last of them were heading down the street, Janice estimated that thousands of spirits had participated in Haversham's Christmas miracle.

And there wasn't a single footprint left behind to mar the blanket of snow on the street.

The rest of the night passed in a blur of congratulations and good wishes as everyone in town stopped by the inn for eggnog and Christmas cookies. This, too, Janice learned, was a tradition in Haversham.

The sun was peaking over the horizon when Janice and Wes retired to her room, tired but happy.

"Tell me something," she said, snuggling against him under the quilt. "Why do we always end up in this room instead of yours?"

Smiling, he said, "Because I swore to myself I would only share my bed with my wife. I know I'm being superstitious, but until we make it official . . ."

"You make it sound like sharing your bed is something worth waiting for," she taunted.

"Aren't all good things?" he teased back.

"Speaking of good things, there's something else I want to discuss."

"You sound serious. What is it?"

She screwed up her courage. "I don't want to write the article about Haversham's spirits."

His smile faded, but he said, "If that's your decision, I won't try to change your mind."

"But I have another idea," she said quickly to erase the disappointed look on his face. "The reason I don't want to help with your idea to save the town is that it would be a travesty. Commercializing Haversham might save it in one way, but in the short time I've been here, I've fallen in love with this place, just the way it is, and I don't want to see it change. Nor would I want your Christmas miracle to be turned into a circus event.

"My thinking is that Haversham would make a marvelous retreat for artists and writers. You could offer scholarships at first, to attract guests. But a more sedate group of guests than what you had planned. Now *that* I'd be willing to write about and help make happen."

He propped himself up on his elbow and looked down at her, his eyes bright with enthusiasm. "Just like

Lady Elizabeth helped the first Wesley start the town." He kissed her on the forehead. "I love it. But what about our miracle?"

"No reservations over Christmas."

He nodded his agreement. "You really think artists and writers would like it here?"

She laughed. "Like it? It'd be like heaven for creative people. Can you imagine all the spiritual help they'd be getting? At any rate—" she traced a pattern in his chest hair, "I know one writer who's looking forward to having her creativity sparked . . ." her fingertips trailed down his abdomen, ". . . forever and ever."

And the sound of tinkling wind chimes echoed through the room.

Christmas Magic

❦

Carole Nelson Douglas

PROLOGUE

'Twas the night before Christmas.

They make a perfect couple.

A perfect young couple to pose on a Christmas card or in the miniature winter bell jar of a snow dome.

They stand paralyzed in time amid the scene's comfortable Victorian bric-a-brac: cheery fireplace, over-stuffed chairs, doilies scattered everywhere like giant, starched snowflakes.

Not a creature was stirring.

Crumpled wrapping paper decorates the small end table beside them. They face each other, hands extended, each bearing the other's gift.

She is a figure from a still-familiar past, in her floor-length dark skirt and long-sleeved white shirtwaist with sleeve tops that puff as extravagantly as a chef's hat. He looks quite modern in his vested suit, except for a stiff paper wing collar. Wax sharpens his neatly trimmed mustache ends into Hercule Poirot-like points.

Not even a mouse . . .

A brown-and-white dog, a mongrel mop of hair, sits between the paralyzed couple, as motionless as they are.

For the couple's handsome young faces are frozen in wonder . . . and touched with other, less seasonal emotions. Surprise. A slow dawning of utter dismay.

Then she moves. A dainty hand, flexed at the wrist, lifts to the back of her high collar, where a large, festive red-plaid bow rests against her thick cinnamon-colored hair.

On her open palm glitters the regal tortoiseshell swirls of a magnificent decorative comb studded with topaz-colored paste stones.

His hand stirs at last also. His fingers press his waistcoat pocket, as if searching for something or touching a sore spot, while the bright gold coils of a splendid pocketwatch chain warms his frozen, extended palm.

The mouse peeking out from the meager woodpile near the tiny hearth is motionless. There is not much wood to feed the pallid fire. Nor is there the expected wealth of cinnamon-colored hair cascading down the back of the young woman's snowy shirtwaist. Nor the golden sun of a pocketwatch emerging from the young man's vest.

Even without a stopwatch, time starts again.

Between them, the dog comes to life. Back and forth, its shaggy tail berates the floor like a fur-bearing metronome, while its ragamuffin head tilts from side to side, its puzzlement comic despite the smothered whimpers.

The mouse darts back under the safety of its woodpile.

The woman's hand lowers, then rises again to her nape as if searching for something familiar, now gone. Once more the man presses his vest as if hunting heartburn. And nothing else moves.

"Oh, Mel, this is my favorite," Natalie whispered.

"I thought you liked the Icicle Ball best."

"That's gorgeous. This is sweet."

"A native New Yorker isn't supposed to be a sap for 'sweet.' "

"Okay, it's bittersweet. Maybe that's why I always liked *The Gift of the Magi* story so much."

Mel smiled at the life-sized scene of her creation. She and her assistant Natalie peered through a crack of the almost invisible door cut into the room's flocked Victorian wallpaper. They were acting like naughty kids who should be in bed.

They *should* be in bed, Mel thought, with all the weeks of work put into this window, and all the others, even though it was only six P.M. on a Tuesday several days before Christmas.

"Showtime," Natalie whispered, nodding beyond the display.

Mel strained to glimpse the window watchers outside, ranks of bundled-up people behind a front row of children's faces. The kids' mittened hands cupped their eyes so they could see into the warmly lit make-believe scenes behind the chill plate glass.

Like the mechanical mouse, Mel and Natalie retreated before anyone caught them peeking. Their presence could break the illusion they'd killed themselves to create.

"Quitting time," Mel said when they were safely beyond the artificial world and they could talk normally. "After all the window displays I've done, I shouldn't be so unprofessional and peek like an amateur."

"But these are your first for Macy's Thirty-fourth Street headquarters," Natalie said, pushing back the dozen strands of wiry black hair that were always escaping her combs, clips, and bobby pins. "You know: Miracle Mall. It's gotta be a thrill."

"Ummm."

The women expertly edged through the shoppers,

past the interior seasonal dazzle of lights and boughs and bows and glitter, heading for the homely, hidden empty spaces of the display department.

"What's the matter, Mel?" Natalie pressed when they arrived. Their Christmas rush was long over, though unused display items littered the workshop along with dismembered mannequins as naked as mushrooms.

Mel shook her head without answering. Her hair, almost as dark as Natalie's, was swept back into a neater version of the revived Bardot beehive Ivana Trump sported on magazine covers nowadays; that's what a midwestern woman got for sticking a curious head inside a pricey Manhattan hairdresser's one day. Still, the style was low maintenance.

Natalie shrugged into a fake-fur leopardskin bomber jacket. Most display people were theatrical, to say the least. Mel smiled at her friend's panache, then pulled her own fake fur off a work table. Hers was a wine-red Fifties swing coat she'd found at an outdoor flea market.

On their way out, they blended with shoppers now, and bumping into people felt a lot friendlier with a muffling layer of fake fur between them.

"What's the matter?" Natalie demanded again on the shopper-jammed down escalator. The elevators were sardine tins.

Mel hated answering in the cheery shout necessary. "I don't know." On the ground floor they inched to the door, pressed together as if by Velcro. "I've got all the presents off to my brothers and sisters and nephews and nieces. Their presents to me are sitting around the television in my apartment. Christmas Eve is only days away, yet it all seems . . . like an anticlimax."

"Postopening letdown," Natalie diagnosed. She

paused by the glassy glitter of Cosmetics to nudge the L'Oreal counter. "Our jobs force us into the Christmas spirit months before; the real thing's a disappointment."

"And it is my first Christmas in a new city," Mel added.

In a tilted countertop mirror she glimpsed herself. She had Ivana Trump's high, eastern European cheekbones, but all of Mel's hair was as dark brown as her eyes, not just the roots.

"What do you think?" Natalie brandished a deep-purple lipstick.

"You with a capital 'Y.' "

Natalie began digging for her Macy's credit card. "You know what I think your real problem is? You miss The Jerk."

"I wish you wouldn't call him that."

"What else do you call a guy who has the kind of job you can do everywhere and who won't budge when the woman in his life gets a career chance of a lifetime in Manhattan?"

"Manhattan isn't everybody's dream city, Nat. I never dreamed I'd end up here. 'Course I never intended to get into window dressing, either."

Natalie summoned a clerk with a quirked jet-black eyebrow and handed over lipstick and card before glancing over her fake-fur clad shoulder. "You know how rare it is for a woman to reach anything higher than assistant in the window business?"

"That's why I couldn't turn down this job."

"And that's why The Jerk wouldn't move. You were doing better than he was."

"I don't want to talk about it." Mel lifted her gloved hands emphatically. She was from Cold Country and didn't mind sweltering indoors to avoid a shocking inrush of cold on the way out. Their earnest conversation had already accomplished the impossible and attracted attention around them.

"I wouldn't want to talk about a jerk just before Christmas, either." Natalie clutched her small paper bag in taloned hands and headed for the ranks of doors whooshing open to the chill dark of New York City streets.

Before they streamed through, Natalie pulled Mel aside at a display pyramid covered with bejeweled evening bags.

"You need a Christmas tree, Mel. Give your own place some of the care you lavish on the windows. What have you got up?"

"Nothing . . . yet."

"See?"

"In my tiny, overpriced broom closet?"

"Listen, you're lucky to get a sublet in a brownstone at any price. There's this little shop—"

For Natalie, there was always "this little shop."

"Up on Thirty-seventh and . . . Madison. Darling place. Unbelievable bargains. The Santa Shoppe. You can find everything there. Take a look. Get a small tabletop tree."

"A fake tree?"

"You're gonna put the White House fir in a broom closet?"

"In Minnesota we always had real trees, no matter how hard times were."

"Sure, you could schlepp out into the local woods and chop one down like George Washington."

"That was a cherry tree."

"Cherry, schmerry. Make merry, get it? Get a tree, throw some of those aluminum icicles around, and buy yourself a bottle of Bailey's Irish Cream. You won't think about The Jerk once this Christmas, I promise you."

"I don't think about The Jerk! I think about my family."

"That's another thing." Natalie hauled Mel through the slipstream of the mob and out the shining brass door onto chilly Thirty-fourth Street. "You think about your family too much. Sending 'em money for school and stuff. They're not here. You are. Get a life. Get a tree."

As usual, Natalie forged a path through the hurrying crowds to the corner, where a constant stream of New Yorkers flowed across the street whether the light shone green or red.

Cars and cabs honked. People brushed against the two women's immobile figures as heedlessly as flotsam. Their intertwined breaths did frosty sarabands on the evening's dark surface.

"Thirty-seventh and Madison," Natalie repeated. Then she plunged into a heedless clump of people rushing toward the opposite red light while yellow taxi fenders edged into their midst.

Mel darted back against the shelter of Macy's. She turned to a window while she decided what to do. Facing her was an icy-white vignette from her northern Minnesota childhood: a pond of frosted Plexiglas surrounded by pseudosnow that glittered like diamonds tossed into soapsuds.

A couple glided around the scene in automated Victorian grace, the woman's fur-edged skirt brushing the ice. Her wine velvet gown sported ermine cuffs and collar. A matching velvet bonnet tied under her chin with a lavish bow, and she carried an ermine muff dotted with black ermine tails. The mustached gentleman beside her wore a velvet-collared chesterfield coat.

Mel had researched the period's clothes, and smiled. Hard to imagine these solemn, sedate Victorians so much as perspiring from their wintry endeavors. They made life look formal and fashionable, and completely effortless.

For a moment her focus shifted to the window's reflections, the passing parade of people behind her. She saw her own cozy, crimson pyramid of a coat, her scarf-swathed face floating above it as if disconnected.

She looked past her faint image to the moonlit scene showcased in the window. This was her true favorite. Mel had adapted the woman's gown from her late mother's sole precious possession: the Royal Doulton china figure of a Victorian woman with the wind ruffling the edge of her long red gown to reveal a froth of petticoats as white as fresh-fallen snow.

The memory decided her. Maybe she could find a similar figurine at this Santa Shoppe Natalie raved about, and consider it a Christmas tree.

On Thirty-seventh Street, Mel reconsidered. Most of these stores sold wholesale only to the trade. Mel was new enough to New York to hate blundering into the wrong place. Natalie not only would blunder in, but then she would insist that they sell to her anyway. Sometimes they did.

The shops were small, only as wide as a door and a pair of bracketing display windows, which were usually jumbled with glitzy apparel, watches, and costume jewelry.

Mel's toes were growing numb in her trusty lace-up walking boots; her nose felt red and runny from the cold. Besides, the display windows were getting more jumbled, even a bit dusty. She was about to retrace her steps to take a bus the few blocks home—if she could

get on a bus during rush hour—when some flaking
gold letters above the window caught her eye.

The Santa Shoppe.

Well. Mel eyed the unappetizing storefront, then
plunged through the glass-paneled door, which also
looked dusty, and smudged besides.

Sure enough, Santa himself sat behind the counter.
Or at least a man in a Santa suit.

As expected, the shop was long, narrow, and disheveled. Still, Mel's trained eye caught a fascinating
mélange of merchandise: tarnished foil decorations
from the Forties and Fifties, old sleds mounted on the
walls like trophies, faded tin toys from the turn of the
century and before. She also spotted wooden nutcrack-
ers and treetopping angels with the spun platinum fi-
berglass hair now outlawed. And—yes!—even some
table-sized artificial Christmas trees.

Mel reconnoitered them. Pretty scrawny. Three-foot-
high orphans draped in dusty strings of pink pearls and
gilded pinecones. Anyone who had seen—or sniffed—
a real Scotch pine year after year couldn't stomach one
of these musty substitutes.

Mel felt a surprising wave of self-pity. She didn't
miss Natalie's villainous Jerk. She understood now that
he was selfish, and she understood why she'd put up
with him: she was congenitally unselfish. They made a
perfect couple until she had to do what she most
needed to do—move. She also knew why she was so
nauseatingly unselfish. Eldest of five in a poor, Iron
Range family. The first to leave home, the first to earn
money and send it back to the others, for college.

No college for Mel Johansen, too busy supporting
herself with her knack for pulling rabbits out of hats.
Then her home-grown design talent pulled her forward
and away, to the Twin Cities, to Cincinnati, to New

York. So she sent letters and love and money home and never made any lasting ties anywhere else, until now she was alone for Christmas in the world's largest lonely city. And The Jerk had nothing to do with it.

"Need a tree?"

Santa's deep, low voice sounded as if it hadn't been used in a while. Mel turned, surprised to realize that she was the shop's sole customer. Oh, no! Now she'd have to buy something, or else feel guilty. No. She couldn't worry about the whole world. What she should worry about was somebody to worry about her, besides Natalie. Somebody of the male persuasion who was not a jerk, which was like hunting for one perfect rose in a weed bed.

"Just looking." Mel hated saying the obvious, but sometimes it was inevitable.

The Santa's question had reeled her back toward the door, to the long counter he commanded. His cotton-wool batting, shoulder-dusting hair and tummy-warming beard were not Ivory Snow white, and his red Santa suit was not only crinkled from storage but moth eaten. Vintage, she reminded herself. Can't expect mint condition at a "Shoppe."

At least Santa's cheeks were rouge-polished to the mandated apple redness, and his eyes twinkled from under the scruffy fake fur rim of his cap, which ended in a drooping point punctuated by a rusted brass bell.

Gee, even her impoverished hometown of Virginia, Minnesota, wouldn't claim this Goodwill Santa! Mel, embarrassed for the tacky mess, glanced down through the glass into the display case. This too was venerable, made of sturdy golden oak, its brass hardware age-dimmed to a sullen bronze color. Yet a fascinating array of items crammed the worn, coral-velvet-covered shelves. She leaned closer and began serious browsing.

"Does that watch work?" she wondered out loud.

"Well, now, we'll see. Which one?" Despite his threadbare attire and deep voice, this Santa sounded terminally cheerful.

Mel wasn't sure she was interested in watches whose workings were so iffy.

"It's old, isn't it?" she asked as he slid open the case's balky rear doors to fumble among the clutter with fat, red-gloved fingers.

"Sure looks it."

The old pocketwatch came swinging above the counter on its long chain, swaying before Mel as if to hypnotize her.

"Is it gold?" she asked doubtfully, knowing better.

Santa shrugged, but his eyes were watching her with a smile. "Probably washed in gold, at least."

No matter how battered, old things sang to her. She pulled off the wool-lined leather gloves she'd bought long ago in Minneapolis to let the watch's smooth shape salve the palm of her hand. It curved to her flesh like a flattened egg, and was egg-heavy, too. Satisfying. Her father would have loved a watch like this. She studied the fine tracery of the cover in the dim light. The watch suddenly became as bright as a star gone nova. She looked up, blinking in the abrupt glare, to find the Santa had pushed an old bronze banker's light closer.

"Do you have a jeweler's loupe?" she asked.

He chuckled. Yes, chuckled like a plump, pleasant, pleased Santa. What a ham! "Does this shop look like it would need a jeweler's loupe?"

Embarrassed again, Mel said nothing. The watch was growing hot in her icy hand, like an ember in the snow. She insinuated a fingernail along the side and gingerly cracked it open to a white face behind glass, marked with dignified Roman numerals. And now she heard the timepiece, ticking like a mechanical heart. The second hand—camel's hair fine—clicked from moment to moment.

On the case's back she read a spidery inscription: *A.G. from P.L.* And a date: *August 3, 1896.*

"How much?" she asked, hating to. When items were unmarked, she knew the price might depend on what she looked like she could pay.

"Two hundred and twenty-eight."

Mel kept silent. A lot of money, but not out of reach. Who needed a sleazy fake tree? This watch had substance, had history. But was it solid brass? Overpriced? She was clever with her hands. Had to be. A thumbnail pried open the thin side seam, exposing the tiny steel-and-brass watchworks. They had balanced, swaying busily, on the fine edge of time for decades. She was sold but tried not to show it.

"Can you do a better price?" she forced herself to say, as Natalie had coached her. Shame on her for trying to bargain with Santa only days before Christmas.

"I just work here." His tone was kindly, rather than the usual indifferent one she had grown used to.

She nodded, balancing the watch in her hand, the sensation returning to her toes, which now burned like hell. Two hundred and twenty-eight dollars wasn't jelly bean money, either. Plus tax.

Idly, she worried at the back piece, surprised when it sprang open on a hidden hinge.

A slender lock of hair coiled there, dulled by the dryness of age, but still a startling, carroty red.

"Oh," she said, charmed. Was this a token of A.G. or P.L.?

Santa leaned into the light, his fake hair a silvery

halo around a face blotted out by the bright light. "Didn't know that was there."

Would he raise the price? Mel's fingers tightened on the watch, snapped the back shut on its relic. *Hey, this is Christmas, have a heart—!*

"I'll get it," she said possessively. Then, "Do you take plastic?"

"Yeah," he said, out of character now that a sale, or a sucker, was at hand.

In moments, the watch was wrapped in plain brown paper tied with knotted string.

"Don't have a box," Santa apologized gruffly.

Mel guessed that she was one of the shop's best customers in days. Was Santa the owner in disguise? Or just an employee? Didn't matter. She had her prize—if only it didn't stop ticking the instant she stepped out the door. . . .

She stepped out the door, her glove still off. Cold seared her fingers. She folded the receipt, thrusting it into the coin purse in her wallet and the wallet into her muff, then drew on her right glove again. The icy air drove daggers into her nostrils as she inhaled. She looked down in the light of some distant streetlight.

She didn't own a muff.

She did now—a capacious oblong of white fur dotted with small black tails. She whirled back to the Santa Shoppe. Its sweeping plate glass windows had sprouted wooden panes outlined by traceries of frost. She pushed her face against the alien glass, as close as the children at Macy's had, and put her gloved hands to her eyes to peer in. Something black that crouched against a wall beamed a fugitive cherry-red—a stove! Why hadn't she noticed it before? And the Santa . . .

She breathed relief. A familiar figure still sat behind the counter. Maybe she had grabbed a prop muff in-

stead of her purse when she had left the store, not noticing in her excitement. Santa was in his seat and all
was right with the world.

Except his costume was green, not red. Had she suddenly gone color blind, like a traffic-scoffing New
Yorker? Mel's panic plunged deeper into disbelief as
she remembered from her research that Santa suits
used to be green . . . in Victorian times.

Mel took a deep breath and started for the shop door,
which was not quite the same as she remembered.
Maybe she'd been more worn out than she thought by
the several months' drive to design and execute the
windows. She looked up for some reason and saw
above the door three milk-white glass globes glowing
in the same distant gleam of light that had revealed the
muff.

Mel recognized the time-honored sign of a pawnshop, a sign that had absotively, posilutely not been
there when she had entered.

Then the dull stare she directed at the alien window
rewarded her. She saw a ghost in the glass, the elegant
skater from her Macy's window, velvet-clad, bonneted,
bowed, and muffed. Herself.

Mel swirled toward the street, feeling the drag of
long, velvet skirts. Streetlights gleamed through the
dimness, faint lights in a flurry of snowflakes. The
sidewalk beneath her feet was blanketed in two inches
of fluff.

A dull thumping seemed like her heartbeat at first,
then something large and dark passed by—a horse, two
horses! And a carriage. A cross-hatching of harnesses
jingled as the horses clopped past, bearing not the bells
of the season, but buckles and harness rings. Their
businesslike hooves churned the snow in the street into
tobacco-brown sludge.

* * *

Half an hour later, Mel—numb with cold and disbelief—could think of nowhere to go but home. She walked familiarly numbered streets faced with unfamiliar buildings. She wandered among edifices no taller than four or five stories. None of the city's soaring landmarks guided her, no silver-petaled top on the Chrysler building, no Empire State skyscraper.

Her furred hem dragged in the snow and she was already exhausted. People still filled the streets, but ignored her to a man. She supposed that she shouldn't have been out unescorted. At every corner, she paused to squint up at the second-story level of the buildings to read the street names. These were her only guideposts, her only signs of reality, despite their unlikely locations. They told her she walked a grid of street and avenue that she knew. Horses were everywhere, bigger and taller than she had imagined, and faster, and more frightening. She avoided crossing streets, for she couldn't move quickly in her cumbersome clothing. And with her icy hands thrust into the now-handy muff, her balance was compromised.

This is a nightmare, she told herself, touching the package inside the muff. I'll get home and it'll be like always, but I'll never call it a broom closet again, and I'll even get a stupid fake tabletop tree, Natalie, I swear—

At last. Her block. The same charming brownstones. The same numbers. You *can* go home again. Mel gazed through teary eyes at the dingy, three-story building that bore her number. A light warmed the window that was hers.

And then a couple of blurred shapes came dashing down the walk toward her, muffled by the snow. Two men in overcoats, running and turning their collars up against the wind-driven sleet, laughing, looking down to keep their footing.

One caromed right into Mel. She gasped, expecting to fall. How would she ever get up in this entangling set of Scarlett O'Hara draperies?

She felt . . . nothing, only a sort of inner jolt.

The man stopped right next to her. Beside her. Practically *on* her.

"What's the matter, Jeremy" The second man stopped as abruptly. "Afraid to go in and face the music?"

"No, I—"

Six inches from her, the man called Jeremy stared into her face, narrowing his eyes. "I must have hit a wind gust. Felt a terrific . . . chill."

"Well, you'll get no warm welcome from your pater, laddie, not with what we've been up to," the second man said.

"Yes, partner, you'd better keep these for now." The man called Jeremy, the man who had stopped so rudely on top of Mel, thrust a sheaf of papers at his companion. "Roll them up so the ink doesn't get wet and run."

He eyed the brownstone and sighed, so softly that Mel guessed only she could hear it. But she couldn't feel it, and she should have, he was that close. She stepped back, but neither man paid her any mind.

"Cheer up, old fellow," the second man advised. "It's Christmas."

"Not quite," Jeremy said a bit grimly. He thrust his bare hands into his coat pockets and loped up the twelve steps to Mel's brownstone, his boots leaving tracks in the soft snow.

She started after him, wanting to slip in with him, for she certainly didn't have the key to the house or her room in the muff. But he didn't unlock the door, he simply opened it, even as a figure met him in the yellow oblong of light behind it. So warm. Mel ached to be inside with a cup of hot chocolate. She rushed up the steps, wondering what she would say.

"Come in, sir." The resident stepped aside, then shut the door in Mel's face as if she weren't there . . . only she had begun running as if Jeremy were disappearing down a rabbit hole and she'd never see him or the brownstone again. She ran right into the door, which was closed, and which didn't hurt her at all . . . or stop her, for she was inside despite her worry that she wouldn't be.

Mel turned to the sidelights of frost-edged glass to gaze on the dimly lit street. She saw Jeremy's footsteps etched into the blanket of snow smothering the steps, but she didn't see hers. She couldn't even find the brushmarks left by her long skirts.

"The master wishes to see you in the study," the doorman was saying.

Of course he wasn't a doorman; he was a white rabbit. In fact, his middle-aged face wore fuzzy white muttonchops and mustache, as if he were planning on auditioning for the role of Santa Claus in a Victorian melodrama. She could see him—them. Why couldn't they see her?

The man, whatever his function, took Jeremy's coat and hat and frowned at his chapped bare hands.

"My gloves are in the pockets, Reeves. I haven't lost them." Jeremy spoke with breezy familiarity even as he glanced worriedly to a set of wooden double doors down the long, chilly hall.

When he moved toward them, Mel felt in sudden need of a guide. This layout was nothing like the lobby of her brownstone. She charged past—through—poor, fussy Reeves, feeling nothing, though the . . . butler!

. . . stiffened as if insulted. Mel swept on, trailing Jeremy's tweed Norfolk jacket as he entered the study. Once again a door shut through her.

"Wow." Mel forgot herself and spoke aloud, but no one seemed to hear her.

She had entered what resembled the *Masterpiece Theater* set on PBS: warm wood paneling, oil paintings, a twinkling galaxy of velvet-matted frames holding sepia-toned photos, tufted leather furniture, and—better than on TV—the smell and snap of burning logs, though the fire was banked low.

The man behind the desk could have been a stand-in for Alistair Cooke, if the former *Masterpiece Theater* host had ever gone in for muttonchops. He had a shock of white hair and pale eyes, and a thin frame and sharpness of feature all his own.

"Jeremy," he greeted Mel's guide.

"Father." Jeremy spoke warily, moving to the weak fire and thrusting his hands into his pants pockets. Mel, forced to accept her strange invisibility, found that the chill in this room went beyond the older man's stern welcome. It was also rude enough to penetrate her heavy period clothing. At least she could still feel.

"You've been out with those theater folk again, I suppose," Jeremy's father noted unhappily.

"Not actors," Jeremy said quickly. "I gave that up, as I promised I would."

"Theater folk are theater folk. What kind of gypsies are you taking up with now?"

"Writers." Jeremy couldn't keep the enthusiasm out of his voice, which was as deep as his father's but much more expressive. "Songwriters," he added cautiously.

"Damn it, lad!" The older man slapped the papers atop his heavy pedestal desk.

Jeremy turned from the fire, his expression flirting with defiance before settling into a certain resignation.

Mel used this first opportunity to observe her guide. Jeremy was in his mid-twenties, with the same lean, tall frame as the older man, but fleshed out with youth and energy. Even standing still he projected imminent motion. Remembering their boisterous encounter on the street, Mel thought he resembled a man on a leash inside the house, using self-discipline to produce the proper behavior, overcoming all his instincts. Despite his troubled expression, his regular features, hazel eyes, and chestnut hair gave him the look of a hero in a horse opera.

The father had also spent a few seconds regarding his son. "Damn it, Jeremy," he said none too gently, "if you're willing to stay up all hours in some drafty theater, you could join me in the office from dawn to dusk like a respectable man."

"I am not a banker, Father."

"And you will not be an actor!" came the thundering reply. "Nor will you stand in my study with your hands in your pockets like a vagrant lounger!"

Jeremy snatched the offending hands from his pockets, his face flushing—but not from the heat of the feeble fire.

Mel automatically opened her mouth in protest. Jeremy's hands were white with cold; he had only put them in his pockets to warm them. Even her own gloved fingers tingled from the chill both indoors and out.

"Yes, sir," Jeremy said in a deliberately dead voice.

"I hope you don't entertain ideas of following your brother Drew in defying me, for I won't have it." The older man sat forward in his high-backed chair, sighing. "If you won't work on Wall Street, I won't have you hanging around Broadway. Apparently, you're handsome enough to make an actor, so you can do the family a favor and at least marry well. If you won't work one way, you'll work another."

"The theater is work—hard work. And it can pay off royally."

His father's dismissive hand waved him silent. "You'll stay home Christmas Eve, not go gallivanting around Broadway. Mr. Blount and Miss Cuthbert and her father are to dine with us. You will be on your best behavior. I expect good tidings out of this by the New Year."

Jeremy's face went as white as his hands. He opened his mouth to speak, but his father's eyes had returned to the papers on his desk. After a moment, Jeremy strode from the room. His father said nothing.

Mel shadowed Jeremy, pausing with him just outside the study door in the icy hall. He glanced up the broad staircase that Mel had never seen before. Of course, the elevators were there now! The wooden railing was twined with greenery and bright-red velvet bows, wafting piney scent down to them.

Jeremy sighed in his turn and sprang up the stairs, energetic despite his obvious reluctance.

Mel gathered up her weighty velvet skirts and tripped after him—quite literally. How was someone supposed to climb stairs in this get-up? she wondered. Jeremy's disappearing heels goaded her upward at a faster pace. This place was a museum set, and he was her only guide.

Huffing and puffing—and apparently unheard as well as unseen—she paused behind Jeremy at another closed door, on which he knocked.

"Come in," a woman's voice said timidly from beyond the coffered wood.

Once again Mel entered an unfamiliar room in a familiar building: a sitting room with a bedchamber beyond it. On a chaise longue near a fireplace a woman sat, her lap covered with a hand-worked counterpane and a writing board.

Jeremy took her extended hands and bent to kiss her pale cheek. Under a lacy wisp of a cap, her hair was a silver-bronze cloud that once might have been chestnut, and her face was as troubled as his own.

"Jem, dear, I was worried—"

"Nothing to worry about," he assured her, edging nearer the fire, his hands behind his back to warm them. "I forgot my gloves, that's all; that's why my hands are so cold. Yours are ice, too; I'll feed the fire."

He bent to the woodbox, but her raised hand stopped him. "No! We must be prudent. Your father won't have a servant let go, but he will tolerate no household waste of late, and we are to have quite a dinner party Friday night."

"I know," Jeremy said grimly. "I assume Phoebe is up for auction, too."

"Jeremy, you mustn't put it that way. Your father is trying his hardest to do what is best for us all."

"He's doing his best to sell Phoebe and me into marital servitude, and all because of brother Drew's defection, I suppose. Father has become a tyrant of late, and it's not doing any of us good. Sometimes I wish I'd done as Drew, run off with a charming milliner to escape the marital sweepstakes."

"Please." The woman's shaking hands began shuffling the notepapers on her writing board, until the slender brass pen atop it rolled onto her coverlets. "Don't talk like that. I don't know what I'd do if you left, too; left me alone here with your father when I don't understand what he is doing, why he is doing it—"

"I'm sorry, Mother." He bent to retrieve the pen and replaced it on her papers. "Perhaps I can sacrifice myself to Miss Cuthbert, for all our sakes, but I'll be damned if I'll let Phoebe marry that old pinchpenny, Silas Blount."

The woman covered her ears. "And don't talk as your father has lately, either! I don't know what has happened to this family. If only Drew hadn't—"

"Drew did what he had to do," Jeremy said. "And I will too."

On that note he turned and left the room. Mel lingered to see his mother sigh again, her once fine face a roadmap of anxiety. She reached to press a mother-of-pearl button on a board dotted with them. How many servants could such a house support?

At the sound of the door clicking shut, Mel realized that she had lost Jeremy. She turned to follow, wondering how she would open the door without attracting his mother's attention. That worry was not necessary. Even as she paused to turn the knob, her hand plunged through solid brass into the hallway beyond. She followed it, feeling as if she were driving against an unseen wind. A faint knock far down the hall drew her to another door. She flowed through its broad wood surface with the same sensation of drag seconds after Jeremy shut it behind him.

"Jem! Have you heard?" The girl who hurled herself into his arms was a vision in lavender wool and linen lace, with tumbling brown curls and red-rimmed eyes. Mel felt another wave drench her, this one as chill as disappointment.

"About Christmas Eve dinner? Yes, I'm sorry to say."

"Oh, I don't want to marry that dreadful Mr. Blount! What can I do? I can't elope like Drew and his Miss Polly Langley. I haven't got the courage."

"Courage has nothing to do with it, Phoebe." He gently untangled himself from her and led her to a tapestry chair and footstool drawn up before the fire. "Desperation, more like."

"It doesn't seem like Christmas at all," she complained, letting him settle her in the chair, "with Father being so fierce and Mother so disheartened, and with Drew gone. What is happening? Are we really to marry only to please Father because one of his children has displeased him by marrying against his wishes? Oh, it is all too medieval!"

Jeremy quirked a smile. "Your despairing monologue would play well on the stage, Phoebe, although I couldn't in good conscience advise a girl of good family to attempt that scandal. Father is right about that much." He sighed and ran a hand through his thick hair, mussing it beyond the services of any pomade. "I can't say why he's playing the melodrama father at the moment. He took Drew's elopement hard."

"He is right; Miss Langley is only a tradesman's daughter."

"Still, that's no reason to disinherit Drew and then put us both up on the marriage block as soon as possible."

Phoebe played with the single lock of hair trailing over her shoulder. "At least your Miss Cuthbert is less than thirty, and not utterly ugly."

"She is not *my* Miss Cuthbert!" he burst out, then laughed when he caught his sister's expression. "Phoebe, you are a dreadful tease, and obviously much too lively for the cadaverous Mr. Blount. Whatever happens Friday night, I promise that you will never have to marry that . . . walking corpse. Besides, if my idea for a show proves out, I shall be filthy rich. We can both leave home in style and do as we please."

"How is it going?" she asked, leaning forward in her chair.

"Philip and I had an interview with Sousa today; he was most encouraging."

"Sousa? The famous bandleader?"

"He's producing comic operas now, and he liked my scripts. If I can dream up enough songs—something really catchy, something . . . unique—he'll produce it. Broadway is begging for good new shows and scores. There's more money in that than in acting."

"Although you wouldn't mind taking a leading role if Mr. Sousa begged you?"

"Well . . . no. And if I had the money from a producible show, not even Father could stop me. Banking! Stocks and bonds!" Jeremy began pacing. "Dull stuff, and risky besides. I know I can write a corking good show, Phoebe, and more than one. Sousa's king, but Broadway isn't a one-man show anymore."

"Still, it's a scandalous livelihood."

He grinned hopefully. "I wager Miss Cuthbert wouldn't deign to marry a Broadway songwriter, rather than the son of a rich financier."

"Oh, I don't know, Jeremy." Phoebe's knowing look belied her probable eighteen years. "Miss Cuthbert may be hard to dissuade. I believe that she'd wed you if you were a chimneysweep."

He shuddered, and not just from the chill room. "I wish to be a dutiful son, but Cora Cuthbert is too high a price to pay."

Phoebe was standing up in an instant, her hands curled into his tweed lapels. "Jem, don't abandon me here in this house. I could never resist Father without

you to encourage me. I'd have to marry that awful man
and live in that lonely old house so far away. That
would leave Mother alone in this house, with Father
the way he is now, and Drew who knows where ...
Oh, Jeremy, you've got to sell your show! You've got
to prove that there is another way to do things than father's old-fashioned solutions that trade in flesh and
blood. Please!"

"I'll try, Phoebe. If I get inspired, perhaps I can finish the show by Christmas Eve, and we can announce
our forthcoming Broadway hit instead of our engagements."

She laughed a little, released his lapels, and stepped
back, shaking her head. "I don't understand what's
happening to us, Jem. I don't understand why."

He nodded, then touched the side of her face in fare-
well and left yet another room.

Mel was tired of scurrying after him like a large,
overdressed, and invisible mouse.

Still, Jeremy was the one active, moving body in this
house of sequestered and troubled people. Something
drew her after him, like a camera following the lead
actor in a soap opera. He was the most compelling person in her strange new world. Somehow, she hoped, he
would lead her out of it.

The last door he opened without knocking. She followed on his heels, wanting to avoid the subtle jolt of
passing through solid mahogany. Mel found herself in
another high-ceilinged room, its walls papered in an
orange and gold Oriental motif of bamboo and bridges.
A desk near the door was covered with odd-sized
pieces of paper and a quantity of antique pens.

Jeremy went directly to the fireplace to stir the pallid
embers before feeding the nearly expired fire a fresh
piece of wood. Above the mantel, the portrait of a

handsome woman in elegant late-eighteenth-century dress looked past the pale sweep of her décolletage down on Jem's chestnut hair. The woman in the painting carried a silky-coated lapdog in one arm. The other forearm lay languidly over the arm of her chair, bearing a folded fan.

Mel had to remind herself that this painting was not a reproduction, but an original; that the gilded pens on the desk were not antiques but contemporary artifacts; that the chilly room would not warm much despite the fresh blaze of the fire on the hearth.

She shivered and looked around. Jeremy was now lighting the oil lamp on the desk, so its two milk-glass globes glowed like full moons. Then he turned up the gaslight sconces on the walls until a soft hiss filled the big, cold room and light dusted its furniture. At last she saw the huge, testered bed on the wall opposite the fireplace.

What a dark, icy, unwelcoming place, Mel thought, glad she didn't have to live here.

And then the arrangement of the windows, which— judging from the muffled sounds of horse traffic— faced the street, struck her with a thrust of sharp familiarity.

This wasn't Jeremy's bedroom—this was *her* cramped apartment, or what it had once been! And there, in the niche where the bureau sat, where Jeremy was brushing his hair before an oval mirror, that's where her tiny kitchen was! Her closet was in that corner near the door, only it hadn't been walled off yet!

Mel felt faint. For the first time during this pell-mell rush into an unfamiliar landscape, finding her dismayed way to a familiar address, feeling the weight of alien clothes, passing through wooden doors like a wisp of fog, discovering herself unrecognized, unacknowledged, unseen . . . for the first time the reality of this unreal situation sank upon her like a cold, soaking wet, smothering blanket the color and weight of pewter.

She was not here. This was not her place. This was not her time. Yet she saw, moved, felt the weight of her antique skirts, felt tired and cold. But not . . . hungry. She glanced to another corner that had not existed in her apartment and saw the ghost of another set of walls—her bathroom. She wondered where such facilities existed here, and wondered even more that she felt no urge to use them. Apparently she sensed some things and not others. Perhaps she had been hit by a taxi on leaving the Santa Shoppe and this was an out-of-body delusion.

Perhaps she was dead.

And a ghost.

While she stood there, stunned, Jeremy, satisfied with his neatened hair, abruptly left the bureau niche. He moved so fast, and her thoughts stirred so slowly at the moment, that he charged right through her.

An ice-cold wave buffeted her, almost took her breath away. If she had any breath to lose.

Jeremy paused, looked around, put a hand to his eyes and simultaneously poked his uplifted elbow into her jaw and down her throat.

She felt only a remote rocking, like a rowboat moving to the last swells of a distant wave.

Jeremy shook his head and moved on to the desk, where he sat down and began scratching one of the pens across some blank paper. His writing was quick and cryptic. He kept dipping the pen in a crystal ink-well, hissing under his breath when the fresh ink blotted at the first strokes.

He also began whispering aloud to himself, repeating phrases.

Mel, drawn from her brink of despair by his puzzling activity, felt her foreign skirts sway over the carpeting as she came to peer over his shoulder.

Notes, he was transcribing musical notes, and words as well. Lyrics. He was ... songwriting. Her glance caught certain words: moon, spoon, and June. Oh, dear. How ... old. Trite. He'd never get anywhere with that stuff.

Sighing, she looked around the strange interior that would later be so altered. Jeremy suddenly pushed his chair back—into her again, causing that seasick swell in her mind or her emotions or whatever was still real in her body—and jumped up to pace.

He kept colliding with Mel, pausing, then looking puzzled. She felt like the Queen Mary in a typhoon and retreated finally to the fireplace.

His mutterings and pacings soon enlarged to include her in his route again, so she awkwardly climbed the sturdy upholstered chair to perch atop the wide wooden mantel, now safely out of reach.

Jeremy stopped before the fire to rub his face until his hair was as disarranged as before. "Something's different," he muttered, then paced some more.

Mel watched him, finding herself less tired now that she wasn't dragging these heavy old clothes around. She felt as if she could sit up here forever—then panicked when she considered that this might indeed be her fate.

Meanwhile, Jeremy hurtled back to the desk, picked up his papers, then returned to pacing and humming and singing under his breath.

"No!" he burst out. "This is worthless!" Bracing his feet, he made to rip the heavy papers apart.

"No!" Mel cried, hating senseless destruction as the antithesis of accomplishment.

Jeremy paused in midtear. "Is there an echo in here?" he asked himself in a low, disbelieving voice.

"No," Mel answered before she could catch herself.

"No." Jeremy waited, his head cocked, while Mel bit her lip and kept silent, as she should have done in the first place. "It's not an . . . echo," Jeremy decided with admirable calm for a man who had just heard a voice when there was no one there. "Echoes don't answer questions. Who's there? Is this a prank?"

He looked around, expecting to see someone. With nothing or nobody obvious, he moved to the window draperies and prodded them away from the wall, one by one. Of course he found nothing, so he went and poked the bed hangings until he was satisfied.

Finally he shrugged and returned to the desk, gazing down at the papers in his hand. "This is still rot." His hands fisted on the abused sheets once more.

"No!" Mel cried, curious to know if he would hear her again.

Jeremy's head jerked up. "Someone *is* there, or else I'm ready for Bellevue instead of Broadway. Phoebe, is this some elaborate joke?"

"My name isn't Phoebe," Mel said, her heart in her throat. If someone could hear her, at least, this state would not be so dreadfully isolating.

Jeremy certainly could hear her. He marched straight for the mantel, his face determined. First he bent to peer up the chimney, which made Mel giggle.

He shot upright again, suspicion shaping every feature, his eyes studying the wallpaper for peepholes. "Is this some newfangled voice box?" he demanded.

"It is *my* voice box," Mel admitted, "and I like to consider myself fairly newfangled."

His hand lifted, turning left and right to place the voice that came from three feet above him. His eyes rested on the lady in the portrait.

"Great-aunt Whoever of Clan Carmody," he said in an awed whisper. "I always thought you looked like a game old gal. Is that . . . you?"

Mel remained silent.

Jeremy eyed the shadowed room again. "I've slept in this room since I left the nursery, but now, I swear, it seems foreign, even frightening. What is your first name, anyway, Auntie? If you're going to converse with a fellow, you could at least introduce yourself. I never took you for the coy sort."

"I don't like my name," Mel said in spite of herself, surprising herself. Until now she hadn't realized that this was exactly the truth.

"Can't be that bad," Jeremy cajoled, his eyes and fingertips still examining the figured wallpaper for newfangled voice machines. "What kind of names did they have in your day? Laetitia, Hypatia, Heliotrope . . . those aren't so bad."

Mel shuddered, for the first time not with cold. "No, not so bad, only dreadful! My name is just . . . ordinary."

"I doubt that." He was still hunting for some hidden trace of human presence.

Mel smiled sadly at his persistence; she knew the feeling. As for revealing her full name, she was invisible, wasn't she? There was no point in not telling the truth; she could always outrun it later.

"Melody," she confessed.

Jeremy stopped patting down the wallpaper and stepped back to regard the portrait. "Melody? Really? That's a grand name! Maybe you're my muse. I'm a songwriter, after all."

"Are you sure?" Mel asked with a smile he couldn't see.

Puzzled for a moment, he glanced down at the crumpled papers in his hands. "Not always," he answered with a rueful grin. "And just now I'm not sure if I'm even sane."

"Then you should make an excellent songwriter," Mel said confidently.

He leaned his folded arms on the mantel—Mel quickly pulling a swath of her velvet skirt out of his way, fearful that he might feel it—and stared up at the woman in portrait.

"I could write a song for you, painted lady. Do you sing?"

"Not much . . . not at all, really."

"You have a lovely voice."

"I'm not singing," she said acidly. "How can you tell?"

"I meant your speaking voice. I'm an actor, too. Or would be one, if it wouldn't destroy the blasted family name. Was Gardner such a high-and-mighty surname in your day?"

She was silent, not having much good to say about his father's outmoded opinions.

"Perhaps you could sing something," he suggested.

"I'm not an actor, and I'm afraid that performance on the stage was far from respectable in my day as well, especially for women."

"Are you a ghost?" he asked suddenly.

"I . . . don't know."

"Do you know why you're here?"

"No."

"Are you . . . from here—this house, this city?"

"Yes . . . in fact—"

"Yes—?"

"This used to be my bedroom."

He stepped even farther back from the fireplace, regarding the portrait with wide but still suspicious eyes. "That's odd; I didn't think this house had been in the family *that* long."

"I'm not *that* old," Mel said, miffed at the implication.

"Of course not," he said quickly. "You have a very young voice. I only meant . . . why are you here?"

"I don't know. Believe me, if I did, I would leave."

"I see." Now *he* sounded miffed. "Can you speak to everyone?"

"I don't know. I'm . . . new here."

"If you're a ghost, then you must have just died."

"I don't think I'm . . . dead."

"Now look here, Auntie. You may feel in the prime of health, but I assure you that you've been dead, oh, since the 1840's, as I recall."

"And I doubt that I'm your aunt."

His eyebrows raised. "Then it really isn't proper for you to appear in my bedroom."

"Apparently, very little is proper in your house."

He nodded in chagrin. "Truer words were never . . . et cetera. Come to think of it, the eighteenth century was a lot less tame than our nineteenth century Age of Nervous Nellies and Stuffy Fellows. I'm not surprised to find you haunting a fellow's bedchamber."

"That sounds like something from a song."

"Haunting a fellow's bedchamber?"

"No, the Nervous Nellies and Stuffy Fellows."

"You're right!" He went to the desk to loft another pen. "Something snappy about how times are changing."

He sat down and began scribbling furiously, humming occasionally, muttering in a singsong voice now and again.

Mel watched him, bemused. He seemed to have forgotten her utterly. Were all artistic types as cavalier toward their muses? Mel considered the artistic types she knew in the display business and nodded sadly to herself. "Forgotten but not gone," she whispered to the lady in the portrait beside her, her partner in time displacement.

"What was that?" Jeremy asked in a rush.

"Forgotten but not gone," she repeated more loudly.

"Great line." And he bent his head to write again.

"Will I get a credit?" Mel asked finally, annoyed at being ignored for so long. She was a genuine phenomenon, after all.

Jeremy looked up and considered. "Probably not. Writers have been stealing from the dead for centuries."

He returned to his verses, humming. Mel watched him. He seemed happy while at work. The papers were filled and shuffled to the back with the speed of true inspiration.

Finally he paused, then pulled a watch from its vest-pocket sanctuary. "Almost seven! Father will fume if I'm late for dinner again." He stood up and glanced at the portrait. "Why am I speaking aloud? I am not obliged to inform you of my every thought, even if you are a most bewitching lady. It's not as if you are really there." He went to brush his hair again, then eyed the portrait once more. "You . . . are there?"

Mel was tempted to hold her tongue. "Yes."

"Good. If I'm going insane, I want to be entertained while I'm doing it. I'm sorry I must leave you, Mistress Gardner, but dinner and father wait for no man, and for no ghost."

"I'm no ghost!" she called after him, but the bed-chamber door shut before she could see his reaction to that declaration.

At last she could reconnoiter the room without worrying about being trod upon at every step. Mel climbed down from her perch and first went to the desk. She picked up some scribbled sheets and read some revised verse.

Like a war a soldier's fought in, you are gone but
    not forgotten
Like a rainfall on a willow, my tears baptize my pil-
    low
If I forgot, what God had wrought,
I'd go to sleep, and no more keep
Watch upon my dreams,
For, my dear, it seems
You are gone but not forgotten
Yet I'm bound to suffer on,
For I am forgotten, but not gone.

Mel guessed it was meant to be a love song, or rather an unrequited-love song. She also thought it would do quite well for a missing brother.

Since she did not have the luxury of being hungry, she prowled the chamber, imagining it in the form of her lost apartment. What would Papa Gardner say if he knew that a mere one room in his brownstone would cost a renter thirteen hundred dollars a month on some distant day? Mel guessed the average boarder at the end of the nineteenth century might pay thirteen dollars a month for a rented room.

She finally wondered whether she could fall asleep in this state, but after inspecting the huge, high bed with its claustrophobic hanging curtains—and consid-

ering the result if she drifted off and Jeremy returned
to lie right atop her—she settled herself in the upholstered chair by the fireplace. She watched the dying
flames dart about like airborne goldfish until she, too,
was forgotten but not gone.

Mel did not dream, was not even certain if she slept.
But she was far enough removed to be startled when
the chamber door cracked open and an unknown
woman bustled in.

Her rusty black clothing rustled as the woman
brought in what resembled an old-fashioned corn-
popping pan with a great, long handle. Deftly, she
slipped the black iron pan under the covers at the bed's
foot, then turned down the sheet at its head. After
prodding the dying fire into a warm whirlwind of embers, she paused by the desk to study the flurry of papers. With a fussy "tsk," she left.

Mel returned to her mentally blank state, exhausted
by all the changes she had absorbed. She thought she
heard Natalie's distant voice calling her to come and
see this wonderful new shop, just in time for Christmas. . . .

Sensation, consciousness, returned like blood to tingling feet, slowly and unpleasantly.

Mel found the room creeping into her mind, forming
before her half-open eyes until it was fully there, and
she was half there as usual, she assumed.

Someone was whistling—a strong, true whistle that
made a shiver run up Mel's spine like an icy zipper in
the dead of winter.

A pale figure garbed in white from foot to neck
stood before her. She shrieked.

It jumped.

The piece of wood it had been holding plunged to
the hearth, sending sparks flying.

Mel leaped out of the chair, sweeping her long velvet skirts from the danger of fire—if ghostly garb could catch fire.

"You said you weren't here," a voice accused.

It wasn't just any voice, but Jeremy's, which Mel recognized even though her back was to the room.

"I said no such thing."

"That's just it; I asked when I returned from dinner, but you were as mute as a mouse. Now," he added with some indignation, "I find that you are still here, spying upon me."

She turned, shocked—no, struck dumb—to see that he was wearing a set of long johns that might have come from a vintage Sears catalog.

She clapped a hand to her mouth, but couldn't help giggling.

Indignation is often clothing enough for the righteous, and Jeremy was most indignant; first, to find that his unseen visitor was still present when he had assumed she was not; second, to realize that she was laughing at his undergarment, which she shouldn't be seeing in the first place.

He hastened to a wardrobe to dig a long, belted robe from the far corner, and donned it.

"You must play fair and announce yourself," he said sternly, returning to the portrait. "Or are you never absent?" he asked with new alarm.

She was still laughing. "Don't worry about shocking me; I have never seen a more modest undergarment in my life."

He frowned. "I understand the eighteenth century was licentious, but I believe that gentlemen wore the same nightshirts then that they wear now." He pointed to the long-sleeved white garment that the maid had laid over the turned down covers, and that Mel had not noticed before.

Her laughter became shrieks she tried to smother. "Goodness, how quaint! It looks like something Scrooge would wear to greet the ghost of Marley."

"How do you know about Scrooge? Dickens wrote the story after you died!"

"Well, I—" Mel was finally able to stop laughing. In street dress, Jeremy had looked reasonably modern. In the privacy of his bedroom, he looked adorably antique. She must remember that dealing with an unseen apparition like herself might unhinge his delicate nineteenth-century brain. Under no circumstances must he know that she was from the future. "Being dead doesn't mean one doesn't hear things."

"Being invisible would lead to one overhearing a lot," Jeremy said astutely.

"But I am not invisible; you see my portrait before you."

"Then you are tied by it to this room?"

"No," she admitted.

He lifted an eyebrow, which gave him a rakish look the robe-covered long johns did nothing to exploit. Mel stifled another giggle. "So you chose to be here?" Jeremy asked.

She shrugged, though no one could see it, and wondered why her garb had been transformed to period dress when no one could see that, either. "It *was* my room."

"And is mine now. I suggest you vacate the premises for the night."

"You would evict a homeless woman?"

"From my bedchamber, yes."

"Even if she is a relative?"

"Especially if she is a relative! Now, go."

Mel had no desire to see the beruffled nightshirt on the bed modeled; her laughter might awaken the house and require more explanation than Jeremy was capable of hearing at the moment, so she wafted by him, feeling very material but knowing she was not.

"Even if she is a ghost, and quite invisible?" she inquired on her way to the door.

"Yes, and I hope that you are more decently clothed, mistress, than your reaction to my garments leads me to believe."

As she passed him, she felt again the odd eddy of some unseen force. He felt it, too, for he reached out for a moment, then drew his hand back as if burned.

"I have no desire to find out, you understand," he said quickly, even as her laughter trailed to the door.

Jeremy stared at the solid wooden surface, waiting for it to open even a crack.

Mel sighed and flowed through. It felt like icy, coagulated Jell-O. The hall was lit only by a lamp at the top of the stairs, and was frigid. At a loss, Mel descended the curving staircase, her heavy skirts dragging three steps behind her. Why could she *feel* so physical and be so immaterial?

A ticking tallcase clock in the downstairs hall said the hour was eleven. The rest of the family had retired, apparently, for no sound but the patient tick-tick, tsk-tsk of time echoed downstairs, and everything was dark, lit only by the lamp atop the newel post. Even the mouths of the fireplaces were dark and cold and mute.

Mel shivered, knowing of no place to go for many hours. Then she recalled the wonderfully warm furnishings of the study and hastened toward the double doors, edging sideways between them and feeling the passing wood tickle her ribs.

She almost laughed out loud before she realized that

the desktop lamp half-lit the room, and that someone sat at the desk and someone sat before it. They spoke in hoarse whispers.

"Another week, I implore you," the man behind the desk begged. His elbows were propped atop the piled papers, and his face was buried in his hands. When he looked up, Mel realized it was Jeremy's father. "One more week, and I'll be clear."

"Can't do it." The man sitting before the desk was a shadowy figure, but he spoke with more authority than Jeremy's father. "I've already let you go longer than most, Gardner."

"It's . . . Christmas," Jeremy's father began in a quavery voice that seemed foreign to a man of his high temper.

"Christmas means nothing to moneylenders, you know that, Mr. Moneybags, Mr. Henry J. Gardner. Now that the bags are empty—"

"Unlucky investments—"

"Moneylenders don't make unlucky investments. I'll have the house, I will, and all that's in it. I'll have you in debtors' court before all your fancy friends."

"Please, Redfern, a bit more time. I . . . expect my children to make good marriages."

"I can't wait for marriages."

"Engagements to be announced this Christmas." Jeremy's father sounded as if he were running out of breath.

"How good marriages are we talking?" The other man leaned forward to extract a cigar from a humidor, and lit it with the harsh scratch of a match against a metal box.

"You wouldn't know the families," Jeremy's father began with some of his old stiffness.

"You wouldn't believe what families I deal with. Try me."

"Miss Cuthbert and Mr. Blount," the older man said.

The end of the cigar burned blood-red as the shadowy head nodded. "Miss Cuthbert's her father's darling, and he's rich as Croesus. Blount's a miser. I wouldn't expect even as winsome a lass as your daughter to tease enough money out of him. But Miss Cuthbert has possibilities if your remaining son is not as headstrong as the other, who upped and ran off with a nobody from New Jersey."

"The girl was a tradesman's daughter," Jeremy's father objected, sounding a bit defensive.

"Let her father bail out the almighty banking Gardners, then! No? I thought not. Until the day after Christmas, then."

The shadowy figure stood in the dim room, his features hidden by the brim of a bowler hat. The live coal of his cigar burned like a cyclops's single eye in the darkness of his face. He left with a clomp of coarse boots, brushing past Mel like a bitter March wind.

Jeremy's father let his face sink into his hands again.

Mel began to feel more sorry for him and his wife— and for Jeremy and Phoebe—than she did for herself.

For the next two days the big house throbbed with activity as the occupants—family members and servants alike—readied themselves for the pre-Christmas dinner party.

Mel drifted from room to room, fascinated by the preparations, despite her quandary. In daylight she slipped into the vacant study to read Mr. Gardner's papers, hoping for a clue to his financial disaster. Nothing in the crabbed handwriting made sense to her, but she discovered a small, brass-framed calendar on his cluttered desk. The heading, *December,* was printed in charming cursive type above a print of a young woman in a red velvet gown skating alone across a moonlit pond. The year, also in cursive vintage numerals, was *1896.*

Mel stood frozen by the desk, then a flash of anger melted her icewater shock as she snatched the small calendar from the desk to stare at the mocking figure dressed so like herself and equally frozen in time and motion.

Her muff swung like a soft pendulum from its wrist cord at her abrupt motion, but the calendar . . . the calendar was in her gloved hands, solid and real. Her forefinger lifted the page to reveal the cardboard backing. She had touched something tangible and it had responded to her as if she were real! Or was this another illusion?

When the study door creaked, she slammed the calendar back to the desktop in breathless guilt and wonder.

Mr. Gardner came in, turning his head quickly toward the desk. He immediately went to examine his papers, then frowned and moved the calendar several inches to one side, to its original position.

Mel watched him, rapt, her gloved hands clasped to her face. She had indeed moved the frame. She had affected something in this time period, in this place. She was not wholly . . . immaterial.

Excited, she sailed through the closed door—and felt the wind half knocked out of her. That trick was getting harder by the hour, but now she had a new one to distract her.

In the warm, steaming kitchen, where teakettle and fire were always primed, she slipped among the servants, moving a pitcher three inches so the hand that reached for it without looking came up empty. She yanked the starched apron bow loose behind the under-housemaid's back and was rewarded to see stuffy Reeves, passing just then, receive an indignant look and a snap of angry eyes as tangible as a slap.

Containing her laughter, she rushed upstairs to Mrs. Gardner's room and amused herself for half an hour by edging everything the lady of the house wanted within closer reach, until the poor woman automatically held her hand out for the needed object as she concentrated on menus and seating arrangements, and never noticed a thing, though the constant furrows on her brow eased. *Lady's companion,* Mel mentally advertised herself for employment to the Victorian world. *Quiet, discreet, and congenial to spiritualists.*

Then, expert at her moves, Mel romped down the hall to Phoebe's bedchamber, where a maid was engaged in sewing an alarming amount of satin flowers, lace, and beadery on a rose velvet gown. Mel anticipated her by placing the froufrou in a more pleasing arrangement, her window display magic at full strength.

The maid frowned and pursed her lips each time she turned back from her sewing supplies to the gown to find a decoration already positioned for her needle, but Mel felt like the helpful birds in Disney's *Cinderella* rather than like the poltergeist she must seem to the maid.

Then it was down the hall, two doors on the left, to Jeremy's room. He was gone. Indeed, when he wasn't dashing off songs at his desk these days, he was dashing out with his friend Philip despite his father's orders. Mel suspected he was defying his father to forge ahead on his Broadway show scheme. The older man was too distracted by the deadline hanging over his head like lethal mistletoe this Christmas season to notice his son's ignorant efforts to save the family finances for his own reasons.

Euphoric because she was at last about to make a physical impression on this world, Mel arranged her velvet skirts on Jeremy's cane-backed desk chair and picked up a brass-barreled pen.

She dipped it in the inkwell, shook it daintily over some scratch paper (which of Jeremy's scribblings weren't scratch paper?) and wrote what she could remember of a contemporary song, "Only a Bird in a Gilded Cage."

It was not original, but it was probably in period, and Mel insisted on authenticity in all her worlds, whether they were behind glass or not.

Her handwriting was appallingly plain and modern, and inkdots freckled the page, but she signed her penmanship "Me" and whisked out the door—ouch—and elsewhere in the house, adjusting evergreens and mistletoe, especially the festive mass hanging from a bell in the dining room archway.

In the front parlor, Phoebe had coaxed her mother to a downstairs divan and was helping the maids decorate the towering fresh Norway pine.

"It would be a perfect Christmas," Phoebe said with a half-happy sigh to her mother, "with snow on the sidewalks and all, if only—"

"What, dear?"

"If only Drew were here."

Mrs. Gardner's head sank under the fragile weight of her cap as she bit her lips. "And if only we didn't have to entertain ... strangers for dinner. I am sorry, Phoebe, that you are to wed so young. I would have wished—" She straightened and stiffened as if suddenly starched. "We must follow your father's wishes, no matter how unpleasant. He is the head of the household."

Phoebe said nothing, but she paused, holding a tiny feathered angel in her hands, to stare toward the street. Talk about birds in gilded cages, Mel thought, whisking the angel up several branches to perch in a prominent place.

Phoebe glanced to her hands as she felt its soft escape, then gazed up to see it free and beyond easy reach. Frowning, she lifted her hand to where it hung—and fell short by six inches. She glanced around, but no one had noticed a thing.

By evening the house was polished and lit until it glowed like a glass of cream sherry. Mel, exhausted as any hardworking brownie must be, had retreated to Jeremy's room, for the Gardner women's maids were assisting them into their gowns, and Mel would be buffeted by too many accidental brushes with busy bodies.

Jeremy had dressed himself, and quite dazzling he looked in his black evening suit, enameled black studs glittering down a seriously starched shirtfront.

He was admonishing his hair before the bureau mirror when Mel eased through the door and heaved a sigh. His own sigh echoed hers as he threw down the brush. "Damn Mr. Moneypincher Blount, and be blasted to Miss Cora Cuthbert with her father's millions and her mother's jewelry! Neither of them is worth a song."

He went to his desk to page through his papers, throwing them down in disgust, too. "One showstopping song and the team of Gardner and Garrett will be launched." He sat down, picked up a pen, hesitated, then pulled out the sheet with Mel's writing on it.

He turned abruptly to the portrait.

"Ghost? Are you there?"

Mel held her tongue.

Jeremy held up the sheet. "It's not in the least original, you know."

She kept silent.

"And what is this 'Me'? Did you start to write 'Melody' and were interrupted?" He tossed the paper down, then stood and walked over to the portrait. "Don't desert me now, Auntie; I'll think I'm utterly mad. I've been writing myself half-crazy anyway, and maybe nothing will pan out. Tin Pan Alley doesn't need dabblers of good family. I'll have to marry Miss Cora Cuthbert and never write another line more than a suicide note," he said darkly, watching the portrait as if he expected the painted face to move.

Mel slipped in front of him and adjusted his black silk bow tie, which was slightly askew.

Jeremy brought an unconscious hand to the center knot of his tie. "I *am* crazy," he declared. "I never heard anything here but my own wishful thinking, my own silly songs humming in my head. Time to be a practical man and confront the family dilemma. Poor Phoebe. I'd marry a Gorgon if it would save Phoebe from the likes of Silas Blount."

Turning like a man facing his execution squad, and looking, Mel thought, like one of her more handsome mannequins come to life—say the Arrow shirt man from the 1910 window—Jeremy left the bedroom for the festivities below.

Mel remained in what would be her own room decades in the future, feeling an appalling sudden wave of utter loneliness. Then she realized, *this* was her window, the window fate had found her, the challenge of two lifetimes, the design assignment of a career. She would just have to arrange things to everyone's satisfaction, even—and especially—her own.

* * *

In the front parlor the Christmas tree, draped in tinsel and paper garlands, clad with a regiment of tiny tin soldiers and a chorus of miniature angels, bearing dozens of small lit candles—hadn't the Victorians heard of fire hazards?—was king.

Mel preened by arranging her festive red velvet skirts, though no one could see her. She had left her muff on the mantel by the portrait and had removed her velvet jacket to discover that the bodice below was shoulder-baring and beaded with jet. The ensemble, she realized, was a "weekender," a Victorian traveling garment that could go from train to dinner party with the undoing of a few buttons. She had filched a black satin fan from Mrs. Gardner's suite—and a ruby-and-rhinestone-studded ebony comb for her unbonneted French twist à la Ivana, and felt herself quite the chic young thing. What a shame that no one could see her.

The fireplaces blazed and snapped that night, banishing the Shadows in Mr. Gardner's study and wafting the scent of burning pine. Mrs. Gardner was a gracious, fragile figure in lace-draped ecru satin, her fine-lined, ivory-pale face a study in resigned sadness.

Mel gazed at the now familiar faces and the beautifully bedecked scene, only to realize that this was her most glamorous, most surprising Christmas ever. For a moment she felt like the guardian angel at the tree's very top, beaming down on everyone unnoticed, and quite, quite content with what she saw.

Phoebe's festive figure shone like the Christmas tree, her gleaming hair as rich as brown satin ribbon against the rose velvet gown.

"Lovely," mother whispered to daughter with a smile. "Quite your best-trimmed gown yet."

Jeremy edged nearer to his sister. "Far too lovely for

the likes of Blubbernose Blount," he said softly between his teeth. "Toast to a Broadway debut in the New Year, sister dear, and we two can live to see Miss Cuthbert wed Mr. Blount. I'll even write the scene into my next show."

Phoebe's anxious face brightened at her brother's levity. "What a delightful imagination you have, Jem. I'll wish that your every Christmas dream comes true with all my heart, but I fear my own fate is sealed."

At that moment Reeves paused portentously on the threshold to announce, "Mr. Silas Blount."

Oh, dear, Mel thought as the man himself entered, *must* he be the very model of a melodrama suitor?

Silas Blount edged into the room like a surreptitious crab, his thin form hunched, though he was no more than forty. A penny-sized wen sat beside the previously advertised unfortunate nose. His fingernails, as he worked his hands on the pockets of a garish brocade vest, were horny, yellow, and ridged, and therefore a perfect contrast for his soft, crimson, bulbous nose.

Neither Phoebe's nor her mother's face reflected the least distaste for this unappetizing, almost Dickensian figure, which made Mel realize how liberated women of her day had become. Both women, she realized, would marry whomever they were told to, and saw no way out of it.

Jeremy did, though, for his lips folded taut and the fire in his hazel eyes promised no happy ending to this courtship, by hook or by crook or by Broadway show.

Reeves returned shortly, celebrating his most officious night of the year by announcing in pear-shaped and brandy-drenched tones; "Miss Cora Cuthbert and Mr. Theolonius Cuthbert."

Cora's father was stout, florid, and quite like a stuffed quail, but Miss Cora Cuthbert was a tall, cool, ash blond, and a beauty in any age. She wore brandy-colored taffeta encrusted with pearls, so she rustled like a serpent with every sinuous movement.

Season's greetings were exchanged, and it was no twist of fate that Mr. Silas Blount ended up seated beside Miss Phoebe Gardner on the chaise longue. It was by a twist of heavy crimson velvet—and the improvised use of a rather sharp doily pin—that Miss Cora Cuthbert was persuaded to avoid sitting next to Mr. Jeremy Gardner on the yellow brocade loveseat.

"Oh," said the lovely visitor, shaking her white-gloved hand, "something nasty on the sofa stabbed me. I never saw it."

Mel smiled with invisible righteousness.

Miss Cuthbert's attentive father seated her in a less aggressive chair before joining Jeremy on the loveseat. "Too much stuffing in me to feel a random pinprick, my dear," he joked. "So, my lad, how go things on the stock market?"

"Oh, rather *boorish,*" Jeremy said with a defiant scowl.

His father looked grim at this two-edged witticism, but no one noticed.

Reeves returned, bearing a tray of tiny, stemmed glasses burnished with sherry, and each glass soon rested in an encompassing hand.

Mel admired the ladies' dexterity at filtering every gesture through gloves, but was glad an invisible guest didn't have to subject herself to such restraints. This made it so much easier for Mel to lift Mr. Henry Gardner's glass ever so delicately while everyone was admiring the Christmas tree and tilt its contents into Mr. Silas Blount's drinking vessel, and to perform the same service for Miss Cora Cuthbert by dipping into Mr. Theolonius Cuthbert's portion.

She even shared some of the senior Mr. Gardner's allotment, which he showed a tendency to bolt, with Mrs. Gardner.

Mr. Henry Gardner regarded his empty glass and frowned. "Short shrift on the sherry, Reeves; a refill for our guests."

Messrs. Blount and Cuthbert nodded eagerly. The decanter came round just in time for Miss Melody Johansen to tip a bit more into Mr. Silas Blount's and Miss Cora Cuthbert's glasses.

Mel even managed to steal a sip from Jeremy's glass while he was watching the shell game with the other glasses, looking most appealingly puzzled.

"Dinner is served," Reeves announced from the threshold all too soon.

Two by two they marched into the dining room: Mr. and Mrs. Gardner; Mr. Silas Blount and Miss Phoebe Gardner; young Mr. Gardner and Miss Cora Cuthbert. Mr. Theolonius Cuthbert brought up the rear with, er, Miss Melody Johansen, unbeknownst to everyone.

Alas, the china-laden table provided no room for an extra, uncounted upon guest. Mel had to content herself with moving around the table with the serving staff, refilling a wineglass here and there—Miss Cora Cuthbert's and Mr. Silas Blount's—when no one was looking. The ever-discreet companion, virtually invisible.

Jeremy grew more distracted by the second, running his fingertips around his wineglass rim, eyeing the slightly tipsy Miss Cuthbert beside him, frowning at his sister and an ever-more-forward Mr. Blount across the table.

But Jeremy had his own battle to fight. Miss Cora Cuthbert leaned nearer than convention allowed on one white-kid-gloved elbow, until her bare upper arm pressed Jeremy's black wool sleeve. She fanned her long fingers on his wrist and drank luxuriously from her wineglass.

"You are quite the bandbox tonight, dear Jeremy." Her whisper duplicated her gown's sinister rustle. "Such a shame that your old-fashioned father forbid you the stage! My father, luckily, forbids me nothing that my heart desires," she added with a sophisticated smirk. "Perhaps, however, you would perform most aptly for an audience of one."

Jeremy stiffened as he began to reply, no doubt with sentiments that would displease his father.

Luckily, at that very awkward instant, Miss Cora Cuthbert's chair skidded inexplicably to the left, nearly casting her to the floor next to Jeremy's chair, had he not caught her trespassing elbow and held her upright.

"Goodness, Cora," her father admonished from across the table with a nearsighted squint. "You are not by nature so clumsy."

The senior Mr. Gardner made quite a display of re-settling Miss Cuthbert into her vagrant chair, while Jeremy smiled into his untouched wineglass, and took a first, happy sip.

"Oh!" said Miss Phoebe Gardner, starting as if a snake had bit her under the table.

When every eye fixed upon her, she blushed and stammered, confessing that a pin left in her gown had pricked her. The grin on Mr. Silas Blount's flushed face put the lie to his dinner partner's polite explanation.

While everyone else simpered sociably, Jeremy glowered at Mr. Silas Blount, who maintained a self-satisfied expression.

Not for long. Moments later a plate of buttered snails and something even less identifiable but equally repellent had slithered onto his lap. Everyone's attention centered on Reeves to the rescue, beating off the attacking mollusks with a damask napkin.

Reeves turned on the unfortunate serving man, who was ready with a defense.

"It's not my fault! Something—someone—tipped the tray from beneath as I was serving."

Before Reeves could protest the unlikelihood of Miss Phoebe Gardner pulling such a trick on a guest of her father's, the master of the house stood, lifting his wineglass.

"A toast," Mr. Henry Gardner cried in a desperate attempt to redeem the evening. He eyed the visitors to his table with a social smile. "To surprising developments in the New Year, and the happiness of my children." At this he beamed in what he clearly regarded as a jovial manner at his son and Miss Cora Cuthbert, at his daughter and Mr. Silas Blount.

The unfortunate Mr. Silas Blount, still daubing his saturated lap, hastened to seize his wineglass—and sighed with relief when he brought it safely to his lips without spilling.

Miss Cora Cuthbert was not so lucky. She had seized the opportunity of the toast to link her forearm with Jeremy's so they would have to sip from each other's glasses.

This forward gesture brought a grimace of paternal relief to Mr. Henry Gardner's face, but Jeremy looked as if he were facing a new onslaught of something slithery and dead. While Miss Cuthbert subtly ran her tongue over the rim of Jeremy's glass, some awkwardness of gesture thrust the crystal against her teeth with a ringing sound.

"Aghhh!" she exclaimed, untwining herself at once

to tend her injured lip and a shower of Burgundy on her pale gown.

"Dreadfully sorry," Jeremy apologized insincerely. "Had no idea I was so deuced clumsy."

"It wasn't you who was clumsy," Phoebe noted from across the table with some spirit, shifting on her chair as far away from Mr. Blount as possible, for the man was now lurching toward the tabletop at a disastrous angle.

Mrs. Gardner surveyed the Christmas board and noted mournfully, "What a festive evening this is; if only dear Andrew could be here."

Into the silence came Reeves and his pair of servers to whisk away the first course and set Mr. Blount upright in his chair again.

"The family is complete," Mr. Gardner announced sternly, "and will soon be more complete still," he added, attempting to smile on the disheveled figures of his future son- and daughter-in-law.

"Oh, don't be such a sentimentalist," Mr. Blount suggested in a tipsy tone. "You know money makes the best matches, and this little honey of yours will well be worth her upkeep—and some of yours."

Another silence, while the servants fled.

Mr. Blount attempted to pinch Phoebe's flaming cheek, but she rose so swiftly that her heavy velvet train overturned her chair as she fled the room.

"Phoebe!" Mr. Gardner bellowed. "You have not excused yourself. Do you wish to ruin me?"

Jeremy stood next, brushing off the clinging fingers of the vacant-eyed Miss Cora Cuthbert. "It's you who should excuse yourself, Father," he declared indignantly, turning to follow his distraught sister.

"I?" Mr. Gardner demanded, eyeing the table now bereft of two more of his offspring, as well as the absent Andrew. "I only said Drew was a conscienceless young fool to marry whom he will, that he was no kin of mine, and that still stands, Christmas or not. I'll disinherit you, too, you ungrateful puppy—" But Jeremy was too far gone to hear his threat.

His wife was not. At that the meek woman stood, her face whiter than the Spode china. She said nothing, only swallowed a wail and ran sobbing from the dining room.

Mr. Henry Gardner eyed the remains of his Christmas dinner party, his matchmaking triumph. Mr. Silas Blount was lying with his head on the tablecloth, setting the butter curls into ranks like soldiers and singing, "On the first day of Christmas, my true love gave to me, a peartridge in a partree."

Miss Cora Cuthbert lounged in her chair, her ladylike manner vanished with her dinner partner, staring after Jeremy with a vengeful pout. "Hasn't a penny to his name, and neither does his silly and boring family, much as they think we don't know. I was willing to overlook the money for other benefits, but he can't treat me like this, can he, Daddy?"

Her father rose, none the better for his own wine consumption. "My daughter is the flowerhood of young woman, sir," he told the dazed host. "I will not stand for her to be insulted. Our discussions are over."

He went to assist his daughter to her wobbly feet and escort her to the hall, where a mournful but prescient Reeves could be glimpsed holding their wraps.

Mr. Gardner sat—or sank, rather—down at his decimated table, staring gloomily at the portrait of a dead hare over the console opposite the head of the table.

"Cheer up," Mr. Silas Blount advised, licking one dead soldier in a butter-yellow uniform from his fingertips. "There's plenty of wine left; the old serving boy left the decanter on the table in his haste. Perhaps you can persuade your deautiful boughter . . . ah, your beautiful daughter . . . to come back down and serve it to us."

"Out!" Mr. Henry Gardner thundered, clutching his head as if to roar away all bad memories.

Mr. Silas Blount took up the decanter in question and, lurching like a sailor, left.

Mel hastened after the dear departed, pausing first at Mrs. Gardner's chamber, where her maid was extracting her from her gown and comforting her with all manner of unlikely assurances.

"There, there, Missus. I'm sure the missing young master will be back in the New Year, and nothing can be so bad it cannot be fixed."

Next Mel peeked in on Phoebe, who sat by her faint fire in full evening dress, staring at the embers through absent eyes, while Jeremy comforted her.

"Don't you see, Phoebe? The row tonight has ruined Father's marital schemes for us both. We're free."

"But Drew's still gone, and it's Christmas," she said without looking up. "I can't understand why Father has done this to all of us. Doesn't he love us?"

"He's our father, of course he does . . . perhaps he wanted us to marry money for our own sakes."

"That won't make us happy, Jeremy. I'd live in a boardinghouse if I could see Drew again!"

"You won't have to live in a boardinghouse if I become a famous playwright. And you will see Drew again, I swear it."

"Where can he have gone after Father made him leave?" Phoebe asked in anguish.

"To a boardinghouse to wait for us," Jeremy answered, patting her shoulder when she looked up to smile at his joke. "One good thing," he added. "The evening's early end permits me to get to work sooner tonight. I'll have a corker of a centerpiece song by morning and everything will be all right."

"Good night," Phoebe said, sounding better but unconvinced.

Jeremy dashed down the hall, wrenching off his black bow tie and popping shirtfront studs as he went.

Mel followed, feeling the breeze of his haste, wondering if she should confess what she had done. What had seemed apt an hour ago looked like sheer irresponsibility now.

Jeremy turned to slam his bedchamber door only a second after Mel had glided through the open portal. The noise made her jump, but he was already pacing in the throes of inspiration.

She understood how creating something could make everything else seem possible. Settling into her old spot atop the mantel, she fanned herself slowly with the borrowed fan.

Jeremy hurled himself into his chair and scratched down some verses. After staring at the page, he bounded up, then fixed on the portrait and came toward it purposefully.

"Well, did you?" he demanded. "You've been quiet of late; too quiet. Did I detect your spirited hand in the proceedings downstairs?"

When Mel was silent, he went on. "Why so shy now, Auntie? The damage has been done, and frankly it was well done, whatever the consequences."

After a pause he spoke more to himself than a presumed other presence. "Perhaps I've gone daft. Perhaps I wanted the dinner party to fail and imagined some unseen hand helping that happen.

"Well," he addressed the portrait in a louder, defiant voice. "I know I'm mad to think you exist, or that you would bother to intervene in our little family drama. I suppose I only imagined that you find my lyrics trite and my undergarments laughable. I will embrace reality and behave as if you didn't exist, which you don't."

With that he finished undoing the shirt, threw his evening jacket on a chair, and sat down to remove his shoes and socks.

Mel was not titillated. Through Jeremy's open shirtfront she could glimpse the odious undergarment, her grandfather's long johns. She understood their services better after spending two days in this cold, drafty house.

Jeremy stood and stripped off his trousers, still clad in an outfit that resembled an early baseball player's uniform, pale and dumpy. He went to the turned down bed for his nightshirt, then glanced over his shoulder at the portrait.

"I'll never see your painted face without thinking of a Peeping Thomasina, Auntie. You laughed at my nightwear, but you're only a figment of my imagination, aren't you? You aren't really there, so it doesn't really matter—"

Mel felt mean for remaining silent, but perhaps it was best to wean him from her presence. Still, where would she go in this alien world? How would she survive unseen, unheard?

He began undoing the long row of front buttons that ran down the long johns. Then he shrugged his shoulders out of the garment—much better muscled shoulders than either his outer- or under-clothes indicated. Mel began to feel nervous, which was ridiculous when she was as safe as one could be, invisible.

Jeremy let the top of the long johns hang from his waist. He would do quite well in modern bathing trunks, Mel decided. And then he—

A flurry agitated the room, like a passing gust of air, as an unseen whirlwind snatched the dresser scarf off the bureautop, overturning a brush and a wooden box.

Levitating, the scarf slapped itself at Jeremy's middle just as the long johns made their last, slow slide to the floor.

"You *are* there!" Jeremy crowed, looping the ludicrous but timely loincloth around his hips. "You're as real as rainbows. I didn't dream you up."

He searched the room for a sign of a presence. "Say something."

"I'm sorry," Mel said in a quiet voice.

Jeremy whirled to face the bed. "For what? Admitting to the truth?"

"For ruining your father's dinner party."

"I'm not," he said with feeling. "We'll recover. Is that all you've got to say?"

The long robe levitated from the coverlet. "Aren't you cold?"

"Seeing ghosts always gives me goose bumps. Kind of you to notice," he added slyly.

The robe, looking oddly occupied, floated to him. He touched it, then jerked his fingers back. "You . . . give me electrical shocks."

"It's this state of mine, I suppose."

"Are you really . . . dead?" he asked, taking the robe and throwing it over his shoulders.

"As I told you, I don't know. You're the only person who can hear me, though, I think."

"That's good." He knotted the belt around his midsection, and Mel relaxed.

"Why?" she asked.

"You were my ghost to begin with, and I want you to stay that way."

"But I can't stay with you—"

"Why not? Are there rules of haunting? Of course you can stay with me. You must. You make me think. You make me laugh. I could even bear the thought of marrying Miss Cuthbert as Father wants, if you could go with me."

"Well, I couldn't!" Mel drew away from him to the desk.

"I won't have to after your dirty work tonight," he said, following her.

She was unnerved that he could sense where she was in the room now. He was trying to cross a line that would always be beyond reach, like her old life in her own time.

"I'm not a ghost, Jeremy," Mel admitted. "I'm a live person—at least I was—from another time."

"You mean that you . . . feel?"

"Yes! I feel cold and weight, but I'm not hungry. I can't explain it!"

"Do you feel . . . emotions?"

"Sometimes," she said carefully.

"So was the eighteenth century really so much more fun than this one, Auntie—or are you really my great-aunt? How can you be? You seem so young; my mother couldn't even have been conceived at your age, so we're not even related . . . yet."

He was very close, as if he saw her almost, as if he knew her. Mel flitted away, alarmed to feel her swaying skirts brush against his robe. Jeremy's hand snatched at the ghost fabric.

"You felt that?" Mel asked breathlessly.

"I think I've always felt your presence. You were out in the street when I came home with Philip, weren't you?"

"I was coming home, too, Jeremy."

"Of course, your portrait is here. You slept in this room, perhaps even this bed, long ago."

How could a ghost blush? Mel felt frantic. "Not long ago, Jeremy! With all your imagination you could never dream what or who I am. I'm not your aunt—!"

His smile became a sigh. "Thank God. I really couldn't sleep with my aunt."

"You can't sleep with *me*! I'm not here. I'm from the twentieth century, practically the twenty-first century! And I'm not going to spend what life I've got here and now peering in on your life. Do you know what it feels like to make no impression upon your environment at all, to be a thinking, feeling mist?"

"You moved my robe a minute ago, and you moved things at the dinner, didn't you?"

"Yes. . . . Jeremy, I'm sorry for interfering with the dinner."

"Forget the dinner. You really can't eat?"

She shook her head miserably, then remembered that he couldn't see. "No."

Jeremy frowned. "But you didn't move anything until you'd been here awhile."

"I couldn't. It was something I developed later, and I find it tiring, like walking through walls and doors. That gets harder and harder, and my clothes are heavy."

"Ah, so you're wearing them. I wondered."

"What exactly did you wonder?"

"If you looked like your portrait, which of course isn't your portrait at all." He came closer. How did he sense where she was? "Melody, it seems to me you're getting better at being here."

"What do you mean?"

"Don't sound so frightened. If you can touch things

here, and move them, perhaps you aren't going to be a ghost forever."

"I might become real?"

"You are real," he said warmly. "You're the most real person I've ever not met. I sense that. Come here."

"No!" She flew to her refuge atop the mantel.

"It's no use," he said, following. "I saw the chair seat dent when you stepped up on it."

"You *saw*?"

"You're leaving impressions on the things around you now, Melody, like you left invisible impressions on the people around you earlier. I heard my mother storm upstairs. She has never defied my father before. I think it will be good for him."

"No," Mel said, shutting her eyes and clutching her borrowed fan.

"Yes," came Jeremy's voice, from very near.

Mel felt a faint, faraway tug on the rim of her person.

"It's velvet," he said, his voice husky with admiration.

"What?"

He chuckled. "Apparently the twentieth century is as forward as the eighteenth was. Your gown, of course."

"You touched it?"

"Didn't you feel it?"

"Yes, but—"

"What do you suppose is making a difference in your physical presence? For you're becoming real, Melody; I can almost feel it happening, as easily as I feel the velvet in your skirt."

She kept her eyes closed, afraid to look, afraid to see what she would see, and might not see. Becoming real. Was he right? Becoming real like the velveteen rabbit in the children's story. Could she live forever in another time, another world, with no one to understand her, to know that her past was this world's future?

The tug on her skirt became imperative. She tumbled from her seat atop the mantel like a doll into a sizzling, semisolid eddy.

"I've got you," Jeremy's voice whispered by her ear.

In fact, she felt surrounded, by a half presence, by his determination, by his need to make her real. Mel pushed off the growing solidity of the past as if it were a series of theatrical curtains, heavy velvet swinging past her yard by billowing yard.

She opened her eyes. Jeremy was as close as when they had collided in the street outside, only now he was not moving through her, but around her, as his arms were, and she felt his possession as partly physical.

"Oh, it tingles!" Mel said.

"Yes." Jeremy's face was as intent as that of a scientist embarked on a dangerous experiment. "It's like being in a storm, up with the lightning."

"Maybe this will ... destroy us."

Jeremy shook his head, closed his eyes, and leaned to kiss her mouth, finding it.

The shock of contact was electrifyingly dangerous. Mel felt her physical self melt and solidify in dizzying turn, even as her emotional self sang with relief and joy.

She felt the smooth sleeves of Jeremy's robe beneath her hands, felt warm lips on hers, breath along her neck, felt as real as the form she touched.

Then she stepped back, breaking the contact that seemed so sweet, ending the union of one time with another.

Jeremy was smiling at her as if he saw her.

"The ghost in the wine velvet gown," he said dreamily. "That's it. That's my signature song for the new show. I've got it all now. It'll be a smash."

"You . . . *see* me."

He nodded solemnly. "You're still a bit faint, but that gives me all the more to look forward to." He reached for her again. "I certainly felt you, and that's all that matters."

Mel backed away. "Why? Why am I materializing now?"

"Perhaps you're becoming accustomed to your new time. Perhaps you're becoming real because I want you to be that way, because I want you with me always."

"But that complicates everything! I can't stay here anymore. I don't know where to go—"

He shook his head, laughing at her. "I do. I'll help you. I'll follow in Drew's footsteps and run off with a lovely, mysterious wife nobody knows anything about." He laughed again at the notion.

"You don't want to marry," she reminded him.

"Cora Cuthbert. I've nothing against marrying you; in fact, I think you need someone to look after you."

"I have been looking after you all," she reminded him.

His face suddenly sobered.

"What's wrong? Jeremy?"

"You've vanished. It's like I've suddenly become blind."

"I'm here," she said, rushing into his arms, feeling his embrace. "I would make a very unreliable wife, popping in and out of existence."

"Some men would find that ideal," he said into the hair at her ear, his breath as warm as steam in the cold room. "Not me."

"Oh, Jeremy, you make me believe that I can gradually solidify in your world and you can pass me off as a mysterious stranger and we can marry and you can write Broadway shows and I can—what can a woman do in this benighted time?"

"What did you do in your own?"

"I do department store windows. Design the vignettes."

He frowned. "Women can't do that. Yet," he added, as if he saw the objection forming on her lips. "You could become a milliner, a costumer, a star in my shows."

"I don't act or sing."

He shrugged. "And I don't do windows. We'll find a way. Where are you going?"

She had drawn away again. "Somewhere else. To think."

He stood still for a moment, then nodded. "Come back soon. Meanwhile, I've got a song to write for you."

As she stood by the door and watched him settle at the desk, she asked, "I'm half visible now, you say."

"For the moment. I'm sure you'll become completely visible when I kiss you again."

"Whatever their time, men are such egoists!"

"What's an egoist?"

"Never mind." She put her hand to the doorknob, and touched cold brass.

Turning it, she slipped out the door in the normal fashion, realizing that passing through walls and doors had become increasingly taxing. She was losing her . . . powers, but she had something to do before they vanished utterly and she was just an ordinary misplaced woman who would marry Jeremy and become a—what? She could become a trailblazer in the history of design, Mel realized, and the first thing she would come up with would be boxer shorts, and then filmy, flowing women's clothes that didn't require yards of weighty fabric, however handsome, and bobbed hair, and oh, the possibilities were endless. . . .

She stopped at Mr. Gardner's door, took a deep breath—even felt the deep breath—and hurled herself through the wood.

It was like getting hit by a wave and pounded into the surf. She froze, quivering, inside the room, changing even as she stood there. In moments her eyes had adjusted to the dark and she moved to the dim kerosene lamp, turning up the light.

"Who's there?" Mr. Gardner started up from the bedclothes.

"I ammm, Henry Garrrrdner," she moaned in a spooky monotone, shaking the bed curtains.

"I see no one," he objected in a nervous voice.

Poor Mr. Henry Gardner. First his disastrous dinner party and now this: psychic indigestion. Her.

"You have been seen, and that is sufficient," Mel intoned, stepping into view at the side of the bed.

"My God, I can see through you, like consommé!"

"And I can see through you, Mr. Henry Gardner. You are not a bad man, but most misguided."

"Who are you?" he demanded, rousing himself.

"The Ghost of Christmas Past."

"No!"

"And Christmas Future."

"The devil you say."

"And this sorry Christmas Present."

"See here, young woman, this charade does not frighten me." He reached to catch her hand.

Mel steeled herself, for she felt a brush of something, but it floated past her senses, unlike his son's impinging presence. What would Mr. Gardner do if she told him he was about to get a ghost for a daughter-in-law?

"You are not . . . r-real," he stuttered.

"I am as real as your secret sins, Henry Gardner. And I tell you that whatever money you have lost in the stock market is nothing compared to what you have lost in your home: your wife's hope, your daughter's loyalty, your remaining son's respect. You cannot sell your children to tomorrow to redeem today. You cannot banish a child for following his heart. Your children are not pawns for your pride and your profit. Heal your family and you will heal your fortunes."

"You have . . . appeared to tell me this?"

"I have come a long way, a very long way, through many decades, to tell you this. And one thing more."

"Yes?" he asked meekly.

"If you invest in the stock market in the future, I would recommend certain enterprises."

Mr. Gardner's shaking ebbed. "Yes?" he demanded sharply.

"An Italian gentleman named Marconi is becoming active in the area of communications. Invest."

"Yes!"

"And you would not go wrong in investing in any project stemming from Mr. Edison."

"Edison? I don't know—"

"I do," Mel thundered in the approved Henry Gardner fashion. "Thomas Alva Edison of New Jersey. He is a man with very bright ideas."

"I thank you, ghost," he said meekly, but his eyes held a new, avaricious glint.

"Merry Christmas," she sighed, backing into the wall until it nudged her, then sighing again—oh, this would hurt—and pushing herself through like cheese through a strainer.

In the hall, Mel shivered from her effort. Jeremy was right, bless him. She was solidifying by the moment. She rushed down the hallway, aware of every creak in the floor, every brush of her gown, and opened his/her/ their bedroom door.

Jeremy was asleep with his head on the desk, the lamp burning down like an artificial sun on his dear, familiar, unique features. What would she do when his father met her in the flesh and recognized her? Perhaps he would not. Mel yawned. She felt . . . sleepy. Come to think of it, she was hungry, too. Hungry and sleepy and an orphan in time.

Jeremy stirred, then opened his eyes and smiled into hers.

"You can see me!" she said, marveling at what she had once taken so for granted.

"Perfectly. Are you tired?"

She nodded.

"Then we should retire." He stood.

"Oh, do you think—?"

"It *is* our room."

Mel awoke in the night, as solid as sanity.

Jeremy slept beside her, but the aftermath of dreams danced in her head. Visions of her old life, her new life in olden times, Jeremy, song lyrics, windows. A woman putting her hand to her hair in dismay. A man betrayed by a pocketwatch. And still love the equation that bridged time and place, that cast lovers in bronze and families in silver.

Words danced in her head. Ghost. Time traveler. Phoebe and Natalie. Skaters in time. Crimson velvet and Broadway shows. Ragtime and rock'n'roll. Jeremy and The Jerk. Jeremy. His father and mother. Hers. Her sisters and brothers. Jeremy's lost brother Drew and his unwelcome wife Polly. Drew. Andrew. And a couple frozen in time with a comb and an absent watch between them, and also welding them and making Christmas what you gave up, rather than what you gave or you got. . . .

"Oh, God," said Mel, sitting up in Jeremy's nightshirt, solid as a self could be, with the recent memories to prove it.

Jeremy, wearing only Jeremy, sat up, too.

"What's wrong? You're not . . . fading?"

She rose, turned up the lamp with an expert hand, and went to the mantel.

"Melody, you're not leaving—"

Oh, God. She saw the muff lying there. The traitorous muff that had introduced her to the fact that when she left the Santa Shoppe she had entered another world.

The box wrapped in paper and string was still inside it, like a gift, a Christmas present from Christmas future and Christmas past.

She went to the lamp and opened the package. Jeremy, wearing his robe, came over.

"What is it, Mel?"

She winced that his worry had found her nickname from ten decades away. "What is your brother's name?"

"Drew."

"His formal name."

"Andrew."

"Andrew Gardner."

"Of course. Melody—?"

"And he eloped with a . . . Polly?"

"Polly Langley."

"A.G. from P.L."

"What are you talking about? Melody, don't scare me."

She held up the watch, whose hands as fine as a camel's hair moved every second, counting time, counting time left.

With her fingernails she opened the back and showed him the lock of hair.

"Polly is a raving redhead, all right. This is his, Drew's! Where on earth did you get it?"

Jeremy held the watch now, held his brother in his hand, held hope.

"A little shop," Mel said through a mist of prescient tears. "I know just where it is. It's a pawnshop. If we go there tomorrow—"

"Today!" he said, happy and even more hopeful.

"We can find the address of whoever pawned it."

"We *know* who pawned it! Drew may be low on funds, but we can find him and bring him and Polly home in time for New Year's. Father will get his surprising developments, after all." Jeremy smiled down at her. "You are magic. I know I've finally got the show—music, lyrics, and script—together now. Mother and Phoebe will be so happy."

"And your father, too, I think."

"Father?"

"He may be a changed man."

"I doubt it, but I am." Jeremy embraced her, as real as rainbows.

But Mel wondered. Wondered what would happen when she went back to—into—the Santa Shoppe.

They stood outside the dusty display window, three milk-glass globes above them, a symbol as old as the Middle Ages.

Mel had not lingered to study the altered Santa

Shoppe when she found herself clutching a muff outside of it, but she knew one thing about this place when it occupied this plateau in time: the address of Jeremy's exiled brother would appear on a ledger here, and nowhere else.

Jeremy clapped his gloved hands together, his eyes alight with anticipation under his dress top hat. She wanted to tell him he looked like a handsome Fred Astaire. "I can't believe that Drew is just a threshold away," Jeremy said.

"He may not have left an address," she cautioned him.

"He would want the watch back if Polly gave it to him. How pleased he'll be to get it back in time for the New Year."

"It may have been pawned by a third party."

"Drew would never let another have it. Melody, why are you so sure this will turn out badly?"

"I don't want to disappoint you," she said.

She couldn't tell him, warn him, of her secret worry. You don't always get what you expect when you toy with time. Before, she had expected nothing. Now, when it counted, she knew what she might be doing. And she had to take the chance. Jeremy's here and now were more important than her "maybe." Jeremy's brother had been key to his life before she had appeared—disappeared—in his life.

She could wait outside—and wonder if Jeremy would step back into his own time, or vanish into hers. She could enter with him and perhaps lose her hard-won solidity here, or perhaps be imprisoned in it for eternity, like an insect in amber.

Mel approached the door, putting her gloved hand on the knob. She turned to Jeremy.

"Melody?" he said, uncertain.

"Hold my muff," she told him, then poised like a second hand between one instant of time and another, between outside and inside, between the threshold to past and future, Mel took the next step, expecting anything.

She turned the knob and stepped inside the pawnshop that held Jeremy's brother.

She opened the door and heard the faint jingle of an alerting bell . . . or the chime of a distant horse's harness. The shop still smelled of aged wood and aging metal, cloth, and paper. She glanced behind her for Jeremy, and saw that she was alone.

The man behind the counter wore a Santa Claus suit, standard red issue. His eyes behind the barrier of false white whiskers and hair were sharp and searching.

Mel tottered for the farther reaches of the shop, her steps feeling oddly long now that no heavy hem dusted the floor. She stood before the familiar stand of phony trees, their shabby glitter blurred by the tear slick of her eyes, and clutched her red Fifties coat close, though the shop was warm and stuffy, if anything.

"Can I help you?" Santa wanted to know.

Too shocked to do anything except respond like an automaton, Mel returned to the front of the shop, to the same substantial, dusty case she had seen before.

She peered through the scratched glass into two shelves of jumbled junk and treasure, staring until her eyes cleared. Although she recognized an item or two—an enameled bumblebee pin, a tarnished Mexican-made sterling bracelet with a broken catch—no gold pocketwatch dimpled the faded coral velvet.

"Do you have any . . . watches?"

A red-gloved finger pointed to a flash of steel—

narrow-banded women's wristwatches from the Fifties. Mel shook her head and glanced to the door and windows. Night had turned the plate glass into a faint mirror in which she saw her forlorn modern self. She glimpsed people streaking past, ordinary modern figures in coats and jackets, most bare-headed despite the chill. No tall, hatted figure waited, not even the deliberately antique form of the driver of a horse-drawn cab in Central Park.

Mel sighed and looked back down the shadowy length of the shop. Empty, except for the tired toys and out-of-date decorations, all of it a wan glitter dimmed by the cobwebs of time, as she herself was, as her spirit had been dimmed by this last, abrupt wrench back into her own time and place and loneliness.

But—Mel sleepwalked back into the shop's depths again, drawn by the single new item that caught her eye—a fresh artificial tree among the tawdry trio she had seen before.

She worked off one glove as she went, pushing her purse strap farther onto her shoulder. Covered with gilded cupids and white satin balls, bright brass trumpets and paper doily parasols and red velvet bows ... populated with tiny tin soldiers and wooden rocking horses, stood a perfect miniature of the Gardner family Christmas tree.

If the pocketwatch was gone, then Jeremy had found it, found his brother! If the long-dead tree was here, even in this stiff and shrunken artificial form, then Mel had found exactly what she came for. Her fingertips touched the tiny cold brass curve of the trumpet mouth, then she whirled to the Santa figure at the shop's front.

"This tree. I'll take it."

"You don't even know the cost." He didn't object so much as comment on her impulsive choice.

"It's perfect. Just what I was looking for, what I'll always be looking for at Christmas," Mel said as she strode back to the counter.

A ratty white cotton batting eyebrow raised. Santa's eyes, she saw, were the required blue, but their expression was perplexed and even a trifle worried.

"What about the one with the gilt and pink feathers and strings of silver pearls? That's a more fashionable tree."

"I'm not interested in fashion. I'll take it." Mel drew—Drew!—her purse around to delve for her checkbook. The tree was hers, made for her, meant for her. Whatever fate had jerked her back and forth over the threshold of time had at least had the decency to leave her with a souvenir of a life she had lost before she was ever born, a token of what could have been a love to last through a lifetime of Christmases past, present, and future.

Tears threatening again, Mel ducked her head to dig blindly for her ballpoint pen.

"Ma'am." Santa sounded embarrassed. "I can't sell you that tree."

"Why not?" An angry consumer, now, intent on her rights.

Santa shrugged sheepishly. "A young fellow came in an hour ago and bought it. Paid for it. He'll be back at six sharp, after work, to cart it home."

"And you just left it out there, to . . . to tempt and disappoint people?"

"It's too heavy for an old man to remove from the display until the customer returns."

Sudden hope sent Mel's heart soaring. "And what happens if he doesn't come back by six?"

"I close, and you can have the tree before I go."

Mel jammed back the thick, plush, crimson sleeve at

her left wrist to expose her sleek Anne Klein watchface. Forty minutes.

She tried to browse, to kill time, but her steps soon turned into pacing on the hard wooden floor. When she glanced at the Santa, he was looking up from his magazine and frowning.

No one came in. The shop was as empty as she had always seen it, like an abandoned railway station nobody had yet bothered to dismantle. Was that what it was, a setting-off place for all times? Could she be sure of stepping out into her own world if she dawdled?

Always she ended up pausing by the tree, to pet the brittle branches, recall the heady pine scent of the real thing, remember her phantom tree-dressing party with the Gardners; how she had played hide-and-seek with Jeremy, how he had followed the path of her prestidigitation, her interference in their lives, until he found her, so to speak.

And then, as she stood daydreaming by the familiar Christmas tree, a breathless possibility appeared full-bodied in her mind like a ghost carrying out a personal haunting.

Jeremy! If she could walk between worlds, perhaps he could as well. Perhaps some latter-day Jeremy waited her on the streets of New York City. Perhaps he had found the Santa Shoppe again when in search of her, and had stepped out into Manhattan a hundred years hence. perhaps ... *he* had bought the tree, needing a souvenir in the same way she did.

Mel whirled again to face the shop door. Her watchface read 5:55 P.M., and any minute he might walk in the door.

"You sure are eager to get that tree," the Santa commented when she bounded once more to the front of the shop. "I got to give him every second, to be fair."

"Then you won't be able to close at six sharp," she said with a smile.

"There are rules," the Santa said grumpily, with a warning look so cold under frosted icing brows that Mel's heart froze in time again.

"I hope he comes," she said, just to confound him.

She was sure now. She knew her Christmas story had to have a happy ending, just as she had engineered a holiday reunion for the Gardner family beyond their wildest dreams. She smiled at the Santa again, knowing that anyone who sat day in and day out in a Santa Shoppe where hardly anybody ever came had to have become a bit cynical. She smiled with all her hope and joy and certainty.

He watched her worriedly, saying nothing, and the unheard seconds ticked away, as they always do.

The door opened to a jingle. A breath of icy air swept up her coat and down her neck. Santa's blue eyes glanced up with recognition . . . and regret.

She turned, resolved to regret nothing.

He was tall, wearing a down-filled nylon jacket. His ears and nose were cold-reddened, his hair brown, his eyes dark, his face possibly fine for his friends and family and the passing people in the street, but not the correct shape, no single feature familiar. He was a stranger.

"I'm here for the tree," he announced in a Southern accent, nodding to the shop's rear.

Santa stood up for the first time in Mel's presence, his fat red gloves braced on the glass counter. "Yes, sir. I'll wrap it in a jiffy."

"No!"

They regarded Mel as if she were mad.

"I'll ... buy it from you." She was thrashing around in her purse for her checkbook again, seeing through tears and panic. "Pay you a good profit."

"No," the strange man echoed her, although more softly. "I've been looking all over for a tree like that."

"So have I—for years and years. I'll pay you twice the price. You can get another." Frantically, she began filling out the check with the date, her name, the shop's name, two *p's,* one *e* on the end ...

The man who was not Jeremy frowned, then glanced at Santa over her head. "Wrap it, please. I want that tree," he told Mel in firm tones.

"Three times!" She tore off the check with amount space blank and thrust it at him.

"Do you even know what it's worth?" Santa interjected.

She supposed she appeared demented. Somewhere in time, Jeremy had her gold watch. She had nothing.

"It's worth everything," Mel whispered.

The man who had brought the cold in shrugged. New Yorkers were wary of inexplicable enthusiasm; New Yorkers knew what they wanted.

She watched the Santa move slowly to the table, lift the little Victorian tree, and bear it through a door into the back.

Her pleading glance got another shrug from the lucky purchaser.

"It's late," he said sheepishly. "I don't have time to shop around and replace it. Sorry, lady, but the race is to the swift."

She said nothing, frozen in her own unwanted time zone. Watching the Santa return with the brown-paper-swathed tree and carry it solemnly to the new owner was like leaving Jeremy all over again.

How could she have talked herself into such a

schmaltzy ending? You don't trick time; time tricks you. Time takes, it doesn't give back. Time doesn't celebrate Christmas, it celebrates New Year's, when the lean, mean old man with the scythe, the antithesis of fat, jolly old Santa with his bulging bag of goodies, comes whistling by, whispering of lost chances and dead dreams.

The man left with the wrapped tree. The Santa Shoppe was officially closed and she had outstayed her welcome. Without a backward look, Mel had no choice but to step into the cold behind the departing stranger, to gaze around until she was satisfied that the New York of December, 1994, greeted her, and to walk home, numb from her toes to her heart.

The brownstone's familiar facade hit her with a double whammy of regret for what she would find—and not find—within. Her keys in her purse admitted her into the warm lobby light. She climbed the stairs, realizing that they had been enclosed at some point into a cramped, graceless necessity. No holly entwined the servicable iron railings.

Her door bore a small artificial wreath, whose purchase had benefited a shelter for runaway children. The waxy leaves were not only lifeless but almost obscenely unreal.

Inside, everything was as she had left it—not always the case in a big city. Colored ribbons tied shut the bright, wrapped packages lying beside her television stand. A tree would have looked good atop the TV, she decided. Not any tree. The right tree.

All right. Mel looked around. She was home, the oversize room with the hideaway bed and the kitchen corner and the closet and the closet-size bathroom was neat, clean, and empty. She would not cling to a delusion, no matter how real it had seemed; she would not expect miracles, no matter what street she worked on; she would not nourish an ache in her heart for a mirage.

And she would make herself a nice hot cup of cocoa, change into something cozy, and get into the spirit of Christmas by opening one or two of the presents early. Then she would count her blessings—her family and the new friends she had made at Macy's. They were real. Jeremy was not. Jeremy was a movie in her mind that she wasn't sure she had ever seen, but that she would never forget.

When Mel delved in the closet for her "something cozy," she pulled out the velour robe she had gotten on sale for a song at Macy's long after last Christmas—and winced to realize that it was a rich burgundy color.

She stuffed her icy feet into fluffy slippers with bunny-rabbit heads on the toes, another post-Christmas sale item. Working for a department store had its benefits.

She heated water in the microwave and dumped in the powdered chocolate with the dehydrated miniature marshmallows, then curled up on her couch. The remote control cruised through a listless selection of holiday fare—reruns and soupy Christmas specials.

Finally she fell asleep, the cocoa cup scummed and empty on the small Parson's table beside the couch.

Like an oven timer going off, her old-fashioned door buzzer drilled into her consciousness. Mel jerked awake, alarmed.

Who would be ringing her bell before the holidays? She glanced at her watch. Ten forty-five! If it wasn't the super with a tale of plumbing woe, it had to be the Boston Strangler, who had moved to Manhatten.

She snatched up her pepper spray and edged toward

the door, uncertain whether to play absent or dead, or to find out what was going on. The place could be on fire, and the paranoid lady in 3G would tremble behind her dead bolt until she burned up.

A second ring startled her as she paused by the door, contemplating her chain lock. She put her eye to the tiny peephole installed after she had moved in.

A man. Who else? Carrying something.

"I didn't order a pizza," she shouted through the thick old door.

"Yes, you did," a male voice returned, loud enough to wake deaf Mrs. Bedard in 1E. "This is just what you ordered."

Now really suspicious, she peeked again. The dim hall made it hard to see more than the obvious: an unknown male bearing gifts. Had her family sent her something . . . but an eleven o'clock delivery? Yet it was almost Christmas, and everybody worked overtime.

Mel turned the dead bolt and inched the door open the length of the chain.

"I'm not expecting anything," she repeated, the pepper spray cocked in her left hand, out of sight.

"That's the best part of Christmas," the voice said jovially.

Someone thrust a large, paper-wrapped object at her that looked suspiciously the size of a poinsettia. Oh, Auntie Lizbeth, nobody sends poinsettias anymore . . . but actually, it would brighten up the place, though she couldn't bear to place it on the TV. . . .

"I'm a moonlighting actor," the man—mostly concealed by the shrouded poinsettia—said in pretty, pear-shaped tones.

A hand thrust toward the crack in the door and she

jumped back. Then she saw the small piece of paper it held out and took it.

Her own unfinished check! How had she lost it?

"You left it behind at the Santa Shoppe," he was explaining in perfect diction in a perfectly pleasant voice that sounded as if it came from a commercial on her muted TV.

"Oh, gosh—" She snatched it.

"Listen, I hate to come by so late, but I had a show to do. Here."

Another paper, this was a pamphlet . . . no, a dinner-theater program.

Mel stared at the woman on the cover. It was obviously an old photograph of a woman in a high collar with a sweep-brimmed hat.

"Open it up to the photos of the cast. That's me, third page, four down. I'm the villain of the piece."

Doing as he said, Mel saw a picture of a man in old-fashioned garb, hair parted unattractively in the middle, with a handlebar mustache. According to the text, this was Jason Fayre, whose greatest claim to fame so far was a run playing Lance Colter on *The Lost and the Loved*, a daytime TV soap opera Mel had never heard of.

Mel peeked through the crack to study the unmustachioed face peering over the package's top. Didn't look a thing like the photograph.

"How did you get my address?" she asked suspiciously.

"Try the check."

"Oh. Just put the package down on the floor. I'll get you a tip."

"I'd rather deliver it in person."

"Why?"

"It's heavier than it looks."

"So am I."

"And it's my job."

"Hah! You know how hard it is to get a deliveryman to drag something six feet inside the door, as they're legally required to do, when you want them to? I'm not letting a strange man into my apartment."

After a pause, he said, "It really is my job to make a personal delivery, and I'm not exactly a stranger."

She heard him deposit the package on the floor and felt better, although she detected no retreating footsteps.

Mel peeked out again. A face was leaning back in at her, a face with blue (not hazel) eyes and a rueful grin, a fair approximation of Jeremy Gardner's face.

"Who are you?" she asked, meaning . . . who really? A dream, a figment, an escapee from his own time?

"Santa," he answered promptly, as if pleased that she didn't know.

Entering the twentieth century must have made him mad, and Mel really couldn't blame him. She found her fingers wrestling with the stubborn chain lock, pushing the door shut in the face she'd been longing to see again. She found herself opening her door to what had to be a stranger, no matter whose features he wore.

He bent to pick up the package, so she still couldn't concentrate on him, to see if he looked like Jeremy or if she was fooling herself . . . or if he, by some unimaginable miracle, *was* Jeremy. And to see if he gave any indication of remembering her, or if hers had been a solitary delusion.

"There you go." He had marched into her room, crossing it to set the package down on the TV. Now he was tearing off the wrappings.

She watched him, looking for familiar gestures,

striving to place the voice, which was similar but not the same.

Nothing quite worked until he unveiled the contents of the package.

The tree. Her tree. Their tree. The tree that had occupied a front parlor in this very building decades ago.

"How—?"

"I saw how much it meant to you, so when I went back to wrap it, I pulled the old substitution trick. He got the feathers and pearls."

"Won't he be furious? Won't you lose your job?"

"No, and no. I put a bunch of tin soldiers and all that old Victorian stuff on the tree, so he got his money's worth, then I paid back the store. Besides, my job ends at Christmas. I'm an unemployed Santa, so I thought I'd play the role one more time. Call it a swan song."

"Said like an actor. Do you sing?"

He smiled. "How'd you guess? That's quite a show," he added, pointing to the program. "Lots of old-time shows are worth reviving. This one's a doozy. The girl on the cover is the composer's wife. It struck me that she looked a bit like you."

So Mel took another look at the program, not worrying now about ax murderers, and saw what she had missed: the title, for one thing.

"The Ghost in the Wine Velvet Gown," she read aloud.

"The title song. Not bad. It's kind of a mystery."

"Why do say that?"

"Well, the songwriter guy married her"—he pointed to the old-fashioned, dark-haired woman on the cover—"but her name was Violet Carstairs. And the song is dedicated 'To Melody, forever'."

"It could be a . . . generic dedication." A good thing

Jason had pointed out the type. Mel couldn't read it through the thick, teary spyglass of time. Drat.

"I was struck by the coincidence," Jason said. "I guess actors are superstitious." He grinned.

"Superstitious?"

"Your name is Melody, too. You sure you don't sing?"

"I'm sure, but I do, in fact, do windows."

He gave the obligatory questioning look on cue.

"I make Christmas magic for Macy's."

"No kidding. That's theater, too, isn't it? Hey, did you do that wild Icicle Ball thing?"

Mel nodded; it was all she was capable of doing.

"You know the one I loved? *The Gift of the Magi.* That was perfect."

"Yes," said Mel without a trace of modesty, but with a smile born to break ice. "It was. Well, Jason. Would you like some hot cocoa?"

Star Light,
Star Bright

Emma Merritt

1

After the train from Chicago to Port Huron lurched to
a halt, Nick Devlin rose from his seat and slipped into
his camel-colored greatcoat. He was taller than the
men who stood around him, and the clean lines of his
coat emphasized the muscular physique he had developed when he was a youth working as a lumberjack
and had kept through the years by doing physical exercise. He buttoned the coat, then picked up his traveling
bag and briefcase. Joining his fellow passengers, he
slowly made his way down the aisle.

As he stepped off the train, the full force of the icy
north wind hit him. It whipped his greatcoat against his
body and swirled raven black hair about his face. His
dark hair and eyes, coupled with a day's beard stubble,
sharpened his angular features and made him appear
more formidable than he really was. His countenance
was grim like the dark clouds that were bringing an
early end to the afternoon, but his was a darkness
caused by desperation and anxiety.

"Need a carriage, Mr. Devlin?" the white-haired porter called out.

"Yes, thank you, George."

The porter lifted his hands to his lips and whistled loudly, quickly bringing a cabriolet beside them. Soon Nick was settled in the small cab and was on his way home. For a while he could hear the clip-clop of the horses' hooves on the paved streets of downtown, the greetings shouted between drivers as wagons and carriages passed one another. All around him was the hustle and bustle of Christmas—bells ringing as shop doors opened and closed; smells of Christmas coming from the bakeries and from street vendors; and people calling out "Merry Christmas" and "Happy holidays."

But Nick wasn't feeling merry or happy. He was worried. He was an architect whose idea for a modern trade center had been rejected out of hand. He had been so sure of himself and of his designs he had concentrated his time and his finances fully on this one project—the Chicago Pavilion of Trade.

Nick knew how he shouldn't have left Alexander and Son. Benton Alexander, Sr., his former employer and the president of the largest and most prestigious architectural firm in Chicago, had warned Nick he couldn't make it on his own. Too young. Too inexperienced. No name and no old money to back him up. But Nick had bucked the man, his money, and his connections. In retaliation for Nick's having left the firm, Alexander had tried to ruin his name and had deviously snatched jobs away from Nick—small jobs that Alexander and Son had not needed and wouldn't have taken if Nick hadn't needed them desperately. Nick loathed Benton Alexander and all he stood for.

Nick leaned his head against the back of the seat and closed his eyes, but he couldn't close out the memory of the pile of bills he had left behind on his desk when he had left for Chicago a week ago. Bills that neither his adoptive mother nor he had the money to pay. Not now. Not since his plans for the trade pavilion had been rejected. Too brash, the building committee had declared. Too futuristic, one had criticized. Too Grecian, another accused. They had wanted architectural designs that were tried, sure, and comforting for the people. They were leaning toward the firm of Alexander and Son.

Tired, disappointed, and cold to the bone, Nick sighed and raked his hand through his hair. He wanted nothing more than to sit in front of the fire in his bedroom and thaw out . . . and brood . . . with a large glass of brandy.

As the carriage moved away from town, clapboard and brick buildings gave way to the countryside. Paved streets became dirt roads. Nick heard only the creak of leather and wood as the carriage dipped and swayed and rolled closer and closer to home. They passed the last intersection before the road forked. The carriage turned right and bumped to the lone three-story house that reposed so graciously at the end of Harmony Lane. Brakes squealed, and the cabriolet pitched to a halt. Three thumps and Rodney was on the ground, opening the door.

"Here you are, Mr. Devlin. Safe and sound."

Nick reached into his pocket and fished out several coins, making sure he gave the lad more than fare.

Rodney's eyes sparkled. "Thank you, Mr. Devlin." He reached for Nick's bag and briefcase. "Here. Let me carry these in for you."

"I'll take care of them," Nick said. "You'd better be on your way. The night is still young, and you can earn some extra money."

"Yes, sir, Mr. Devlin."

The cabriolet rolled away, but Nick stood outside the

wrought iron gate and gazed at the blue house trimmed in white. It represented the world of Adeline Peabody Stimms, the woman Nick affectionately called Addie, who had adopted him after his parents died of cholera when he was twelve. The house, worn and comfortable, was full of warmth and love and pets and people whom Addie had rescued through the years. Cook— she had no other name—had been with Addie for twenty-five years; Perry, the housekeeper, for twenty-one; and Nick for twenty. Then there were the dogs and cats—too many to count anymore. Yet Addie had given each one of them a special name and knew each individually.

Nick felt a new wave of regret. He had promised himself that this year he would build Addie the kind of house she needed to accommodate her extended *family*. He knew she wanted to take in Mr. and Mrs. Merriweather and their ten orphans. So did Cook and Perry. And it was a wonderful idea. Leiland and Bessie Merriweather were young, and they loved and respected Addie. They needed her guidance as much as she needed their youth and strength and assistance. Like Addie, the couple had a mission to rescue the less fortunate. Now Nick didn't have the money to finance such an undertaking. In fact, he didn't know where the mortgage money for their present home was coming from.

The front door opened, and a Christmas tree glided through the opening onto the veranda. Or course it wasn't a tree. It was Addie who was totally obscured by garlands that looped several times over and around her shoulders and arms, hanging down and dragging on the ground.

Then a round and smiling face emerged from among

the greenery and peered in the direction of the gate. "Nicholas Lucien Devlin, is that you?"

"Yes, ma'am." Addie was the only person whom Nick allowed to call him by his full name.

"Get yourself in this house immediately before you catch your death of cold." She spoke to him much as if he were a child, something that Nick tolerated only because he loved his adoptive mother so much.

"Yes, ma'am." Unlocking the gate, he stepped onto the boardwalk and moved toward the porch.

Although Addie gave the greenery a good fight, it was winning the battle. "I made more garlands today," she announced. "The door looked so bare."

Nick set his luggage down, and in one swipe lifted the decoration from Addie's shoulder and hung it over the tiny nails he had tacked around the glass panes that formed the upper half of the door. He wasn't surprised when Addie didn't ask about his meeting. She had favorably predicted the outcome, had accepted the prediction as truth, and nothing Nick reported would change her mind.

"Oh, Nicholas." Addie stepped back and gazed first at the door, then at her adopted son. Over her long-sleeved blue dress, she wore a pinafore apron. Her white hair was combed back in waves and coiled on the top of her head. Blue eyes twinkled. "This looks so much better."

Nick wasn't sure it looked any better, but if Addie thought so, that was all that mattered.

"And you, young man," Addie announced, "into the house. What you need is a cup of hot chocolate."

"What I need is a brandy," Nick growled and picked up his luggage, following Addie into the house.

Many cats were draped over the furniture, and four dogs—Jack, a Boston Pug; Colleen, an old Irish setter;

a Scottish terrier named Duncan, and one they called
Wolf—lay on the rug in front of the fire. All rose and
padded over to Nick, each patiently awaiting his turn
for affection. After Nick greeted each and gave it a
treat, dried beef jerky he always tried to carry in his
pocket, the animals returned to their place in front of
the fire.

Glad to be home, Nick straightened and inhaled
deeply. Warm, familiar odors greeted him—homemade
bread, apple pie, shortbread cookies, coffee. The fresh
odor of pine and cedar and birch garlands. Yes, he was
home, and he was glad.

"Dinner will be ready shortly," Addie informed him.
"While we're waiting, I'll have Cook make a pot of
hot chocolate."

Long strides carried Nick to the first-floor bedroom—an entire suite of rooms he had added to the
house so that he could come and go at his leisure without disturbing his adoptive mother and her menagerie
and so that he could have his privacy.

Once in the commodious room that was dominated
by a large four-poster bed, he set down his luggage.
Grateful for the warm blaze in the fireplace, he moved
around the room lighting the oil lamps. Their glow
quickly dispelled the gloom of the winter evening.
Shrugging out of his coat, he laid it negligently over
the back of the wing chair close to the bed. Next came
his suit coat, and his vest followed, landing in the same
pile.

Down the hall Nick heard the tinkle of bells.

He knew it was Tommy, a street woman whom
Addie had rescued. Because Tommy was forgetful and
had a tendency to wander, Addie had sewn bells to her
shoes so they would know where she was.

Nick liked Tommy—he judged she was close to one

hundred years old—but she lived on a higher plane than earth and believed in spiritual beings. She had been a nameless beggar when Addie found her in an alley off Main Street. Addie couldn't leave the old woman there to die, so she invited her—as she did so many others who were down and out—to *board* with her for a while, until she was on her feet again.

Addie had brought the woman and all her bundles home. Then she had christened her Thomasina. When the old woman hadn't been able to remember her name, Addie had shortened it to Tommy. Soon Tommy was installed in the cook's quarters on the first floor, and Cook had been moved to one of the larger bedrooms on the second floor. Cook and Perry, having been with Addie for so many years, were accustomed to running the boarding house and to moving to other quarters when one of their boarders needed special concessions.

A kettle in her hand, Addie walked into the room.

"Is Tommy still trying to find her way to heaven?" Nick asked.

"Don't make fun of her," Addie chastised softly as she crossed to the washstand and filled the basin with warm water. "She can't help it if she's more in the other world than in this one."

"That's just it, Addie," Nick argued. "Only her mind is in the other world. Her body is in this one. And somehow we've got to put the two back together again."

"Yes, dear," Addie said. "That's what I'm trying to do. Just be patient. Tommy's angel is coming for her soon."

Exasperated, Nick hiked a brow. "Not you, too, Addie!"

"No, the angel's not coming for me," Addie answered, a decided twinkle in her eyes. "Just for Tommy."

A door opened and closed. A dog barked—an unfamiliar bark. Nick tensed.

Quickly—a little too quickly—Addie announced, "Perry's back. I'd better go."

The dog barked again.

"Addie," Nick said, "have you . . ."

Footfalls heading toward Nick's bedroom beat heavily against the wooden floor. Into the room raced a huge silver-haired mutt.

"Addie . . ."

The dog reared into the air, planting a paw on each of Nick's shoulders. He stumbled backward.

"Damn it, Addie! Not another mongrel!"

A large tongue darted out and licked him in the face.

"Down, Rumples," Addie ordered. "Get down this minute."

Whining happily—or so it seemed to Nick—the dog kept on licking. Breathing deeply, counting to ten, Nick gently caught the dog's two front legs and lowered him to the floor. In a tight voice he asked, "Where did *Rumples* come from?"

Bending over, Addie ran her hand over the dog's head. "While you were in Chicago, I found him in the ditch off Summons Street. You know, I couldn't leave him there, not with the snow and all. He would have died."

"Addie!" At his wit's end, Nick plunged his hand through his already tousled hair. "We can't take in any more strays." Addie opened her mouth, but Nick said, "Or boarders. You're almost out of money, and—"

"The Lord will provide, Nicholas. He always has and always will." Blue eyes gazed steadfastly and confidently at Nick. "Besides, Rumples isn't a stray. He's going to be our watch dog."

Nick understood all about Addie's watch dogs. They had a house full of them. Nick and Addie fed them, then stood and watched as they devoured the food, the furniture, and the clothes—especially his shoes. But Nick couldn't bear the forlorn expression on his dear mother's face. Shaking his head, he smiled.

Addie did also. "Good." She patted his cheek, a gesture Nicholas Lucien Devlin would tolerate only from Adeline Peabody Stimms.

"Addie." A prim, feminine voice came from the doorway. "I'm back."

Both Nick and Addie turned to see the reed-thin form of Julep Periwinkle, known to all her friends as Perry. Over her gray dress she wore a white bibbed apron. Her hair, liberally streaked with white, was pulled back and pinned into a small chignon at the nape of her neck. Kindly gray eyes softened her sharp facial features.

"Dr. Walters wasn't home, so I left word with his wife," the housekeeper reported. "She'll send him around as soon as he returns."

"Thank you, Perry," Addie said.

With a nod the housekeeper disappeared.

Addie looked at Nick and explained, "Tommy. Perry found her wandering barefoot in the garden earlier. She's been more disoriented than usual, and I've been worried. So I sent for Jasper. But with the weather being what it is, I don't know how long it will take him to get here."

"Addie," Nick said, "the time has come for you and me to talk about your ... er ... your *boarders*."

Addie flexed and unflexed her hand nervously around the handle of the kettle. "Knowing how worried you were about me and my health," she said, "I did something while you were gone, Nicholas. I . . . er . . . I—"

"Yes?" Nick prompted, but dreaded to hear what she was going to say.

"I hired a young lady to help me take care of Tommy, especially at night."

"Addie!" Nick exploded. "We don't have the money."

"But we'll have it, dear. You've got that contract you've been working on," she said. "I told you you'd get it before you left."

Nick caught his mother's hands in his. "Addie, the building committee rejected my ideas. I'm not going to get the contract. They're going to award it to Benton Alexander."

"No, they aren't, and yes, you are," Addie said. "And even if you don't get it, the good Lord will provide. In fact, Nicholas, I've told Leiland and Bessie that they could move into the house come spring."

Dumbfounded, Nick said slowly, "You've invited the Merriweathers and their orphans to come live with us in *this* house!"

Addie nodded. "They no longer have the money to pay their rent, but the landlord told them they could stay through the winter. Come spring, they must move."

Nick released Addie's hands and turned, rubbing his hand over his forehead. There was no need to argue with Addie or to point out that they were in the same boat as the Merriweathers. She wouldn't listen to him. He loved his mother, but he hated it when she began to soar in the clouds and to quote her Christian platitudes. Dear God, but he didn't know how they were going to make ends meet. And now he could look forward to more burdens.

"She's trained in the Nightingale manner," Nick heard Addie say.

He faced her.

"The nurse, dear," Addie explained. "She's trained in the—"

"I heard you."

"She'll be here directly."

"I'm surprised she agreed to come out on Christmas Eve."

"She was in dire need of a job," Addie replied. "Besides, watching Tommy will not be a tiring job. As long as we make sure Tommy wears her bells so the young lady can hear them, she can get some sleep during the night and be home to enjoy Christmas dinner with her family."

"How did you find out about her?"

"Bessie Merriweather told me about the service," Addie answered.

The vague answer bothered Nick. "Just whom did you communicate with?"

"A Mrs. Creighton in Chicago. She has a registry of young women who are in need of jobs and who will be sitters. some of her girls are even trained in medical nursing."

"Who is the woman?"

"I don't know her name," Addie replied, "but Mrs. Creighton promised that the girl would be trained in the Nightingale manner."

With a grace that belied her seventy-five years, Adeline Peabody Stimms straightened to her full five feet and one inches, indicating that the interrogation was ended, and swept across the room. "Now you relax a bit while I go see about Tommy. But if she knows you're home, she'll be in here to see you. So you'll have to mind her, dear."

So you'll have to mind her, dear.

Addie's words rang in Nick's ears long after his mother was gone. Finally, he chuckled. All his life he had tended to Addie's losers and strays. And he hadn't cared or objected because she had taken care of him all his life. At least her rescue mission hadn't concerned him when she was younger and stronger. Now he worried about her, and he was the only one who did.

Addie was everyone's pillar of support; they couldn't imagine her being in need. Nick was the only one who seemed concerned. On that eventful day after his parents had died in the plague and he had thought he was doomed to an orphanage, Adeline Peabody Stimms had arrived. To a frightened little boy she had seemed so tall and strong.

"Well, Nicholas Lucien Devlin," she had announced briskly, "I guess the good Lord means for you to be my son. Don't you?"

"Yes, ma'am," He would have sworn at that moment that Addie was the good Lord herself. From that day forward Addie and he had rescued any and everything that had needed rescuing and some that hadn't wanted to be rescued.

Nick walked over to the ornate wood box by the hearth, picked up several logs, and threw them onto the fire. Then he stepped to the sideboard, pouring himself that long overdue glass of brandy. Sitting in the chair, he stretched his feet toward the fire and settled more comfortably into the occasional chair. He took several swallows of the brandy. Dear God, but he was tired and angry and frustrated.

He should have remained a lumberjack and not become an architect.

A year's work gone, all because a group of short-sighted men wanted to stay in the past. They hadn't awarded the contract to Benton Alexander yet, but they would. Even if they didn't, Nick felt he didn't have a chance. Only one man on the committee had been interested in his plans, and the man didn't seem to carry too much weight.

Without this contract Nick also knew he would have to return to Chicago and take a job with a larger firm. He laughed bitterly. Benton Alexander, Sr. had invited Nick to return to his firm, had even offered him a junior partnership. The man could afford to be magnanimous, Nick thought bitterly. His son had married the woman Nick had wanted to marry, and he was about to pull off the biggest architectural coup in years.

Nick nearly choked on his swallow of brandy as he remembered what Alexander had said later. He had intimated they would incorporate many of Nick's ideas into the final plans for the Chicago Trade Pavilion should Benton be awarded the contract . . . and should Nick return to the firm. Ideas shunned when Nick Devlin had presented them would be readily accepted if they were presented by Alexander Benton, Sr.

No, Nick swore. He would not be blackmailed or bribed to return to the firm. He had conceived the idea for the trade pavilion during the time that Alexander was pulling jobs away from him. It was Nick's idea and he would fight for it. He wouldn't let another take credit for his work.

But Nick would return to another company in Chicago . . . if he had to. This compounded his worries. He couldn't leave Addie behind, and he knew she wouldn't willingly go with him. He didn't know what he was going to do.

The mantel clock struck six.

Nick didn't stir, and he hoped Addie was right, that God would provide. Enjoying the warmth and solitude of his bedroom, Nick settled more comfortably in the chair and listened to the soft sounds of the room—the ticking of the clock, the sputtering of the fire.

Then he heard a gentle ping and glanced out the window. Snow, It was splattering like white glitter against the pane. He took another swallow of his brandy. He appreciated the warmth slowly pervading his body. From down the street he heard the carolers sing, " 'Tis the season to be jolly." Christmas. Nick couldn't believe it was Saturday, the twenty-fourth of December. Christmas Eve!

He rose, walked across the room, and glanced out the window. The cabriolet was long gone, and the snow had been falling so heavily there were no traces of it left behind. Mother Nature had covered the world around him in a pristine white blanket. Farther down, where the lane forked off the main road, he saw a wagon lumbering through the snow. Then he saw a child running into the intersection. Neither the driver not the boy saw each other.

"Watch out!" Nick shouted.

Dropping his glass, he rushed out of his suite and down to the foyer. With one turn of the knob and a jerk of his arm, he opened the front door. He crossed the veranda in two long steps, leaped over the stairs, and raced down the boardwalk, out the gate.

He heard the scraping of brakes against a metal wheel, then skidding. A man bellowed. A child screamed. The wagon slid across the street, teetering to one side, then to the other. A small body flew through the air.

By the time the driver had descended from the wagon, Nick was hunched over the lad, who lay deathly still on the icy, snow-covered ground. He picked up the boy's hand and touched his fingers to his wrist. He felt a pulse—faint, but there.

"I didn't mean to hit 'im," the driver said. "Is he dead?"

"No." Nick unbuttoned the boy's coat and gently examined him.

Addie rushed up. "What's happened?"

"The boy." The driver rubbed his gloved hands nervously together. "He ran out in front of the wagon ma'am. I didn't even see 'im. It was snowing so heavy, and by the time I got the horses—"

"Is he badly hurt?" Addie knelt beside Nick.

"No broken bones I can see," Nick answered, "but he's unconscious."

Addie looked up at the wagon driver. "Do you know who he is?"

"Sure don't."

Nick pushed a shock of unruly hair from the child's forehead and revealed the swollen and discolored flesh. "He's sustained a heavy blow to the head."

Addie lifted first one lid, then the other, and looked at the boy's eyes. "Let's get him inside." She rose, the front of her long skirt wet and ringed where the snow had melted and soaked into the fabric.

Nick eased his arms beneath the small, limp body, pausing when the boy moaned.

"We'll need to notify the authorities," Addie said, "so they can start hunting for the child's parents." She turned to the driver. "Will you report this to Loren Gage for me?"

"Yes, ma'am." He bobbed his head. "Sure will."

"Also let Loren know that the boy is at Adeline Peabody Stimm's house on Harmony Lane."

"Yes, ma'am," he said and climbed up on the wagon.

In the distance Nick saw a brilliant explosion of light. The air glowed with glitter. Then he heard the soft ring of bells. Ding-a-ling. Ring-a-ling. Far, far away. Sleigh bells? He looked around, but saw nothing . . . no one.

As he followed Addie down the lane, he had the feeling he was being watched. He stopped and slowly turned, looking in all directions. He saw no one, nothing, except the falling snow. Shrugging aside the eerie feeling, he began to walk again, quickly catching up with Addie.

"Put him in your bedroom, Nicholas," she ordered as they entered the house. On she marched past the kitchen. "Cook," she shouted, "I need some hot-water bottles as soon as you can get them filled. Perry, get some bricks to heating. We can use them, too. And chop me some ice."

Nick walked straight to his suite and laid the boy on his bed. He slipped off the boy's shoes and socks. Then trying not to move or to disturb the child, he removed his overcoat, his overalls, and shirt. He went through the pockets, searching for a piece of identification. Nothing. When the boy was clad only in his underwear, Addie covered him with a soft, thick blanket.

"I'm worried about him," she said.

So was Nick. The boy couldn't be more than seven, Nick thought, staring at the pale face that was illuminated in the soft glow of lamplight. He tucked the cover under the boy's chin and lightly brushed the shock of hair from his forehead. Nick gazed at the swollen purple knot.

"He's suffering from a severe concussion," he said.

Addie hesitated, then said, "I'm afraid he's in a

coma." She wrung her hands together. "I wish Jasper would get here."

"What can we do?"

"We'll pack ice around his head to keep down the swelling. After that, we keep him comfortable and wait," She paused. "Then we do a lot of praying."

Feeling helpless, Nick curled his hand into a fist. "This would be good time for one of Tommy's angels to show up."

"She's here," a fragile voice from behind him said. "Didn't you see the stardust?"

Nick turned and looked at the tall, delicate woman who stood in the doorway of his bedroom, clad in her white flannel dressing gown.

"Some people call it starlight," Tommy said, "but it's the same."

Her hair, gleaming like polished silver, hung in deep waves about her shoulders. A smile wreathed her wrinkled face. Nick relaxed and forced himself to smile.

"No, Tommy, I didn't see any stardust or starlight."

"Someday you will, Nick. Mark my word."

2

Nick had believed in stardust, magic, and romance at one time, but not anymore, not since Carolyn Hansen had walked out of his life for the younger Benton Alexander. Nick left those fanciful emotions for others. He found solace in having his feet rooted in reality. He prided himself on being a pragmatist.

The door bell chimed.

"That may be the doctor." Addie whisked out of the room.

"It's not," Tommy said. "It's her."

"Her?" Nick asked.

Tommy nodded. "The angel. There's so much unbelief in this house she's probably coming in the form of a human."

Gazing into Tommy's big, brown eyes, Nick didn't have the heart to argue with her. Truly, she was in another world, one that he no longer believed in. Smiling at her, he walked toward Tommy.

Softly, he asked, "Do you have your slippers on?" He knew she didn't because he would have heard the bells.

Tommy looked blank, nodded, then shook her head. She pulled up her gown and revealed her bare feet.

"Come over here by the fire." He kept his voice soft.

"I'll get your slippers." He caught her by the hand and led her to his chair in front of the fire. He seated her, then asked, "Do you know where you left them?"

She thought a moment, then shook her head. "There's really no need for you to get them, Nicholas. The angel is coming for me. She's been here before, you know. She's the one who took Mr. Dunlop home."

Nick sighed. Horace Dunlop, another one of Addie's *boarders*. A year ago when Addie had learned that the old man had no family of his own, she had whisked him out of his house and brought him here. Dr. Walters had told them that he hadn't much longer to live. Addie had seen to it that those few days had been memorable for Mr. Dunlop. He died six months ago, only two nights after Tommy had arrived. Ever since, Tommy insisted she had seen an angel taking him home. Addie never tried to convince Tommy that she hadn't seen an angel, and Nick argued in vain.

Not wanting to leave the boy or Tommy alone, Nick moved into the adjoining room. As soon as he had changed into dry trousers, he rummaged through the wardrobe for a clean pair of thick, woolen socks. He returned to the bedroom.

"Here, Tommy." He knelt in front of her and gently encased each foot in a sock. "This should keep your feet warm until we find those slippers." He lifted the afghan from the chair back and laid it over her legs.

Tommy smiled tenderly at him. "You're a kind boy, Nick. I just regret I'm not going to be here when that wonderful woman finds you."

"So here you are, Tommy." Addie, carrying a tray laden with a food, medicine, and a large crock filled with ice, entered the room. "I thought perhaps you were here. Since Cook figured that none of us would be sitting down to dinner tonight, she sliced the roast and made us some sandwiches."

Nick crossed the room and took the tray from her. He held it while she set the food, the cups and saucers, and the hot chocolate pot on the low table beside Tommy's chair.

"Be sure to eat something, Tommy," Addie admonished. "You, too, Nick. You must be famished."

At the moment food was the least of Nick's concerns. "Was that the doctor?" He carried the tray over to the night table and set it down.

"No, it was someone else. When I saw it wasn't Jasper, I decided to let Perry handle the matter, so I could get back in here to the boy."

Tommy picked up one of the sandwiches, took a bite, and returned it to the plate. Then she poured herself a cup of hot chocolate. Holding it in both hands, she leaned back in her chair.

"Is there any change in the boy?" Addie asked.

Nick shook his head and touched his finger to the child's neck. "His pulse is weaker. Is there nothing more we can do?"

"I'm doing all that I know to do," Addie said. "Now it's up to God."

Nick walked to the window and gazed out. Again he had that eerie feeling he was being watched. Through the flurry of snow he saw the pale golden ring of light from the street lamp, but he saw no one.

"I'm looking for the angel, Nick," Tommy said. "Do you see her out there?"

"No," he answered.

He heard the sleigh bells in the distance.

"I knew she was out there," Tommy said, standing right behind Nick.

He started. She had moved so quietly he hadn't

known she was this close to him. He turned to see the room filled with a sparkling glow ... the same glow he had seen earlier.

"Starlight," Tommy said softly. "Surely you see it now, Nick."

"Yes," he murmured. "I see it."

"Good evening, Mrs. Stimms." The voice was soft and feminine and almost ethereal.

Nick jerked his head up and stared at the young woman standing in the open doorway.

"Your housekeeper told me to come in here," the woman said. "She said you were expecting me."

"We are, my dear," Addie said.

In an instant Nick forgot his objections to Addie's having hired the young nurse. She was the most beautiful woman Nick had seen during his thirty-two years. She was tall, and although she wore a long, flowing cloak, he could tell she was slender. Her eyes were radiant, and her cheeks and lips glistened with a rosy glow. Golden hair, like a halo, framed her face and hung around her shoulders.

"You're the angel!" Tommy's wrinkled face glowed. "Have you come for me?"

The woman smiled and said gently, "I've come for—"

"—for Tommy," the old woman suggested.

"Yes."

"I knew it!" Two tears coursed down the wizened cheeks. "I knew you had come for me."

"I'm so glad you're here, dear. There's been a terrible accident." Addie waved her hand over the bed. "I fear the child's in a coma. I've put a cold compress on his head, but I don't know what else to do for him."

Although Nick was concerned about the child, he was enchanted by the nurse. He couldn't take his eyes off her. She was the most radiant creature he had ever seen. If ever a woman looked like an angel, she did. *Angel!* Nick pulled himself short mentally. Tommy's talk was getting to him. After Carolyn, the only angel he believed in was the devil.

"I'll take care of him." The nurse's soft, warm voice brushed like velvet over Nick. While it settled the anxiety that had been hovering over the room in regard to the boy's condition, it unsettled Nick personally. He didn't like this instant feeling he had for the woman. He wanted to be in control of his life and feelings. This attraction made him feel out of control.

At the bed she stood beside Nick and looked down at the child. She reached out to touch his forehead the same time as Nick. Their hands touched. Although she still wore gloves, Nick felt a shock run through his body. She quickly drew her hand back and lifted her head to stare into his face.

Nick heard her quick intake of breath as he stared into the most beautiful eyes he had ever seen. Blue. They were heavenly. Then they clouded, and she lowered her lashes. They fanned like a dark crescent over her cheeks. She brushed the lock of hair from the boy's forehead.

"He was hit by a wagon earlier this evening," Nick explained. "We've sent word to Dr. Walters and to the authorities."

She raised her head. "The authorities?"

Nick nodded. "We don't know who he is, and we want to let his parents know about the accident. I'm sure they're concerned about him."

"Yes." She pulled off her gloves and reached down to touch the child's brow lightly with her fingertips. She softly outlined the flesh around the knot. The boy breathed deeply, then a small smile played around his mouth.

"Is he going to be all right?" Nick asked.

As she had done earlier, she brushed the shock of hair from the boy's face. But once she had removed her hand, the strand spread across his forehead once more. "Oh, yes, he's going to be just fine."

Relief rushed through Nick. She was a trained nurse, and she would know.

"You don't have to worry about the boy any longer, Mr. Stimms."

"Devlin," Nick said.

She lifted her head. In the lamplight her hair shimmered around her face like spun gold.

"I'm Nick Devlin. Mrs. Stimms is my adoptive mother." Lost in the beauty of her eyes, he murmured, "You know my name. May I know yours?" When she didn't answer, he asked, "Or am I doomed to calling you Nurse?"

"Nicholas!" Tommy exclaimed, clearly impatient with him. "How many times must I tell you, she's not a nurse."

"Sara," the woman said. "Sara Finley."

"She's an angel."

Sara smiled and turned to look at Tommy. Kindly, she asked, "How do you know that I'm an angel?"

"I saw you the night Horace Dunlop died."

In case Sara should not understand how disoriented Tommy was, Nick said, "She believes she saw an angel take him to heaven."

"I did." Tommy's gaze never wavered from the young woman's. "I did see an angel."

"Yes," Sara said, "I'm sure you did."

Nick breathed a little more easily. He had been afraid that Sara would have no patience with Tommy.

He didn't ask that she believe the old woman or that she even pretend to believe, but he did want her to understand and to treat her kindly ... and she did.

"Are you the same angel who came for Horace?"

"No."

"Oh." Clearly, Tommy was disappointed.

Again Nick took charge of the conversation. "Nurse Finley, you say the child is going to be all right?"

Sara looked at him. "Yes."

Moving around the bed at the same time Nick did, Sara bumped into him. He caught her by the shoulders to steady her. Her hair brushed over his hands—silky smooth, caressive. Her face was so close to his he could see the smooth texture of her skin.

"May ... I help you take your cloak off?" Nick gazed at her mouth, an extremely kissable mouth.

She looked at if she were about to refuse, then smiled and nodded. "Please." She reached up and unfastened it.

As Nick swept it from her shoulders, he heard the far away tinkle of the sleigh bells. The air was again filled with luster, like a million fireflies on a dark night.

"Starlight," Tommy murmured.

Yes, Nick thought, as he stared into the beautiful, upturned face. Starlight. Romance. Magic. Ethereality. This woman, a stranger, seemed to embody all the ideas that Nick had ceased believing in long ago—the day Carolyn Hansen had walked out of his life.

For the past year Nick had felt nothing but loathing for women. Yet Sara Finley was arousing emotions in him that Carolyn had never tapped. While it excited him, it also frustrated him. Since Carolyn, he had not wanted a woman in his life, casually or seriously, that is, not until this moment.

He heard the front door open and shut. Still he and

Sara stared at each other. Then a man's voice boomed out.

"Cook, I declare I could find this house if I were blind. I'd simply follow the odor of your coffee."

"Jasper!" Addie exclaimed.

The mesmeric bond broken, Sara stepped away from Nick.

Addie rushed from the room. "Thank God, he's here."

Tommy sat quietly in front of the fire, warming her sock-covered feet and sipping her drink.

A large man, dressed in black, followed Addie into the room.

"Evening, Jasper," Nick said.

"Evening." Jasper Walters nodded his balding head and moved directly toward the bed. "Bad weather tonight. Not fit for man nor beast."

For a big man, the doctor moved quickly and gracefully. He set his black satchel on the night table, then searched through his pockets until he found a small black case. Opening it, he extracted his spectacles. When he was putting them on, Addie introduced him to Sara. After he unfastened his bag and pulled out his stethoscope, he sat on the edge of the bed beside the child.

"Addie, you say he was hit by a wagon?" Jasper raised the boy's lids and looked at his eyes.

"Yes," she answered.

"About an hour ago," Nick added.

"Hmm," Jasper mused. As Nick recited the chain of events that led to the boy's comatose condition, Jasper pulled the covers down and unbuttoned the boy's underwear, pulling his shirt aside. He pressed the silver-colored stethoscope against his chest.

"Is he going to be all right?" Addie asked.

The doctor listened.

"Jasper!" Addie's voice was tinged with desperation. Nick moved to the other side of the bed. Circling his mother's shoulders with his arm, he pulled her against his chest.

The doctor straightened. "I'll do the best I can for him, Addie. But I can't make any promises. It's up to the Man in the Sky. Right now I want all of you out of the room, so I can tend to my patient. Miss Finley, if you don't mind, I'd like you to help me."

Tommy's cup clattered to the saucer. Her hands were shaking, and tears sparkled in her eyes. "But she was sent here for me!" Her frail voice quivered.

Nick rushed to her.

"She's my angel!" Tommy cried out.

"Yes, Tommy." Nick took the cup and saucer from her and set them on the table. "She's your angel. But the little boy needs her."

Her lips quivering, Tommy looked at Nick, then at the bed.

"Will you share her with the boy?"

Tears slid down Tommy's cheeks.

"Please."

"All right," she mumbled.

"Go with her, Miss Finley," Jasper said softly. "Right now she needs you more than I do. Keep her calm and see if you can't get her to sleep. Addie can help me here."

Nodding to the doctor, Sara walked to Tommy and placed her arm around the frail shoulders. She guided the woman out of the room.

"Are you going to take me home tonight?" Tommy asked.

Sara looked at Nick. Silently, he pleaded with her to

be understanding with the old woman. "Do you want to go home?"

"Yes," Tommy said, "more than anything else."

"Then rest up. You'll be making your journey soon."

Tommy stared into Sara's eyes a long time. "You promise?"

"Yes."

"All right, dear. If you'll help me to my room, I'll go to bed."

Nick brushed past Sara and led the way down the hall to Tommy's room. He watched in amazement as Sara gently settled the old woman into bed. Carolyn had never liked his family. Choosing to believe them insane rather than eccentric, she had wanted Nick to put Addie in an asylum. On more than one occasion she had grumbled about the prospect of their having to take care of a "batty old woman and her menagerie of idiots" for the rest of their lives.

After a heated argument over his refusal to commit Addie to an asylum, Nick and Carolyn's relationship had become strained. Carolyn had issued an ultimatum. Either he committed Addie, or Carolyn would leave him. Other men—better men—wanted to marry her, Carolyn announced. Furious, Nick had ordered her out of the house, telling her he never wanted to see her again. Carolyn had accused him of being the devil incarnate and wished him in hell. Not many days later, Nick's already battered ego suffered another blow: Carolyn and Benton Alexander, Jr. announced their engagement. For a while Nick had thought he was living in hell.

Sara tucked the cover around Tommy and asked, "Are you warm?"

Tommy nodded, and Sara leaned down and kissed her on the forehead.

"Good night," Sara said. "Sweet dreams."

"Sweet dreams," Tommy murmured, then added, "Why don't you go into the kitchen and have Cook make you a cup of hot cocoa? And have her give you one of her roast beef sandwiches." Taking a deep breath, she closed her eyes.

Nick remained in the room until he thought Tommy was asleep. "Well, Miss Finley, is there anything I can get to make you more comfortable?"

"No, thank you."

"The cocoa," Tommy mumbled. "Take her into the kitchen, Nicholas, and get her a cup of hot cocoa."

Nick really wanted to get away from Sara. Already she had resurrected emotions he no longer wanted to feel. She definitely made him feel out of control. Yet manners compelled him to follow Tommy's bidding.

"I'm not hungry," Sara said.

"Perhaps you would like to have a cup of hot cocoa?"

"Yes," Sara said. "I would."

Nick sighed. "Follow me." He led the way into a kitchen that was brightly lit with several oil lamps and the fire in the hearth.

Three of the dogs—the Boston Pug, the Scottish Terrier, and the wolflike mutt—rose and walked over to Sara; the Irish Setter just cocked open one eye.

"This is Jack," Nick said when the Boston Pug sniffed at her dress. He fished in his pocket and brought out a small piece of brown food. "Jerky," he explained. "Dried meat. I always carry some with me so I can treat them." He handed her several pieces of the dried meat. "Now, you feed the others."

"Wolf," Nick called.

The wiry, silver-gray dog came close, sniffed her hand, but backed off without taking his treat.

"He's suspicious," Nick said and held his hand out to the Scottish terrier. "Duncan."

The dog, his tail swishing, swaggered closer and gladly accepted the tasty morsel.

Wolf growled.

"He's ready for his now," Nick said. Then he walked to the Irish setter. Bending, he scratched behind her ears. "And this is the queen of the lot, Colleen."

Kneeling beside Nick, Sara gave Colleen her treat, then patted her.

"She may be the queen of the lot, but she's not the last," Cook said. She opened the back door, and Nick heard the heavy beat of paws against the floor. "Rumples!" His exclamation ended in a grunt as the silver-haired mutt leaped onto his back and knocked him to the floor.

Nick pulled a face and swatted at the dog to keep him from licking him in the face. Sara and Cook laughed. Finally, Nick joined in.

"Miss Addie has her work cut out for her on this one," Cook said. "He's young and feisty. He's going to be hard to train."

"Addie has a way with animals." Nick pinned his gaze to Sara who sat in the middle of the floor, playing with Rumples. She had a way with dogs also.

"That she does," Cook muttered.

Towels draped over her arms, Perry walked into the kitchen. She was shaking her head and mumbling, "I'll swear. I don't know what I'm going to do. Addie promised those kids that tree and they'll—"

"The Christmas tree!" Nick exclaimed. He leaped to his feet and reached out to help Sara up.

"That's right." Cook, her arms full of dry goods, stamped out of the pantry. She laid the sacks of flour and sugar on the worktable and reached up to swipe a strand of dark brown hair from her face. "The Merriweathers and their orphans are coming over here tomorrow for dinner. They'll be expecting the tree. Don't tell me you've forgotten, Nick Devlin?"

Looking into Cook's accusing face, Nick nodded.

"Somebody's got to get our Christmas tree." Cook planted two hands on her ample hips and glared at Nick, leaving him no doubt who that somebody was. "Me and Perry are too old to be out in weather like this."

"Of course you are," Nick agreed.

Cook walked to the black woodstove that dominated the corner of the room. Lifting the kettle, she said, "I'll make each of you a cup of hot chocolate and serve you dinner. Then the two of you can go find us a tree."

"I don't think so," Nick quickly said. Among all these people Sara Finley unsettled him. He certainly didn't intend to be alone with her.

"Thank you for including me in your Christmas plans," Sara said, "but I really can't accompany Mr. Devlin. I must stay here."

"That's right," Nick agreed. "Addie hired her to sit with Tommy, and that's what she should do. She can't go with me."

"Nonsense!" Addie exclaimed. She bustled into the kitchen in time to hear Sara's last remark. "Jasper is going to stay for a while longer. He and I will look after the boy and Tommy."

"Do you reckon that wagon driver told Loren about the boy and the accident?" Cook set out two places, laying a slice of home-baked bread on each. On each piece of bread she laid two slices of roast beef. Over this she ladled a thick brown gravy filled with potatoes, carrots, and green beans. "Should expect that his ma and pa would be here by now."

"Yes, you would think so," Addie said, "but we'll make sure the driver delivered the message. Nick, will you and Sara stop by Loren's and find out what's been done?"

"Really, Mrs. Stimms," Sara said, "I don't think it is wise for me—"

"I hired you, Sara," Addie said, "and I can send you on an errand if I choose. I need you primarily to keep an eye on Tommy so that she doesn't hurt herself, but we have enough eyes in the house at the moment to watch her." Addie smiled. "Besides, you're young, and you'll enjoy the evening."

Setting two mugs on the table in the center of the room, Cook filled them with hot chocolate. "Your dinner's ready, and I expect you to eat every bite."

Her brow wrinkled, Addie glanced toward Nick's bedroom. "I just hope we find the boy's parents soon. I know they must be worried." As quickly her frown disappeared, and she smiled brightly. "But we shall. The lad will recover and will have a happy Christmas day."

3

Sara paced the parlor as she waited for Nick to hitch the sleigh. She wanted to go sleigh riding. She wanted to hunt a Christmas tree with him, but knew she shouldn't. Walking to the window, she gazed into the starlit heaven, then at the blanket of snow covering the ground. She saw the spontaneous glow, the sprinkling of starlight, then felt the presence in the room. She turned. A huge man dwarfed the room with his presence, with his radiance, but he didn't daunt Sara.

"Hello, Gabriel."

"Hello, Sara." He gave her a lopsided smile. "It is Sara?"

She nodded. "Yes, I'm more comfortable using my earthly name. That way I won't forget."

"You know the rules," Gabriel said.

"Never interfere with the affairs of mortals."

"You were sent here for one purpose—"

"I know, Gabriel, and I shall do it. I have never failed yet. I shall bring Tommy home."

"This is the first time you've been this tardy."

"More has happened than I originally thought," Sara answered. "Tommy can see angels, and the family is concerned about the boy who was hit by the wagon. And this is the season when people celebrate the birth of Christ. I haven't had the heart to take Tommy yet."

Gabriel's blue eyes pierced hers. "This is also the first time you have assumed corporeal form for an assignment like this."

"This is an unusual household," she answered truthfully, omitting to tell him that the most unusual and compelling member was the dark and brooding man called Nick Devlin. "As I told you, Tommy can see angels. I must be careful." She smiled. "Another directive is that we are not to reveal ourselves unless Father has given us permission."

Nodding, Gabriel smiled gently. "You make a beautiful human."

"Thank you," she said shyly. "It's been so long since I was human, I've forgotten how it felt."

Gabriel caught Sara's hands in his and squeezed gently. "Much is at stake here, little one. If you perform your task well this time, you will no longer be a messenger angel. You will join the archangels."

Sara nodded. "I've worked so long for this."

"If you're not careful, you'll lose it all."

"Miss Finley," Nick called.

Sara heard footsteps in the hallway.

"I'm in the parlor," she answered.

"In human time you must be at the gates of home no later than six in the morning. Or else—"

Sara nodded. Gabriel didn't have to outline the "or else." She knew she would lose all her supernatural powers. No longer would she be an angel of the highest order. She would be a human, subject to their limitations and frailties and to living an earthly life again.

"Good-bye, little Sara," Gabriel said softly, then disappeared.

Nick stood in the arched doorway, Sara's cloak draped over her arm. He stared at her oddly. "Did you see it?"

"What?"

"The ... er ... the—" He shrugged. "Tommy calls it stardust or starlight."

Sara smiled. "Yes, I saw it. I'm surprised you did. Few humans witness it."

Nick laughed shortly. "Miss Finley, you fit into this family just fine."

Yes, Sara thought, she did. And she liked it. She was excited about going to hunt for a Christmas tree. When she had been a human before, people hadn't celebrated Christ's birthday in this manner.

"Are you ready to go?" he asked.

"Yes."

He caught her hand in his. His clasp was firm and warm. She looked down at his hand. It was large and tanned and strong, his fingers lightly shadowed with tiny hairs, his palm covered in calluses. A warmth seeped through her body, and it had nothing to do with the fire blazing in the fireplace. Nick's touch infused her with emotions she had never experienced before, that she wanted to feel.

"Jasper says the boy is resting better," Nick reported. "He thinks he is getting better."

"I told you he would be all right," Sara said.

Nick settled the soft material of the cloak around her, his hands clasping her shoulders. In the soft light of the lamp, Sara gazed breathlessly into his face. Not beautiful, but ruggedly handsome, she thought.

"Your hair," he said. "It's beautiful."

"Thank you," she murmured, not knowing how to react to compliments from humans.

"I've never seen this shade of blonde before." As if he could not help himself, he reached out and wrapped a curl around his finger. "It shines like pure gold."

"Your hair is beautiful also, Mr. Devlin." Sara ventured.

"Nick."

She stared into eyes that were dark and fathomless. If she allowed herself, Sara knew she could easily lose herself in their beauty and mystery.

"Nick."

"Sara," he murmured.

He gazed at her so intently, Sara felt warmth rising in her cheeks. "I've ... I've never been sleigh riding before," she said in an effort to cover her confusion.

As if he understood that she was embarrassed, he smiled and said, "Then you're in for a treat."

In only moments he had her out of the house and was swinging her into the seat of the sleigh. As quickly he was beside her, stacking warmed bricks under their feet and tucking the blanket over their legs. He clicked to the horses, and soon they were gliding over the winter wonderland.

They hadn't traveled far when Sara heard the barking; then a huge dog streaked by them. "Rumples," she cried out. "He's going with us."

"I'd tell him to go back," Nick said, "but it wouldn't do any good."

Rumples trotted back to the sleigh and looked up at Nick. Then he barked, danced around, and bounded away again. Nick and Sara laughed at the dog's antics.

Nick pulled Sara closer to him. When she looked at him, he said, "For warmth."

She smiled and scooted closer, loving the feel of his strong body next to hers.

"You said you've never been sleigh riding before?"

"No."

"You're not from around here?"

"No."

Nick chuckled. "We're not going to get acquainted if you give me only one-word answers."

Sara laughed also. It had been such a long time since she had been a human, she was having difficulty in remembering what it was like, what she had been like, what she had thought, what she had felt. She snuggled closer to him, liking his warmth and feeling protected by his strength.

"Tommy thinks you're her guardian angel come to take her to heaven." He gazed down at her, his eyes dark and mysterious.

Sara felt Nick's warm breath fan against her cheeks. They were in a clearing, the glow from the lanterns on the front of the sleigh dancing shadows over the snow and the moonlight casting them in silver. She saw the shadow of beard stubble on his face.

Not interested in what Tommy thought, she asked, "What do you think, Nick?"

"I don't believe in guardian angels, Sara, but I think you're a woman who could carry a man to heaven—if but for a little while."

"Perhaps I could carry you there forever." She was surprised at how breathless her voice sounded.

"At one time I would have believed a woman could," he answered sadly. "But not anymore, Sara."

"You've been hurt," she said.

"Just learned a lesson the hard way," he answered.

"Whoever taught you the lesson, evidently didn't know you, Nick."

He laughed shortly. "Oh, she claimed to know me all right. I just didn't know her."

"What did she think she knew?"

"She accused me of being the devil," he answered, remembering Carolyn's parting words to him. "Possibly I was . . . or am. Certainly my names bears witness to the fact. Nicholas Lucien Devlin."

Giving the horses their lead, he twisted more fully toward her, pressing their bodies more closely together.

"Does it frighten you to think that I may be the dark angel?"

"I believe in angels," she confessed, "but I don't believe you're one. Even if you were, I don't think you're dark."

Nick lowered his head and touched his mouth to hers. At first her lips were cool . . . and certainly they were innocent. They never moved beneath his. But he felt her warm breath and smelled the faint odor of cocoa. He put his arms around her and drew her into his embrace, and his lips began to play with hers, gently, tenderly. She whimpered and pushed away.

He made no effort to pull her back into his embrace. "Do you want me to apologize?"

"Do you want to?"

Surprised, Nick stared. "No."

"Then don't. I enjoyed it."

"I want to kiss you again."

"I know," she whispered. She wanted it too, but knew she mustn't let it happen again—that she shouldn't have allowed it to happen the first time.

Sixteen when she died, Sara had never loved a man, had never been loved by a man. Now she wanted to love and to be loved by Nick. But this could never be. She was an angel, he a mortal.

"Do you believe in love, Nick?" she asked.

Nick tensed and moved away from her. "No."

"I do."

"I know." He caught her chin in his gloved hand and lifted her head so that they were gazing into each other's face. Softly, he said, "But you mustn't fall in love with me."

"I didn't say I loved you." Sara wouldn't let him know that his warning had come too late, that she had fallen in love with him the moment she saw him bending over the helpless child. "I only said I believe in love."

"I did at one time," Nick confessed, "but not anymore." He smiled, the gesture endearing him to Sara. "Besides, I'm not marriage material. I come with a ready-made family. At the worst they are accused of being insane, at the best eccentric. Addie. Cook. Perry. And all Addie's other friends."

"I can see where people would think your family is different," Sara said, "but I like them. I also think you are marriage material. From the way you treat your adoptive mother and her friends, I know you love them. I also know, Nick Devlin, that you would treat your wife with the same kindness and understanding. You say you don't believe in love, but I say you do."

"There's a difference between love and responsibility," Nick said. "I believe in responsibility."

Sara's smile told him that she didn't believe him.

Scowling, Nick lowered his hand and raked it through his hair. "Don't look at me like that."

"How am I looking at you?"

"Soulful," he muttered. "With your big eyes and your parted lips. Sara, you're beautiful."

She could only gaze at him.

"Do you have any idea what you're doing to me?"

"I know what you're doing to me," she whispered. "Am I . . . doing the same to you?"

"Oh, God, yes." A hunger, unlike any Nick had ever felt, gnawed at him. His voice lowered to a seductive level. "I'm jealous of the moon, Sara. It's kissing your eyes and your lips." With the tip of his finger he touched each part of her face as he spoke. "The tip of your nose. Your cheeks. It's touching you, and that's what I want to do. What I can't do."

"No," she whispered, completely ensnared in the sensuous web that Nick had woven around them.

"Sara, I can't allow myself to care for a woman." He had cared once, and she had stepped all over his heart.

"Can't or won't?"

"Both," he answered.

"You have so much to give a woman, Nick. You must allow yourself to love. You have to take the risk."

Sara was treading too close to Nick's heartstrings, and it disconcerted him. "Besides, I don't have a cent to my name and no job prospect. I'm an architect without a job. I have so many responsibilities."

"Those are excuses, not reasons," Sara softly pointed out. "If a woman loves you, she will help you with your responsibilities. If you find a woman whom you love deeply enough, you'll find a way to earn a living."

Pondering the wisdom of her words, Nick stared at her.

"I'm not being critical or trying to make you feel guilty," she said. "I only want you to understand that you have no reason to think of yourself as not being

marriage material and every reason in the world to
love . . . again"

Nick knew Sara wasn't deliberately trying to make
him feel guilty, but he did. He also felt ashamed of
himself. Desire burned hotly through him. He wanted
her, but because of Carolyn, he was afraid to love
again. He was afraid to made a commitment of love
. . . of any kind . . . to her. For the first time in a year,
he desired a woman, Sara Finley. But he was afraid to
reach out again. He still smarted from Carolyn's re-
buff, from the humiliation he had suffered when she
renounced their engagement and married Benton Alexander, Jr.

Sara evoked a sense of regret in Nick by reminding
him that he was growing older with nothing to show
for his life. Since she had walked into his home a
few hours ago, he had begun to feel an emptiness in
his heart . . . an emptiness he feared only she could
fill.

All this time he had been hating Carolyn and thinking that she had broken his heart. But his heart was in-
tact. His pride had been trampled. And he had been
judging Sara by his distrust of Carolyn. Now was the
time for him to take down the barrier around his heart
and to forget about pride. Sara was not Carolyn; she
wasn't like her at all.

"I've made you angry," Sara said.

"No, just made me think."

"Is that good or bad?"

"Good."

"I'm glad."

Drinking in the beauty of her countenance and the
radiance of her smile, he said, "Time is passing, and
we need to get along. We have chores to run and a
Christmas tree to get."

Flicking the reins, he clucked to the horses and set them into a trot. They wound their way through the thick forest. Rumples raced ahead of them, sometimes looping back to run beside the sleigh.

They had ridden a ways when Sara said, "I don't understand this custom of Christmas trees, Nicholas."

Surprised, he said, "You've never had one?"

She shook her head. "Why do you have them?"

Nick shrugged. "According to Adeline Peabody Stimms, the old church calendar designated Christmas Eve as Adam and Eve Day. The day after is naturally the day of Christ's birth since Christians generally believe he is the second Adam. Supposedly, the first Adam brought an apple from the Tree of Knowledge with him when he was expelled from Eden. Thus, the apple tree is symbolic of both Adam and Christ. On the eve of Christ's birth, the apple tree blossomed, and on the day of His birth it bore fruit."

"The legend is beautiful," Sara said. "But you are cutting the tree down and taking it to your home. What do you intend to do with it?"

"We're going to decorate it," he answered. "We put the tree in a heavy stone crock filled with sand and water and set it up in the house. Most people put it in the parlor. Then we hang ornaments on it and attach candles to the ends of the branches. The candles represent the blossoms, the ornaments the fruit. The candles are lit for about twenty minutes on Christmas morning while we sing Christmas songs. Afterward we exchange our gifts."

Even in the moonlight Nick could see the animation on her face.

"This is a wondrous custom, Nick," she said. "I think I shall truly enjoy it."

"You've never celebrated Christmas like this?" he asked.

"Not with a tree. We had Christmas dinner and exchanged gifts that we had made during the year with our family, but we never had a tree. Where do we get the ornaments?"

"We make them," Nick replied, then added, "home-baked cookies and little cakes and handmade ornaments such as cotton-batting Santas and silver-paper cornucopias. We also make garlands of stringed–popped corn. And since you are with us tonight, I'm sure Addie is going to volunteer your services."

"She doesn't have to," Sara said. "I'll volunteer myself." She grinned up at him. "What happens if you snitch some of the goodies while you're preparing the ornaments?"

He grinned down at her. "That's your privilege as an ornament maker."

Sara caught her breath as she stared into Nick's teasing face. Then she reluctantly turned her head, exhaled, and looked at the trees around them. "Do you know which one you're going to get?"

"I don't, but Addie does. She marked one several months ago. When we return this way, we'll get the lantern and find our tree with its ribbon flying in the wind."

They lapsed into a comfortable silence as Rumples darted ahead of them, and Nick skillfully navigated the sleigh through the forest. The runners whooshed over the thick, silver blanket of snow that softened the austerity of winter. Lantern glow and moonlight blended to guide them through the woods to the edge of town.

"Where are you from?" Nick asked. "I had assumed Chicago—"

"No, the south." She had been too inquisitive about the tree, Sara thought, and Nick had been thinking about it. "New Orleans. I've seen lots of ice and sleet, but no snow that really counts."

"Did your family move to Chicago?" he asked.

"No," she replied, "I'm alone. All of them are ... dead." The human word for the crossing sounded so harsh and ugly. Sara hated to use it, but she felt that Nick would classify her as either insane or eccentric if she were to do otherwise.

She vaguely remembered her family when they had been in their corporeal forms. Life and time was so different in heaven it was difficult for her to translate it back to the human experience.

"I'm sorry."

"Thank you." Sara had wanted to manifest herself, but now she was finding it difficult to converse with him. There was so much she wished she could tell him, but couldn't. And what she remembered from her past life had taken place about seventy-five years before. She had to be careful not to give herself away.

"I admire you," Nick said. "I would imagine that being a nurse and sitter can be a thankless job at times."

"That hasn't been my experience. I love helping people."

Nick laughed. "Most people would love to have you as their nurse. I know I would."

Although the wind blew against Sara's face, she again felt heat flush her cheeks. She was glad Nick couldn't see the color that surely must tinge them. As they emerged from the forest, Nick took a turn that threw Sara against him.

"Careful!" He reached out and caught her, much as

he would do if she were a child who would go sailing out of the sleigh.

When she straightened up, he held her close to him, and she was glad.

Nick pointed. "That's Port Huron, but we're not going into town proper. Loren's house is on this side of the tracks."

In the distance she saw the lights of town, and he began to recount its history and to describe the people. The roads widened, and houses were closer together, although there were huge open fields between them. They traveled quite a ways when Nick stopped in front of a two-story house. He pushed the blankets aside and leaped out of the sleigh.

"Wait here where it's warm," he said. "I'll be back in a minute."

As if he really were a guard dog, Rumples sat by the sleigh, making no effort to follow Nick.

At the gate Nick turned. "I won't be long."

Leaning her head against the cushioned seat, Sara watched Nick as he strode to the door and knocked. A man answered, stepping onto the porch to join Nick. The man was large and muscular, Sara noted, but beside Nick he looked small. In fact, she decided, if Nick were standing in a crowd of men, he would stand out. There was something about him that set him apart from other men.

Sara smiled. Nick was special. She could so easily care for him, but she mustn't. At all costs she must protect him, must shield him from the pain that caring for her could bring him.

Nick glanced out toward the sleigh, and in the light that poured out of the house through the glass-paneled door, she saw him smile and wave at her. Sara's heart began to beat so fast she was light-headed.

She had always thought him handsome, but now he was endearing. His facial features were still angular and hard, but gone was the harshness and bitterness. For a moment he seemed softer. A moment ago she had thought how easily she could care for him, but she had been fooling herself. She more than cared for him. She loved Nicholas Lucien Devlin.

4

Christmas Eve, Nick thought as he drove away from Loren's house—supposedly the season of joy and good tidings, a time of celebration. But he felt no joy or good tidings and had no inclination to celebrate. He was worried. How was he going to make ends meet until he could find himself a new job? Never had his responsibilities felt so heavy.

"Is something wrong?" Sara asked.

"Everything," he replied, then surprised himself by opening up to Sara and repeating his conversation with Loren. Law officers had been combing the town and surrounding area all evening and had found no trace of the boy's parents. But they were still looking.

Finding Sara to be a sympathetic listener, Nick confessed that Loren, also president of one of the local banks, had reminded him that the mortgage on his home was coming due in a couple of months. And Nick didn't have the money.

With Sara asking a question or making a comment, Nick was soon talking to her about his plans for the trade pavilion and the meeting with the architectural committee. He even told her about Wilson Grumly, the one man who had liked his designs but who seemed to have no influence with the committee. Nick then told her about his plans for Addie's boarding house.

"Will you be able to pay your mortgage and have all of this if you return to Benton Alexander's firm?"

"I'll be able to have most of it," he answered. "With a job I'll be able to pay the mortgage and can even build Addie's boarding house."

"But you'll also be adding to your responsibilities," Sara said softly. "You'll not only have Addie's friends to take care of, but the Merriweathers and their orphans."

Nick nodded. "And in returning to the firm and in letting them have my design, I lose control of the trade pavilion. It will be Alexander's dream come true, not mine."

"Perhaps Mr. Grumley will have more influence than you think."

"Perhaps," Nick answered.

"Even if you don't get the contract," she said, "you'll get others. I know you must be a great architect. I believe in you, Nick."

He stared at her through the dim glow of lantern and moonlight. "Do you really?"

"Yes."

Nick felt the strength of her conviction, and it imbued him with the same strength, the same confidence. Sara Finley was an optimist just like Addie, and he found himself pleased with the comparison. Right now, right here, he felt as if Sara might be telling the truth. That he might still have a chance of being awarded the contract for the trade pavilion. That he and she might have a chance!

"Sara Finley, I think it's time for us to find that tree."

He stopped the horses, tethered them, then lifted

Sara out of the sleigh. He held her against him, enjoying the feel of her body against his. Her eyes sparkled, and her cheeks were flushed.

"You know," he whispered, "I could get used to this."

"What?" Her word came out as a silver vapor.

"Holding you."

He let her slide down his body until her feet touched the ground, but still he did not turn her loose. He had fought his feelings for her, had convinced himself that he wasn't going to become involved with her, but he was losing the battle. He liked Sara Finley, and she liked him. She believed in him.

"Where are you staying while you're here in Port Huron, working for Addie?" Nick asked.

After a pause she said in a low voice, "I'm not staying over. I'm only here for the night."

Surprised and disappointed, he said, "Addie was under the impression that you would be taking care of Tommy for us as long as we needed your services."

"No, I just came for the night," Sara replied. "If Addie needs a sitter for a longer time, she'll have to go through the registry again."

"But you're so good with Tommy," Nick argued. "You understand her. You must stay. If it's a matter paying you more money—"

"It's not." She smiled sadly. "I have to go home."

"Sara, earlier I was telling you why I shouldn't become involved with a woman, why she shouldn't become involved with me."

She nodded.

"You were right. I was giving you excuses, not reasons . . . because I was afraid to risk loving again, because a woman had trampled on my pride."

The wind blew, a shock of black hair falling across

his forehead, and Sara wanted to brush it back. She wanted to touch him, to know him in every way that a woman could know a man.

"Sara, please stay a few days longer."

"I can't."

"You and I are attracted to each other, Sara. Let's see if we can't find a way to make it work."

"No, Nick," she whispered. "I *shall* be leaving in the morning."

In the flickering light of the lantern she saw disappointment darken his countenance. More than anything in the world she wanted to reach out to him as he had reached out to her, but she could not. She couldn't stay here with him, so it was better to end matters now rather than prolong the hurt. And she had hurt him . . . perhaps as the other woman in his life had hurt him. He tried to mask it, but she could see it in his eyes, in his rigid stance.

He lifted the lantern and handed it to her. Moving to the side of the sleigh, he reached for the ax and slung it over his shoulder. Then he struck out through the trees, politely guiding her, but drawing away from her. Rumples darted behind him and on several occasions tried to play with Nick, but he ignored the dog. When Sara and Nick were unable to find the tree together, Nick suggested they separate. Finally, in the distance Sara saw darkened shadows fluttering in the sky. She raced forward, held up the lantern, and saw the red ribbon.

"Nick," Sara called out, "I've found the tree. I've found our Christmas tree."

He waded through the snow and found her standing in front of a tree that was taller than he. From one of the branches a red ribbon flew in the breeze.

"Oh, Nick," she cried softly, turning to him, "I have

never done anything like this in my life. I didn't know Christmas could be so beautiful."

Earlier Nick had allowed himself to be taken in with her childish wonder and air of innocence. And he had gone against one of his basic principles. He had begged her to stay with him. He had been willing to take a risk to find out if he could love again, if she could love him. But she had rebuffed him. Even so, he was still under her spell. But he must not let her know. He had to keep his emotions under control. He wouldn't let another woman play him for a fool.

"For some Christmas is beautiful," he agreed. "To me it's just another day in the year." He pointed. "Hold the lantern over there."

Sad because she couldn't tell Nick that she loved him, because she was going to have to leave him, Sara moved to the spot he indicated. He stripped out of his greatcoat and his suit coat and handed them to Sara. Then he began to chop down the tree.

Entranced, Sara watched the pull of his shirt across the bunched muscles of his shoulders as he chopped the trunk. He handled the ax with such ease and grace that it seemed to be one with him. Effortlessly the blade sliced through the wood. Strong, solid, stalwart, Nick reminded her of the trees around them. How she loved him and wanted to stay here with him, but she could not.

But she could taste the joy of being his for a little while, she thought. As quickly she rejected the thought. She wasn't of this world, and if she pretended otherwise where Nick was concerned, she would only hurt him more, and she would hurt herself.

As he chopped down the tree, she felt something moist and wet on her cheeks. Snow? But it was no longer falling. She took off her glove and touched her hand to her cheek. When she pulled it back, she saw the droplet of water. A tear! She was crying ... and angels did not cry.

"Hold the lantern still!" Nick ordered. "I can't see what I'm doing."

Still marveling that she was crying, Sara raised the lantern again and brushed the tears from her face. When the tree fell, she watched Nick encircle the branches with a thin rope. Then he hoisted it onto his shoulder.

As she followed him back to the sleigh, she said, "You carry that as if it weighs nothing."

"When I was young, I worked as a lumberjack. I've kept myself in shape during the years by doing a lot of outdoor work. Maybe I should have continued doing this."

Once the tree was secured to the sleigh, and Nick had seated Sara and covered her with the blankets, he slipped into his coats. After he had settled himself into the sleigh, Rumples joined them.

"Get out," Nick ordered.

"He's tired," Sara said.

The dog looked at Nick, but didn't move.

"Out!"

Whimpering low, Rumples edged closer to Sara. "He's not bothering me," she said.

"He is me."

Sara knew what was bothering Nick, and it wasn't the dog. It was the attraction they felt for each other—an attraction she could not encourage. Now she knew why one of the directives warned angels against taking on a corporeal form.

Finally relenting, Nick allowed the dog to ride home with them. Sara tried to breach the barrier Nick had erected between them, but the camaraderie and warmth they had shared during the earlier part of the evening was gone. If Sara asked him a question, he answered, then lapsed into silence. When he pulled the horses to a halt in front of the carriage house, Rumples jumped out of the sleigh. Sara laid her hand on Nick's arm.

"I'm sorry if I've angered you."

"You haven't. I'm just disappointed."

"Nick, more than anything in this world, I would like to stay. But I can't." She wished she could make him understand. She wanted to make a full confession to him, but even if she did, he wouldn't believe her. Nick felt a responsibility for people who believed in angels, but he didn't believe himself.

"You've made your choice, Sara. We'll have to live with it."

He debarked, helped her out, then walked to the side of the sleigh. The back door opened, and Perry stepped onto the porch.

"How's the boy?" Nick called out.

"He hasn't regained consciousness, but he's moving about," Perry answered. "Jasper says it's a good sign. Did you find out who he is?"

"No, Loren's men are still searching for his parents."

Cook poked her head around the door. "Glad you have that, Nick. It'll be really nice if the boy can wake up to a Christmas tree. Is it a pretty one?"

Grinning, Nick shrugged. "It's a Christmas tree."

"It's more than pretty," Sara said. "It's beautiful."

She raced ahead of Nick, holding open the gates and doors. She followed him into the parlor where he stuck the tree trunk into a crock filled with sand and water. He untied the rope and brushed the branches out to their former fullness.

"Here is your tree, ladies. You may do with it as you

wish. As for me, I'm going to put up the sleigh and take care of the horses."

"Raleigh will do that for you," Perry said, referring to the yard man. "You can help us with decorating the tree."

"Yes," Cook chimed in, "the cookies need to be cut and baked, the cakes wrapped, and the corn popped and strung."

"Not right now," Nick said. "I promised Raleigh that I'd let him leave as soon as I returned."

"Who's going to lick the cookie bowl?" Cook asked.

"I think Miss Finley would like to do that." Nick winked at Sara. "She also said she would be volunteering to help with the tree decorations. What you three haven't finished by the time I've taken care of the horses, I'll help you with. Until then, ladies." He walked out of the house.

"I do want to help with the decorations," Sara said to Cook and Perry, "but first I'd like to check on the boy and on Tommy."

Moving into the foyer, she took off her cloak and hung it on the hall tree. Then she walked to Nick's bedroom.

Addie, sitting in the wing chair in front of the fire with her eyes closed, opened them and looked at Sara when she entered. "You're back, dear. Did you learn anything about the boy?"

Shaking her head, Sara repeated all she and Nick had learned. By the time she was finished, Jasper had thrown more wood onto the fire and was stretching his arms above his head. Sara walked to the bed and gazed at the child who lay between the white sheets. The purple knot on his forehead stood out against his pale face.

He seemed so small and helpless Sara wanted to

hold him, to rock him, to assure him that everything would be all right. She wondered what it would be like to be the mother of a child like this. A black-haired boy with dark eyes like his father . . . like Nick.

Mentally, Sara shook herself. She shouldn't be fantasizing like this.

Addie walked to stand beside Sara.

"How is he, doctor?" Sara asked.

Jasper shrugged. "All we can do now is wait."

"And pray," Addie added. "He's so young and has so much to live for. No telling what his destiny is in this world."

"No," Sara murmured.

Closing her eyes, Sara touched the boy's head and measured the life force that flowed through him. Strangely, it was strong and vital. He wanted to live. Sara lost herself in his energy field and felt his creativity and his ability to help others. Then she fully melded with him. Silently, he begged her to let him live, to let him fulfill his destiny. So powerful was his cry, his desire to live that Sara wondered if some mistake had been made. Had God really intended to bring this young soul back to heaven? Moving beyond the child's spirit into the universal spirit, she reached into the future and saw that if he lived, he had the ability to change the course of history. Mankind needed him.

"A doctor. Attorney. Musician. Farmer." Tears tracked down Addie's weathered cheeks. "Dear Lord, please don't let him die if there's the chance that he'll do something good for our world."

Removing her hand from the boy's head, Sara turned to Addie. The two women seemed to fall into each other's arms.

"Perhaps, it's not his time, Addie," Sara said.

"I hope not."

The two women stood there for a long while, each gaining strength from the other. Finally, Addie pushed away and smiled up at Sara.

"Thank you, dear," she said. "You're very kind. And you've renewed my hope."

"You're fortunate that Mrs. Creighton sent Sara to you," Jasper said.

"Yes, I am," Addie replied. "God always supplies my needs."

Sara said. "I'll go see to Tommy now."

Addie nodded.

Quietly, Sara left the bedroom and moved down the hall to Tommy's room. The old woman lay on her side, curled into a tiny ball. Tiptoeing into the room, Sara saw that she slept soundly. Her hands, palms together, her fingers intertwined, lay beneath her cheek. Her silver hair fanned out on the pillow around her face. No sooner had Sara sat down, than Tommy roused.

She pushed up on her elbows. "I thought I heard you."

"I went with Nick to see if we could find the child's parents," she said. "And we chopped down the Christmas tree for the children."

"That's nice." Tommy sat up. "I wish Nick were married and had children of his own."

Sara said nothing.

"He was engaged once, but Carolyn broke the engagement when Nick wouldn't kick out all of Addie's friends and have her committed to an insane asylum."

Sara understood Nick's pain, his distrust in women, and his fear of being hurt again. Wanting to hear more, she rose and walked to the foot of the bed.

"It's true," Tommy said. "I've heard Addie and Cook and Perry talk about it. But Carolyn didn't understand love, and Nick does."

Sara disagreed with Tommy, but she didn't argue the point. Nick understood responsibility, but Sara didn't think he understood love.

"He promised Addie that he would build her a big house so she can take in the Merriweathers and their orphans. Then Addie can have as many friends stay with her as she wants." Tommy paused. "But I heard him tell Addie today that he didn't get the contract."

"The contract hasn't been awarded," Sara agreed, "but Nick doesn't think he'll get it."

Benton Alexander, Sr. was going to get it, and Nick was going to have to return to work for a man whom he loathed in order to save the world of his adoptive mother.

Tommy patted the side of the bed. "Come here, Sara."

When Sara sat beside Tommy, the old woman clasped both of her hands, enabling Sara to meld with her and to measure her life's force. It was ebbing. Tommy was ready to go home.

"I know you're an angel," Tommy said. "I've seen the starlight."

"I believe you," Sara answered.

"Why did you wait so long to come get me?"

Gently, Sara said, "I wasn't sent for you."

Tommy studied Sara a long time before she said, "You didn't materialize until after the wagon hit the little boy. Were you sent for him?"

"Yes."

"He's too young," Tommy said. "Take me in his place."

"I can't," Sara argued. Yet she remembered her melding with the boy. She remembered his silent plea for her to allow him to stay here on the earthly plane. "I have my orders."

"It's time for me to go home," Tommy insisted, more lucid than she had been since Sara had arrived at the house. "I'm an old woman who has outlived all her family and her usefulness on earth. The boy's life has just begun. Please take me home."

"I would like to," Sara said, "but—"

"You can," Tommy said, "if you want to."

Yes, Sara thought, she could. The repercussions would be monumental, but she could escort Thomasina home in place of the boy. Tommy wanted to go home. The little boy wanted to remain on earth. And in melding with him, in reaching into the future of his life, she had seen that in leaving him she would not be condemning him to unwanted misery and sorrow. She would be helping mankind.

"A mistake has been made, Sara. The heavenly Father doesn't want Tommy, the little boy. He wants me." After a pause Tommy added, "If you must take him, will you take me also?"

Sara sighed. "Yes."

"When?"

"At daybreak. Once you are inside the gates of the city, Tommy," Sara said, "the Father will not make you leave. You will leave only if you want to."

Tommy nodded.

"You may hear loved ones calling your name, begging you to return to your former life, but you don't have to . . . unless you want to. Remember, the choice is always yours."

"Yes, dear," Tommy said quietly, "I understand. When the angels learn that you have delivered the wrong person, they might try to entice me to return to this life."

Sara nodded.

"Believe me," Tommy promised, "they won't succeed."

"Also," Sara said, "you mustn't let anyone know that I'm the angel who will be taking you home. Others here don't believe."

"Yes, *he* does," Tommy answered. "He just doesn't know it yet."

Sara rose and walked to the window. She looked into the barn and in the golden glow of lantern light saw Nick rubbing down the horses. Once more he had discarded his coats and was wearing only his shirt. Again she was drawn to the pull of his muscles, clearly outlined and emphasized by the fabric of his shirt as it stretched tightly across his back.

"I want to say good-bye to everyone." Tommy pushed back the covers and slipped out of bed. "While I'm combing my hair, dear, look for my dressing robe and my slippers. And do take those infernal bells off them. I'm tired of jangling when I walk." When she sat in front of the dresser, brushing her hair, she smiled. "I know Addie will be sad to see me leave, but it's for the best, Sara." After a few more strokes she laid the brush down. "Now, where are my slippers?"

Sara knelt beside her and slipped the soft shoes on her feet. "Why don't you sit in front of the fire, and I'll have the family come in here to see you?"

"Thank you, dear," Tommy said. "I would like that. I'm feeling a little tired now."

"Yes," Sara murmured, "I knew you would."

Once Tommy was seated, her feet propped on an ottoman and her legs covered with an afghan, Sara eased out of the room and quietly summoned the family.

Addie's eyes darkened momentarily. "Is it time?"

Sara nodded.

"You gather the others, dear. I'll go to her."

"I'd better look in on her," Jasper said.

"You must for your own sake," Addie said, "but you're not going to find anything wrong with her, except a great desire to go to heaven."

After Sara sent Cook and Perry into Tommy's room, she slipped out the back door and raced to the stable. Nick stood beneath one of the overhead lanterns, his black hair gleaming in the golden light. The front of his shirt was unbuttoned, and in the opening she saw the line of black hair that ran from his chest to the waistline of his trousers . . . and lower.

"Nick," Sara said. "Tommy wants to see you. She's . . . she's going home tonight."

Nick stopped brushing. "What does Jasper think?"

"It's not up to him," Sara replied. "Tommy has chosen this night to make her journey."

Their gazes locked. Sara nodded, letting him know that she spoke the truth.

"Tommy wants to speak to you, to tell you good-bye."

Nick threw the brush, and it clattered as it landed on the nearby shelf.

Stepping closer, Sara caught his arm. "It's all right. She's ready."

"Damn it! It's not all right. We're not ready." He pulled away from her, but not before Sara saw the glint of tears in his eyes. He strode out of the stables, across the yard, and into the house. She ran behind him.

When she entered the bedroom, Nick was kneeling beside Tommy's chair. "So you've finally found the way," he said.

Leaning her head against the back of the chair and drawing a deep breath, she smiled and nodded. They talked together for a long time before Tommy began nodding off.

"I think I'll go to bed now," she said. "I'm tired, and I want to be rested for my journey."

Nick helped her to bed, gently tucking the blanket beneath her chin. He was so big and strong, yet kind and gentle.

Jasper remained in the room with the boy while Nick and Sara stayed with Tommy. Addie moved back and forth between them. In the wee hours of the morning, Sara rose and excused herself, leaving Nick alone in the room. He sat in a chair next to the bed, his hand on Tommy's chest. She took a deep breath. In the distance Nick heard the faint sound of bells. Tommy smiled, mumbled, and drew her last breath. The room was filled with glitter.

At first Nick thought he had imagined it all ... and maybe he did, the bells and the drizzle of light. But Tommy was dead. Blinking back tears, he remained where he was sitting. Finally, he rose and walked into his bedroom.

"Addie," he said, "Tommy ... she's found her way to heaven."

5

"Sara," Tommy called as she floated toward the glorious white light above her, "is that you?"

"Yes," Sara answered.

Tommy became part of the light.

"I knew you were my angel the moment I saw you," Tommy said.

She and Sara were flying out of the house, through the sky, beyond the clouds, and through the stars. Starlight. Divine. Golden and silver. The stars sang. Never had Tommy heard such a wondrous melody. Brilliance and glory surrounded her; it infused her.

In the distance Tommy saw the city gates, haloed by the rainbow. When they arrived at the heavenly portal, an aged man, wearing a white robe, greeted them.

"Your name," he said.

"Thomasina." She chuckled. She had finally remembered the name Addie had given to her.

He searched his list. "Thomasina," he repeated.

"That's what Addie called me," she admitted, "but my name is really Tommy."

"But"—he looked at Sara—"she's not the one."

"She's the one," Sara answered.

"No, she's—"

"You know better than to argue with an escorting angel."

He sighed and turned to Thomasina. "Are you truly ready to enter into the city?"

"Yes."

With his golden quill he marked the parchment. Then he held out his hand to Thomasina. "Come with me."

Tommy took his hand, then turned to Sara. "Are you going with me?"

"No," Sara answered, "I have some unfinished business downstairs."

"The little boy."

"Remember what I told you, Tommy."

"I remember."

Quickly, Sara journeyed back to the three-story blue house in Port Huron. By the time she stepped onto the front veranda, she had reassumed her corporeal form. She heard the swish of wings and felt the invisible presence beside her.

"Sara, are you aware of what you've done?"

Out of the brilliance Gabriel materialized.

"Yes." Tears in her eyes, she gazed into the archangel's face. "The boy is young, Gabriel. He has his life ahead of him."

"It isn't for us to give or to take life," he said. "We're supposed to obey."

"I was sent after a soul named Tommy," Sara argued. "I brought home a soul named Tommy."

"Why have you returned to earth?"

"I want to be with Nick."

Gabriel gazed at her sadly.

"I love him," Sara cried.

"Does he love you?"

"I don't know, but I want the chance to find out."

"You're giving up so much, Sara, and for what? For

a man who doesn't believe in love—the very essence of the soul."

"I'm going to him, Gabriel."

"What if he rejects you?"

"What if he doesn't?" Tears spilled down her cheeks.

Gabriel reached out and dried them off. "You're crying, Sara. If you don't give up your corporeal form soon, you will be human and can't return home until you have completed another earthly journey."

"I am home, Gabriel." She smiled.

"Think of all the pain and sorrow."

"Possibly I'll have some pain and sorrow," she admitted, "but I'll also have a chance to know the kind of love that's shared between a man and a woman. I'll also know happiness and joy." The archangel opened his mouth, but she laid her hand over it. "I want this, Gabriel."

Finally, he nodded, and she lowered her hand.

"Wish me well."

"I do, Sara."

From the midst of glory, she heard him say, "You have until midnight tonight by human time to change your mind. I'm sure Father will understand your having brought Thomasina home rather than the child."

"Addie," Nick said. "Did you hear me? Tommy's—"

"Yes, Nicholas, I heard."

Addie rose. About that time the boy on the bed moaned; his body convulsed, and he drew in a deep breath. He opened his eyes and gazed at Jasper.

"Papa," he murmured.

"No, little man," Jasper said, "I'm Dr. Walters."

The child frowned, then reached up and touched his head. "The wagon hit me."

Jasper nodded. "We've sent for your papa and mama. They should be here soon. Can you tell me your name?"

The boy nodded, smiled, and mumbled something.

Jasper leaned closer. "Say it again, son. I couldn't—"

"What did he say?" Addie demanded.

Jasper straightened. The boy's eyes were closed, and he was sleeping again. Jasper shook him gently, and the boy's lids fluttered open.

"Can you tell me your name?"

The boy mumbled again.

"He's sleeping," Jasper said, "but at least he was lucid. When he wakes up again, maybe we'll find out who he is."

"Where's Sara?" Addie asked. "I must tell her."

"I'm here," Sara replied from the doorway.

Addie turned toward her. "Nick said that Tommy—"

"Yes, she's crossed over."

"She's at peace now," Addie said. "She's been wanting to go for a long time."

"Addie," Perry said, "are you going to have Christmas dinner here?"

Addie breathed deeply. "Yes, Tommy would want that."

"Adeline," Jasper said, "I'm going to go home for a few hours. I'll send the undertaker for Tommy's body."

"Thank you," Addie said.

"Send for me if the boy's condition changes for the worse. Of course, I expect a full recovery."

While Jasper and Addie said good night, and he gave her further instructions for the care of the child, Sara walked into Nick's bedroom. But he was gone. She returned to Tommy's room, but he wasn't there either. Looking out the window, she saw him in the stable. He was pitching hay. Without taking the time to put on her cloak, she ran out of the house to him.

By the time she reached the stable, she was short of breath. Nick, looking up and seeing her, leaned on the pitchfork. Quivering beneath his intense scrutiny, she lowered her head and encountered the line of dark chest hair.

"Go back to the house, Sara." His voice was low and thick.

She raised her head and looked into his eyes. In their sultry depths she saw his desire.

He turned the pitchfork loose and walked toward her. "Sara."

Each step brought him closer and cause her heart to beat harder. Sara could hardly breathe. Yet she wouldn't have moved for the world. There was the possibility that Nick didn't love her, that he only wanted her, but she loved him with all her heart. She would make him love her . . . she would.

"I'm staying, Nick," she said.

"Why?"

In two steps he stood directly before her.

"I love you."

His expression was closed, his eyes guarded. "Are you mistaking love with desire?"

"No, I feel that, too. Earlier you said you were jealous of the moon. That it was touching me as you wanted to touch me."

His eyes grew darker.

"I want you, rather than the moon, to touch me, Nick." Sara knew she sounded brazen, but she didn't care. Her love for Nick transcended convention and custom. "I want you to make love to me."

Nick's expression didn't change, but Sara saw his chest rise as he inhaled deeply.

After a moment's hesitation he shook his head. "Call me a fool, Sara, but I'm not going to make a confession of love to you, then have you walk out of my life. I made a fool of myself over a woman once before—"

"I'm staying ... as long as you want. I love you, Nicholas Lucien Devlin."

Before Sara quite knew how it happened, she was wrapped in Nick's arms, her face nestled against his chest. She heard the thunderous beat of his heart ... and it was because of her. He rubbed his hand down her back.

"I love your family, too, Nick."

"Sara." His voice was thick. "I don't deserve a woman like you."

She lifted her head so that she could look into his face. "People don't love each other because they deserve to be loved, but because they need and want to be loved."

Nick lowered his face and kissed her sweetly. He whispered, "I love you, Sara. Will you be my wife?"

"Yes," she cried. "Yes, Nick, I will."

Although she was innocent when it came to the ways of the world, when it came to physical expressions of love, Sara knew that Nick was going to kiss her again. She trembled with happiness.

She lifted her face, welcoming his kiss, yearning for his most complete possession. His lips were both firm and soft, demanding and giving, urgent but gentle. She had known all kinds of sensation, but the fire of desire that Nick set ablaze in her was the most glorious sensation she had ever experienced and would ever experience.

Breathing deeply, Nick lifted his head and broke the sweet bonding. Bereft, Sara whimpered. He ran his hands through her hair, down her neck, and pushed the offending cloak from her shoulders.

"I want to touch you, Sara," he whispered. "All of you."

"And I want you to," she answered, "but first I must tell you something."

"No. No confessions," he said. "I have my past, Sara. You can have yours."

"I'm not a nurse from Chicago," she said, "and I've never been trained by Florence Nightingale."

"Don't tell me," he teased. "You're the angel sent to get Tommy."

"Yes."

Nick pulled away from her.

"I really am, Nick. Remember, the starlight and the soft tingling of the bells when I entered the room. The starlight you saw when Gabriel, the Archangel, came to visit me before we went for the Christmas tree." When he didn't answer, she said, "Do you remember?"

Staring at her strangely, he nodded. "Tommy always claimed you were her angel."

"Tommy was right about my being an angel, but she was wrong about my being her angel. I wasn't . . . at first."

Sara stepped away from Nick, and he listened as she explained about her mission to come get the child. Instead, she had taken Tommy. Then she started talking to him about previous life as a mortal. She had lived in New Orleans in the late 1770s. Her parents had been Irish immigrants who had taken refuge in the Catholic colony in the New World. At age sixteen she had died prematurely when she was thrown from her horse. Her head had hit a rock, and her neck had been broken. Afterward her guardian angel had escorted her to heaven.

"Sara," he said quietly, "I want to believe you, but I can't."

Nick heard the ting-a-ling of distant bells. Then a familiar feminine voice said, "You must believe her. She's telling you the truth." He saw the burst of light, the glitter. Then Tommy materialized. "She loves you, Nicholas, and has returned to earth at great cost to herself to be with you. If she does not return to heaven by midnight earth's time, she will become mortal like you."

Then Tommy was gone.

Nick prowled through the barn, pushing his hand through his hair. Finally, he halted in front of her. "You're really an angel."

"Was."

"But you can still return?"

She said nothing.

He caught her arms. "Answer me, Sara. Can you still return?"

"Yes."

"Then you must. You can't stay here."

"I've already made the decision. Whether you love me or not, Nick, I'm staying here."

"Sara, you haven't been a human in almost seventy-five years. You don't know what you're doing."

"Yes, I do."

"I couldn't bear it if you grew to regret your decision and—" he broke off.

"And came to hate you," she finished.

"Yes."

"I could never hate you, Nick," she said. "And the only regret I'll have is not taking the opportunity to live one more time. I love you, and I always will."

Silence stretched between them.

"Then let me have what I was denied so long ago," she whispered. "I've waited several lifetimes for your love."

He ran his hands through her hair, letting the silky strands flow through his parted fingers.

"Let me have love, Nick, the kind of love that you and I can share."

She laid her palm on his chest. Her soft, tentative touch excited Nick and aroused him to a fevered pitch that he had never dreamed possible. But he also knew that he could not . . . would not . . . take advantage of her.

He caught both her hands in his. "Sara, my darling, you don't know what effect you have on me. We must stop now, or there will be no stopping."

"I don't want to stop. I want you to make love to me, Nick."

"I want to make love to you," he confessed, "but I don't want your first time to be in a barn. I want it to be in a bed where I can tutor you gently, where I can truly love and adore you."

"Oh, Nick"—tears seeped from the corners of her eyes—"I'm so afraid of losing you now that I've found you."

"You're not going to lose me, darling." He licked her tears, then gently kissed her again. "I love you, and I want to marry you. Now, as Addie would say, let's go inside before you catch your death of cold."

Slowly, Nick and Sara walked across the yard into the house. As they passed through the kitchen, Perry said, "Are you about ready to help us with the decorations?"

His arm around Sara's shoulder, Nick said, "How about our popping the corn?"

Cook scoffed teasingly. "I know you, Nicholas Devlin. You'll eat more of it than you string."

Perry rocked back on her heels, squinted her eyes, and peered at Nick and Sara. "You two look like you have a secret that doesn't want to be a secret much longer."

"We're going to be married, Perry," Nick said.

"Well, now," the housekeeper said, "I reckon that sounds like a good idea to me. It's time we had our own children in this house."

Cook picked up her apron and wiped her eyes. "Yes, sir, Nicholas Devlin, I reckon it's time you found yourself a good wife."

"You know, Cook," he said, "I think perhaps my wife found me."

"What's all this commotion?" Addie asked, walking into the kitchen.

"Nick and Miss Sara are going to be married," Perry announced.

"How wonderful!" Addie exclaimed and looked at Nick with glistening eyes. "I'm happy for you, Nicholas, so happy." She turned and opened her arms to Sara. "Nick couldn't have found a more wonderful wife, Sara. Truly you are an angel."

"Well," Cook said, "the closest to an angel that we'll ever come."

Nick winked at Sara.

"Addie," Perry said, filling a basket with small cakes wrapped in colored paper and with decorated cookies. "we're going to have to start planning a wedding."

"Yes, we are," Addie agreed as she and Sara stepped apart. "When do you think you'll be getting married?"

"As soon as possible," Nick answered.

Perry, having walked into the parlor with her goodies, shouted, "Addie! Company's coming. I do believe it's Loren Gage and Jasper and a woman. Addie, it may be the boy's mother."

"Thank God!" Addie exclaimed and rushed into the hallway. Nick followed. Sara walked into the bedroom and stood beside the bed. She tucked the cover more closely about the child's face.

"I hope you've rested well, Tommy." She leaned over to kiss him lightly on the forehead.

The boy opened his lids, blinked several times, then gazed solemnly at Sara.

"You have a great deal you must accomplish during your lifetime," Sara said. "That's why I escorted Thomasina over rather than you."

The front door opened, and Sara heard a mingling of male and female voices, then footsteps moving down the hallway.

"Sara," she heard Addie call.

"In here," Sara returned.

"The boy's mother is here," Addie said from the door.

The words were hardly out of Addie's mouth before a woman pushed past her. The boy saw her and smiled. He tried to sit up, but grimaced and touched his hand to his head. He fell back against the pillows.

"Thomas Alva Edison, you've given me the fright of my life." Her smile and tears softened the words. "I thought you were staying with Stanley. I had no idea until—"

In between hugs and kisses mother and son talked, their sentences garbled and disjointed. Then they turned to Nick, who recounted the incident in detail for them. Later, after a lengthy discourse over what she must and must not do in regard to the boy, Jasper Walters allowed Mrs. Edison to bundle up her son and take him home.

Standing on the veranda, Sara and Nick waved at the child until he was out of sight. Then Nick brought Sara inside and settled her in the parlor in front of the tree she loved so much. She smiled when she saw Perry's basket of decorations sitting close by. In front of the fireplace was a long-handled wire popping basket and a fruit jar filled with golden yellow kernels of corn.

"Loren delivered more than Mrs. Edison." Nick remained standing. "He delivered two telegrams that came late last evening. The first one was from Mrs. Creighton. She informed Addie that she was going to be unable to send her a sitter."

Sara grinned. "As Addie says, God always provides."

Nick chuckled with her. "I tore that telegram up. But the other one—" He took a piece of paper from his pocket and handed it to her.

Sara unfolded it and read, then waving the telegram in the air, leaped to her feet and threw her arms aground him. "Oh, Nicholas, you did it. You've been awarded the contract for the Chicago Pavilion of Trade!"

"Evidently, Wilson Grumley had more influence than I thought."

"According to his telegram, he's an international land developer!" Sara exclaimed. "And he wants you to design more buildings for him, more trade centers. All over the world." Catching Nick's face in both hands, she pulled his head down to hers. "You're so wonderful."

"The most wonderful thing about me," he whispered as their lips touched, "is you, my angel."

In the distance, the far distance, he heard the faint ting-a-ling of bells, and the room was filled with glitter.

"Starlight," he murmured, then closed his eyes and gave himself to the wonder of his love.

It's a Wonderful Christmas

❦

Edith Layton

England, December 1835

It was bitterly cold, but there had been visitors to the well that morning. There always were, though no one in living memory had tasted the well water. It was for wishing, not washing or drinking, after all. And it had been since the first man on English soil became human enough to wish. Down through the ages wishes had been made here—and sometimes were answered. It was said that when a wish was granted the surface of the water would dimple, as though more than a prayer had been thrown in it. It didn't take tokens of blood or money, only faith. Once, a religion had been built around it; now, a different church lay down the road. The well had a saint's name, but it had been an age since the church considered it more than a relic. The saint's holy day was in midsummer, and yet there were fresh footprints in the snow now. Perhaps because the well lay in a grove of oaks covered with mistletoe and ivy, and Christmas was coming. The local people used the trappings of one religion to celebrate another, the way they did the well itself. It was only plain sense. The well was older than time or religion. It was said angels as well as fairy folk tarried there. And the season for miracles was near.

* * *

The woman in green ran through the snow. She was so small and slight and ran so lightly she could have been mistaken for a girl. Surely a lady would have been more careful of her step. The hood of her cloak had fallen back and long auburn hair streamed over her shoulders. Her piquant face was ruddy from the cold: her cheeks and lips were red as holly berries, as was her small upturned nose. But the curved form beneath the cloak was a woman's. And though her clear skin had no wrinkles, a few fine lines at the corners of her shining green eyes showed that they'd seen their share of snowbright December mornings.

A lady, then, and a fine one, too. Her cloak was thick and her boots fine Spanish leather, her skirts belled out wide and her hands were covered with soft doeskin gloves. She carried a wicker basket filled with fresh-cut holly over one arm. She stopped at the well and paused to look around. Then she raised her heavy woolen skirt and hopped up on a fallen tree trunk. She stood on tiptoe and stretched far as she could toward a branch above her.

"Bother!" she muttered to herself as her fingers just missed snagging a prime cluster of mistletoe. "I thought I was early, but the little folk got here before me."

"Little folk?" a voice boomed in mock astonishment. "And here I always thought you were a good Christian woman, Lady Maude!"

She spun around so fast she almost overbalanced. A tall, thin man in a baggy coat, with a red muffler wrapped several times around his long neck, stood near the well. He smiled at her. There was another man she didn't recognize coming up behind him. She put a hand on her heart.

"Goodness! You startled me, Mr. Potts. I only meant

that children must have got here before me. See? They've stripped all the lower limbs. And I'm too small to reach the rest without a struggle. Philip could do it, he'd swarm right up the tree like a little monkey. But I couldn't send him, he's just getting over a cold. And Zoe is too little and may be coming down with Philip's cold, besides. It's been Simon's job for years. He's coming home from school today. That's why I'm here. His letters have been so full of home lately. I know it's right for him to go away to school, he must be educated for his position, but oh, it seems he misses us as much as we miss him. He's bringing a friend home for the holidays, and I wanted the house to be just the way he remembers it being every Christmas. . . ."

"And you couldn't send a servant to gather greens?" the vicar, Mr. Potts, asked with merriment. "Or gather them elsewhere?"

She looked uncomfortable for a moment, and then grinned just as merrily. "I'm not of the old faith, Mr. Potts. Or even superstitious, really. It's just that it grows thicker here. Why, just look at the size of the berries. The holly, too, from down the path. It's greener, lusher here. Everyone knows that. Well, I suppose it might be just custom. But it *is* a tradition that we get our mistletoe and holly from the grove, you know."

"And the viscount?" the vicar asked.

"Oh, well," she said, looking down, truly embarrassed at last, "he doesn't hold with supersti—I mean to say, he likes the look of it," she said, her chin coming up a jot. "But since I'm the one who insists on it, I don't want him to go to the bother of gathering it. Anyway, he's busy with Mr. Martin and the grooms this morning, some problem with the stable wall or somesuch."

"The Viscount Southwood is a first-rate horseman," the vicar told the young man at his side. Then he added quickly, "Oh, yes, how remiss of me. Lady Maude, may I present Mr. Clarence? Mr. Clarence: the Viscountess Southwood. He's a visitor to our shire, Lady Maude, a bible scholar touring ancient holy sites for a paper he's writing. He was interested in the holy well and so I brought him to see it this morning."

Maude stared at the young man. He must have been used to it because he stood patiently, smiling at her with neither conceit nor amusement. He was blond and fair, with fine features ... with beyond fine features, she thought dazedly. She'd seen pictures of someone very like him in her hymn book when she'd been a little girl. And then again on her honeymoon, in Rome. She was sure she'd seen him high on a ceiling in the Sistine chapel, draped in celestial robes. And then again in a more earthly pose, on a pedestal, in bronze, in Florence. Without the celestial robe. She blushed, remembering.

"Would you like me to cut some mistletoe for you, my lady?" he asked.

"Oh, no, that's not necessary," she said quickly, blinking. "But thank you ... I'll come back later, with a stepping stool. I must go now. I hope you have a nice visit. At least, try a wish."

She took the vicar's hand and stepped down from her perch. Then she turned a bright face to them. The wind whipped streamers of her hair across her face, like an Arab woman's veil. But few Arabian ladies peeked up at men with bright-green eyes over a distinctly freckled nose. "But my wish to you is: Happy

Christmas. I'll see you on Sunday, Mr. Potts," she said with a grin. Then she left them.

"Such a *nice* lady," Mr. Potts said with admiration as they watched her slight figure disappear down the path. They didn't see Maude's expression when she heard him.

Nice, she thought on a sigh. But it was what everyone said, after all. She supposed she only resented it now because of the dazzlingly handsome young man. It would have been nice to have been called *fiery* or *fascinating.* Yes, and it would have been nice to fly up into the boughs to get her mistletoe, too, she thought sourly.

But it didn't matter what they said, she thought with rising spirits. Because she had Miles, who was so much more than merely handsome, and who loved her even though she was only *nice.* She could have told young Mr. Clarence that the well was truly magical. Because she had gotten her wish. Hadn't she wished for Miles at the well every year of her life since she'd learned how to wish? Until she'd turned seventeen. That was when he'd actually asked her to marry him. And then she never wished for anything else, because there was nothing more she needed. Because against all odds, and for no reason she could ever understand, he—who could have had anyone, *anyone*—had asked for her hand in marriage. She, who had never had anything anyone ever wanted before that. She, who had never been wanted at all.

She'd been a surprise to her parents, coming to them late and unlooked for. To give them credit, they'd welcomed her when she arrived. But then they promptly forgot about her. She was only a girl, and they'd two strong sons to dote on, after all. But she was the squire's daughter, and so she was raised properly by the very best servants, and inspected every so often to see how she fared. She grew, but not very tall. She was pretty, but not a great beauty. She was clever, but girls didn't need to be that. But her governess said she was a very *nice* child, and that seemed to please them. So she tried to be the nicest child anyone had ever known. And succeeded, had they cared to see it.

But then there was an epidemic of measles, and she caught it. She looked like a robin's breast, or a speckled egg—or so her brothers said. It tickled them. That was the only thing that made it bearable to her. It was a source of great amusement to them, since they'd never had the measles. When they caught it from her, from spending long hours in her sickroom entertaining her, it was only a silly bother to them. But then they both died of it, and she didn't. So then she was her parents' only child—an unwanted honor for all concerned.

Her parents took in Cousin George, because he was now their heir, and his own parents were glad to have him come to live with them and learn to manage the estate that would be his. He was a serious boy from humble beginnings, and greatly impressed by the honors that would fall to him someday. And while they never forgot their own two bonny boys, in time her parents came to love and respect George for all his good qualities. George was *good* the way she was *nice,* and so Maude never really took to him. She greatly feared her parents had thrown them together so they'd make a match of it someday. She needn't have worried. He had his eye on increasing his fortunes, not consolidating them. And was no more impressed with her than she was with him. Besides, she'd thought when George became betrothed to the heiress from London, he always called her "Maude". Always. And her bonny brothers had called her "Maudie" and "Moogie" and sometimes "Mad Maude," just to make her really deliciously angry.

Not that it mattered. She'd wanted only Miles, from the moment she'd set eyes on him—and that was perhaps the same moment she'd learned to focus them. He'd been her oldest brother's age, their near neighbor and friend, and an idol to her. She'd made her wish at the holy well from the first time she could lisp it whole. But she'd never really believed she had a chance for him.

First she'd been a nuisance to him, and then a source of amusement, and then when her brothers were gone, a reminder that they were. He had gone into the wide world, and she'd stayed home, haunting the well like a will-o'-the-wisp, whispering his name. He'd finally come home from the war, safe but limping and pale. And had needed someone to talk to that whole long seventeenth summer of hers.

He'd asked for her hand at the end of it. If that wasn't a miracle, Maude didn't know what was. It made the loaves and the fishes look like mere sleight of hand. He, Miles Randal deForest, Viscount Southwood, had asked for her hand in marriage. And had been kind enough not to laugh when she'd grown pale, then red, then pale again, and almost fainted. She would have, except that she'd refused to let anything make her miss that first kiss.

Now, three children and almost two decades later, she still couldn't entirely believe her good fortune. Merely nice little Miss Maudie had married Miles deForest, Lord Southwood, and was living happily ever after. And still not quite believing it.

She was almost out of breath by the time she reached the drive, and so she lost it altogether when she saw him. Because the sight of him, even now, even after all these years, always caused her breath to hitch. Tall, elegantly made with wide shoulders and narrow hips, his thick dark hair was black as night against the background of sun-dazzled snow, his gray eyes danced with dark light as he saw her. He was not handsome, not as young, blond Mr. Clarence was. Not in the least. He was less, and more. He was craggy and lean, and outrageously attractive, as only he could be.

She flew into his arms and rested one moment there before she danced away so as not to embarrass herself, or him. He was her husband. She'd gone to bed with him last night and waked with him this morning as she had for almost a score of years, and yet she never got over the thrill at seeing him after an absence. Even if it was only of an hour. She shook her head, causing a cascade of hair to cover her blushes. After all this time—it was a miracle. She wasn't sure if the miracle was the joy she took in him, or the fact that he remained with her, and didn't want to know.

He looked at what she was carrying. "Holly," he said in a deep voice warmed by withheld laughter. "All the way from the woodland? But you could have saved yourself the trouble. There's so much in the drive. We could have Cullen cut all you want. They need trimming anyhow."

"You know better than that," she giggled.

"Oh, yes, my little witch woman must have her holy holly. Now aside from being difficult to say," he mused as he fell into step with her and they paced toward the house, "isn't there a contradiction there? Considering it's a heathen plant, growing by a pagan well?"

"Indeed?" she said, as if she hadn't said the same thing every Christmas for years. "Tell Saint Ethelinda that, then. It's *her* well now."

"Only because the church decided that if you can't

get rid of it, you might as well name it and call it your own idea. Saint Ethelinda isn't famous for much around here but coming to grief by that well—and mistletoe and holly are Druid charms, and grow on Druid oaks . . . but where's the mistletoe?" he asked, peering into her basket. "Or have you decided you don't want my kisses at Christmas anymore?"

She blushed. She wished she could say, "Oh, but I do!" and cast herself into his arms. She couldn't. She hadn't been able to when they were first married because she'd been too overwhelmed by him. And she couldn't now because he'd think she'd run mad, to fling herself at him after all these years—although she yearned to do it.

"Children had stripped the lower branches by the time I got there. I'll go back with a stepping stool later."

"I'll do it for you if you like," he said.

"Oh, no," she said, embarrassed by what he must think was her childishness. "It's a cold, damp day and a long way, and you have to be at the station when Simon arrives."

"My leg's not bothering me today," he said quietly. "And even if it was, I can ride."

"Oh, I know, I know," she said too quickly. "But you don't have to trouble yourself. Truly. It's my pleasure, you know."

She cast a worried glance at him. He didn't seem to be in pain, although a west wind often caused his old war wound to ache like a bad memory. He had a slight limp. Damp and cold made it worse. She often thought that the one small impediment must vex him even more because he was otherwise all grace and fluid movement. She thought that was why he made far too much of it when it was new. It had taken her weeks of coaxing and joking to get him to partner her in the waltz that long-past summer.

"You're *supposed* to slip and sway when you waltz. Dips are built right into it," she'd argued. "I don't doubt you'll be better at it than anyone there because of your leg," she'd insisted as he'd sat beside her, laughing, the lines of pain in his face momentarily erased by his merriment.

He had eventually danced with her. And she had been so overjoyed to find herself in his arms that she hadn't had to say a word—hadn't dared to—her stunned delight was so obvious.

He paused by the door and looked down at her now.

"I could get you the mistletoe," he said again. "I've time, if you wish."

"*I* could drive to the station to collect our son and his guest, you know," she said as gravely. "But I've my jobs, and you have yours." And the wind was picking up, and though he denied it, she knew his leg could not be entirely free of pain, not with more snow coming. She listed her chores: "I have to get the mistletoe, visit Zoe and promise her I'll send Simon to her straightaway when he arrives, set Philip some tasks so he doesn't go mad with boredom, get Mother's and Father's rooms set just the way they like them, see to the puddings and cookies, and make sure Cook has everything—and then set out all the ornaments for that walloping great tree. Christmas used to be simpler," she complained. "Our queen has given me a great deal more work to do, now that we must drag in a whole tree as well as half the woodland at Christmastime."

"And how you hate that," he said gently, "don't you, little ladybird?"

Her gaze grew tender as his half smile was. He'd called her that on their wedding night, when she'd been so ashamed of all the freckles on her white skin. "Ladybird," he'd breathed as he'd taken her two hands in his to stop her covering herself. "Ladybird," he'd said against her skin as he'd kissed each tiny one of them as she'd shivered in shocked embarrassment and sheer delight. "My own little speckled ladybird. Fly away home, to me."

She shivered now, in sweet remembrance. He knew it, and dropped a light kiss on her cheek. She held his shoulders for a moment, closing her eyes and breathing in the clean scent of him. Then she remembered herself and her duties.

"Off with you," she said brusquely. "I've work to do, and so do you."

"Yes, ma'am," he said, then added as he began to walk away, "Oh, yes, I've set Martin and the lads to cleaning up the stables for you."

She looked at him in puzzlement.

"In the spirit of the season," he said with a smile, "though I didn't tell them why. But there is a certain *un*superstitious young woman, who doesn't believe in mistletoe, who nevertheless manages to pay a visit to the stables every Christmas Eve—and has since she was a tot—to hear the animals talk. As they are supposed to do."

Her fair skin turned holly-berry red. To think he knew that! And had never said, not in all these years.

"Nonsense," she said gruffly. "I only go to give them a carrot or a bit of sugar cake. Christmas, you know."

"Oh, I know," he said, laughing, as he strolled away.

She drove the pony cart into town. She didn't have to; any of the servants would have done her chores for her. But she was too excited and anxious to sit still. Simon was coming home! He'd been at school for months, but for this brief beautiful holiday season he'd be hers again. She was too impulsive and she knew it, but she couldn't just sit and wait for him. She had to be doing something. Last-minute Christmas chores were a wonderful excuse.

She waved at the vicar and his glamorous guest as she saw them standing in conversation in front of the old church. It was as old as the religion itself in this area, but not a famous place. It was too ancient to appeal to more than scholars, and though it was beautiful, it wasn't ornate. Famous men and kings had prayed and been buried elsewhere. In fact, Miles was the most elevated man in the vicinity. That thought made her smile, because a less conceited fellow would be hard to find anywhere. Her own father, the squire, had more self-importance than did the viscount Southwood.

She kept smiling as she drove down the main street—the only street. It was a very small village, a collection of old tilted shops and eccentric cottages. But everyone was proud of the fact that an eminent journal had once called it one of the prettiest towns in all England. Not a shop that didn't have flowers in front of it in summer. Nor one that wasn't swagged with green now. The snow powdered it over until it looked more like a gingerbread treat than an actual town. It didn't offer a single thing that couldn't be found cheaper and in more quantity in London. But she and Miles preferred it to London. The city made her nervous, and although Miles had cut a dash in his youth there, he'd come home from the war and said he never longed for it again.

She waved to John Phelps, the blacksmith, as she passed his shop, and found friendly hands to take the reins for her when she stopped the horse and stepped out to shop. She bought extra candies and spices, threads and spools at Jessup's emporium, and was given holiday greetings with her purchases. Then she went into *The Fox and Glove*, the village's only inn. It was tiny, but so old and well preserved it had actually been noted in a guidebook once. Mr. Apple, the proprietor, served excellent ale and the finest cider in the county. Or so everyone claimed. They ought to know, since everyone in town eventually ended up there sometime during the day.

"A glass of the finest elixir ever coaxed from an apple, my lady?" Alfred the innkeeper asked with a wink when she stepped inside his snug parlor.

He didn't have to ask. But like his father before him, he always did. She grinned and accepted a glass of cider. "Happy Christmas!" everyone said, just as they did in the street when she left—as if they wouldn't be seeing her on Christmas Eve, when the carolers went through the village and then on up to The Hall.

She'd see them again at the church on Christmas Day. And then at The Hall. Everyone in town, all their tenants, most of Miles's family, and all of their friends—they'd all wend their way to The Hall during the holiday. Only her own family was coming to actually stay at The Hall. And her son! she thought with glee as she took up the reins again. Simon was coming home!

She returned to The Hall just as two other coaches pulled up in the drive. One held Miles and Simon, and another boy. Maude scrambled from the gig and stood in the drive with a great, glad, foolish smile on her face. But no one saw her.

Simon clambered down from the coach.

"There he is! I say! Why, look, there he is!"

Maude's father called, pounding with his cane, making his laborious way down the little stair of his coach.

"Dear boy, dear boy!" Maude's mother sang. She scurried from the coach and, bustling past her husband, got to her grandson first. After a shrug at the boy still sitting on the driver's seat of the carriage, Simon gallantly allowed himself to be swallowed up by the attentions of both his grandparents.

"I say, he's grown!" Maude's father said as Miles stepped down. He slapped Miles on the shoulder to congratulate him on his son.

"Like the veriest weed," Miles agreed, smiling.

"But what's this I hear about Philip being ill?" Maude's mother asked, looking from Simon to Miles with anxiety.

"A trifle, a nothing, don't fret," Miles said calmly, knowing they would; knowing that having lost two fine boys in their prime, they'd panic at a hint of illness in their darling grandchildren.

Her mother looked up to see Maude and immediately demanded, "Have you had the doctor in?"

But Maude was watching Simon. He'd grown. She'd seen it when she'd last visited the school, but it was more apparent here, where he'd taken his first steps. He hadn't grown tall so much as he'd lengthened: his body contours changing from those of a boy to a young man, losing softness and gaining length of limb, and just beginning to show true shoulders. He'd always resembled Miles, but now he was beginning to look like a relative she had met but couldn't quite place. He was changing, and a part of her ached for the little boy she'd been waiting for.

"Simon," she said, only that.

He saw her then. She put out her arms, expecting him to run to her and hug her, as always. He took a step—then hesitated. He looked back at the boy sitting high on the carriage.

"Come along, Tim," he said. "Hello, Mother," he continued calmly, then, and walked to her. He let her hug him, and as she did, she felt shoulders and elbows and bones, and not the wonderfully warm boy she'd sent away.

"Mother, this is Timothy Plummer, from Kent. His father's abroad, as I wrote in my letter."

"Good of you to have me, ma'am. Terribly pleased. Lonely back at the school, don't you know," the boy said nervously. He was a thin lad with spectacles and a tentative smile. Maude remembered then: he'd no mother, and nowhere to go for the holidays. If he had, if he hadn't come to her, maybe Simon would have hugged her back and chattered to her the way he used to, instead of standing like a stick, enduring her. She resented the boy being there. And hated herself for it.

"Well, then, welcome, Master Plummer. I've got your rooms ready," she said quickly. "But Simon, first—see that pink blob bouncing up and down in the parlor window? That's your brother. He's been sick and so he's not allowed out for another day. He's on fire to see you. After you escape his sticky fingers—Cook's been plying him with jam tarts, the way she used to do to you when you were ill—there's your sister. Poor Zoe looks like she's coming down with the same thing. She's in bed, *breathlessly* awaiting you."

"What?" the squire said, stopping, his cane hitting the ground like it was struck there with a mallet.

"Zoe's in bed, Father. Nothing serious. I think she's getting the cold Philip had," Maude explained.

"Then Simon mustn't see her, until the thing blossoms, or goes away entirely," her mother said.

"Certainly not!" her father trumpeted.

"But she's been desperate to see him," Maude argued, "and it's only a cold."

"*You* can say that?" her mother asked.

There was a silence. Only a second of silence, and after only four words. But there was a world of pain opened up.

"Of course you're quite right," Maude said dully, looking away from her parents. "We'll wait to see how she feels in the morning. There's time enough. She'll see him tomorrow night—or Christmas morning. It will be her present."

She hurried to the house alone. But Miles was soon by her side.

"She meant nothing by it," he said quietly.

"Of course she did," she said in wonder at his foolishness, and then fled into the house before he could try to deny it again.

She wouldn't let it ruin her Christmas. It was a thing, like her husband's lame leg that he'd had to cope with, that she had to learn to live with, however much it pained her. She'd make the holiday merry, because she, of all women, knew how tenuous happiness was, how fleeting it could be. And so she kept herself so busy she had no time to fret or chat with her parents or children until it was time to dress for dinner.

"You look very nice in that, is it new?" Miles asked.

He leaned against the door, looking in at her. She was dressing as best she could without her maid. She'd sent Betsy away after she'd laced her stays. There was too much to do this afternoon; the girl could be better occupied than wasting time trying to make her mistress look beautiful.

"This?" Maude asked, looking down at her gown as if seeing it for the first time. It was crimson velvet, a daring color for a lady with auburn hair. But it was a deep, rich shade, as close to black as it was to blood-red, and it made her eyes green as the great tree she'd decorated. The skirt swept wide and full as the bottom of that tree. The gown showed off her white shoulders, and its wide sleeves accentuated how narrow the waist was. She turned in place to let him see. She thought of her usual game, of saying, "This old thing?" But she needed more than his laughter tonight.

"I had it made for the holiday," she said. "It was my gift to me."

"No, I don't think so," he said, levering a shoulder off the door and reaching her in a few long, uneven steps. "No. It is your gift to me."

He held her close as she held him, and when his lips left her cheek and sought her lips, she sighed against his mouth before she surrendered all thought and feeling to him.

"No," he eventually muttered, as his hand left her breast. "Too much to do," he said on a shaky breath, stepping back. "But if you would wear things that were sensible instead of merely beautiful, we could have made something of it."

She opened her eyes in anger and saw the laughter in his.

"I distinctly felt buckram and whalebone as well as cotton and silk and whatnot beneath that velvet second skin of yours," he said. "Getting you out of it would be a pleasure. But back into it again? Before dinner?"

"*That* is, supposing I intended to get out of it now," she said haughtily, putting her nose in the air as she straightened her gown and swept from the room. But she felt much better.

She stopped in to visit with a sad and sleepy Zoe.

Her fever had gone down, and she was cranky only because she missed seeing her dear Simon.

"Tomorrow, Christmas Eve, I promise," Maude said. *"If* you've no fever and are bright-eyed as I know you can be if you get enough sleep tonight. Then there'll be nothing wrong with you seeing Simon. But you know how Grandmother and Grandfather are."

"I know." Zoe said on a weary little sniff. "But I am not a—a *pestilence,* like Philip said."

"No," Maude said, smiling. Then she remembered that neither had she been a pestilence, but still there were always two bonny ghosts at her side at Christmastime, sadly watching her grow older than they had ever been. "No, never," she said more softly as she kissed her goodnight. "But now you rest and be better, and all will be well."

Maude went down the stairs to hear that more company had arrived. Their voices announced them better than the butler could. It was the rest of her family. She sighed.

Cousin George and his wife were already in the salon, asking the children the questions they always did, and nodding as they didn't listen to their answers. Their own two sons sat in a corner of the room, ignoring their younger cousins with as much boredom as they did each other. Both obviously thought themselves too good for the family they were in. They were dressed with care in cutaway coats and embroidered waistcoats with double rows of buttons, outsized winged collars, and high cravats. One studied the ceiling, and the other an unread book held in a languid hand. But since they were both plump and heavy featured and resembled their parents as closely as piglets did their littermates, their attempt at bored sophistication looked like little more than acute indigestion.

Her parents nodded with pleasure as they listened to George explaining something to the children. Maude heaved another sigh. George was always explaining something to someone. The fact that he was usually right didn't make it any better. Not for the first time, she wondered why the idea of having the family all together at Christmas was always so much better than the reality of it. She loved them all, and not having them with her at this joyous season would have pained her. But it was always a shock to discover how much having them always did pain her.

Maude told herself it was a very *small* family, after all. She stepped forward to greet them. And then froze in the doorway as she heard a trill of unfamiliar laughter. It stopped her in her tracks, and she tilted her head the way that a rabbit does when it hears the high, keening cry of a hunting hawk overhead. Because it was delicious laughter—light, giddy, artificial, flirtatious laughter. A quick glance showed her Miles standing in deep conversation with a woman. An unknown woman. His wide shoulders blocked her face, but Maude could see the bell of a golden gown in front of his long, black-trousered legs.

She wasn't a jealous woman. Even though she knew she wasn't worthy of Miles, she didn't begrudge other women eyeing him or seeking him out on all sorts of ruses at village picnics and parties. She might as well resent people gaping at her house or gardens. He was simply worthy of attention. He'd never given her real cause to worry about his faithfulness—he couldn't help it if it was her nature to worry about why he stayed constant to her.

But something elemental in her nature stirred now. Maybe it was the way Miles stood as he spoke with the unseen guest, his head to the side—as her own was as she listened to a new burst of that trilling laughter. He was enchanted. Or fascinated. She could see it in his stance. And in the way his head was inclined, politely, but also as though to catch every note of that silvery laughter. She looked upward at the swags of evergreen over the heads of the couple, and was suddenly delighted to remember that with all the fuss of getting the house ready she had forgotten to get the mistletoe.

She also remembered that she was wearing her new gown. And that the light of the winter evening subdued the color of her hair until one could almost think it was brown or black—not the despised, unfashionable red she was afflicted with. She looked as well as she ever had—or could, she thought. And so she took in a deep breath and walked into the room prepared for anything—except for not being noticed at all.

Cousin George was expounding about why steam engines would never replace the horse, and his wife stood at his side, bored and inattentive as ever. But since Simon and his friend were obviously bursting with impatience for a chance to refute him, none of them saw Maude come in. Or cared, if they did, she thought as she walked past them. Her parents had gotten Philip to themselves, and were being entertained by him. Not a hard task, Maude thought, since all Philip had to do was to breathe in and out to accomplish that. They didn't so much as look up as she passed by.

And Miles was talking with the most beautiful woman Maude had ever seen—aside from those shown on the top of chocolate boxes. She had golden hair and larkspur-blue eyes, alabaster skin and a gown that showed as much of it as was descent. She had a deep bosom and an even tinier waist than Maude did, even laced up as she was. But she was much taller, Maude thought with incredulous envy, and every statuesque inch of her was willowy and graceful in spite of her sumptuous bosom. She belonged in miniature, on the top of the newly cut Christmas tree, or gracing the label on an expensive soap. She was merely magnificent, Maude decided. And obviously fascinating Miles, because Maude was certain he'd never have noticed her as she came and stood by his elbow if those celestial eyes hadn't turned to look at her, causing him to turn to see what she saw.

"Oh, there you are. Cressida, let me introduce you to my wife. My dear, this is Cressida Lampert. Cressida, my wife, Lady Maude."

Maude inclined her head, but the beautiful Cressida curtsied. It was so gracefully done Maude wondered if she were a dancer.

"My dear Lady Maude," Cressida said in a beautifully modulated voice, with undertones of amusement, "how very good to meet you at last. I've always wondered what the fortunate lady Miles decided upon looked like. Now I know. You see, I've envied you half my life, my dear," she said with a gurgle of irresistible, throaty laughter.

Maude could only stand there, shocked. And jealous. Because she could never say such a thing, even if she'd ever thought it. Only such a woman could. And because there was absolutely nothing clever she could think to say in answer. She could only stand there with a stupid grin and say, "Oh. Oh, really?" before she could think to ask, "Have—have you known each other very long?"

"A long while ago," Miles said, just as Cressida said sadly, "Yes, Long—and well."

Miles grew still.

"Oh, you've never told her!" Cressida exclaimed as she saw Maude staring up at Miles in confusion. "Oh, dear, that makes it even more ... We were engaged to be wed, once upon a time," she told Maude.

"Before I went to war," Miles said.

"And after," Cressida put in quickly, and Miles frowned.

"Not long after," he said, and Cressida looked at him in hurt surprise.

Maude began to feel that neither of them knew she was in the room anymore, and curiously like she was a little girl listening to adults talking about something she oughtn't know.

"Oh, I see," she stammered, though she didn't, and suddenly didn't want to anymore.

"My brother, that rogue over there in the corner," Cressida said, tilting one shapely shoulder toward a niche near the fireplace where two men Maude hadn't noticed were sitting, deep in conversation, "was a companion-in-arms with Miles. They were in the same unit and then fought in the Peninsula together. We were leaving a friend's house in Torquay, on our way to London for Christmas. But one of the horses threw a shoe and while we were having it seen to in that charming little village of yours, Charles remembered Miles lived nearby. He had the notion of dropping in to pay a call. Just for a Christmas greeting. And yet this rogue," she said, smiling up at Miles, "insisted we stay to dinner. I hope it's no inconvenience?"

No more than the moon loosing from its moorings in the sky and crashing down into the dining room, Maude thought, but smiled and said, "Good heavens, no! It would be our pleasure."

She was widowed. She was wealthy. And she'd never forgotten Miles. Cressida was merely magnificent, Maude thought, her head aching as dinner wore on.

Soup gave way to fish, which made room for shellfish and aspics, which in turn gave way to meat and fish patties and cutlets, and on to fowls, with only a token nod to the hostess . . . who didn't know what she was eating, if she was eating, she was so busy thinking and watching.

Malign Fate had seated the marvelous Cressida at her host's right hand, down the table from Maude. Because Maude would have seated her in the coal bin. But custom said a lady guest must sit next to her host. And that was on the opposite end of the table from her hostess. Maude was stranded at the foot of the table by herself. Or as good as. She'd drawn Cressida's brother on one side, and his friend, Sir Blaise, on the other. Charles had his sister's coloring, but twice her weight, and Sir Blaise was thin, brown, bland and smiled a great deal. But even if she'd been seated with Apollo and Michelangelo's David, both with the conversational skills of angels, she wouldn't have been able to ignore the way Miles and Cressida were carrying on. Well, she had to admit, not so much carrying on as looking to her as if they wished they were.

But things became more interesting when Charles had his sixth glass of wine. "Tolerable, very tolerable, eh Blaise?" he asked, after he'd swallowed it. "Trust Miles to have a nose. And eyes." he said, inclining his bulky body forward as he tried to sketch a bow to Made as he sat. "Women and wine, the fellow's a connoisseur. Absolutely. Always was. He had a way with both, didn't he though?"

"He did, did indeed," Sir Blaise agreed.

"Could have used a nose like that in the family, eh?" Charles said on a gusty, wine-laden sigh. "Richard would drink cat pi—Oh, pardon, my lady. Wine got my tongue, don't you know. But the truth is, my late brother-in-law didn't know distilling from ditch water. Scotch whiskey or French wine, it was all the same to him. Drink it down, and wait for it to smack him silly, that was all he knew." he said, then sighed with pleasure at his refilled glass and drank it down again.

"Women, too," Sir Blaise said. "Miles had an eye. Don't know how Richard got Cressie a'tall. Lucky fellow.

"Got her when she broke with Miles, don't you know," Charles said sadly. "A love match gone wrong, and before he could change his mind, she upped and took Richard. Married him in a fit of pique. Acted in haste, repented at leisure. Hot and hasty. She knows better now. Just look at her now," he said, with the outsized sadness that can be achieved only after seven glasses of wine.

They did.

"Well, then! Lovely, Christmas coming and all," Sir Blaise said, suddenly remembering who they were talking with when he saw Maude's face as she watched Miles and the beautiful Cressida.

But he had never told her! Not a word. She knew about his war experiences. He'd told her those during those first long afternoons, when she'd finally gotten him to talk as she'd paced by his side, trying to get his mind off the pain of trying to walk again. She knew about his experiences with women in London from rumor. But not that he'd been engaged to marry! And to such a paragon.

Cressida held court from her end of the table. She was a wonderful storyteller. She even had Cousin George sitting with his mouth closed, and his two greedy sons stopped feeding long enough to listen with their mouths open. She spoke about her travels in Spain. She had a way of talking about the terrible war with Napoleon as though it had only been a diversion. She could talk about herself and her brother and Miles in the days when they were all young and free in ways that made Maude wish she had been there. Until she realized she'd have been nothing to them then. And maybe still was not. Miles sat listening, too, laughing in the right places, but his grave gray eyes were troubled as he watched Cressida.

The fowl came and its bones went; the roast arrived, was dealt with, and left the table in shambles. Then the desserts were paraded in. They were a disappointment only because the house had been filled with the scents of gingerbread and mince, cinnamon and spicy plums and puddings all day. But those treats were waiting in the wings for Christmas.

So, evidently, was the magnificent Cressida. Because when the ladies left the men to their port, Cressida found her way to her hostess.

"We only meant to stop an hour," she said, coming to sit beside Maude, the golden silk of her skirt making Maude's wine-red gown look merely dark, "and here we've stayed to dinner. Now Miles has asked us to stay the night, because of the hour. I do hope you don't mind."

"Mind?" Maude said. "Heavens, no! It's the very thing." She swallowed hard and smiled as though delighted.

"He mentioned our staying over Christmas, but we've so many obligations in London," Cressida said. "Still . . . we shall see," she said gaily.

Maude knew she ought to second Miles's invitation, for courtesy's sake. She knew she should find a way to ask about that long-vanished engagement, too. Instead, she asked about London as though it were her life's ambition to live there one day.

When the men joined them, they grouped around the piano. They sang carols. At least some did. Cressida's brother and his friend snored bass accompaniment from the depths of their chairs near the fire, in concert with Maude's father. Her mother went to bed early, and Cousin George's two sons sat gobbling sweetmeats and trying to look pained.

Maude wasn't surprised to hear Cressida had a clear, lilting soprano and could sing harmony to any tune. So could Maude, but unintentionally. She never sang, because she loved music and knew she couldn't carry a true tune. So she sat and watched and listened, as always. But not quite as always.

She watched Miles, and couldn't fault him. He was a perfect host. If he smiled at Cressida at all, she couldn't say it was any more tender than his smile at Simon or his old friend Charles, for that matter. If his gaze met Cressida's with approval it was only in the secret, silent language of singers. Maude had often seen and envied the way singers acknowledged each other that way, as if to say, "Isn't this fun? See how we two make this one thing better together?" In truth, only their voices met, touched, toyed, moved with each other, and found joy together. Maude saw that, and knew the fear that gripped her was folly and foolishness. But it was no less keen for that.

Watching Simon was better. She'd missed him badly, not because she doted on him more than the others, but because when he'd left she'd felt his absence like a piece missing out of the puzzle of her life. There'd been no more children after Zoe, though she wouldn't have minded. Simon's leaving had made her realize one day they'd all be gone. Then it would be just herself and Miles again. She wondered if that would be enough for him now. After all, she no longer had youth to recommend her, or the promise of a new family in her.

Miles smiled at her, and often, too. He knew she loved his voice. So he sang on. But he sang with Cressida. And Cressida sparkled in the gaslight like the frost on the outside of the windows of the warm room.

When it was time for the boys to go to bed, Maude excused herself from the room, saying she had to see Zoe . . . and not saying she didn't want to keep seeing Miles and Cressida. She managed to intercept Simon on the stair as he was dashing up to bed.

"I forgot the mistletoe," she said breathlessly.

Simon paused and looked at his friend. "Yes, I saw," he said.

"I didn't forget it at first," she explained. "Children had stripped the lower branches. I couldn't reach the higher ones and was going to come back with a step stool, but then I forgot."

"The local people believe mistletoe from our wood is best," Simon told his friend. "Because there's a holy well there. The vicar says it was in a Druid's grove once."

"Oh, keen!" his friend said.

"My mother's superstitious," Simon explained, with a slight blush.

"I'm not," Maude said. "It's tradition. I'd hate to have Christmas without it. Will you come with me in the morning and harvest some? You don't have to," she said, grinning. "You can always dare to be the first in the family to have Christmas without mistletoe from the grove."

He looked at the other boy again, and she grew impatient. Couldn't he do anything without looking for his friend's reaction?

"Well . . . certainly," he said, finally.

She held out her arms so she could gather him in and kiss him goodnight. But he grew tense at her first touch. She hesitated. It would be absurd to shake his hand. She settled for kissing his forehead, and then watched him race upstairs with his friend. She was almost bowled over by Philip as he tore after them, eager to be invited to his brother's room so he could chat with the older fellows. She stopped him for a quick hug and a kiss, thought about insisting he go to bed at the proper time, and then sighed. She remembered how brief the holiday was, how brief boyhood itself was. She walked up the stairs very slowly.

Zoe was sleeping. Daisy, the nursery maid, whispered, "Cool as a cucumber, my lady. She'll be right as rain in the morning, just you see."

"Then off you go to bed," Maude said. "I'll stay with her awhile."

"Oh, no, ma'am," Daisy said in shock. "I'll stay the night, to be sure."

Daisy was as much part of the family as the house itself. She felt an outsized obligation to the family. Dismissing her for the night would hurt as much as dismissing her from service. Her mother, Lucy, had been a downstairs maid with a problem—in the shape of an unborn Daisy. Maude hadn't considered it such. Keeping a good housemaid on in spite of her having a child out of wedlock hadn't been a burden. Others might not have agreed, but Maude made her own rules and judged people by them. She'd judged right. Daisy's father had eventually shown up. He'd made an excellent stable man, after he became a husband as well as father. Although Daisy was young, she was wonderful with Zoe.

Maude looked wistfully at Zoe. She wished she could have some hours alone now, watching her youngest child sleep; there was warm peace in that that she needed tonight. But even that sanctuary was breached.

"How's our girl?" a voice from the door demanded. The squire's whisper was like the whisper of a storm through the pines.

"*Shh!*" her mother hissed, louder than the question she was shushing.

"Mama?" Zoe murmured, swimming up from sleep.

"See, there? Now you've waked the child," Maude's mother said triumphantly. "Now, now, Zoe, my love. You'll be alright."

"She *is* all right," Maude said, but she might as well have spoken to herself.

"How's Grandmother's best girl?" her mother cooed as she sat on the bed and a sleepy Zoe scrambled into her arms.

"She's hot as a furnace!" Maude's mother said in alarm.

"Flushed with sleep, Mum. She was cool as could be moments ago," Daisy protested.

"Nonsense, feel her forehead!" Maude's mother demanded.

"Hot," the squire agreed.

"Cool!" Maude insisted.

Zoe's eyes, beneath a forehead covered by so many hands, grew wide.

"Oh, dear! Have I come at the wrong time?" a sweet voice asked.

They all grew still and looked at the vision in the doorway to the nursery. The firelight's shadows flirted with Cressida, outlining her golden curls, making her gown radiant. Zoe's eyes grew even wider. She was groggy and a little frightened by all the sudden attention, and the wonderful lady, who looked like a fairy out of one of her bedtime books, was smiling at her.

Zoe automatically held out her arms, and Cressida floated across the room like thistledown to settle beside her.

"She might be coming down with something," Maude's mother warned, but in a smaller voice than she'd used with Maude. Maude wondered if that was because she wasn't sure she wanted to save Cressida from whatever contagion Zoe had, or if she was as intimidated by Cressida as Maude herself was.

"Miles said she was fine," Cressida said, as though that settled it. "He said he and her brothers had visited her earlier and stuffed her with sweetmeats. That could give anyone a difficult night. Isn't that so, little chick?" she asked sweetly, taking Zoe's two hands and smiling down into her transfixed face.

The worst of it, Maude thought, was that they looked so right together: blond and radiant Cressida, with the baby girl with a headful of fair curls in her arms, intent on each other.

Maude's mother stared at them for a moment. "He did, did he?" was all she said, in an awful voice, before she took her husband's arm and stalked from the room, intent on finding Miles.

"Sweet chick, poor babe, Zoe-Zoe dearest," Cressida murmured, as Zoe stared at her, charmed by the lilting nonsense. "Are you sick? No, I don't think so. Are you sleepy? Oh, I do think so. Let me sing you a little sleepyhead song. Yes?"

She began to sing a pretty little tune, light as the snow that fell outside the windows, drowsy as the cozy room they were in, all to do with little lambs. She sang sweetly, in a soft, breathy voice. As Zoe listened, her eyes were shuttered once by her long lashes, and then again, and then she dozed in Cressida's arms. Cressida sang on. And Maude stood in the shadows and felt as though she might as well have not been there. So she left.

Maude lay stiff and cold in bed, though she was covered by eiderdown and wore a long flannel nightgown. She decided to pretend she was sleeping when he came to bed. If he touched her, she'd mutter and turn away as though she were too sleepy to do anything else. If he persisted, she'd pretend she was having an awful time waking up, so that he'd know that even if he woke her, it would be like making love to a statue. Not that it had ever happened. His lightest touch could always rouse her, his lips could bring her up from a coma, she thought; the feel of his hard body against hers could raise her from the dead, she believed. But tonight, she'd pretend she was sleeping like the dead.

Because she didn't know what to say. She couldn't ask why he'd never said a word about a woman he'd loved and almost married. At least not yet. Not without sounding hurt, or petty, or catty. Nor could she fight something that wasn't anything. Or at least might not be. She didn't want to seem to be such a poor creature as to envy a woman who was only beautiful and kind, witty and sweet, and still wholly in love with him. And too, she thought nervously, sometimes an unjust accusation led to mischief—if it became inspiration.

He came in quietly, much later, and undressed by the fire. They slept in the same room, in the same bed. He didn't have a valet. He often said one of the greatest joys of living in the countryside was that they didn't have to worry about any fashion but their own. She watched through slitted eyes as he took off his clothes. It was unnatural, she knew, but the sight of his naked body still thrilled her—even after all these years. But it wasn't the same body she was watching now, after all.

Now he was no longer all supple masculine grace, like the statue of a youthful Mercury she'd seen in Florence on their honeymoon. Now he was the adult Achilles, his body all experience and tough male muscle. Even the terrible scars on his leg no longer pained her to see, they were as familiar to her as the bark on a sturdy tree.

His body had changed, but she thought it had gotten better. As had their lovemaking. It wasn't the sweet shock of the new that so enticed her now. It was that he had learned every way to please her, as she had him. They always made love on cold winter nights like this, the snow without making it so much cozier within. And always found joy in each other at this joyous season. It was an old joke of theirs: the best Christmas present of all. It would be hard to refuse him tonight. But her heart ached with confused jealousy even as her traitor body roused at the sight of him. She saw his broad chest and narrow waist and that which the firelight caressed and showed to be growing as roused as she herself was. But no.

She'd pretend to sleep no matter what he did, try as he might, she thought. And turned away from him to lie on her side, before she could change her mind.

He came to the bed. She knew he was looking down at her. She heard him breathe a heavy sigh. Then he got into bed, turned on his side away from her, and within moments, he slept. Leaving her to lie awake until the fire died, thinking of why he'd not even tried to rouse her.

He was gone when Maude awoke. Staying up half the night fretting had made her oversleep. She rose and looked out the window. A thin snow was still falling. She scrambled into a heavy woolen gown. It was old and faded and had flannel petticoats instead of lace ones, but she doubted Saint Ethelinda would care how fashionably dressed she was. That was the only adult who might see her this morning, if she was quick about it.

Cousin George and his family slept until noon, and dressed until teatime. She was sure Cressida would sleep until noon, too, as elegant ladies did. Maude paused for a moment to fret about how many more days Cressida would be there. The thought of sharing Christmas with her was terrible. But if she could endure Cousin George and his family each year, she thought, she could endure one radiantly beautiful woman who . . . She was suddenly grateful for all the chores she had to do.

When she went into the nursery Zoe was sitting up in bed.

"How's my little girl this shiny morning?" Maude asked brightly.

"I'm fine," Zoe said in a sturdy little voice. She peered over Maude's shoulder as Maude bent to feel her forehead. And angled away from her kiss, frowning. "Where's the pretty lady?" she asked.

Maude's smile slipped, even though Zoe seemed wholly well again.

"Now, Zoe-Zoe," Daisy said, "remember? She said she'd see you later today. Must be patient. Come, get up and we'll have a wash. Is that alright, Mum?" she asked Maude.

Zoe-Zoe? But no one had ever called Zoe *Zoe-Zoe* before, Maude thought, startled. "Oh. Yes," she managed to answer absently. "Fine."

Children were very impressionable, she told herself as she peeked in Philip's room to see how he was. He was already gone. He had looked "right as rain this

morning, ma'am," the butler assured her. Even his
grandparents had seen that. And so they'd promptly
taken him out for a ride in their carriage, to keep him
from "mucking about in the snow and getting sick
again."

Maude smiled, and skimmed down the stairs to meet
Simon. She'd miss breakfast rather than make him wait
to go harvest mistletoe with her. She hummed to herself as she thought of her other chores. Presents to
wrap. Be sure the punch bowl is glittering clean, she
cautioned herself, because the carolers would be in for
some after the wassailing tonight. And, yes, don't forget baskets for old Terrence and the Reeds, their poor-
est and proudest tenants. The poor felt need and the
shame of needing more keenly at this time of year. But
they couldn't be offended if their baskets were over-
filled, because Christmas giving didn't look like
charity—if you were clever about it. So, a turkey for
the Reeds *and* a ham, along with woolen goods. And
two sweaters for old Terrence this year, and a stout
new scarf to go with the usual treats, yes, and the bundles for the parish poor ... but first, the greens—for
the luck of the season.

But Simon and his friend were nowhere to be seen,
although he'd known she'd be waiting for him. Then
she remembered where he always liked to wait. She
threw on an old, warm, hooded cloak, picked up her
wicker basket, and hurried out to the stables.

But he wasn't in the stable yard.

"Left an hour past," Daisy 's father told her, "with
the whole company, my lady."

"Whole company?" Maude asked.

"Aye. The master and his friends. The lot of them:
the viscount hisself, the lovely lady and the gents, and

the boys—they all went off together, singing and laughing to wake the dead."

But they hadn't wakened her, Maude thought dazedly. Because she was worse than dead to them—she had been out of sight and mind as though she'd never been at all. She had dreamed of bells and laughter and light, airy voices singing, but had thought it was a dream of the fairy folk. But it had been another bright, cruel company she had overheard.

"And they went . . .?" she asked humbly.

"Don't know, ma'am. They didn't venture to say."

To me, either, she thought. And swallowed. She picked up her chin and walked away calmly. She didn't start to run until she was in the woods, where there was no one to see her, or her face.

When she reached the grove she went to the well, and braced both mittened hands against it, and stared down into the darkness at her distant reflection. It was like looking into a dark mirror. The water reflected her mood: black and still. She'd been running hard, and she bent her head, catching her ragged breath.

It was as if the worst of her nightmares were suddenly true. She was alone on Christmas Eve because no one wanted to be with her. She'd always known she wasn't worth anything. And now they all knew it, too.

Even little Zoe hadn't wanted her. Her parents hadn't for years, poor things, they'd always only been making do. Their grandchildren were the prize they'd won for putting up with her when they'd lost their hearts' desires—because of her. And Simon was no longer a baby who had no one to love but his mother. He'd grown up enough to choose his companions. She was not to be one of them. Philip was on fire to follow in his footsteps. He would. And Miles . . .?

Miles could have had anyone, but he'd chosen her.

Even then she'd thought it might have been pity, or obligation to the memory of her brothers, or out of kindness for the squire's daughter, whose heart was in her eyes every time she'd looked at him. Or maybe because of a sense of honor, once he'd realized he'd passed the whole summer with her, every idle hour. He'd only been whiling away the time until he was well again. But maybe he'd realized that by doing so he'd raised her expectations—and her father's. Had Father spoken to him? She'd always wondered. Now she wondered if she knew at last.

Had Miles asked her to marry him because of a broken heart? Because when he'd seen he couldn't have what he'd always wanted, he'd settled for her?

They'd discussed so much in those days. She'd chattered like a magpie to amuse him when the pain was bad. He'd come home from the glorious wars a shell of his old self: worn and weary, his fine-featured face drawn, his shapely lips thinned by constant pain. She'd been his jester, his newspaper, and then, his audience. She'd listened to him talk as they'd walked—as she'd walked, and he'd had to force each step to accompany her around his grounds. But he'd never mentioned Cressida.

He'd always been kind to her, gentle with her, loving to her. But he was a kind and loving, gentle man. Who had not touched his wife last night. Who had stood by the bed with a troubled gaze instead of taking her in his arms. Who had watched Cressida every minute last night, and then gone off with her today, without a word. As had his son. As his daughter would have, if she could have. Beautiful Cressida. And merely Maudie. It would be laughable if it weren't so sad. He'd never mentioned Cressida, though his eyes said he'd never forgotten her.

It seemed to Maude, then, in that quiet glade alone, that it was all of a piece. That the only difference she'd ever made in anyone's life was in taking up the space of someone else they'd really wanted. One daughter in place of two fine sons. One ordinary mother instead of a fascinating stranger. One plain young woman instead of the woman of his dreams. And now she was not only a substitute, but a positive barrier to happiness. But then, she had never been of any real use, except for harming those she loved, by simply being. She leaned her head against her clenched fists and wept wrenching, silent tears of shame.

"I wish I had never been born!" she whispered passionately as tears rolled down her face unchecked.

One fell a long way, splashing into the well without a sound. The surface of the dark water dimpled as it received it. She didn't notice. But it grew colder.

Eventually, she stopped crying. The snow had stopped, too. But a biting wind blew round the glade, turning soft snow to ice, hanging the old oaks with crystal beards. She drew her cloak closer and wiped the last tears from her eyes. She looked up at the oaks, with their burdens of white-berried, green mistletoe. There was some on the lowest branches that she'd missed seeing, she noticed now. But now her basket weighed her down, empty as it was. Hang the mistletoe! she thought rebelliously. And didn't even giggle at her inadvertent joke as she turned to go home—and saw the heavenly handsome young Mr. Clarence watching her.

Of course, she thought with weary embarrassment, her eyes and nose would be as red as her cheeks now. Not that it mattered. No other man, however handsome, mattered except for Miles. Even now.

"Good afternoon, Mr. Clarence," she said. "Have you come for a wish?"

"Yes," he said, smiling, "I have."

"Then don't let me stop you," she said. "Wishing should be done in private, and I'm just leaving."

"Oh, the wishing's done," he said pleasantly. "But you can't be. Where's the mistletoe? I see, you've forgot the ladder again. It doesn't matter, I'll get you some. I insist."

"And I insist you do not," she said with determination. "I don't want any now. Good day."

"I'll just stroll along with you, then, if I may," he said amiably, and fell into step beside her.

She looked at him out of the side of her eyes. He couldn't be flirting. She was older than he, and he knew she was married, and besides, she didn't have any illusions about herself. He might just be lonely, in a new place so near to Christmas. She didn't feel very companionable, but supposed she had to say something pleasant.

"The well is very old, you know," she said, and stopped. It was an inane thing to say. Of course he knew that; Mr. Potts must have given him chapter and verse on the old well. But he just smiled, and so she kept chattering nonsense to do with the well. She heaved an inward sigh of relief when they neared the vicarage. He was a nice young man, but she hadn't the heart to be sociable now. She'd leave him with Mr. Potts, and hurry home the moment his back was turned.

She saw a figure leave the vicarage and go to the one-horse shay halted in the little drive. She didn't want the vicar driving off before she could detach herself from Mr. Clarence. So she picked up her pace and waved, calling, "Ho! Mr. Potts!

"I didn't want to miss him," she told Mr. Clarence. "I've—I've a Christmas errand to ask of him. A visit to one of our tenants, you see."

It sounded foolish, even to her ears, but she didn't care. Nor did she care for the fact that Mr. Clarence only smiled wider, as though he knew just what she was thinking. It was unsettling. She hurried on.

"Mr. Po—," she began as she approached the vicar. And then paused. It wasn't Mr. Potts at all. At least not the Mr. Potts she knew. This man was much older: a bent, gaunt, gray-faced old fellow who stared at her without recognition. She imagined he might be a relative of the vicar's, because there was some resemblance. But she couldn't even imagine Mr. Potts's ready smile on this narrow, bitter face. He wore unrelieved black, not the magpie, merry assortment of woolens Mr. Potts threw on against the cold.

"Oh. Terribly sorry," Maude said. "I thought you were the vicar."

"I am," the man said abruptly. "What is it you want of me?"

"No. I mean *our* vicar: Mr. Potts," she said.

"I don't know who *your* vicar might be," the man said impatiently, "but I am the *the* vicar, Mr. Potts. What is it you want? I can guess," he said with resignation, looking her up and down, noting her serviceable old cloak and windblown hair, "but charity is given on Christmas Day, and there's little enough to go around. First choice goes to those who live around here, anyway. So you might as well be on your way, young woman."

Maude gaped at him. Then she shook her head to clear it. She took in a deep breath, straightened her spine, and said in an awful voice copied from her mother at her worst, "I beg your pardon? I am the Viscountess Southwood. And who may you be, my good man?"

"I may be calling for someone to cart you back to Bedlam, where you belong," he said in annoyance. "No more nonsense now. Get you gone, missy, and be quick about it."

Now she was speechless.

"Well? Be off with you!"

"Where's Mr. Potts?" she said fearfully. "What have you done with him?"

"Look, girl, no more of this! I've better things to do than stand here and listen to your foolishness." His words were hard but his eyes were concerned—for a moment. "Tcha! Drunk, that's it," he exclaimed with sudden inspiration. "Well, if so young woman, then this cold wind will sober you up soon enough," he told her irritably. "But I haven't had a drop, and my bones are colder than charity. So good day to you."

"But I'm not drunk!" she protested.

"Whatever you are, I'm not interested," he said, turning as if to go. But he glanced back and saw her staring at him in incomprehension. He clucked his tongue in vexation.

"Are you deaf as well as drunk or mad? Just my luck. As if there weren't enough sorrow in this world," he grumbled to himself in exasperation, "and my lot weren't hard enough this time of year. Now mad strangers . . . Well, I haven't the time, even if I had enough pity or patience left to deal with it. Enough. Go on, be gone, be gone now," he told her, a distinct threat in his voice as he flapped his bony hands at her.

She backed away a step, afraid of physical harm for the first time in her life. But she couldn't leave yet; it wasn't in her nature to give up so easily.

"But—Mr. Potts is the vicar here," she said, her eyes

wide and dark with fear. Perhaps it moved him, because he seemed to relent, and spoke to her again, although grudgingly.

"Aye. I've been vicar here for twenty years, the more bad luck," he muttered. "It's a poor living, in a poor parish, with few worshipers and a mad master, but such is my lot."

"But my husband, the viscount, appointed the vicar here when he first came into his honors," she said.

"That much is true. The viscount did, damn his black soul. But if you've a mind to indulge in wild fancies, young woman, I'd suggest you imagine a demon lover as a husband instead of Southwood. Even a demon would be better. You may be many things to the viscount—most of them things decent men wouldn't speak of, I don't doubt—but wife, you are not. He never married, thank God for that. One of his stripe is enough. He's the last of his line—the last legitimate one, anyway. Now be gone!" he snapped. "I don't know why I even troubled to talk to you, with the wind biting so keen, and me with so many desperate errands to do for decent people before I can get back to my meager fire. Leave, and don't think you can pass the night in a haystack, either. They're a fierce lot around here. There's little to go round, as I said. I don't know what they'd do to you if they thought you were trying to share it with them. No, I don't *want* to know what they'd do."

Then he marched off to his carriage, got in, gave the horse the whip, and drove off. Leaving Maude to stare after him. When she was sure he was gone, she went to the door of the little house and sounded the knocker. She knocked on the doors and tapped on the windows, going round and round the old house, calling. No one answered. There wasn't even a yip from Mr. Potts's fussy old pug.

"I don't understand," she murmured at last. Then she saw Mr. Clarence looking at her with sympathy. "He was so rude. And where's Mr. Potts? I'll go straight home and ask Miles. . . ." She paused and flushed and then raised her chin and said, "But he's not home just at the moment. So I'll have to go into town and find out. It's a way, but I'll walk."

She marched out into the road. Mr. Clarence fell into step beside her.

"And another strange thing," she said, almost to herself. "Why . . . why, he acted as though he didn't even see you, Mr. Clarence."

"He didn't wish to," Mr. Clarence said simply.

Maude shot him a puzzled look and was about to speak when she saw a lone figure standing in the old churchyard.

"Oh, good!" she cried in relief. "Look, there's Daisy. My nursery maid," she said before she picked up her skirts and ran through the snow toward Daisy. She had to weave to avoid all the mottled old gravestones age had thinned to wafers. They leaned in random drunken patterns in the hilly graveyard. The frost must have made the ground heave, she thought absently, because they usually stood tall as sentinels against the centuries.

"Daisy!" she sang in sudden relief. And then, "Daisy?" she asked in astonishment.

Because Daisy had chosen strange clothes to wear to the churchyard. She had a thin coat trimmed with ratty fur at the sleeves and the breast, and wore it open, despite the cold. She had on a tight, stained red gown more suitable for evening under it. Daisy's sandy hair was frizzed into clumsy curls, and her young face was covered with badly applied rouge. And she was wearing lipcolor!

Daisy startled and backed away, afraid. "Yes'm?" she asked warily.

"What are you doing here? Who's with Zoe?"

"I couldn't say, ma'am," Daisy said nervously.

"You couldn't say? What's the meaning of this? Have you lost your mind, Daisy?"

"No, ma'am," Daisy said anxiously as she backed off. "I never meant to be in the way, I swear I didn't. I waited till they was all gone, 'specially him, Old Potts. He'd skin me if he found me here. But it's Christmas," she said, pleadingly. "I just had to come to say Merry Christmas to Mum."

"Well, why don't you go home and do that? Daisy, are you alright? Who did you leave Zoe with?"

"Me? I'm fine," Daisy said with a little more confidence, stopping to stare at Maude. "It's you maybe you should be worried about. And I told you, I don't know no Zoe."

"Don't know . . . ? Are you feverish, Daisy?" Maude demanded.

"No, I ain't. And I tell you, ma'am, I don't know you neither. Nor do you know me. Because if you did you wouldn't be telling me to go home and say hello to my Mum, 'cause she's buried right here, and all the world knows it, and the only home I got is that room in the back of The Fox and Glove, and everyone knows that, too."

"Back of the inn?" Maude asked in confusion. "What would you be doing there? You've left us to work for the Apples? But you're too young, surely."

"Too young? You are dicked in the nob, ma'am, and no mistake. Fourteen ain't too young for what I do,"

Daisy said wearily. "Some gents like them even younger."

"What are you saying? Daisy, your mama would be appalled by how you're behaving. As am I. I can't understand it."

Daisy's face grew cold, and she suddenly looked much older than she was. "Easy enough to understand," she said angrily. "Ma got cast out of The Hall when she got with me. She worked like a slave at the inn—only just doing the floors and housework, mind, 'cause there's few gents who want a wench who's about to drop a babe. Just like there's none who'll keep a housemaid on if she carries a babe without a name. She worked herself to death, and that's an actual fact. They brought me up there and had me working on my knees, too, and on my back, but not at scrubbing floors," she said bitterly, "when I turned ten. They start them even younger in London. I guess I got that to be grateful for this Christmas. That—and the fact that whatever I am, I know what I am. Not like you. Here's something for the season. Buy yourself some hot soup, and keep your mouth closed. They'll have you in Bedlam for sure if they hear you. Goodbye, and Happy Christmas to you, poor lady."

Daisy dropped a coin in Maude's hand and then fled down the snowy hill, back toward the village.

Maude stood watching her in shock.

"I must go back and tell them poor Daisy's in a taking," she muttered at last. "I suppose someone's watching Zoe, but I must go back to The Hall at once and tell them about poor Daisy. Do you think she's run mad?" Maude asked fearfully.

"I think you should read that first," Mr. Clarence said quietly, pointing to the stone Daisy had left one ragged artificial flower on.

Lucy Standish
1803–1826
May God Forgive Her

"But Lucy is alive and well, and her name is 'Martin' now!" Maude said in confusion.

"No. She's not. She's buried here. And she never married," Mr. Clarence said quietly, "because no one gave her a chance to live long enough for Joe Martin to come home and take on his obligations. It was a shame and a scandal for an unwed girl to be in her condition. No respectable household would employ her."

"Nonsense!" Maude declared. "*I* kept her on. And he came back two years later, filled with repentance, with a proposal of marriage."

"No," Mr. Clarence said gently, "you didn't. You couldn't. Because you were never born."

Her eyes grew wide and she stared at him. She wanted to run, but she wasn't afraid of him so much as of what he said.

"Your wish," he reminded her gently. "The well always obliges the pure of heart."

"How did you know . . . ? No," she said, backing away from him step by step. She stumbled on a stone, then caught herself, holding on to a crooked tombstone with one hand as the other flew to cover her mouth as she stared at him.

"I know because I came to see to it," he explained. "You weren't happy," he said with a sad smile. "Not really. Not so happy as you deserved to be. So I was sent to see to making this a truly happy Christmas for you. I was charged to do as you wished. And so I have."

He was clearly mad, Maude thought. He didn't look

dangerous, but he was not in his right mind. She gave him one long last disbelieving look and then began to run. It wasn't easy because the snow was so thick, but she stumbled on. She ran toward the village because it was closer than The Hall. She didn't hear him pursuing, but her breath was coming so hard and the snow was so soft underfoot, she wouldn't hear if he were. She could only hope he wasn't violent and wouldn't follow . . . and that she would stop wondering about how he knew.

She stopped when she came to the main street of the village and stood there alone, hand on her heart and head down, dragging in breath until her heart slowed. But then she glanced up and lost her breath again.

The gingerbread town was gone, replaced by a row of shabby, sagging shops. Even Jessup's proud emporium had no wide front window, and no gilt-lettered sign. Half of the shops were boarded up, the others deserted, their windows open, black and gaping, like empty sockets, blind to the empty street in front of them. Which was for the best.

The snow in the street was filthied by soot. Looking up, Maude saw that the clouds themselves seemed muddy and brown, heavy with something other than the promise of snow. The air bore the smells of sulphur and brimstone, not woodsmoke and pine. She wondered if she had died and gone to some version of hell.

Maude began to walk, slowly, woodenly. She went down the street, peering into empty windows, shaking her head, murmuring to herself.

"Something I can do for you?" the man standing in front of the inn said.

Her head came up. Again, she saw someone who looked very much like someone she knew. He stood in front of what looked like the inn, but this inn badly needed a coat of whitewash, and its timbers were broken and dented. And this fat fellow with a greasy waistcoat straining across his belly couldn't be jolly Mr. Apple. She knew Alfred Apple and had known his father before him, both born innkeepers. They were happy, laughing fellows, as quick to quip as they were to sympathize. This man resembled them, but he was staring at her insolently, openly, appraising her like a leg of mutton he was thinking of purchasing for his dinner.

"What's happened here?" she asked dazedly. "Where is everyone?"

"Back of my place, having fun," he said, taking a toothpick from his mouth to speak. "Like you could be, if you were of a mind to. I've been expecting you. Daisy told me you were wandering about, looking for a meal. I can offer better. Employment."

"Employment?" she asked in confusion, suspecting a jest.

"Aye," he said.

"At the inn? But why?" she asked when he nodded, curiosity getting the better of her confusion. "The Apples never needed to hire strangers, neither James nor his son ever did."

"The *Apples*, is it?" he said, gazing at her narrowly. "You knew old Jim Apple, then?"

"Of course," she said in wonder. "You must be joking; he was famous here."

"Aye. So he was," he said in a softer voice, "and with good reason. He was an innkeeper, a fine one and proud of it. As I dreamed of being . . . But I've not got that pleasure, and for all I've missed him sore these past years, I'm that glad he's not around to see it, too. But needs must as the devil drives," he said briskly, "and he drives a hard bargain around here. And a man has to eat to keep body and soul together—aye, well, at least to keep body together," he added with bitter humor.

"So, down to business," he said, eyeing her. "Like I said, I've an offer of employment for you. In short, I've got two girls: Daisy and Sal. But our Sal is getting old. Clients complaining she lays there like a log these days. A chap wants some bounce to his pleasure. You'd clean up well, I think. Well? I pay by the customer: you get a quarter of the fee, but I give you room and board. The food's plenty and good, too, there's that unchanged at least. Times being what they are, you won't get a better offer. It's easy work. None of the lads hereabouts go in for much fancy. Straight in and out, and a half hour at most, even for the randiest of them. What do you say?"

She stared at him, wide-eyed. His wife, she noted with numb horror, stood right behind him, nodding, waiting for her answer. Or at least the grossly fat woman somewhat resembled buxom, merry Mrs. Apple.

But then she saw a tall, broad-shouldered man leaving the inn. At last she someone she clearly knew and trusted absolutely. It was the blacksmith, John Phelps. She recognized his honest face immediately, although he looked tired and older than he had just yesterday.

"John!" she cried. "John Phelps, please, what's happening here? Is this some kind of elaborate joke? What happened to the shops, the street, the inn?"

"What is always happening here," he answered sadly. "Who are you?"

"I'm—oh, please, John, not you too. You know me. I've lived here forever. You used to let me sit in your shop and watch you at the forge when I was a little girl, remember? You made me a horseshoe-nail puzzle once, for my birthday."

"Oh, you knew this place when you were a girl? Can't say I remember you," he said, peering down at her. "Well, but then, my eyes aren't what they used to be. As to this sorry town, well miss, folks started leaving when the old squire died. Before your time, I expect. When that fool George sold off the manse, they put up the mill there. Mill means good business, they said. The future's in manufactories, not farming, they said. Some future. They pay cheap and work you long hours, and you never see the sun again except when it's rising and you're going to work, or setting when you're done. And just smell it. Works on coal and cooks up glue. I used to shoe horses. Now I help to melt them down.

"Some folks left right then," he said sadly, "the smart ones, I guess. The rest stayed for the work. After the war, work was hard to get, you know. But the mill's not doing well these days. Too many others in the land. There's not much left here now. A man has to take his pleasure where he can," he muttered shamefacedly, looking down and rubbing his chin. Then he looked up again, his eyes narrowed. "What did you say your name was?"

"Maude. Please, John, look closely. You saw me just yesterday. I'm Maudie Atkins, the squire's daughter, Lady Southwood now, you know. But . . . but you said the squire died . . ."

"Crazy." Alfred muttered, "just like Daisy said."

"Squire? Sure. Years ago," John said, eyeing her, his concern clear to see on his brood, honest face. "Everybody knows that. Him and his wife. Right after their two boys did. Boys died of a contagion. But squire and his wife died of broken hearts, folks said. Then that fool George came in and took over and didn't know his bottom from his hindleg and lost the lot. For us as well as himself. Lost us a town. Lost himself an estate and a life. Now he's a sot, they say. Drinking himself to death in London on the last of the money he made. They say it's a race to see which goes first."

"No, no," Maude said, her voice shaking with incredulous nervous laughter. "George married an heiress. And my father is still alive. He's up at The Hall, even now. With Miles, my husband, please, you know that."

"Crazy as a bedbug, doubt if Bedlam would even take her," Mrs. Apple said. "We can't use her, pretty as she is. Can't use that kind of trouble. Be off with you," she told Maude.

"True," Alfred said on a sigh. "A pity, but it's true. You heard the missus," he told Maude. "We've enough trouble on our plate as it is. Best get on, go on now, clear out!"

"No," Maude protested, her thoughts reeling. "This has gone too far. No more. Wait! I see. Is Miles behind this? Or my father? Is it some part of the Christmas pantomime or something? Some holiday jest? Well, if it is, it's not funny anymore. Now stop it."

"A nutter," Alfred said. "I think we'd better call the sheriff."

"I'm not mad!" Maude said. "You know that, and you have to stop now!"

"Walking about town, muttering to herself, pretending to be someone that never was," John said sadly.

"Thinks she's the viscountess," Mrs. Apple said, her heavy jowls shaking as she shook her head. "There's *true* madness."

"Poor lady," Daisy said, coming out of the inn, fas-

tening up her gown. She peered over John's shoulder at
Maude. "Maybe you should lock her up for her own
good."

Maude backed away, as terrified as she was appalled. Surely she was dreaming. But she could feel
the cold snow beneath her feet and smell the rank air,
and if they tied her up she was afraid she wouldn't
wake and find herself in her own bed. They watched
her. When John took a tentative step forward, she suddenly knew what to do. She picked up the hem of her
skirt and ran. Back toward The Hall. Miles. In all of
this, there was one constant, as there had been her
whole life: Miles. Wherever he had gone, he would be
back. Whatever he wanted now, at least he would tell
her the truth. Whatever terrible thing had happened, in
her mind or in the world, he would protect her.

She didn't stop running until she reached the holy
well, and only then did she look back. No one had followed her. She stopped to catch her breath and rested
there, trying to reason things out. But there was no
rhyme or reason to anything that had happened. It
seemed a real as she was. That wasn't saying much.
But the bleak afternoon light was growing dimmer, and
so she picked up her courage and started back to The
Hall again.

Halfway there she knew she wasn't alone anymore.
She sensed him before she saw him. Mr. Clarence,
hands behind his back, was pacing along beside her
again.

"You got what you wanted," he said reasonably.
When she turned her head and walked faster, he went
on, "And the squire and his lady didn't want to live after their bonny sons died. Because they didn't have
you to care for. They didn't have a lovely girl-child

they adored. They couldn't forget their sorrow by watching you grow. And so they grieved, unbearably."

Maude wheeled around to face him. None of it made sense, she didn't believe any of it. But this was a thing she could argue.

"How could the boys have died if I wasn't there?" she shouted with as much triumph at his faulty reasoning as pain.

"There was an epidemic," he said. "All the children who hadn't had the contagion before got it then. It's the way of measles. Were you the only child in the village? Didn't they play with others? Your husband himself, for example?"

"Yes, but he had it before I did. . . ." her voice trailed off.

"Yes. Just so." Mr. Clarence said.

"But—but they didn't see him when he had it," she protested, but weakly. A new, wild hope was dawning. An expiation of the guilt that had been her lot since that sad day she'd followed two coffins to the graveyard and come home by herself. She didn't dare believe it; it was as if she were unwilling to lay her burden down. Heavy as it was, it was a part of her now.

"The sickness comes before the spots. The spots only prove it. Didn't they ever tell you that?" he asked gently. "Or did you never ask? Why did you assume it was your fault?"

"It was *someone's,*" she cried.

"Ah, yes. Perhaps. But no one you can blame." he said gently, "unless you can claim to understand Him. And even I do not."

She thought about that. It might not have been her fault. It was too much to hope to believe in. She'd borne the guilt too long to set it down now; it made her feel too light-headed.

"But they, my parents, thought . . ." she began.

"Did they?" he asked. "Or did you? They couldn't go on without you in any case, could they? And look what the lack of them did to the village."

"They said that was Cousin George," she said. "Cousin George lost the estate, and sold it to the mill. That ruined the village."

"No," he said and smiled, "that was you, too. Your parents invited George to come and live with them— for you. At first they only wanted you to have company. Then they hoped you'd make a match of it. They didn't mind when you didn't. They liked George for his own self by then. But if they hadn't let him live with them he'd never have learned how to manage the estate. He wouldn't have learned how to be a gentleman who planned for the future, and wouldn't have won his boring heiress, either. When you weren't born—as you wished not to be—he inherited and lost it all, didn't he?"

She thought about that so long and hard she wasn't aware she'd reached home until she found herself in the familiar drive again.

She ran toward the house, forgetting everything but the need to go home . . . until she noticed it didn't look quite like home. There were no carriage-wheel tracks in the snow. The facade of the house wasn't softened by wisteria and ivy, and none of the towering evergreen rhododendrons she had planted along the drive were there. There was nothing green at all: The Hall stood stark and cold against the coming winter night. And the great front door was locked. It hadn't been locked in her lifetime.

She raised the great brass Griffin door knocker, and

let it fall. Someone was playing a terrible prank, she prayed.

"Yes?" the butler said when he swung open the door. He saw her and sighed. "I'm sorry," he said wearily. "There's no work to be had here, my good woman. If you like, Cook can give you a parcel of food to take with you. But that's all. We're lucky to hold our own positions here. Though Heaven knows it's a queer sort of luck."

He began to close the door.

"Wait! Joshua, don't you know me? I—I may be a bit disheveled, but it is I. What's happening here? Please, I'm weary of this. Tell me."

He paused. Her clothing was plain, but her voice was well bred.

"Please, let me in. Miles will be wondering where I am," she cried.

"Oh, *Miles,* is it?" he said with weary patience. "I see. Very well, go in. He usually tells your sort to go in the back way. Remember that in the future—if there is a future; he usually likes them younger, and dressed brighter. Go on, go on. He's in the library. He doesn't expect me to announce you. That, at least, he does not ask of me." He pointed to the library and shuffled away, leaving her alone in the great dark hallway.

That was the first thing she noticed. It was dark. She always had the lamps lit as evening approached. Lots of them, because she didn't like shadows. But the whole house lay in gloom. She didn't hear the children's voices, or the company, or even any of the servants going about their tasks. She'd never heard the place so still and lifeless. But it wasn't lifeless so much as empty. She wrapped her arms around herself and shivered. This was silly; it was her house. She walked through the gloom to the library.

There, at least, there was a fire in the hearth. It lit the room with dark and dancing shadows.

"Miles?" she asked, her voice quavering. She was close to tears. If this was madness, it was a cruel madness. She thought lunatics were happy in their own little worlds. This was a hell. And if it were real . . . But it couldn't be real. "Miles?" she called again.

"Yes?" he said.

She saw him then, sitting in a chair facing the fire, the light harsh on his face. She fairly flew across the room to him, and fell to her knees at his side. She picked up his hand and lay it against her cheek, weeping over it.

He didn't cry out in alarm at her distress. He didn't take her in his arms and ask what was wrong. He didn't even move. That frightened her more than anything had this long, strange day. She dropped his hand and drew away from him. She was still on her knees as she stared into his eyes.

It was Miles—and yet, it was not. His face was pale, not tinged by the weather, tanned from all the hours of riding he did. His hair was still lustrous and jet-black, his features were his own—and yet different. It was not Nature, but his own nature, that seemed to have changed them. Because they were not so much different as altered. His shapely mouth was thinner and his lips set tight. There were lines bracketing that hard mouth, and his whole thin face was notched, as if by pain. There were shadows beneath his darkened eyes.

His voice was the same, but laced with sharp sarcasm.

"Ah," he said, "this is new. Who told you to try it? Never mind, it doesn't matter. I like it, I think. Subservience. Cowed worship. Utter devotion. It's a new slant. It has possibilities." He lifted her chin with one long finger. "Pretty little thing. Not my style, but charming. Yes. But this fawning and cringing. Very diverting. How much further are you willing to take it, I wonder?" he asked with a twisted smile.

"Miles," she said frantically. "what are you talking about? Good Lord, what's happening? Nothing is the same since I left. Where are the children? My parents? The family?"

"Ah, the family," he said in a deep, slurred voice. "A very good question; I have often wondered the same. But as to where the children are, I hardly know. I don't want to know, to tell you the truth. Are you claiming a son or a daughter? I've a parcel of both. Bastards are inevitable in my line of work," he said, and laughed, and took a drink from the glass of amber liquid that had been sitting on the table at his elbow.

He was drunk, she realized, and was shocked. Because Miles seldom drank deep, and never when he was alone. When he did overindulge, he became almost too merry. Not dark and troubled, like this.

"I don't remember you," he went on, "but that's nothing new. Was it good, with us? It's always good for me. That must be why I keep doing it. How much do you want? I'll pay for the brat. Within reason. Don't be greedy and you'll do well. And then I'll pay for tonight. I've no one else here with me tonight. Not that it would make any difference to me if I did. That's always diverting too."

"Miles, I don't want money," she cried. "I just want you to remember me. I'm Maudie. Your wife!"

"Less amusing," he said, staring hard at her. *"Much* less amusing. I've no wife, my dear doxy. Drunk I may be, and a reprobate certainly. In fact, there's no evil I have not done. Except to marry. I'm certain of that. I've never been that drunk. I've never even asked; the words are not in my vocabulary. Find another way to get my gold. I can think of quite a few tonight. Christmas is coming, and I've a notion to, too," he said, grinning.

"You asked me to marry you," she said, looking into his eyes to try to find him there. "Don't you remember? In the apple orchard. I was so thrilled and happy I couldn't answer. So you kissed me, and after, you said, "There. Now you must marry me, my Maudie."

"*Certainly* not me!" he roared with laughter, and took another drink.

"You asked Cressida, too, have you forgotten that?" she asked, her pain making her say what she'd been thinking all the night before this terrible day.

But now he stopped laughing. His face grew darker still. He looked suddenly sober, or so drunk that there was cold murder in his eyes. "Who are you?" he demanded. "Did that bitch send you here? God. I thought I'd forgotten her, drunk her out of my system with all the other pain. Yes. I asked for her hand. And she gave it back to me—across my face, or as good as—when I came home from the war less of a man than when I went. Willing enough to marry me when I was sound. But not after I was crippled. Took one look at me, ended the engagement, and waltzed off with another— who could waltz, I assume." His laugh had no humor in it. "She'd have no part of me if my legs wouldn't work."

"But that's nonsense," Maude protested. "You're not a cripple. You weren't one then. Yes, it was hard for you to walk. I knew it caused you pain. But you did it. And you went farther every day, just as the doctors said you would."

"Miserable little thing from hell!" he cried, rising to tower over her. "Who—no, *what*—has sent you to me?

Yes, they said I'd walk again, *if* I'd walk again. A wonderful riddle, isn't it? One with no answer. Because how could I? Each step was excruciating pain. I drank it away. Then each step made me fall. Then I gave up." He grew a twisted smile and added, "Walking, not drinking, of course. I was alone then, as I am now."

She rose to her feet, too, and touched his arm. "But you are not. Miles, this is madness. Let me help you. I've never wanted anything else."

"There's only one way you can help me," he snarled, reaching out to her. He pulled her close and kissed her hard. It was like no kiss she'd ever known from him. His mouth was ruthless, slanted against hers; she felt his teeth as he forced her to accept his tongue. She would have given him what he wanted, but this was no lover's silent quest, it was a wild intrusion. He fondled her roughly as he kissed her. He meant to hurt, he meant to shame her. And he did. But she felt his arousal. He seemed as surprised by it as she was. He chuckled. "Well, well, who would have thought it? Nice, very nice, little—Maudie, is it? You're a nice little package, aren't you? With a new game. I see. You inflict pain, and then I do. You arouse me to lust—no mean trick these days—and then I service you. Different. I suppose a fellow could get to like that. Shall we see?"

She pulled away from him and stumbled back. He followed her. That was when she saw that he was lame. He'd snatched up a walking stick from the side of his chair, yet even so he couldn't walk very well. The effort contorted his whole lean body into a parody of its usual grace. She stared in pained pity as he limped toward her. That made his face contort with rage, and he rushed at her. His knee buckled and he fell hard, to the floor. He lay there, groaning.

She bent to him without thinking. "Miles!" she cried, touching his hand.

Only to find her own wrist gripped tight in his rough clasp. "Bitch!" he snarled. "Now we'll see who wins."

But she wrenched free, and staggered away. And left him lying on the floor cursing. She ran through the hallway to the door, and then out into the night. She didn't stop until she wondered where she was going. And then she foundered, discovering herself once again in the Druid's grove, by the holy well. She held onto the rim of the well and sobbed for breath, and when she got some back, she wept.

"He didn't want to live, that summer you finally met as adults," a familiar voice said sadly.

Mr. Clarence was sitting on the rim of the well. A cloud blew off the face of the moon, and she saw him clearly—or as clearly as she could through a haze of tears. He seemed to be surrounded by silvery nimbus, and he was beyond beautiful.

"She—Cressida—had just thrown him over," he said. "He *was* crippled, you see. And hadn't the heart to heal himself. You gave him the courage. You teased and chattered, flirted and giggled, and generally nagged him into it. He couldn't show pain when you were there. Of any sort. You prattled on, to entertain him. You kept walking, so he had to follow, even if it did hurt. Because he couldn't show you his pain. You were only a girl. And then he discovered you were far more than a girl. You were the woman for him."

"But he could have had any girl," she protested. "I was merely his neighbor."

"You were merely Maudie," he said gently, "yes. The only woman for him. Just as you were merely

Maudie, the girl who kept her parents from despair. Merely Maudie, the woman who held the fortunes of everyone she knew: George and his heiress, Lucy and Daisy, the Apples and the blacksmith and the vicar—everyone in the village. Without you, their lives were different. You lent light and laughter, you gave hope and meaning to so many. Yes, you. Merely little Maudie. Merely one little life, one good, little life. There are so few of those. You touched them all. Too bad, really that you wished you hadn't been."

"I wish I hadn't said that!" she cried. "Oh, please, I wish I had not. I didn't know—I cannot bear that they should suffer because of me."

"But they didn't. They suffered because you were *not* you," he said. "Can you see that? Finally, Maude, do you see?"

"I do!" she cried. "Please. Put it back the way it was. I cannot bear this. I want Miles, and I want him whole and happy again. And the children. Oh, the children! They never were; let them *be* again, please. And everyone else: my parents, Mr. Potts, the Apples ... oh, and take down the mill, please. I didn't know how much I had. I didn't know how much I meant. I wish I'd never said a thing. I want it all back again. . . . Oh, please."

But when she looked to see his reaction, she saw only that he was gone. He wasn't sitting on the edge of the well, or anywhere in the lonely glade. She looked around frantically, but she was alone. On a sudden, wild surmise, she put both hands on the rim and peered down into the well itself. But all she saw was dark water rippling.

She closed her eyes, her hands gripping the rough edge of the well. She prayed to everything she had ever prayed to, and threw in a few words to the ancient spirits of the grove, too. But when she opened her eyes again, she could see no change, except that it had started snowing again.

She was too cold and heartsick for tears. She put her head down and waited for enough courage to move again.

"Why, my lady!" a shocked voice said. "What are you doing here so late? I wouldn't be out this late myself, except that I've just seen that charming Mr. Clarence off on the afternoon train. He's gone, said he had to be home for Christmas. Nice chap, incredibly well-versed biblical scholar. I shall miss him." Mr. Potts said. "But what are you doing here? The mistletoe! Of course. Oh, dear me. Don't you worry, my dear lady. I'll have some for you in a trice."

"Mr. Potts?" Maude asked, looking up. She gaped at him. And saw the vicar she'd known all her life. "You know me?" she asked, astonished.

"Why, yes," he said, taken aback. "Er . . . why? Should I not?"

"It *is* you!" she cried. "It is. It is!" She jumped up and danced around him in her glee. "Yes! Why, there's your muffler, your dear, lovely, ratty old red muffler, knotted around your neck. It's you! Oh, Mr. Potts. Oh dear, dear Mr. Potts. You aren't frowning. Of course, I never see you frowning. And you aren't grumbling. Oh dear, dear Mr. Potts," she cried, before she whirled around and threw her wicker basket toward the sky. "Oh, wonderful!" she shouted.

Mr. Potts watched her hurry down the path to The Hall.

"The lady," he murmured to himself, "certainly loves the old traditions. I never guessed. I shall have to gather a great deal of mistletoe."

She ran to The Hall, never pausing, even though

she'd a stitch in her side. The Hall! she thought in ex-
ultation when she saw it. It was her home again. There
were her shrubs, there were ruts from carriage wheels
from all their visitors, and the place was aglow. Every
light was lit, inside and out, for Christmas, and against
the night.

She raced through the front door and fairly skidded
to a halt when she saw her parents gawking at her.

"Maude? Whatever is the matter?" her mother asked.
"You look as if you were dragged through a hedge
backwards."

"Through a *well,* Mama," Maude said, dropping a
kiss on her mother's brow. "Oh, it is so good to see
you!"

"I cannot think who you expected to see," her
mother said, but she grew flustered, the way she always did when she was pleased.

"Perhaps Father Christmas, although he can't be
bearing better gifts for you, daughter, than I am," the
squire said, and earned himself a hug from his daughter for that. That got him red-faced and started him
saying, "Well, well, there, there, very good, my dear,"
in pleasure.

Maude spun around from them and found herself
face-to-face with Simon. It stopped her. She'd never
been face-to-face with him before, simply because he'd
never been tall enough to look her directly in the eye
before.

"Mama," he said, his fair face reddened by more
than a day in the December cold, "I'm sorry. Please accept my apology. I absolutely forgot we were going for
mistletoe so early. We usually go in the afternoon,
don't we? I was so busy showing Tim The Hall, you
see, I started the minute we awoke. I did remember,
but when I did you were gone. I felt like a beast. Not

just because of the mistletoe, but because I missed going with you, the way we do every Christmas. I went out and got you heaps of it, when I remembered."

"Oh, dear," Maude muttered, "poor Mr. Potts!"

"Now you have it, but I wish I could have spent the time with you," Simon went on. "We have such a good time when we go out to get it, don't we?"

"There's next year, thank the Lord, there's next year," Maude cried, and hugged him hard. This time he hugged her back—harder, because he was older now, and could.

While she was getting her breath back she felt a tug on her skirt.

"I'm better," Zoe announced. "Even Grandmother says so. Where were you, Mama? I've been looking for you."

"As have I," Philip complained. "We looked everywhere. Where were you today, Mama?"

"A long, long way away," Maude said, through her tears and smiles. But then she couldn't say more, because she saw Miles.

He came into the room with his usual grace, and she stared. There was only the slightest hint of a hesitation in his long, easy stride. She couldn't look her fill at him; he was tall and straight and altogether beautiful to her. She raced into his arms.

He caught her and wrapped his arms around her and chuckled. He held her close and she reveled in the feel of his strong, beating heart against her cheek. But then she remembered. She stepped back and gazed up at him.

"Yes, you were a long, long way away," he said. "Where were you? I looked everywhere."

Maude could only grin until he added, "And Cressida was wondering, too."

"Oh," Maude said. She couldn't say more. This was worse than her dream. Because she was sure this was real.

"Yes," he went on. "She wanted to say good-bye. I told her I'd do it for her. I took her and her brother and their friend to town, to the blacksmith, so they could be sure of getting their newly shod horse in time to start out for London before dark. I bundled all the children I could find in the carriage and made a game of it. But I made sure of it. I didn't want to risk them staying another day. They came a week too early. Christmas is for family and close friends. Old acquaintances are the ones who are tolerable on New Year's Eve, *if* they are tolerable. And if they are really old friends," he added, his gray gaze somber as he looked at her.

"They're gone?"

"I took them to town to be absolutely sure of it," he said, watching her gravely.

"She was a pretty lady," Zoe commented, "and she used lots of perfume. Can we have dinner now, Mama?"

Maude laughed until tears came. But everyone knew how easy tears were on Christmas Eve. They trooped in to dinner, where Cousin George began to explain about Christmas customs. Then they heard the carolers on the lawn and left the table to open the door and listen. Then nothing would do but the carolers had to come in and raise a cup of cheer, and have a bite to eat to take the bite out of the winter wind. Mr. Phelps, the smith, sang his deep bass in perfect counterpoint to Mrs. Apple's high soprano, and Maude cried and cried when Daisy and her father joined in. Half the town was there that night; there never had been a merrier Christmas Eve. And at the very end of the festivities, when even Zoe couldn't keep her amazed eyes open any longer, Mr. Potts came in, frozen to the bone and bearing an armload of mistletoe. But he soon thawed out before the fire and got into a wondrously complicated discussion with Cousin George about Druid customs.

It was only when it was very late, and all the guests had gone to their rooms or back to their homes, and the children were all abed, that Maude relaxed. Only then did she dare believe who she was, where she was, and how lucky she was, at last. Now the terrible day she had passed seemed like it had been a fevered dream. It could have been.

Philip and Zoe had both been sick and then better in a day. Maybe she had caught that same contagion, she thought. It would explain much. A fever might make her imagine many things: make a simple bible scholar into something supernatural; turn her familiar village into a nightmare. What had preyed on her mind could have taken shape in her fevered thoughts. It all could have happened in her mind as she sat in the snow by the well by herself. It didn't matter anymore. It was over. She'd seen the world without herself in it, and she hadn't liked it. And never had her own life looked more wonderful.

She was resolved that it should go on the way it always had. She waited until the house was still and the servants were in bed. Miles was in his study. She suspected he was wrapping a present for her. Others might get their gifts on Boxing Day, but they always exchanged theirs on Christmas Eve. But before they did, she had something to do. She scooped up her old cloak and slipped out the door into the cold and starry night.

The stable was warm with the smell of hay and animals. Maude closed the door carefully behind her. She was alone in the night, with the animals and Christmas Eve. She put down her lantern, then almost jumped out of her skin when she saw a shadow loom up out of the shadows to stand before her.

"You were right," Miles said with a smile. "I've been listening. The farm animals do get gossipy on Christmas Eve. But they haven't said much yet. Oh, the old milch cow told the horses how glad she was to see the company leave. But that was hardly news. No one wanted them here."

His smile faded. He took Maude's hands in his. "No, no one did," he said gravely. "I never told you about Cressida because I wanted to forget her. I asked for her hand when I was young and foolish. When I came home from the war battered in heart and mind—and limb—she took one look at my infirmities and broke the engagement. It was the best thing she ever did for me. I tried to forget what a fool I'd been. But I ought to have told you. She tried to make it seem very different. I couldn't say anything for fear of making it worse. And poor old Charles was once a good friend to me. What could I say to you? Actions speak louder than words. I could only make sure to see her on her way as soon as I could.

"Forgive me, love," he said, his gray eyes searching hers. "I never meant to cause you a moment's distress. When I got back from town to find you gone, I worried. I wondered if you'd ever come back."

"Where else should I go?" she asked.

"Oh, I can think of a great many places. Too many. Because I know very well I don't deserve you. I've always known it. I'd no right to burden a lovely young creature like you with an old battered soldier like myself. But I did. And I'm glad. Thank you for coming home to me, my Maudie."

"Oh, Miles," she said, resting her head on his shoulder. "Thank you for *being* home to me."

He kissed her gently, as gently as he had the moment she'd said she'd marry him, all those years ago. Then he kissed her more deeply, as he'd done the next moment, all those years before. And then deeper still, as he pulled her into his arms.

It wasn't until they were deep in a bed of fresh-cut straw that she remembered where she was.

"Heavens!" she said, her eyes flying wide. "In the straw? And on Christmas Eve?"

"Exactly," he breathed into her ear. "Precisely," he said, as she sighed against his. "No better place in the world, my love. There's no one here but the animals. So let's give them something to talk about."

"Merry Christmas, Miles," she said tenderly.

They came to each other then as they had for so many Christmases before. Even as they did, she heard the sound of all the Christmas bells ringing. Some rang out from the old church and drifted through the night. Some tolled from the collars of the cows as they shifted in their sleep. But none were so joyous as those in her heart. She wished the night would never end . . . and then remembered to be very careful of her wishes. Then Miles made her forget everything.

And far away in the grove, the water in the ancient well lay deep and still. The angelically fair young man standing beside it sighed. He bent his bright head, gazed down into the water, and saw no reflection but that of the stars above him. But they were very bright. He looked up to them and smiled, and then walked off into the silent night.

With thanks to the great Frank Capra for the wonderful concept. And with a wish for a wonderful Christmas to all.

The Crystal Dove

Justine Davis

It was impossible.

The thing couldn't be there, but there it was. Sitting absurdly in an intricately woven nest of straw, right there on his desk. On top of the papers he'd been working on last night. Actually this morning, Case Rafferty amended, remembering it had been well after three A.M. when he'd finally gone to bed for his requisite four hours of sleep. It was a nuisance—having to sleep—but at less than four hours a night he'd found his efficiency began to fall off, and he couldn't afford that.

He stared down at the small, dark-blue glass dove. He wasn't quite sure how he knew it was a dove; the smooth, flowing lines of the glass merely suggested the lines of a bird, with a plump, rounded body, head tilted as if to look at the watcher, and the merest suggestion of wings and tail. Yet he knew it was a dove.

What he didn't know was how the hell it had gotten on his desk. He was the lightest of sleepers, waking at the merest rustle of sound, and he hadn't heard a thing.

He turned on his heel and stalked over to the far wall. He studied the control panel of the intricate alarm system. All the lights unhelpfully glowed green. And there was no record on the thermal tape that printed out such things that any zone had been disturbed for even a second. The last entry was when he had returned from dinner in the hotel restaurant last night at nine.

A rap on the door distracted him from the puzzle for a moment. He flipped off the front door alarm zone and had taken two steps toward it when he realized that, except for his watch, he was stark naked, having come directly out from the bedroom. He'd better do something about that, he supposed. He knew he already had quite a reputation with the hotel staff; he didn't want to add exhibitionism to their list of his probable sins.

He detoured to the bathroom and grabbed a towel to wrap around himself. If it was one of the female butlers, she'd just have to live with it; he sure as hell tipped enough for them to put up with a few idiosyncrasies now and then.

"Breakfast, Mr. Rafferty!"

The voice calling through the door was male, thankfully. He undid the dead bolt and pulled the door open. The young man was a stranger, but the smile he wore was familiar, the first thing every hotel employee was indoctrinated in. Case stepped aside and the young man came in. He held the tray with ease; he might be new at the Seattle Host hotel, but he obviously had had some practice somewhere.

"On the table," Case said, gesturing toward the small dining table in one corner of the spacious suite. The young man nodded, set down the tray, and proceeded to set the table with exacting precision.

Case eyed him with interest, glancing at the name tag that proclaimed him to be Raphael. All the hotel staff was efficient, but few were this precise. He wondered if the young man had been warned about the "hard case" that lived in the penthouse suite; he knew that was his nickname here, just as it was at his office across the street. He also wondered if the hotel staff still drew straws to see who would make the trek up here; he'd never been able to determine if the one who got the short straw was considered the winner, because of the tips, or the loser, because of his exacting nature.

In either case, he appreciated the extra effort and added an even larger than usual tip to the bill the young man handed him before he signed it.

"You get this from Kestra?"

Case looked up from the bill, surprised at the question; the people who served him usually never spoke except in answer to his rare questions. But his surprise turned to astonishment when he saw that the butler named Raphael was looking at the dove . . . which now sat on the table in front of his breakfast.

He knew it had just been on his desk. He knew he hadn't moved it. He knew the butler hadn't moved it. But he knew too, it hadn't been on his desk last night. He temporarily put aside impossible to answer questions and asked the obvious one.

"Who's Kestra?"

Raphael smiled, a smile that told Case incontrovertibly that this person with the odd name was female. But Case saw a touch of resignation in the young man's smile as well; he knew he was right, he'd seen that look too often on an opponent who had finally realized he was going to lose. Whatever this Kestra was to this young man, it wasn't what he would like her to be.

"I thought everybody around here knew Kestra," the young man said. "She runs Celebration."

Case's dark brows furrowed. "Celebration? You mean she works for the hotel, for parties?"

Raphael's eyes widened in genuine surprise at his ignorance. Case didn't like that expression turned on him, not one bit.

"*Celebration* is the name of her store," the young man hastened to explain, as if he sensed he'd offended one of the hotel's richest guests. "The one in the big office building across the street. You know, right in front."

Case blinked. His building? He didn't remember the name of the store, but then he wasn't involved much in the leasing end of the property. He didn't have time. Nor, he realized suddenly, did he have time to stand here discussing some unknown shop owner with a kid who obviously had a crush on her. He started to wave the waiter out of the suite, but then something occurred to him.

"What made you think that"—he gestured at the dove—"came from her?"

The young man shrugged. "She knows a lot about things like this. And since you work right there in that building, I thought you must know her."

I do more than work there, Case thought to himself. *I own the place, and I don't have a clue who this woman is.* He rarely took the time to look at retail shops, even those on the ground floor of his own building, and paid little attention to them unless there was a problem.

Well, he thought when Raphael had at last gone, there was a problem now. This damned bird had shown up in the middle of the night, and whoever had put it there hadn't triggered the alarm, or awakened him. And now the thing was jumping from desk to table, apparently under its own power.

He stared at it for a moment, then stalked over to the phone and dialed hotel security. Moments later, after being assured no one could possibly get to the penthouse level without clearance or their knowledge, and after further unctuous assurance that they would thoroughly check all the videotapes from the security cameras on his floor, he finally sat down to his breakfast. And wound up staring instead at the tiny glass bird in front of him. Impossibly in front of him.

Case Rafferty was not a man who dealt well with the concept of impossibility. Told something was impossible, he felt compelled to prove it wasn't. He had admitted long ago it was that compulsion that had pushed him to build the small but extremely profitable business empire he now ran. He also admitted that he had little time to indulge in that kind of demonstration of proof anymore. What he wasn't comfortable with was the knowledge that he missed it, missed the challenge of taking on a problem he wasn't completely sure he could solve.

But he wasn't quite ready to put this silly bird into the unsolvable category, not yet. There was a simple explanation, and it would present itself soon enough.

In the meantime, breakfast was waiting. He lifted the cup of coffee. He spat out the first sip; it was cold. Startled—they wouldn't dare serve the hard case cold coffee—he tested the toast. Equally cold. And the ice in the bowl that held the orange juice had melted. All of it. His forehead creased. He lifted his wrist and looked at his watch. His eyes widened in disbelief. He rose and walked to his desk, to look at the always reliable clock there. And faced the third impossibility of this impossible morning.

Three hours had passed since he'd sat down.

Kestra knew who he was the moment he walked in, but that didn't lessen her shock; she'd been in this building for nearly five years, and never once had its owner set foot in her small shop. Not that she minded; Case Rafferty was far too high-powered for her comfort.

He barely glanced at the bright lights and cheery Christmas decorations, although she thought she saw his nostrils flare slightly, as if at the scent of the luscious—and hunger producing—pumpkin spice potpourri she kept simmering in the back room.

Then he spotted her amid the exquisitely stitched needlepoint stockings she was rearranging over the fireplace—a gas fireplace, to her regret, but anything else was impossible in here—and started toward her. After one look at his face, she abandoned her plans for an early lunch.

Her first thought was that the pictures she'd seen, and the glimpses she'd caught of him as he made his way—always hurrying—across the street, hadn't done him justice. He was bigger than she'd imagined, taller, and broader than she would have guessed from his long, leanly muscled legs. His hair was much darker than she'd realized, gleaming nearly black in the shaft of winter sun that poured through her doorway. And his eyes were startlingly, vividly green. A feral sort of green. If he lived in the jungle, he'd be wearing stripes, she thought as her breath seemed to catch. Tiger stripes.

But then, he did live—and work—in a jungle of sorts, she realized. And he was bearing down on her as if she were his next meal.

When she saw his glowering expression, her next thought was to frantically reassure herself that yes, she had paid the rent this month, and on time. Then the absurdity of the idea of Case Rafferty, who owned this entire twenty-story building and Lord knew what else besides, coming personally to collect her miniscule rent check struck her, and she laughed aloud.

He stopped dead in his tracks. He stared at her. Stared at her as if he'd never heard anyone laugh before. More likely, Kestra thought ruefully, he'd never had anyone laugh at him before, especially if he were approaching them like this, predatory eyes fixed, muscles ready for the pounce. She drew in a breath and composed herself.

"I'm Kestra Shepherd. Can I help you?"

"Do you always laugh at potential customers?"

Lord, even his voice matched the image; that low, raspy undertone resembled nothing less than a growl. And she'd been right; he didn't like being laughed at. She hastened to explain.

"I'm sorry," she said quickly. "I was thinking of something else."

"Something quite amusing, apparently."

He *was* angry, she thought regretfully. But she'd been growled at by the best, and she wasn't about to cower before this man. Even if he did—literally—own the roof over her head. So she grinned instead.

"Actually, after seeing your expression, I was trying to remember if I had paid the rent or not."

He blinked. The tiger actually blinked. She didn't know if it had been her rueful words or the grin he no doubt hadn't expected, but she felt a small rush of mild satisfaction that she had rattled him, and she couldn't find it in herself to feel guilty about the sensation.

Then his eyes narrowed, the dark brows lowered, and she suddenly wished she'd held her tongue; only a fool provoked a tiger.

"You know who I am?"

"Mr. Rafferty," she said quietly, appalled now at her own folly, "I'm sure everyone in this building and probably in all of Seattle knows who you are."

Kestra Shepherd, you *are* a fool, she told herself sternly. You're happy here, your business is at last doing well in this unlikely spot, you're going to show a profit this year, so what do you do? You annoy your landlord. You try and tease a man who, by all accounts—and by his current expression and demeanor—had been born without a sense of humor. She knew the type all too well, yet she had tried anyway. Sometimes, she thought, her perpetual optimism got her into more trouble . . .

She tried to change the subject.

"Can I help you with something, Mr. Rafferty?"

His focus shifted almost visibly, and she breathed an inward sigh of relief. He reached into the pocket of his coat, unbuttoned despite the chill of this crisp, clear winter day, and drew something out. He held it out to her on his palm.

"Do you sell these?" he asked bluntly. "Was this purchased here? And if so, who bought it?"

Kestra wondered if he always asked questions in threes. Probably so, she thought, to save time. Men like him were always in a rush, the precious crumbs of their time carefully doled out. She ignored the reflexive pang that thought gave her; those kind of people were, after all, what kept her shop going here in this district full of them. She also ignored for the moment the spate of questions. Instead she looked at what he held.

The first thing she noticed was that he had a very strong hand, with long, supple-looking fingers. Artist's hands, she thought. Then she chided herself for being fanciful. According to the business section of the *Seattle Times*, Case Rafferty was many things; a shrewd businessman, a tough negotiator, and if you crossed him, your worst enemy. The man lives in a hotel, for heaven's sake, she told herself. No doubt because it then took him only two minutes to get to his precious office. Hardly artist material.

She turned her attention to the thing he held. Here was the artistry, she realized. The little bird, barely three inches high and four inches long overall, was a beautiful piece. Subtle lines that suggested rather than detailed, yet missing nothing of the softness of the gentle body, the fragile curve of wings, the hopeful tilt of the tiny head, as if the creature were searching for something, perhaps a light in a dark, dreary world.

"It's beautiful," she whispered. "What a marvelous piece of work. May I?"

She was reaching for it before he answered, but he didn't protest so she picked it up. As she did her fingertips brushed his palm, and the most amazing sensation seemed to leap in her, a flooding rush of heat and something else she couldn't quite define. Startled, she cradled the bird in her hands as her eyes shot to his face.

"It's very . . . warm."

"Of course it is," he said impatiently, but he was shaking his hand slightly, as if he'd felt it too. "It was in my pocket."

Well, at least she hadn't blurted out the truth; that besides the warmth, besides that odd sensation, for one incredible instant she could have sworn she felt the beat of a tiny heart.

But it was gone now, and the piece was no more than a lovely crystal shape, warmed by the body heat of a man who apparently had it to spare; while others outside were wearing heavy overcoats, he seemed quite comfortable in a light trenchcoat.

She held up the bird, marveling at the rich, deep color. "It's beautiful," she said again.

"Never mind that." He sounded even more impatient than before. "I asked if you sold them. I presume from your reaction that you don't."

"No, I don't. Nothing like this."

He frowned. "I was led to believe you handled this kind of thing."

His tone put the crystal bird on a par with the latest in cartoon-character Christmas ornaments. His lack of appreciation for what she held struck an old, raw nerve in Kestra. Nothing irritated her more than people who wouldn't—or couldn't—take time for the beauty in the world.

"I believe you're mistaken, Mr. Rafferty," she said coolly.

The dark brows shot upward. "Excuse me?"

Words he obviously didn't hear often, Kestra observed in silent satisfaction.

"You said 'them.' " She held up the dove once more. "I doubt very much that this is a mass-produced piece. I've never seen such a deep, dark blue before. Or such lines, or weight, in such a small piece. In fact, I'd say you have the work of a master craftsman here."

He looked astonished. "A glass bird?"

She smiled, knowing it was a pitying rather than a friendly smile, and knowing as well that it would irritate him; she doubted very much if Case Rafferty was a man who would take well to pity. Her theory was proved in the next instant when she saw irritation replace the surprise in his expression.

"It's hardly just a glass bird, Mr. Rafferty. It's crystal, very fine lead crystal. And it's a dove."

Was she mistaken, or had a sudden new alertness come into those green eyes, like the watchfulness of a tiger who had just spotted an adversary he hadn't quite assessed yet? But his next question was so simple, she doubted her conclusion.

"How do you know it's a dove?"

Indeed, how did she? Kestra wondered.

She looked down at the crystal bird nestled in her hand. How could she explain how the simple yet eloquent lines of an unknown artisan made her so certain of something that wasn't distinct in the work itself? Especially when she wasn't at all sure that there wasn't more to it; the memory of the peculiar sensation the dove had sent through her lingered.

Finally, she shrugged. "I just do."

She'd half expected him to laugh at her answer, which rose purely from a gut-level reaction, but instead she saw that wariness again, as if her rather inane answer had sounded some kind of warning only he understood.

Then he seemed to shake it off. "You seem to know about crystal. Do you know where something like this would be sold?"

"A gallery, perhaps."

He looked puzzled. "An art gallery? What about department stores? They sell crystal, don't they?"

Obviously he still thought the dove was just of the knickknack variety. She tried to explain. "Some of them. But those who do probably wouldn't carry a one-of-a-kind piece like this, even if the maker would sell it to them."

The dark brows furrowed again. "If? Why not sell it?"

She lifted one shoulder in a shrug. "I just can't see whoever made this selling it to a department store, to be pawed over by any passerby."

"Maybe he needed the money."

His voice sounded dry, almost bitter, and Kestra lifted a brow at him. "Then there are other ways to sell. I don't know any art galleries in the area that specialize in crystal, but several do carry individual pieces." She hesitated, then plunged ahead. "Why is it so important? If you didn't buy it yourself, wasn't it a gift?"

"No," he said flatly, staring at the bird now nestled in her palm. "It just showed up in my suite."

She smiled widely. "Sounds like a gift to me. And the best kind, given anonymously, so there's no worry about returning the favor."

He looked startled once again. Then irritated.

Kestra smothered a sigh. Mr. Rafferty apparently didn't like being surprised, either. And she doubted if he was the type to just accept the bird as a lovely piece of serendipity and enjoy it. No, Case Rafferty was the kind of man who had to solve every puzzle, reason out every occurrence until he had an explanation that satisfied him. She knew the type; her father had been one of them. She didn't like it any more now than she had when she was a child. She'd put up with her father because she'd had to, but she—

She'd have to put up with this one, too, she thought rather gloomily, remembering suddenly that he was her landlord. Reluctantly—she hated to spoil someone's surprise, even as she wondered who on earth would have the nerve to try to surprise Case Rafferty—she decided the only polite thing to do was offer to help.

"If it's truly so important," she said, "I could make some calls. I know some gallery people. Perhaps I can find out something about where it came from."

He looked at her with a curious expression, as if he was wondering why she'd offered. His words confirmed her guess.

"Afraid you didn't pay the rent after all?"

She laughed, choosing to take his words as a joke, although she wasn't at all certain they were meant to be.

"I'll pay you for your time," he said then, and her

laughter faded away. Everything had a price. Hadn't her father said it a thousand times? This man was apparently cut from exactly the same cloth.

"That's hardly necessary." She didn't quite succeed in keeping her voice from showing her disappointment, although what she had to be disappointed about was beyond her. "I'll do it after lunch, when I'm not busy."

He glanced around, as if only now realizing something. "You don't seem very busy now."

"No," she agreed. "But I will be soon. My busy times are lunch and after the area businesses close. People stop in on their breaks, or after they get off work. And I'll be very busy up until Sunday, of course."

He looked blank. "Sunday?"

Her brows arched. "Christmas?" she said.

"Oh."

For an instant he looked disconcerted, but the expression was gone so quickly she could be no more sure of that than she was of that odd feeling she'd gotten when she'd first touched the bird in his hand. He glanced around her small shop again, as if only now seeing what it contained. Wonderful, she thought. I run a shop dedicated to holidays, and he doesn't even know that the biggest one of all is practically here.

"Do you make enough money on this Christmas stuff to keep going year-round?"

Spoken like a true Scrooge, Kestra thought, not missing his slight derogatory emphasis on the "stuff." And suddenly she was feeling as she had so often as a child, when her father had ruined her pleasure in what should have been a joyous day with his gruff annoyance at the holiday that interrupted his business.

But she wasn't a child now, she told herself. She was old enough not to be hurt by the intonation of a man's words. Especially when that man was a virtual stranger.

For some reason she thought then of the game she'd played as a child, wishing for a miracle to make her father change. Later she'd expanded her wishing to include anyone like him—including strangers—feeling sorry for their neglected families. As she grew up, she realized she had been feeling sorry for herself, and that it had just felt less like self-pity if she widened the wishing well a little.

But it would take one heck of a miracle to get through to a hard case like this one, she thought.

"I make a lot of my money this time of year," she said evenly. "But the other holidays do all right for me, too." It was none of his business, she thought, even if he was her landlord. "I pay my rent," she added pointedly.

"I know you do, or you wouldn't be here," he said, sounding more bemused now than angry. It was that simple for him, she thought. If she didn't pay her rent, she'd be gone. By his order, no doubt. "And you make a living at it?"

"I manage. There's always something to celebrate."

"Always?"

"Well, almost."

She forced herself back to her usual cheer; she wasn't going to let this man ruin her day. Smiling, she began to tick off holidays on her fingers.

"January is New Year's, of course, and February, Valentine's Day. March is St. Patrick's Day, and April is Easter. May and June have Mother's Day and Father's Day, and of course July has the Fourth. September has Labor Day and Grandparent's Day, October Halloween, November Thanksgiving, and here we are back at Christmas and Hanukkah. And there are lots of others along the way, too: Flag Day, Groundhog Day, all the presidents' birthdays, the first day of spring—"

She stopped as he waved a hand at her. "I get the idea. But there's money in all those other holidays?" he asked. "What do you sell, fireworks on the Fourth of July?"

"No. I sell flags, copies of the Declaration of Independence for those who want to remember the true reason for the day, and picnic lunches. On Valentine's Day I sell the usual things: candy, flowers, plus a selection of the most romantic movies on video, the best romance books, music, and I pack romantic dinners for two." She shrugged, nodding toward the banner over the counter that proclaimed the store's name. "In other words, I help people celebrate. Whatever they want to celebrate."

"Groundhog Day?" he said, sounding incredulous.

"Sure. I sell hot-buttered-rum kits in case he does see his shadow, and spring flower seeds if he doesn't."

He shook his head, looking utterly amazed.

"More importantly," she added, "I enjoy what I'm doing."

He studied her for a moment, as if she were a spreadsheet that didn't quite add up.

"What happened to August?" he said abruptly.

So he'd caught the omission, she thought. "Poor August got shorted. No official holidays. So that's when *I* celebrate"—she grinned—"by taking a vacation."

He suddenly backed up a step, that watchfulness glowing in his eyes again. She had no idea what had brought it on; all she'd done was grin at him. But she was aware of something beyond the increase of distance between them. It felt oddly like a chill, as if his body heat had warmed her and now she felt the loss.

"I would appreciate it if you would make those

calls," he said formally. He pulled a card out of an inside coat pocket and handed it to her. "Call me if you find out anything."

She took it, nodding, still somewhat preoccupied with that strange sense of loss.

"Here," she said, holding the bird out to him when it became obvious he intended to leave.

He shook his head. "You keep it. In case you . . . have to describe it, or something."

Why did she have the feeling the little piece of crystal made him nervous? That he didn't want to take it back? She must be imagining things, she told herself. From what she knew of this man, nothing made him nervous. Yet when—after a final, doubtful glance around her shop—he turned and left, she couldn't help feeling that it was the tiny bird she held that was driving him away.

For the third time in as many hours, Case caught himself staring out his office window. The first time he'd been able to write it off to a natural interest in the huge freighter that was pulling out of Elliott Bay, heading for the shipping lanes. The second time, he'd put it down to the realization that the sparkle of the winter sun on the water was lessening as the cloud layer built up. But this time there was no excuse except the truth—he'd been utterly, totally distracted all day.

It was that damned bird, he thought. Showing up as if out of thin air. And for all he could prove otherwise, that was exactly what had happened. There had been a message from hotel security waiting on his desk when he'd arrived at the office. A review of the security videotapes of the anteroom for the elevator that led only to the penthouse showed it had been empty all night, except for his own return from dinner and the waiter's arrival this morning.

And they had anticipated his request and checked with the housekeeping staff, the only other people who had access to his suite. No one had been inside. Not that he had truly suspected them; most had been with the hotel for years, and he knew the head of the service usually supervised the cleaning of the penthouse himself, keeping the key separate from the master key used for the other rooms.

Yes, it was the damned bird. His distraction had nothing to do with that Kestra woman. Nothing at all.

Not that she wasn't attractive enough to be a major distraction. In an offbeat kind of way, that is. That mass of smooth, shiny red hair, burnished with highlights that were almost gold, that laugh that felt like feathers up his spine, that softly curved figure that made a man think of cuddling it against him in the dark . . . and her eyes. Gray eyes. A soft, clear gray. Dove gray, he'd thought when he'd first seen her, then had winced inwardly at the "dove" reference.

But she was hardly his type. He preferred his women blond, whip-thin, and razor-sharp, and Kestra Shepherd was none of those. She looked more like some fey creature from the woods, all curves and eyes and fiery hair.

Damn it, he was doing it again. Staring out the window instead of concentrating on the pile of work on his desk. He had that prospectus to read, an annual report to finish going over—he'd been waiting days for it so he could assess that fiber-optics company's takeover value, and he was still only halfway through it—and he had a stack of letters to sign. Yet here he sat, doing nothing more productive than watching the clouds start to pile up over the Olympic Mountains. Soft-gray clouds, although they would darken later when the promised storm hit. Soft gray, like a pair of wide eyes framed by a mass of silken red hair . . .

He swore—short, sharp, and heartfelt.

The phone on his desk buzzed. Probably Mrs. Russell, wondering why he hadn't gotten to those letters yet, he thought to himself. He picked up the receiver.

"Mr. Rafferty?"

Who else? he thought, but kept it to himself; Mrs. Russell was the best assistant he'd ever had, and he worked to keep his naturally slicing impatience from irritating her. She was too good at keeping his life organized just the way he liked it, including fending off unwanted interruptions. But now she sounded hesitant, doubtful, which was highly unusual for her. He wondered what had caused it.

"Yes?"

"There's a woman on line two. A Ms. Shepherd. She says you're expecting her call. Something about . . . a dove?"

Case smiled wryly. So that explains it. If you only knew, he told the woman silently, you'd be even more dubious.

"Shall I take a message?"

That was the obvious answer. He didn't really have time to talk now; he was too far behind. He'd have Mrs. Russell take a number and he'd call her back later.

"No, put her through," he said, and the instant the words were out wondered where the hell they had come from. But he picked up the receiver before the first ring had died away.

"Mr. Rafferty?"

They were the very same words, in almost the same

tone, that Mrs. Russell had used just moments ago. So why did a spurt of heat trace its way down his spine, like a pulse of light through one of the fiber-optic cables he'd just been reading about? It must be her voice, he decided, that rich voice with the depth of a mellow woodwind and the sweetness of clover-honey.

God, I'm losing it, he thought. That's the sappiest thing I've ever heard. He spoke quickly, briskly, denying the uncharacteristic reaction to something as simple as a woman's voice.

"Yes, Ms. Shepherd. You've found out something?"

"I'm afraid not. I've called everyone I can think of, and no one's been much help. All I got were names of people I'd already called, and a fanciful story from a sweet little old customer of mine. A couple of people referred me to a curator at a museum in Chicago that specializes in unusual glassworks, but I didn't know if you wanted to go that far."

"I don't need to know who made the thing, just who bought it."

He thought he heard a sigh. "I don't suppose you could just ... accept it, for what it is? A lovely piece of whimsy someone wanted you to have?"

"That piece of 'whimsy,' as you call it, got into my suite past twenty-four-hour video cameras and a state-of-the-art alarm system. I damned well want to know how."

Definitely a sigh this time. "I'm sorry, then. I wish I could have done more for you."

She meant the words sincerely, in the most innocent way possible. He was sure of that. So why did his mind suddenly start conjuring up all the many different and mostly sexual things he'd like this fiery-haired woman to do for him? And to him? So that he could return the favor?

"—tonight?"

Yes, he thought. Tonight. If he could wait that long.

"Mr. Rafferty?"

He snapped out of the lascivious haze he seemed to have slipped into, and realized what she'd said had—thankfully—nothing to do with his suddenly fevered imaginings.

"I'm sorry. I was . . . distracted."

"I probably should have just left a message," she said, "but you seemed kind of . . . anxious about the dove."

You don't know the half of it, he muttered to himself. "It's no problem. I told you to call. Now, what were you asking?"

"I wondered if you wanted to come by and pick it up tonight."

That was the last thing he wanted. He wasn't sure if it was the dove or the woman with dove-gray eyes he was avoiding, but his answer was swift.

"No. Keep it."

"Keep it?" She sounded startled. "I mean, I don't mind holding it for you until tomorrow, but I don't really have anywhere to keep something like that safe—"

He'd meant permanently—he certainly didn't want the thing—but he realized she would never accept it if she reacted so strongly just to the thought of keeping it overnight. Too bad; she was so impressed by the thing, she ought to have it. It meant nothing to him. All he wanted was an explanation. And then the damned thing out of his life.

"Don't worry about it. I'll get it tomorrow."

"All right," she said after a moment. "I suppose I could take it home with me."

"Don't worry about it," he repeated.

"Mr. Rafferty," she began, in the tone of one very

aware she was talking to the man who owned the place where she made her living. He'd heard that note in other voices before, often, but somehow it bothered him in hers.

"What?" It came out more sharply than he'd intended, but she went ahead anyway; which was more than some of those others had had the nerve to do, he thought.

"I don't think you realize how special this piece is—"

"What I realize, Ms. Shepherd, is that I have work to do."

That came out more sharply than he'd meant it to as well, and this time she took the hint he hadn't consciously intended.

"Of course you do. Pick it up whenever it's convenient. I open at eight. Good afternoon, Mr. Rafferty."

Before he could respond, he was listening to a dial tone. And feeling as if his face had been slapped. And he didn't know why. She hadn't been rude, nor had she sounded particularly angry. She had sounded . . . resigned. As if something hadn't turned out the way she'd expected.

Or as if it had.

Somehow that thought bothered him more.

And that disappointed tone in her voice haunted him for the rest of the afternoon. For the first time in his life he signed the half-dozen letters Mrs. Russell had left for him without even looking at them—he, who never signed anything without reading every word. And when he called research with a question on the fiber-optics company, the department head rather puzzledly reminded him they had discussed that very thing three days ago; he'd completely forgotten. When he reached the last page of the annual report and realized he didn't remember anything he'd read, he knew it was profitless to continue.

He hadn't left the office before eight in longer than he could remember, but he got ready to do so now. He threw the annual report and the prospectus into his briefcase, added what was in his tray for tomorrow, and snapped it shut. He'd drop it off in the suite, head down for an early—for him—dinner, maybe work for a couple of hours, then go to bed early. Maybe even before midnight.

That's all he needed, he told himself, a little sleep. Maybe he'd just been pushing it a little too hard lately. It wasn't like he had anything to prove, not anymore. He'd already surpassed even his own highest dreams. Of course, there had been a price, but everything in life had a price. He wondered idly if Sandy and her new husband had that brood of kids yet. He hoped so. She'd be a wonderful mother. Just as he'd make a lousy father. He supposed she'd known that, and that it was one of the reasons she'd left him, so long ago. Sometimes it didn't seem as if they'd ever really been married at all.

I really am tired, he thought as he rode down in the elevator. I haven't thought about that in years.

He pointedly avoided even glancing toward the shop that took up one small corner of the ground floor. That it took a concentrated effort perturbed him, and by the time he opened the door of his suite, he was well on his way to being completely irritated about his wasted day. And at the woman who seemed to be the cause of it all.

He tossed his trenchcoat over a chair, shrugged off his suit coat and tossed it down as well, unknotted his tie, and dumped the briefcase unceremoniously on the sofa as he considered his options. He could stew over what he hadn't gotten done, and no doubt take another step down the road toward an ulcer. He could go out for a run, and try to burn off his aggravation. He'd done his ten miles already this week, mostly on the enclosed track on the roof of the hotel, but a couple more wouldn't hurt him. Or he could forget about sleeping and try to make up for those ridiculous hours he'd spent today staring off into space.

With a disgusted sigh he walked over to flip on his computer. And realized he wouldn't be sleeping anyway, no matter which option he chose.

The dove was back in its nest.

Kestra typed the last set of numbers into the spreadsheet program, entered the equation, and smiled in satisfaction as the computer neatly updated her month's totals. She'd resisted the machine at first, but once she'd figured out how it thought—like a child, doing absolutely nothing unless you told it exactly what to do—it had saved her hours of frustrating accounting work. It was before nine, and she was already done with what once would have taken her until nearly eleven.

The fact that it was still new to her, and that she had to concentrate on the input, was a side benefit she hadn't really appreciated until now. Now, when she had something she was trying hard not to think about.

Or someone.

She smothered a sigh as, once more, her guard was down and the image of Case Rafferty crept back into her mind. She'd had excuse enough this afternoon; when she'd been making all those calls about his dove, it was impossible not to think about the man it belonged to. But when she'd finished the fruitless inquiries, and had set the crystal bird out of sight in a cupboard, she'd told herself that was that. But she hadn't been able to stick to her resolve.

She leaned back in her chair, tapping her pencil on the table that served as her desk. It irritated her that she was still thinking of him at all, especially after that last phone call. She told herself she should have expected just what she'd gotten; a few terse minutes from a man whose work was his life, and who couldn't disguise his impatience at her wasting of his precious time. After growing up with a man like that, she should have known better than to expect anything else. But he'd seemed genuinely intent on finding out where the dove had come from—and if it had appeared as impossibly as he'd said, she could understand why—so she had called.

Maybe Mrs. Gilhooley was right, Kestra thought, smothering a smile as she saved her spreadsheet. Maybe the dove was magic. Maybe—

"I'd like an explanation."

Kestra gasped, barely able to bite back a tiny scream of shock as the deep voice came from directly behind her. She whirled, her fingers dragging on the keyboard making the computer give out a protesting beep. She stared at the man standing there, wondering if somehow she had conjured him up out of her restless thoughts. But he was real—undeniably, overpoweringly real.

"My God, you startled me!"

He shrugged. The gesture could have been taken as an apology, but somehow Kestra was certain it hadn't been meant that way. He was angry; she could see it in the depths of those intense green eyes. And for some reason, that anger seemed to be directed at her.

Deciding the best defense—especially when she didn't know what had brought on the attack—was a quick offense, she asked, "How did you get in? I know I locked the door when I closed up."

His mouth twisted. "I own the building, remember? I have a master key."

"Oh."

She felt a little foolish for having forgotten that, but every logical cell of her brain seemed to have short-circuited at the first sight of him standing there.

"Well, you could have knocked," she protested.

"Yes."

He said it with no trace of apology, not even a shred of abashment at having violated not only her privacy, but possibly a law of some kind; she was certain a landlord couldn't just walk into his tenant's property without warning. But she doubted if anyone, least of all she herself, would call him on it. Not when faced with the steady stare of those eyes which looked not quite domesticated.

"I said I'd like an explanation," he repeated.

Her forehead creased. "Of what?"

"This." He reached into his pocket and drew out the dove.

"Oh. You decided to pick it up after all?"

He didn't answer, just stared at her until she began to feel like a helpless small animal staked out as bait for a man-eater. Then something else occurred to her.

"How did you know where I'd put it? I mean, among the tea bags is hardly the first place you'd look—"

"Cut the games, Ms. Shepherd."

His voice flicked at her like a steel-tipped lash, his obvious anger adding to the fierce intensity of his eyes. She came as close to screaming then as she had when he'd so startled her. And then, as it had as a child, her natural rebellious streak came to her rescue; anger rose up in her. She'd long ago sworn never again to be intimidated by men like this, and she wasn't going to let herself be now.

"If you'd like to explain what you're talking about, I'll be happy to talk to you, Mr. Rafferty," she said, her voice cold. "Otherwise you can take your high-handed self out of here, landlord or not."

He drew back a barely perceptible fraction, but enough so that Kestra felt a small sense of gratification; he hadn't expected her to stand up to him. She wondered if anyone ever did.

"High-handed?" was all he said.

"What else would you call it? You sneak in here, into my own shop, try to intimidate me—"

"And fail miserably, I see," he said.

He wasn't angry anymore. Kestra sensed it immediately. She had no idea what had caused the change, but she had a suspicion it was probably amusement at her refusal to be cowed by him. And she discovered, to her dismay, that she didn't like being laughed at any more than he did. At least, not by him.

"You have your property back," she said stiffly. "Please go. I'm closed."

"May I apologize first?"

"Do you know how?" She blushed furiously as she realized that her first reckless thought had popped out in words.

He gave her a half smile that could only be described as rueful. "Probably not, not suitably, anyway. But I am sorry I startled you. I thought if I surprised you, I'd be able to tell if you—"

He broke off suddenly, and lowered his eyes. That simple act startled Kestra; she doubted he very often avoided anyone's gaze.

"If I what?"

He sighed, then looked up. Only then did she realize how very tired he seemed. He lifted his hand and set the dove down on the table before her. When he spoke, his voice sounded as weary as he looked.

"It was on my desk again."

Kestra's gaze flicked from his face to the dove, then back. "What?"

"When I got to my suite, it was there."

Her brows furrowed. "But it was here."

"I know. I thought you'd done it somehow."

She stared at him. "But I haven't left all afternoon. I put it in the cupboard, over the microwave, behind all the tea bags, because I thought it would be safest there. Really, Mr. Rafferty, I didn't—"

"I know," he said again. Then, with a weary sigh, "I think I knew before I even came over here."

"But how did it get there?" Kestra asked, bewildered.

"Probably the same way it got there in the first place," he answered, sounding disgusted.

"But I thought you said you didn't know how—"

"Exactly."

Kestra laughed, a little nervously. "Maybe Mrs. Gilhooley *is* right."

"Who?"

"That customer of mine I told you about. A sweet little old Irish lady. A bit off-center, but sweet. She thinks it's magic."

He blinked. "Magic?"

"Yes. She said there's a local legend in the village she's from about a crystal dove that magically appears at Christmas, but only to the people who need it most."

His mouth quirked. "Is that her opinion, or yours?"

"Just the legend. It's supposed to heal people who have lost their way."

"Or drive them into losing their mind?" he suggested sardonically.

This was not the time, Kestra thought, to tell him the rest of the legend Mrs. Gilhooley had imparted to her. He was in no mood. Nor was he the type of man who put any faith at all in legends, Christmas or otherwise. In fact, she wondered if this man had any faith at all in anything that couldn't be shown on a balance sheet.

"It was just a story," she said after a moment.

"Makes as much sense as anything else, at the moment." He shook his head. "I'm not in any heavy negotiations right now, or anything that might make somebody want to distract me. But somehow, for some reason, somebody's doing this. If they were good enough to bypass the alarm, then they could have seen me bring it over here, and where you put it afterward. And if they're that good, they could have gotten it back."

Kestra shivered at the thought of being watched so closely. And at the thought of living the kind of life where you expected people to try and play with your mind, just to get an edge. For a long moment they both just stared at the crystal dove.

"Is it my imagination," she said at last, "or is it . . . lighter than it was?"

"Yes," he said, taking up the tiny bird with a sweeping gesture that spoke volumes about his mood. He shoved it into his coat pocket, out of sight once more. "I noticed that, too."

He obviously didn't want to discuss the dove any longer.

"Kestra," he said suddenly. "That's an unusual name."

"I suppose," she agreed. "My mother was a bit of a bird-watcher. She saw a kestrel the day she found out she was pregnant with me. When I was born, she decided it fit. The kestrel is one of the most"—she smiled crookedly as she tugged at a strand of her bright hair—"colorful of the hawk family. I shudder to think what she would have called a boy. She always—" The loud ding of the microwave oven interrupted her. "Oops," she said, "dinner's ready."

He glanced at his watch, then to her in surprise. "Isn't it a little late?"

She eyed him speculatively as she walked over to the oven. "And what time do you usually eat?"

From what she knew of him, she could guess the answer. To her surprise, he smiled. She wished he hadn't; the sight of a smile on that face, even a slightly sheepish one, sent her pulse racing, and that was a fact she didn't want to acknowledge.

"About now," he admitted. "Or later. But I know most of the rest of the world doesn't keep my schedule."

"Which is why the rest of the world isn't where you are, isn't it?"

His brows lowered slightly. "That sounded rather . . . intense."

Kestra let out a sigh. She knew she had sounded bitter, and she hadn't really meant to. Just as she hadn't really meant to go icy with him on the phone today. Something about this man just seemed to weaken the restraints she'd worked so hard to put on her naturally loquacious personality. And now she had to apologize to him.

"Sorry," she said, "that's one of my emotional buttons."

She opened the small oven door and a luscious odor wafted out. She sniffed appreciatively, and out of the corner of her eye, caught him doing the same.

"I'm trying a new vendor for my baskets," she explained, "and they sent over this lasagna."

"It smells great. You put lasagna in picnic baskets?"

"Sometimes. In a special container that keeps it hot for up to three hours. It's been quite successful." And then, before she could stop herself, the words were out. "There's far too much for just me here. Want to help me test?"

He looked startled, then wary. Just like she felt, she thought ruefully. Startled that she'd done it, and wary now that she had. And wondering what had ever made her think she had learned to keep her mouth shut when something foolish leaped to her lips. For what could be more foolish than inviting Case Rafferty, millionaire several times over, to sit in the back room of a tiny shop and eat microwaved lasagna?

"Never mind, I'm sure you have other plans—"

"No," he said suddenly. "No, I don't. I'd like to stay."

Minutes later, as she scrabbled in the back of the tiny refrigerator for the half-full bottle of rosé she knew was there, she was thoroughly regretting her rash invitation. Not because of the absurdity of the situation—he'd alleviated much of that by taking off his trenchcoat and revealing a shirt unbuttoned at the throat and sleeves rolled up over his forearms, as casually as if he took dinner in back rooms regularly—but because he seemed to so fill the small room just by his presence.

She wondered how much of her reaction was because of the image, the sheer overpowering reputation of the man, and how much was due to the solid, muscled strength of those bared forearms and the wedge of bronzed skin visible in the opening of the shirt.

"This is all I have for wine," she said, as she set the

bottle on the end of the table that also served her as a spot to eat. He, no doubt, was used to the best in wines as well as everything else. "Strictly grocery store variety."

"Relax," he said, his tone dry. "I grew up in a house where wine that cost over two dollars a bottle was saved for New Year's Eve."

She *had* sounded defensive, she realized. And the personal information he'd unexpectedly just given her wasn't really a surprise; she remembered reading somewhere of his humble beginnings. It merely enhanced the reputation; the added cachet of poor boy making good was irresistible to those who built people into legends. And she supposed she should admire him for all he had accomplished. She just wondered what it had cost to do it. And who had paid the price.

"At least you know when New Year's is," she said lightly. He lifted a brow at her. "Well, you weren't real sure about Christmas. But I suppose you have to know when New Year's is, to change all those appointment calendars."

He reached for the bottle of wine and filled the two glasses she'd set out. "Are you saying I'm . . . What are you saying, Ms. Shepherd?"

"If we're going to eat together, at least call me Kestra. And I'm saying that you work too hard, if you can't even remember when Christmas is."

He glanced at his watch, around them at the shop, and then pointedly back at her. Kestra couldn't help it; she laughed.

"I know, I know, the pot labeling the kettle. But I don't do this year-round. Except for the Christmas season, I'm usually closed and out of here by seven."

"That's still a long day . . . Kestra, if you open at eight."

She heard the pause before he said her name, and she wondered if that was why she almost shivered when he finally did say it.

"I get a lot of prebusiness-hours customers that way," she explained. "It's one of the things I knew I'd have to do, if I was going to survive here."

She tasted the lasagna, and immediately decided to do business with this company; it was delicious. He took a bite and agreed with her before going on.

"This is an unusual spot for a . . . shop like this."

"Yes, but it's proving my theory, that with the right hours there's enough traffic here from working people who are usually too busy to think about things like holidays until the last minute." She gave him a crooked half smile. "But I get the feeling you think anyplace would be an unusual spot for a shop like this."

"It's true, I don't have much time for . . . celebrations. Or holidays. The only advantage I see is that I get more work done when everyplace else is closed."

Just as I thought, Kestra said to herself. "I rest my case," she said aloud.

He studied her, took a sip of wine, a bite of lasagna, then asked casually, "Tell me, are you always so quick to assess people?"

"No," she said, swirling the wine in her glass. "You're somewhat of a legend in Seattle, so I admit to a certain number of preconceptions about you."

"And I haven't done anything to disprove them, is that it?" he asked wryly.

"Not yet, Mr. Rafferty. Not yet."

"I'm glad you're keeping an open mind. And I thought we were on a first-name basis."

"I was. I didn't know about you."

He raised a brow at her. "You've already written me

off as hopelessly holiday illiterate, but you're waiting for permission to use my first name?"

Kestra laughed at the obvious silliness of it. "My apologies, Mr. Ra—" He held up a hand and she corrected herself, "—Case. You've caught me in a social absurdity."

He smiled, as if the sound of her laugh pleased him. She supposed he didn't hear much laughter at his level of business; everything must be much too serious for jollity.

But when she found herself staring intently at the unexpectedly sensuous curve of his lips, Kestra felt a spurt of fear, fear that she'd done something very foolish by not turning tail and running like mad the moment this man had walked into her life.

He hadn't meant to do this at all. He'd gone barreling across the street with every intention of calling Ms. Kestra Shepherd on whatever game she'd been playing. He'd even used his key—another first—to catch her off guard, knowing her culpability would show on that wide-eyed, innocent-looking face the instant she realized he knew she'd been behind the mysterious appearance—twice now—of the dove.

But it hadn't. He'd taken one look at her startled eyes and known, with the experience born of long hours of negotiations with people expert in hiding the truth, that she'd had nothing to do with the dove's return to his desk. Or its original appearance. She'd been as bewildered as he had been. And so instead he'd impulsively, and utterly foolishly, committed himself to spending time alone with the woman who had disrupted his entire day.

And he was enjoying it.

He'd enjoyed listening to her enthusiasm about her

odd—at least to him—little shop, and been surprised at how well she apparently did with it. And been amazed at how many different, off-the-wall little holidays she knew about, from all around the world.

"February sixth, Waitangi Day in New Zealand. And November second is Melbourne Cup day in Australia."

He was laughing by then, and when she suddenly jumped up with an exclamation about missing the eleven-fifteen ferry, he was startled to realize it was nearly midnight.

"Which ferry?"

"Winslow," she said. "I live on Bainbridge Island. I'll have to hurry to make the twelve thirty-five."

"That's really late. It'll be after one by the time you get there. Do you have to go back?"

She gave him a wry smile. "I'm not up to sleeping here tonight," she said, gesturing at the tiny back room. "Not that I haven't done it before."

"There's a hotel across the street," he reminded her.

Her smile turned a bit wintry. "Sorry. My budget doesn't run to a hundred and fifty-plus a night."

He felt himself flush, and was so astonished by the fact that the offer came tumbling out before he thought—another first. "I have a suite with an extra room."

She went very still. She stared up at him, searching his face. When at last she looked away, he had a feeling she hadn't found whatever she'd been looking for.

"I don't think that would be a good idea."

Relief warred with disappointment in him, and he wasn't sure which one was winning. "You're probably right," he muttered.

"Besides, I have some deliveries to make on the island in the morning, before I come over to finish up my deliveries here."

"You deliver yourself?"

"On the island, I do. It gives me a chance to see all my friends there, so I don't feel so guilty about not accepting invitations to join them for the festivities tomorrow night."

"Festivities?"

She sighed. "Christmas Eve, Case. Christmas Eve."

He was beginning to see her point; he'd actually forgotten. Again. Hastily, he tried to divert her. "You don't join them?"

She shook her head. "I love the island people, but Christmas Eve is my time to myself. I have little enough of it, since I started *Celebration,* so I try to hoard what I have. They understand." She grinned. "I think they've always considered me a little . . . eccentric."

"Always? How long have you lived there?"

"Off and on, all my life. I spent every summer there with my grandfather. He gave me his house, so I live there full time now."

"Oh." He shifted his feet uncomfortably as she bustled about, cleaning up. He thought of offering to help, but he didn't know where anything went and figured he'd probably be more of a hindrance. "I'm sorry."

She glanced at him. "About what?"

"Your grandfather."

Her wide. gray eyes looked puzzled. "What about him?"

It was his turn to be puzzled. "You said he gave you his house . . . "

Her expression cleared and she laughed, a lovely, husky sound that sent that flash of heat down his spine again. "You mean you thought he died and left it to me? No, he's hale and hearty and living it up in sunny Florida. He's having a great time, even though I think he moved mainly to have an excuse to give me the house. I think he thought it might make up for my father.'

"Make up for him?"

She looked away then, the first time he'd ever seen her avoid his eyes. "I shouldn't have said that."

Finished cleaning up, she turned and lifted a long, navy-blue coat from a rack on the far wall and put it around her shoulders. Silently.

"What about your father, Kestra?" he asked, uncertain why it was important to him, only sure that it was. When he said her name she looked up sharply, as if startled. Or as if she liked the sound of it. She didn't speak for a long, strained moment, then the words seemed to come in a rush.

"He's . . . what's commonly known as a workaholic. He always said he was doing it for us, but . . . I always thought he was hiding. Using his work to cover up the fact that he'd never been able to really relate to another person in his life. My grandfather raised me more than he ever did, after my mother died . . . of neglect, I think."

A connection leaped to life in Case's mind, and the flippancy of her last words did nothing to soften it. *Sorry, that's one of my emotional buttons. I'm saying that you work too hard, if you can't even remember when Christmas is.* She had obviously put him in the same category. And he couldn't really say she was wrong.

"Better than a father who never worked at all," he said, not even realizing the words were coming until they were already tumbling out. "A father who felt he didn't deserve a family if he couldn't take care of them."

She turned then, her eyes much softer than they'd been a moment ago. "Is that how your father felt?"

He wished he'd never started this now. "I just know he used to say a man shouldn't even have a family if he couldn't take care of them."

"Does he still feel that way? After how successfully you've turned out?"

A chill swept through him. He reached for his coat and pulled it on. "He's dead," he said at last.

"I'm sorry." Her response was instant, but he couldn't doubt the sincerity of it; it was glowing in those dove-colored eyes. He couldn't look at them.

"Don't be," he said shortly. "It was his choice."

She blinked. "What?"

"He drove off a bridge."

"My God, Case—"

"They said it was an accident, that he hit black ice, but we knew better. He'd driven in the winter around here all his life. Then we found out he'd spent the last of our savings on life insurance six months before." His mouth twisted sourly. "He finally found a way to take care of his family."

He buttoned his coat, then turned to look at her once more. She'd gone pale, her eyes wide and troubled as she looked at him. He saw now that it wasn't a coat she'd put on but a cloak or cape of some kind that fell from her slender shoulders nearly to the heels of her leather boots. A hood lay across her back, and driven by a need he couldn't resist to see the fiery red of her hair against the navy wool, he reached out and gently pulled the hood up over her head. It framed her face, seeming to soften already delicate, pixielike features. It turned her fair complexion, which had only a scattering of tiny freckles, even creamier, and made the color of her hair even more vibrant, more alive. He pulled his hands back, accidentally—he was sure it was accidentally—brushing her cheek with the back of his hand.

She seemed to shiver, then gave a little shake of her head. "Ironic, isn't it?" she said softly. "Both our fathers, for the same reason but in such different ways, took away from us the one thing we wanted most. Themselves."

Pain stabbed through Case, an old, harsh pain he'd thought himself long over. She saw things too clearly, this fey creature who looked nothing less than mystical in her swirling cloak. Too, too clearly, with those soft-gray eyes.

"You'd better go if you're going to make the next boat," he said, a little gruffly.

"Yes," she said, her voice barely above a whisper. She looked up at him, and the steady regard made him swallow tightly.

Don't, he told himself. *Don't do it.*

The warning went unheeded, and in the next moment his mouth brushed hers, tentatively, barely tasting. It was so sweet, the feel of her breath so soft and warm, that every muscle in his body tensed, sensing the delicate, seductive danger here. He pulled away, his pulse accelerated and his breathing quickened all out of proportion to what had just happened.

And Kestra said nothing, only looked at him with those wide, wise eyes before she turned to go.

Long after she'd driven away, in a tired old compact that had him worrying about whether she'd make it, he was still there, a man who resented the time stolen by holidays, staring into the dimly lit windows of the shop run by a woman who found a holiday worth celebrating in the simplest of things. A man who realized the impossibility of such a combination.

When at last he walked back to the hotel, he entered by way of the garage. And tossed the crystal dove into a trash bin.

Case felt the satisfaction of difficult decisions made and put behind him. The decision not to waste any more time on the mystery of the dove. The decision to throw the damned thing away. The decision to remove himself from the temptation of a curvy redhead with an obvious, deep-rooted aversion to men like himself. He wasn't running, he told himself, just doing what was best for both of them.

So, if he'd accomplished all that, why the hell wasn't he sleeping? Why did she persist in haunting him every time he closed his eyes? Why did his lips still tingle with the memory of the feel of her mouth beneath his, while his suddenly unruly body demanded more, much more, than just a kiss?

He purposely, determinedly ignored the fleeting thought that she was just what he'd admitted he missed—a problem he wasn't sure he could solve. He doubted if anyone could ever be sure they had solved the complex puzzle that was Kestra Shepherd.

At last, as the first light of dawn crept from behind the blackout curtains, he gave up. He rolled out of bed and stumbled into the shower, cranking it up as cold as he could stand it while telling himself it was to help him wake up, not to tame a certain uncooperative body part.

He'd just go over to the office now, he thought. He certainly had enough work to catch up on, after yesterday. Yes, he'd get an early start, and not quit until he was caught up, no matter how long it took—

Christmas Eve, Case. Christmas Eve.

Kestra's words poured over him like the water over

his body. Like he wanted her to pour over his body, all hot and sweet and fiery ...

He swore as he slapped at the tap and shut off the water. Holidays were a nuisance, had always been a nuisance, and would always be a nuisance. He grabbed a towel and began to scrub at his wet skin. He stalked into the bedroom and grabbed the first clothes that came to hand, a pair of jeans and a pullover sweater; not his usual office attire, but comfortable.

Consider it my contribution to the holiday spirit, he muttered silently as he pulled on a pair of socks and dark leather running shoes, not sure who exactly he was addressing the thought to.

He was going to work, like he always did. He was going to forget about that flame-haired pixie who wasn't his type anyway, any more than he was hers. And, he added as he ran a comb through his tangled, wet hair, he was going to start all this progress by getting rid of that silly wad of straw on his desk. He should have done it last night, when he'd dumped its pesky occupant in the appropriate receptacle.

He felt almost cheerful as he strode into the living room. Much more cheerful than he had a right to feel, after such a sleepless night.

The truth of that mocking thought slammed home the moment he flipped on the light over his desk. The nest he'd come to throw away was still sitting there.

And in it was the crystal dove.

"Sir?"

"I said, forget breakfast. And tell housekeeping there's some broken glass to clean up."

"Yes, sir."

Case watched the waiter—one of the familiar ones, this time, not Raphael—disappear from view as the elevator doors closed. His jaw was clenched as the slow descent began. He stared at the framed poster on the wall of the elevator car, advertising the hotel's four-star restaurant, showing happy diners seated at a window overlooking the sound beneath a wondrously clear sky. Blue sky. Sky blue. The color the dove was now. Or had been, before he'd grabbed it and hurled it to smash against the tiled entryway of his suite.

The change in color had made him think for an instant that it was a different bird, but the moment he had picked it up, he'd known it wasn't. It was that certain but inexplicable knowledge, he supposed, that had driven him to throw it. He hadn't even thought about what he was doing. He'd merely reacted, violently, in a way he'd never done before. His entire life had been lived by a careful plan, set in motion the day he'd realized what his father had done. Driven by an odd combination of determination never to be as desperate as his father, and a need not to let his sacrifice go to waste, Case Rafferty had set his course and never wavered. And he'd succeeded, beyond his greatest hopes.

And he had never, ever acted impulsively. Yet in the past twenty-four hours, that was all he seemed to be doing. And his first impulse after destroying the dove this morning had been to run to Kestra.

He wouldn't have done it, of course, even if he could have. It didn't matter that she was out making her deliveries—in that unsafe rattletrap of a car, no doubt—and therefore not here for him to run to; he knew he wouldn't have done it even if she had been here. He just wouldn't have.

Besides, he'd already handled it, albeit in a most uncharacteristic way. The dove was shattered now, ruining the plans of whoever was tormenting him. He could get on with his life, get on with business. And maybe, after a while, when the images of red hair and gray eyes had faded a little, he would seek out one of those sharp, racy blonds who knew the rules and didn't mind playing by them if enough was in it for them.

The thought left him as cold as the winter air. So cold that he wondered if he would ever be warm again, he who had barely needed a coat in the coldest of Seattle winters. So cold that he wondered if his breath would even raise a vapor when he stepped outside. So cold that the only thing he could think of that would warm him was a shining mass of fiery hair.

He locked himself in his office, with orders to Mrs. Russell not to disturb him for anything short of a fire—and then only if it was on their floor. He summoned up every ounce of his old determination he could muster and threw himself into his work. Ruthlessly he forced his mind to cooperate, yanking it away from dangerous paths, most especially from the owner of the shop on the ground floor below him.

Crazy, he muttered to himself once, when he hadn't yanked quite in time and she'd popped vividly into his mind, the dark hood of that cloak lying soft on her hair as she stared up at him after he'd kissed her. Crazy that it was she who kept creeping into his mind, when, if he was going to stew about something, it ought to be that omnipresent bird. Maybe he should hire a detective to try and solve this little mystery.

The thought of trying to explain the appearance—and reappearances—of the dove was more than he could deal with. And he supposed it explained why he was thinking about Kestra instead; there *was* no explanation for the dove. But then, there was no rational explanation for the way he reacted to her, either.

He forced his mind back to his work. He was moderately successful, because when Mrs. Russell buzzed him to tell him that unless he had something he needed her to do she was leaving, he was startled to find it was already afternoon.

"No, go ahead," he told her. Then, remembering, he added, "Have a Merry Christmas, Mrs. Russell."

The startled silence on the phone line was as cogent a comment as he would ever get, he thought, except perhaps for the astonishment in the woman's voice when she returned the wish.

"Why, thank you, Mr. Rafferty. You too."

Just call me Scrooge, he thought glumly as he sat back and stared out his window. He rubbed wearily at his eyes. Maybe that woman—what had Kestra said her name was?—was right. Maybe the dove was magic. Or a message. Like Marley to Scrooge. Wake up, buddy, you're walking the wrong path.

He shook his head at his own folly, then went back to work.

When he caught himself dozing off over his accountant's tax estimates, he decided it was time for a walk. A little turn in the winter chill ought to wake him up enough to come back and put in a couple more hours. That should catch him up, he thought. It had nothing to do with not wanting to go home, where that damned bird kept showing up. That was over now, and the dove was in pieces on some housekeeping cart in the hotel somewhere.

He yawned, stood up, and turning again to face the big window, stretched. The city looked deserted below him, and he glanced at his watch. Nearly seven. No wonder he was stiff; he'd been working steadily since Mrs. Russell had left at two. She was probably home with her family now; Case had lost track of the number of grandchildren some time ago. He nearly smiled at the thought of the calmly efficient woman marshaling her troop of toddlers with the same effectiveness as she ordered his office.

He wondered where Kestra was. Had she finished her deliveries? Had she been here and gone? Was she already home, ensconced before a fire, enjoying her peaceful evening? Or was she scurrying to finish at the last minute? He stared out the window as if he could see the answer from here.

He could look, he supposed, as he went out for his walk. It couldn't hurt, since she was probably already gone anyway. He yawned again, absently considering that he hadn't eaten since the sandwich Mrs. Russell had brought in at noon. That would explain this hollow feeling; it was simple hunger. He was grateful for the acceptable explanation; he'd been running a little short on those lately.

So he'd go for a walk and get something to eat. He didn't particularly care what. It would be hard to top that lasagna, though. He should have asked Kestra where it had come from. Maybe he would, if she was there when he went downstairs. No, he wouldn't. He couldn't. He didn't dare.

He turned away from the window at last, disgusted with himself. Indecisiveness had never been one of his characteristics, and he wasn't about to let it start to be now. He would take his damned walk, and he wouldn't even look—

He froze, unable to move, unable to even breathe. For in the pool of light cast by the desk lamp he'd been reaching to turn out, in that damned straw nest, sat the dove.

Whole. Unmarked. In one piece. As if he'd never thrown it, never smashed it against hard, cold tile. Exactly as it had been before.

No, not exactly, the small portion of his logical mind

that wasn't stunned into numbness reported. It was even lighter now, a pale, robin's-egg blue. But it was the same bird. He knew it was, could feel it. And it had . . . what? Followed him here? Appeared while his back was turned, when he knew absolutely that no one else had been in the room?

He shuddered, and a creeping, growing fear that he'd refused to acknowledge until now overtook him in a rush. Was he going crazy? Had he already slipped into some shadowy insanity, and just hadn't realized it yet?

Panic welled up inside him. Was this how his father had felt . . . caught, trapped, losing his grip, but unable to stop it? Had he really not meant to drive off that bridge; had he been instead driven off it that night? God, was it hereditary or something?

He grabbed at the dove, meaning to destroy it if he had to break this top-floor window and heave it to the street below. And for an instant, an instant that terrified him, he thought of following it. But something, some odd warmth that emanated from the small crystal shape, stopped him, and he found himself instead running for the elevator. When it didn't immediately answer his call, he ran for the emergency stairs and started down. He was moving blindly, gasping for air, afraid to stop, heading for a haven he wasn't even sure existed.

Kestra yawned as she cleared away the last of the clutter. Her final delivery had been made, she'd filled all her orders, and was at last free. She could hardly wait to go home, light a fire, and curl up and simply stare at the flames for a long, long time. She would—

The sudden pounding made her jump. Instantly she thought of the other occasion when she'd been startled recently, and just as instantly fought off the memory.

Please, she muttered, she wasn't sure to whom, *isn't it enough that I kept thinking about him all day?*

And couldn't whoever it was at her door read? The sign said closed, in letters six inches high. After all, it was seven o'clock on Christmas Eve; who would be out in this business district now?

One possibility—the same individual she'd been fighting thinking about all day—came immediately to mind, but he hadn't shown any inclination toward the niceties of knocking before, so why would he start now?

The pounding came again, and she reluctantly made her way through the darkened store to the door, half expecting some forlorn shopper who'd forgotten until the last minute to buy something for his secretary. When she got close enough to see, she knew that it wasn't that shopper at all, but the man the other, foolish, hopeful half of her mind had expected: Case.

She unlocked the door with a strange combination of eagerness and reluctance, wondering what she was letting herself in for this time. The memory of that brief yet searing kiss had never left her; at odd moments all day she had thought she could still feel his lips on hers. She made herself sound casual as she pulled the door open.

"Forget your key?"

"I . . . yes."

Her eyes narrowed as she looked up at him. Her first thought was that he looked even more devastatingly attractive in jeans and a sweater than he did in business clothes. And that was saying something.

Then she looked closer. His hair was tousled, and his eyes were a little wild with a look she didn't recognize. His skin glistened with perspiration, yet he was shivering. Literally, physically shivering, this man who had astounded her with his heat. Concern kicked through her with a stomach-tightening wrench.

"Case, what's wrong?" She stood aside and he stepped inside, a little unsteadily. "Are you sick?"

"No. Yes. God, I don't know."

He sounded desperate. She closed the door after him and urged him back to the small office. There, she smothered a gasp; he looked even worse in the light. And with a shock, she realized the look she'd seen in his eyes, seen and not been able to recognize since it seemed so impossible in this man, was fear. A deep, gnawing fear.

"My God, Case," she whispered. "What is it?"

He leaned on the edge of the table, as if his legs had lost strength. Only then did she realize he held something, so tightly his knuckles where white with the pressure.

The dove.

She came up close before him, instinctively putting her hands over his. A sudden flash of utter turmoil shot through her, as if she were feeling his confusion, his fear.

"What happened?" she asked gently.

Slowly, painfully, he unwrapped the fingers cramped around the little crystal shape. She let her hands slip beneath his then, but she didn't break the contact. It seemed important, somehow, to keep touching him.

"It . . . came back," he muttered.

"I know, you told me, but—"

"No. You don't understand. I threw it away. And broke it. But it came back."

"Case—"

"God, I think I'm cracking up, Kestra." His head came up then, and she saw him try to control the fear. It took a kind of strength she'd never seen, but he did it. "After you left last night, I . . . threw it away. In the trash bin at the hotel. This morning it was back on my desk. I . . . freaked out, I guess. I smashed it. Broke it. Into pieces. I knew I was rid of it. I knew it. But it came back. In my office. Just now. While I was standing right there. No one came in. It just . . . appeared."

Kestra's breath caught. She stared at the dove, noticing now that it was an even lighter blue than when she'd last seen it. Even as she saw the change, he spoke of it.

"It's getting lighter, can you tell?" He shivered. "It's getting lighter, and I'm getting darker, like it's pouring all the darkness into me. . . ."

"Oh, Case . . ."

"This whole thing's crazy. Or I am. I'm scared, Kestra."

She knew she couldn't begin to imagine what it had taken for him to admit that. And for the first time she understood the impulse that had made him want to be rid of the beautiful little bird. Because suddenly she didn't care how beautiful it was, what master artisan had crafted it, what talent and vision had gone into the crystal sculpture. All she cared about was that it was tearing him apart, reducing this strong man to a shivering, wild creature on the edge of shattering. She didn't know what to do, but she knew she couldn't bear to watch it happen.

She moved to take the bird from him. In the instant when her hands touched the crystal, the bird seemed to come alive, and as she had the first time, she felt the leap of warmth and the odd pulsing of energy that felt almost like a heartbeat. Even Case, as ragged as he was, felt it; he looked up, startled.

"What . . . ?"

"I don't know," Kestra said. And it only added to

her bafflement when as she lifted the bird away from him, the sensation faded away. But it left her something; the certainty of what to do.

She looked for someplace to put the dove out of sight, and settled for the microwave. She slammed the door on it, then turned back to Case.

"Come on. You need to get away from here."

"I don't . . ."

His voice faded away, and she knew he was even closer to shattering than she'd thought. She gave him no time to argue, but hustled him out the door and into the car she'd left parked on the street. That he didn't protest, even about getting into the vehicle he'd already told her shouldn't be on the road, she took as a grim measure of his state of mind.

He didn't even seem to notice that they were moving, let alone where they were going, until she stopped the car.

"Good," she said, surveying the neat lines of vehicles; they were in the fourth line, about five cars back. "We'll make the seven forty-five boat. I didn't think we would, not on Christmas Eve. Luck must be with us."

"Boat?" He blinked then, as if coming out of a daze. He looked around at the ferry terminal. "Ferry boat?"

"None other. Nothing like a good boat ride across the sound to clear out the cobwebs."

"But—"

"Trust me," she said. "I've solved more problems on this run."

"I'm not sure you can solve this one."

"Maybe not. But perhaps we can decide if it's even important that we solve it."

Before he could answer that, the cars started moving. Once they were loaded on the ferry, she dragged him out of the car and chivied him up to the open-air deck, just as the horn sounded their departure. It was one of her favorite parts of living here, this ferry travel, this anachronism in a world of jet travel and telecommunications, and the novelty had never worn off. And at night it was even more special, the sound and smell of the water seeming stronger, more potent somehow. She stayed quiet when she realized Case was breathing deep, looking out at the retreating skyline. And looking a little less tattered around the edges. They completed the trip in silence.

"Thanks," he finally said as the boat began to dock in Winslow. "It helped."

"We're not done yet."

"We're not?"

"I think a hot toddy and a fire are in order."

His eyes widened in surprise. "But . . . you said you always spend Christmas Eve alone."

"See?" she said, grinning. "We're already making progress. You know what day it is. Who knows what else we can accomplish?"

She wondered if he came along so easily because he wanted to, or because he was too weary—or shaken— to argue. And she had to admit, that dove had pulled some pretty fancy tricks, enough to rattle anyone, let alone someone as pragmatic and grounded in pure reality as Case Rafferty. If Gramps hadn't taught her to believe in wondrous things, she'd be pretty shaken herself.

She felt a glow of pleasure when they stepped inside her little house and he looked around appreciatively. It was small, and old, but it was snug and tight and as colorfully cozy as she knew how to make it, and she loved every beam, every floorboard of it. It glowed with the warmth of wood, and the gaily decorated tree in one corner brought the fresh scent of the Northwest inside.

"This is nice," he said. "Warm."

"It'll be warmer as soon as we get that fire going."

"I can do that."

She didn't argue. "Good. I'll fix the drinks."

They'd been sitting on her overstuffed couch, sipping at hot apple cider and brandy for several minutes before she said casually, "You're not crazy, you know."

He looked at her sharply, then let out an exhausted-sounding breath. "I wish I was as sure as you are. I'm open to any other possible explanation."

"Christmas."

"What?"

"Christmas," She shrugged. "It's the time of year for miracles, Case. Maybe this is one of them. Maybe we're not supposed to explain it."

"Miracles? You call driving me insane a miracle?"

"No." She couldn't help grinning at him. "But it's Christmas Eve and you're not working. You took a boat ride, just for the heck of it. You even *know* it's Christmas Eve. And you admitted you're scared. That there are things that even Case Rafferty can't control. Sounds like a whole pocketful of miracles to me."

For a long moment, he just looked at her. Then, slowly, a tired smile curved one corner of his mouth. "Funny you should say that. I was thinking, just before . . . the dove appeared again, that maybe it was . . . a message. Sort of like Marley coming to Scrooge, you know?"

Kestra's heart leaped. If he could even think of that . . . "Mrs. Gilhooley said according to the legend, the dove heals people who have lost their way," she repeated softly. "That it goes to those who need it most."

"So I'm supposed to just accept it? That some glass

bird just magically shows up because I've . . . lost my way? And that it apparently decided that convincing me I've lost my mind was the way to help me?"

"Maybe that was the only way to really get your attention. You're not exactly the most"—she hesitated before going on—"receptive of audiences for anything outside of work."

He studied her for a long, quiet moment. "Do you really think I'm like your father, Kestra? That I use my work to hide behind, because I can't relate to anyone?"

He didn't sound like he was looking for an automatic denial. He sounded like he was afraid it was true. And that was enough to convince her that it wasn't. At least not irrevocably. Not yet.

"No," she said quietly. "But I think you were headed that way. You don't live in that hotel just because it's convenient, do you?"

His brows lowered. "What do you mean?"

"Isn't it mostly because it's so . . . impersonal? You don't have to . . ."

"Relate to anyone?" he said, his voice dry. Then he let out a compressed breath. "Maybe you're right."

"Maybe I *was*" she amended. "But . . . you've made a turn, haven't you?"

"Maybe," he said thoughtfully. "Maybe."

"Then the legend is at least partly true, isn't it?"

His mouth twisted wryly this time. "Does the legend warn you that the cure is nearly worse than the disease?"

"I don't think legends have to do that, do they?"

He took a long sip of the brandy-laced cider, staring at her over the rim of the glass mug. She could see the flames from the hearth reflected in his eyes. And suddenly she saw something else there as well, something that nearly took her breath away.

"What they should warn you about," he said, his voice low, "is redheads with dove-gray eyes who don't know when to give up on hard cases like me."

She swallowed, made unbearably nervous by that new glint in his eyes. No, that returned glint, that flash of feralness that had been absent when he'd been so shaken. She had to struggle to answer him.

"I couldn't give up. Not when you were hurting. Besides"—she lowered her eyes—"I was hoping for that miracle."

He let out a long breath. "Why?"

Her eyes shot back to his face. "What?"

"What on earth made you think I was worth a miracle?"

"What on earth made you think you're not?"

Eyes widening, he stared at her. She saw the dawning of a kind of wonder in the green depths. It shifted, changed the feralness somehow into something softer and yet more primitive at the same time. And then, as he looked at her, she saw him stifle a sigh. His jaw tightened slightly and he closed his eyes. And when he opened them again, the wildness was gone, as if he'd snuffed it out with full intention.

And you, she told herself at that fanciful thought, are getting carried away with this miracle stuff.

"I've got some homemade clam chowder in the fridge," she said, purposely bringing in the ordinary topic of food. "I'll heat some up for us."

By the time she came back to ask if he wanted crackers with his soup, he was sound asleep on her couch.

Case came awake slowly. He gradually became aware of several things: that he was somewhere much softer than his own bed, that he was comfortably warm, that he could hear the occasional cozy snap of a fire, and that he felt more relaxed than he had in . . . he couldn't remember when. He opened his eyes slowly, almost reluctantly.

It came back in a rush the moment he saw the room he was in, warm with firelight and the sheen of natural wood. And when he realized he was stretched out, covered with the richly colored afghan he vaguely remembered seeing on the back of the couch when he'd first sat down. His head was pillowed on a soft, furry thing of some kind, although he didn't even remember lying down. Or taking his shoes off.

He turned his head, and his breath caught at the sight before him. A woman dressed in a soft, flowing, green dress, flame-colored hair tumbling in smooth waves past her shoulders, firelight painting her soft curves in light and shadow, stood before a large bay window, staring out into a wonderland. A white wonderland. It had snowed.

He rose quietly, telling himself he should stay away, that he was no good for this gentle, hopeful woman. But he was unable to resist the tableau before him. Besides, every instinct in him told him that while she might have soft-gray eyes the color of a dove, she had the fierce, fighting spirit of her hawk namesake, and it would take more than a hard case like him to bring her down.

She looked up, and the smile that curved her lips welcomed him as surely as if she had held out a hand to him. And then she did just that, and he took it with a sense of wonder he'd felt only once before in his life: when Kestra Shepherd had thought him worth a miracle.

"It started just before midnight," she said softly. "Isn't it wonderful? It so rarely snows here. . . ."

That wasn't the only rare thing that was happening here, Case thought. But he tried to rein in senses that had begun reeling the moment his hand had touched hers.

"I'm sorry I fell asleep on you—"

"Ssh," she said, lifting a slender finger to his lips, "you needed it."

Fire shot through him at her touch, and before he even thought about it, he had pulled her into his arms. Then he was kissing her hungrily, her forehead, her cheeks, the tip of her nose, like a starved man suddenly faced with a banquet so sweeping he didn't know where to begin. Then at last he took her mouth, fiercely, almost needily, expecting at any moment that she would, with that gentle kindness, pull away.

She didn't. She clung to him, kissing him back, her hands rising to thread through his hair as it tangled in the fiery satin of hers. His hands slid down her back to pull her close. It took a moment for the message to get through to his pleasure-hazed brain; beneath the soft velour dress she was naked. He could feel the luscious curve of her waist and hip, and against his chest the unbound softness of her breasts. And within an instant he knew he was hot enough to melt every bit of the snow that had fallen outside. And very, very close to being out of control. He wrenched his mouth away.

"Kestra," he said, nearly gasping. "Look, I know this is crazy, we've only known each other for two days, but I—"

He shuddered, trying to regain the control he'd been so proud of, worked so hard for, all his life. Years of it, shattered in a few fevered moments, by this woman. Had she meant to do this? Was her nudity beneath the rich green gown a signal of her willingness? There had been a time in his life when he would have assumed it and forged ahead. But with this woman, he found himself suddenly unwilling to assume anything.

"Kestra," he said again, "I know I don't have much of a track record with . . . this kind of thing. I was married once, and . . ." He grimaced before going on shakily, "It turned out about like you would expect. You were right, I am . . . was a workaholic. It destroyed my marriage as surely as not working destroyed my father. So I figured I was damned if I did, damned if I didn't. But as long as I kept working, as long as I didn't let anything else in, I didn't have time to think about it. But I swear, Kestra—"

For a second time, she put a finger to his lips, silencing him. "Before you say any more, Case, I think there's something you should see."

Her voice was soft, unthreatening, yet somehow Case got the feeling his entire future was hanging in the balance, as if he were being tested somehow. He didn't understand how or why, but neither could he deny the odd sensation.

"Look," Kestra said quietly, gesturing toward the cushioned seat of the bay window.

He looked. And there, glistening in the silver light reflected from the snowy world outside, in its tiny nest, sat the dove. He tensed instinctively, waiting for the shiver of fear to overtake him. But it didn't come. He just stared at the crystal bird, accepting its presence as part and parcel of the extraordinary string of events that had brought him here, to this house, to this woman.

It was even lighter now, he saw. A pale, almost powder blue. Or icy blue, perhaps, considering the weather.

"Aren't you going to ask if I went back and got it from the store while you were asleep?"

Her voice was still level, even gentle, but he had the

same feeling he'd had before. This, then, was the test he had sensed. And knowing that he owed her no less, he answered quickly. And without hesitation.

"No. I know you didn't."

Joy, pure and radiant, lit her face. She hadn't expected him to accept it, he realized. She had hoped, but hadn't expected. It was all so clear on her face, that enchanting, open, loving face. . . .

"If you can believe that, then maybe . . ." Her voice trailed off as she bit her lip. "Pick it up, Case."

He hesitated. Accepting the dove's appearance and accepting the weird feeling he got when he touched it were two very different things.

"It's not the dove, Case. It's you you were afraid of. What you were becoming. And there's no reason to be. Not anymore."

He couldn't say no. He couldn't look down into those soft, honest eyes and say no. He picked up the dove.

He would have, logically, expected it to be cold, sitting so close to a snowy window. It wasn't, of course. It was warm and heavy and solid in his palm.

"We have to . . . touch it together," she said.

"What?"

"I can't explain it, or even how I know, just . . ." Her voice trailed off. She lifted her hands and placed them over his, and at the same time over the dove.

It began almost instantly, that odd leap of sensation he'd noticed before. A rush of heat, of energy, that odd pulsing that felt almost like a heartbeat. Only this time it was more intense, much more intense. It flooded him, until he had the crazy thought that he should be glowing with it.

The odd sensation heightened, the pulsing deepening until it was hammering in rhythm with his own heart.

The dove seemed to shimmer beneath their hands. His fingers curled, tightened, as if he were literally hanging on for his life. He could feel Kestra's slender fingers, and as clearly as if he were measuring them, he knew her own heartbeat had matched the same rhythm.

And then the images came, fragments of scenes, people in strange places, other times. And emotions, powerful, searing . . . and everlasting. It should have thrown him back into that state of panic, but this time he had an anchor; the feel of Kestra's hands on his. As long as she was there, he knew he was safe.

At last the flood began to ebb. The images faded, but the emotions remained, settling into an understanding he'd never had before of his life, his place, his future. And the knowledge that he had something he'd never realized before; the capacity to love, endlessly, eternally.

And the little crystal dove had turned sparklingly, serenely clear, the last of its color gone as surely as the last of the darkness within him had vanished. It hadn't been giving him the darkness, he realized, it had been drawing it out of him, purging him of the pain, the anguish, and the grief he'd had locked up inside for so long. It had been freeing him.

When he at last lifted his gaze to her face, he saw reflected there everything he was feeling himself.

"It all makes sense now, doesn't it?" he whispered.

She nodded slowly. "The legend was true. All these years, the dove has appeared, over and over, to those who need it most . . . to show them the way."

He smiled at her, putting every bit of the lingering warmth and understanding he could into it. "You never told me the rest of the legend."

A blush colored her cheeks. "I . . ."

"You thought I'd take off running?"

"Yes," she said simply. "I didn't think you were ready to hear ... that part."

"I wasn't," he admitted. Then, curiously, he added, "Did you know? I mean, when you learned that the dove's main purpose was to ... bring lovers together, did you know it was meant to be you?"

Her color deepened. "No. Not until ... just now. I got some of the images earlier, when I picked it up while you were sleeping. But not ¯ . . ."

"The ones of us?" he asked gently. She nodded, lowering her eyes. "So you never thought of it, until now?"

Her lashes lifted quickly as she met his gaze. "I didn't say that."

He let out a breath of relief; he hadn't been alone in his immediate response to her, before he'd even known the incredible person she was. Before the dove had pulled them together and shown them the way.

"I never would have guessed," he said, shaking his head in wonder, "when Raphael told me about you, what would happen."

"Raphael?" she said, sounding startled.

He explained about the waiter at the hotel who had first told him about her, and inspired him to come to her in search of an answer to the mystery of the dove. About halfway through his explanation, she began to smile.

"What?" he asked.

"Don't you remember? In *Paradise Lost?* It was the angel Raphael who was sent to warn Adam."

Case blinked, then swallowed. His mouth quirked. "I suppose you won't buy coincidence, will you?"

Her smile widened. "Nope."

He sighed. "Me either."

Then, slowly, he leaned over to set the dove gently

back on the cushioned seat. He straightened, fastening his gaze on her, knowing now that he would be waking to this lovely face for the rest of his life, and that it would still never be enough.

"I'm glad you thought I was worth a miracle," he said softly.

"I'm glad your miracle came," she answered.

And then she was in his arms, and as he swept her up and carried her back to the warmth of the fire, Case could have sworn he heard the soft, satisfied cooing of a dove.

And later, when they went to gather up the dove and put it in a place of honor on the tree, they found only the empty nest. With tight throats and misty eyes, they hugged each other as they looked at the little cluster of straw. Then both of them, as had all the couples that had come before them, sent along a silent prayer for the next pair to be visited by the tiny miracle worker.

"I wanna hang it!"

"You did it last year; it's my turn!"

"Did not, you did! It's my turn!"

"Okay, knock it off, you two." Case swept up his fierce, redheaded daughter—named Casey, after him— who continued to glare mutinously at her brother.

"Tell you what," Kestra, ever the peacemaker, said as she picked up her son and smoothed back his tousled dark hair. "Your father and I will pick the branch, and you both hang it together."

The two children, the carrot-topped, green-eyed girl and the dark-haired, gray-eyed boy—who had a serviceable first name but was known affectionately as Hawk, for the kestrel his mother had been named for— eyed each other warily and then grudgingly nodded.

Kestra smiled as Case picked up the unusual ornament with tender care. It always had a place of honor on their tree, and it never failed to give her a little thrill every time she looked at it. That sense of reverence had been passed on to their children; the two tiny hands carefully handled the golden thread as they looped it over the selected branch. The children smiled; the little straw nest was in its place, and all was right with their world.

"Tell us the story again, Daddy," Casey commanded imperiously.

"Yes," Hawk chimed in, "tell us."

"Aren't you two tired of hearing it?" Case teased.

"No!" Hawk said instantly. "I wanna hear about the man with the angel name, who sent you to Mommy and then disappeared."

"It wouldn't be Christmas if you didn't tell us the dove story, Daddy!" Casey exclaimed.

"No, it wouldn't," Kestra agreed gently.

Case looked at his wife, and a smile curved his mouth. It was a smile reserved only for her, never given to anyone else. A smile full of treasured memories of lonely lives left behind, of new discoveries, of hot, passionate nights—and days—and of children born of a love stronger than either of them had ever dared hope for.

And memories of a tiny crystal dove.

ANNOUNCING THE

TOPAZ FREQUENT READERS CLUB
COMMEMORATING TOPAZ'S
1 YEAR ANNIVERSARY!

THE MORE YOU BUY, THE MORE YOU GET

Redeem coupons found here and in the back of all new Topaz titles for FREE Topaz gifts:

Send in:

 2 coupons for a free TOPAZ novel (choose from the list below);

☐ **THE KISSING BANDIT**, Margaret Brownley

☐ **BY LOVE UNVEILED**, Deborah Martin

☐ **TOUCH THE DAWN**, Chelley Kitzmiller

☐ **WILD EMBRACE**, Cassie Edwards

 4 coupons for an "I Love the Topaz Man" on-board sign

 6 coupons for a TOPAZ compact mirror

 8 coupons for a Topaz Man T-shirt

Just fill out this certificate and send with original sales receipts to:

TOPAZ FREQUENT READERS CLUB-1ST ANNIVERSARY
Penguin USA • Mass Market Promotion; Dept. H.U.G.
375 Hudson St., NY, NY 10014

Name_____

Address_____

City_____State_____Zip_____

Offer expires 5/31/1995

This certificate must accompany your request. No duplicates accepted. Void where prohibited, taxed or restricted. Allow 4-6 weeks for receipt of merchandise. Offer good only in U.S., its territories, and Canada.